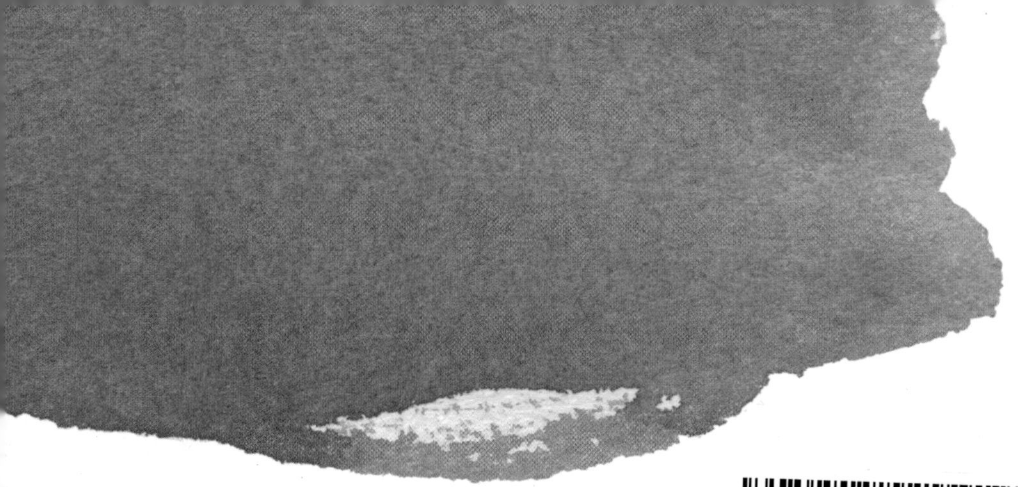

First published in the US by Athenum in 2020
An imprint of Simon & Schuster Children's Publishing Division
First published in the UK in 2020
by Faber & Faber Limited
Bloomsbury House,
74–77 Great Russell Street,
London WC1B 3DA

Printed by Short Run Press, Exeter

Text copyright © 2017 by Jason Reynolds
Illustrations copyright © 2020 by Danica Novgorodoff
Adapted from *Long Way Down* by Jason Reynolds,
published by Atheneum in 2017 and Faber in 2018

Published by arrangement with Pippin Properties, Inc. through Rights People, London

Book design by Danica Novgorodoff and Sonia Chaghatzbanian.
The text for this book was set in Danica Novgorodoff.
The illustrations for this book were rendered in ink and watercolor.

A CIP record for this book is available from the British Library

ISBN 978-0-571-36601-9

MIX
Paper from
responsible sources
FSC® C014540

2 4 6 8 10 9 7 5 3

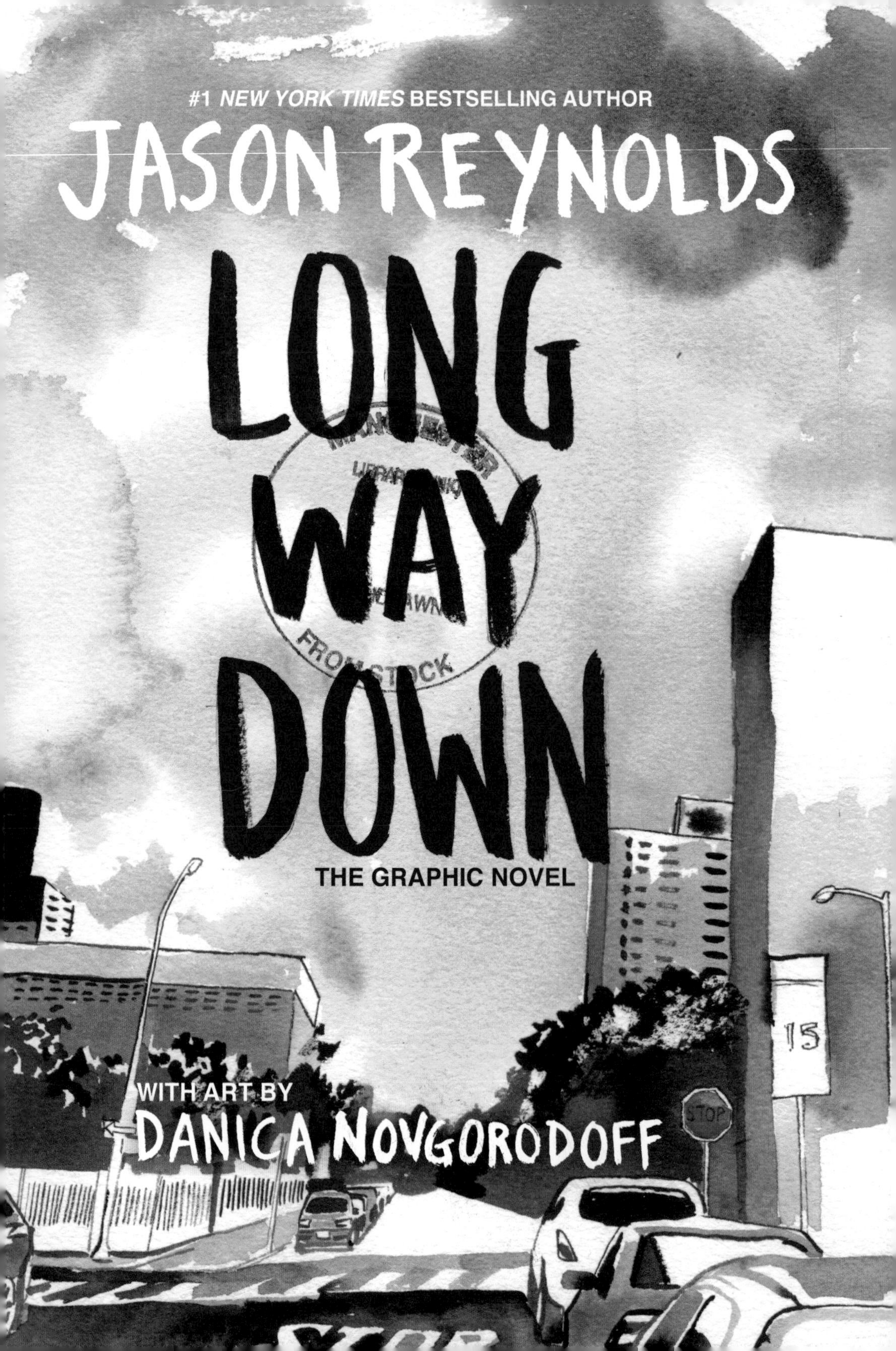
#1 NEW YORK TIMES BESTSELLING AUTHOR
JASON REYNOLDS
LONG WAY DOWN
THE GRAPHIC NOVEL
WITH ART BY
DANICA NOVGORODOFF
15
STOP

For all the young
brothers and sisters in
detention centers around
the country, the ones
I've seen, and the ones I
haven't. You are loved.
—J. R.

To the young artists,
writers, and activists
working for justice.
Tell your stories.
—D. N.

LONG
WAY
DOWN

faber

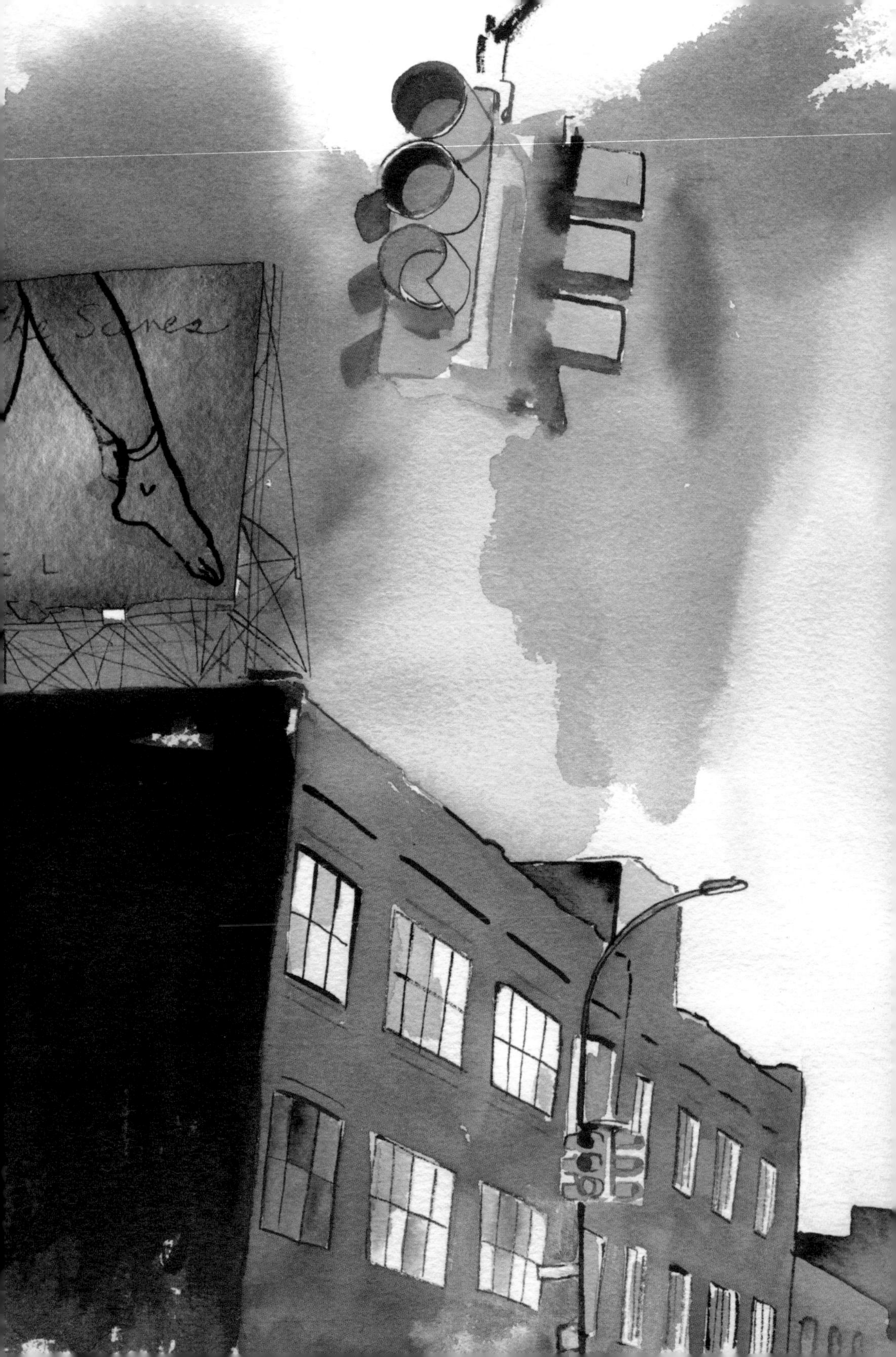
Scenes

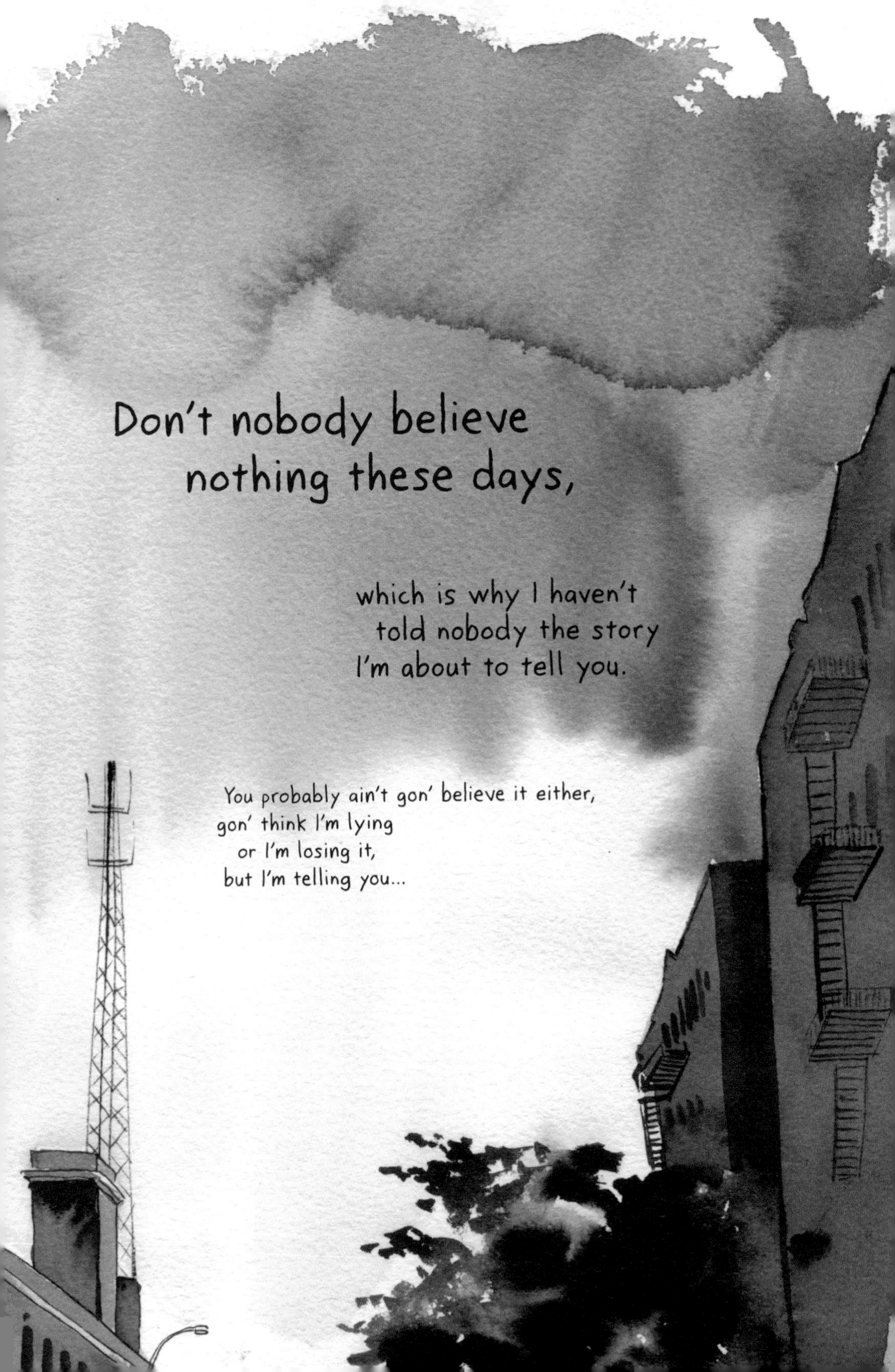
Don't nobody believe nothing these days,
which is why I haven't told nobody the story I'm about to tell you.
You probably ain't gon' believe it either, gon' think I'm lying or I'm losing it, but I'm telling you...

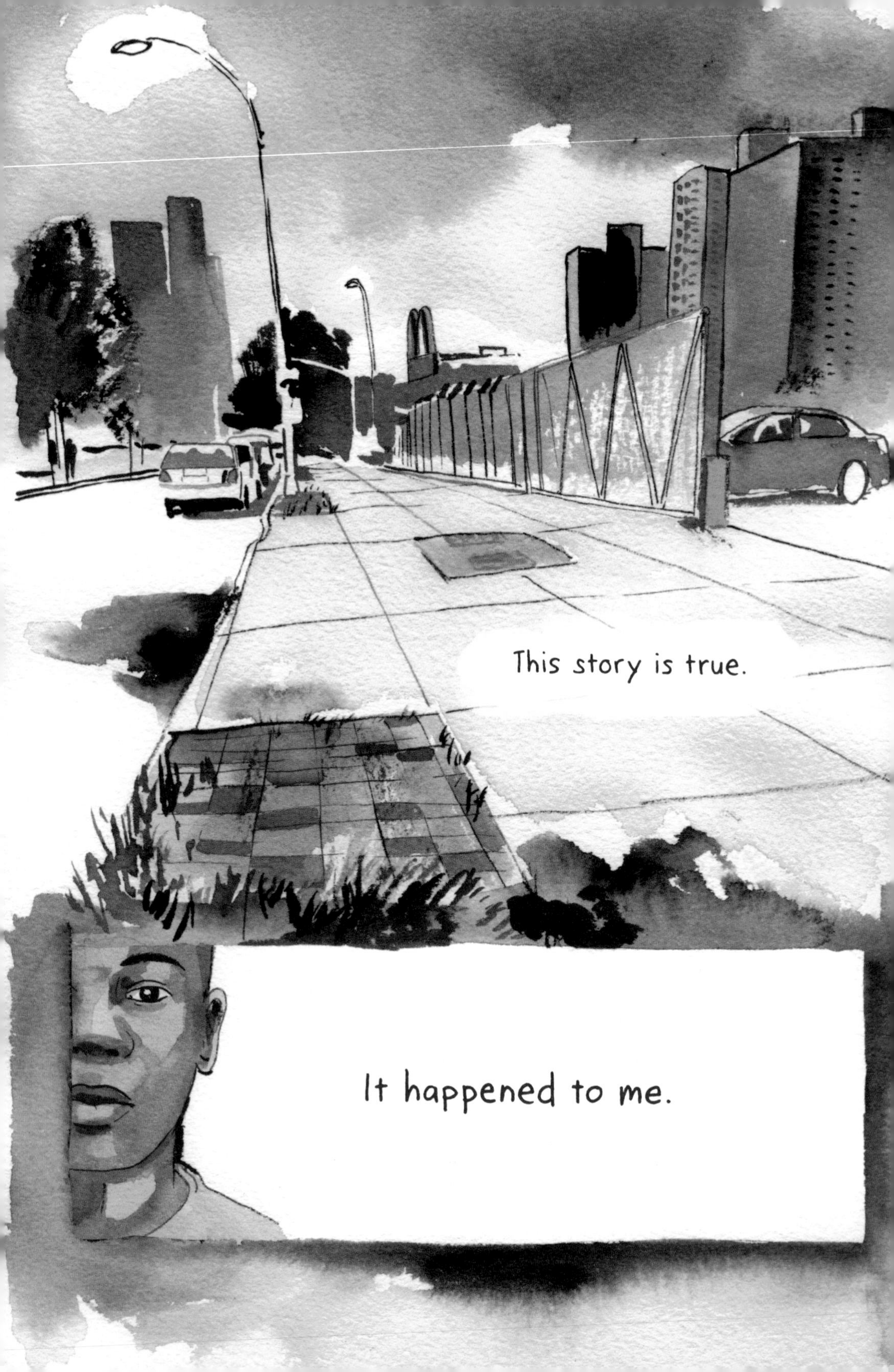
This story is true.
It happened to me.

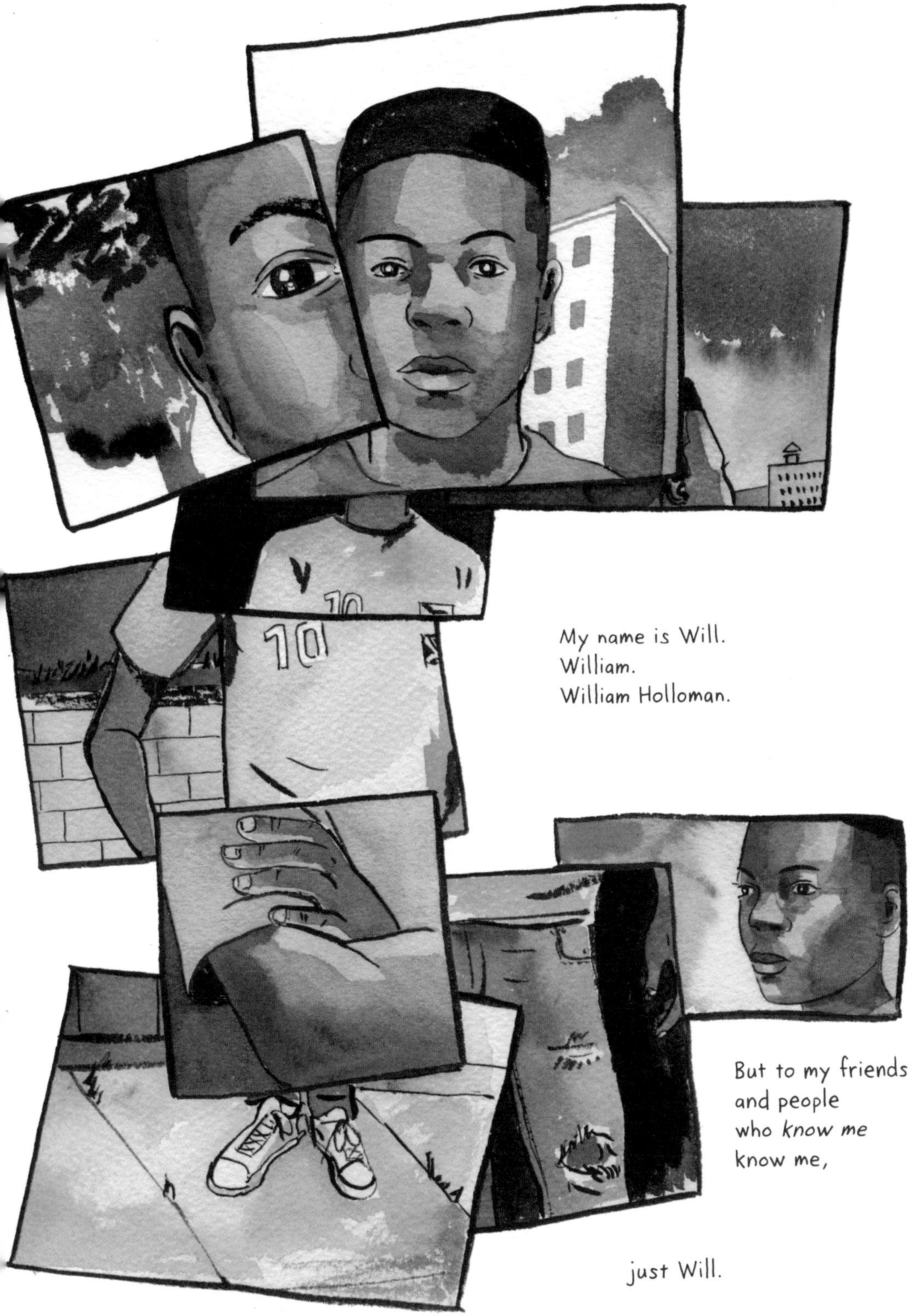
My name is Will.
William.
William Holloman.
But to my friends
and people
who *know me*
know me,
just Will.

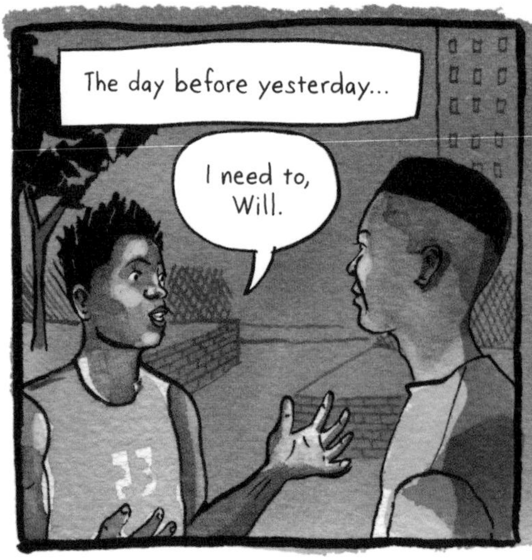
The day before yesterday...
I need to, Will.

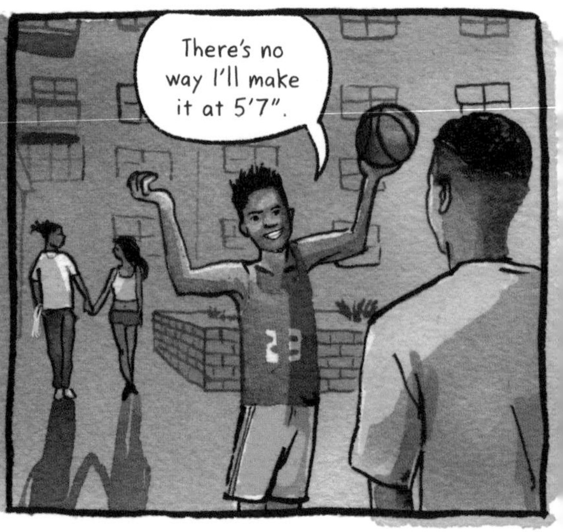
There's no way I'll make it at 5'7".

I'm only William to my mother

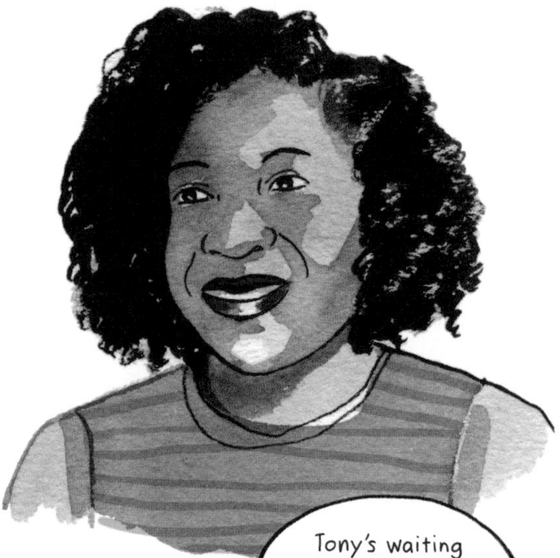

and my brother, Shawn, whenever he was trying to be funny.

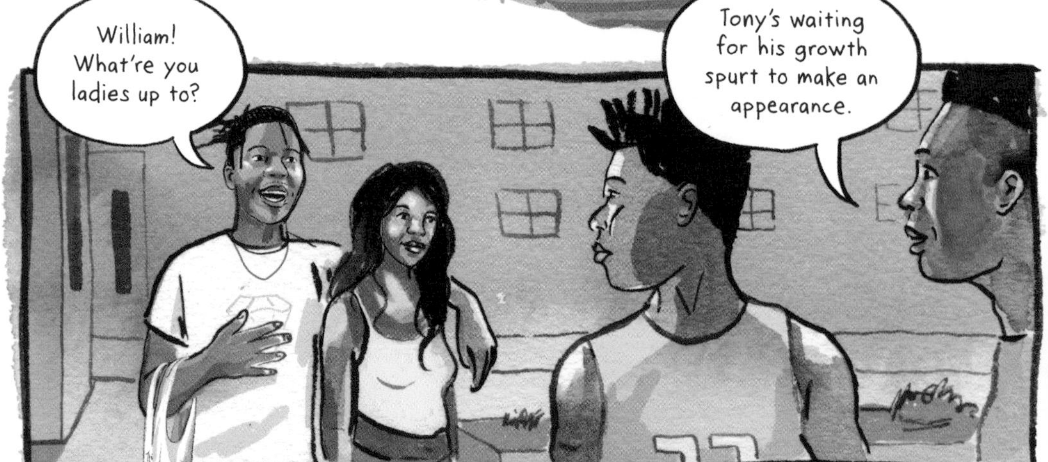
William! What're you ladies up to?
Tony's waiting for his growth spurt to make an appearance.

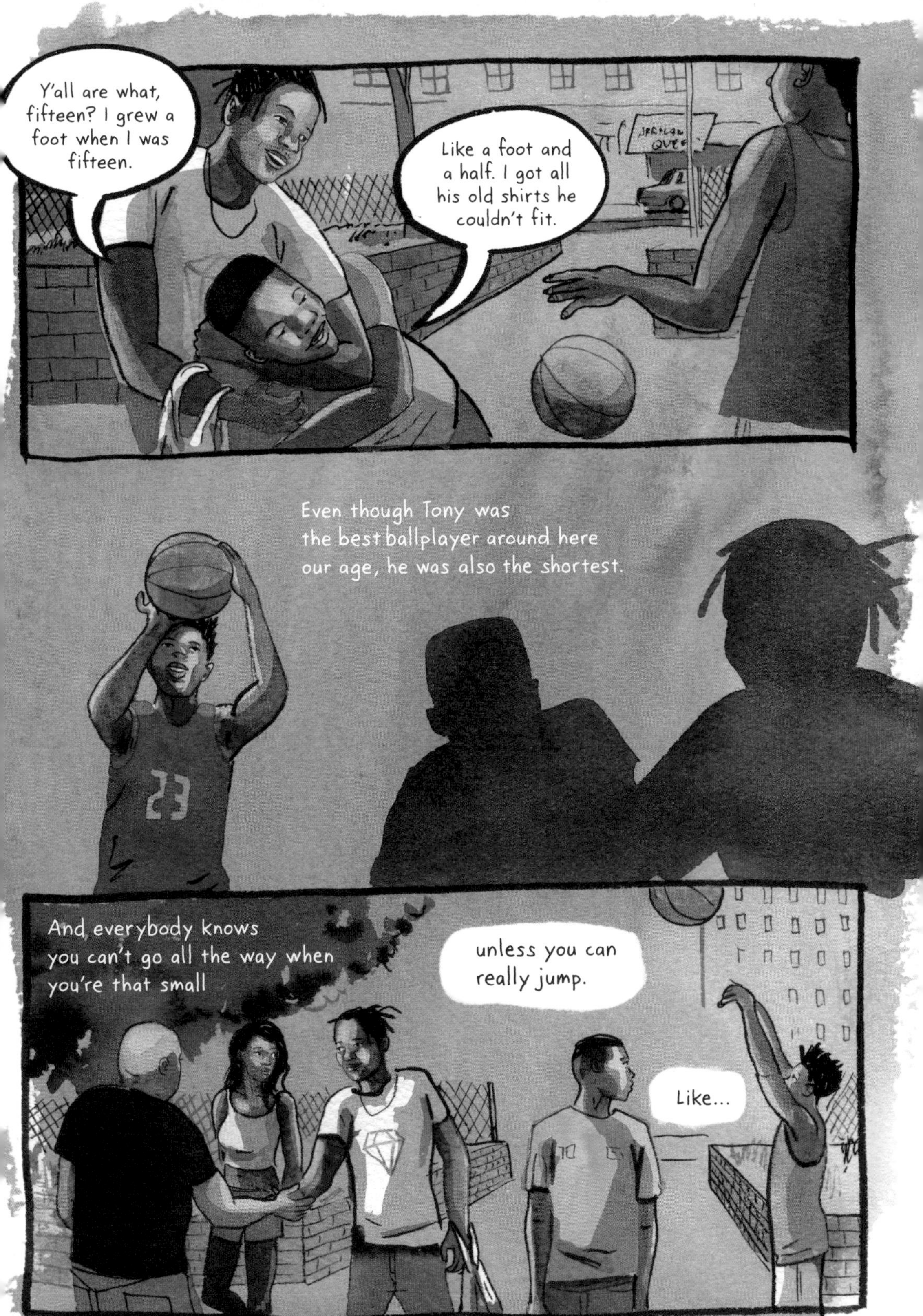
Y'all are what, fifteen? I grew a foot when I was fifteen.
Like a foot and a half. I got all his old shirts he couldn't fit.
Even though Tony was the best ballplayer around here our age, he was also the shortest.
23
And everybody knows you can't go all the way when you're that small
unless you can really jump.
Like...

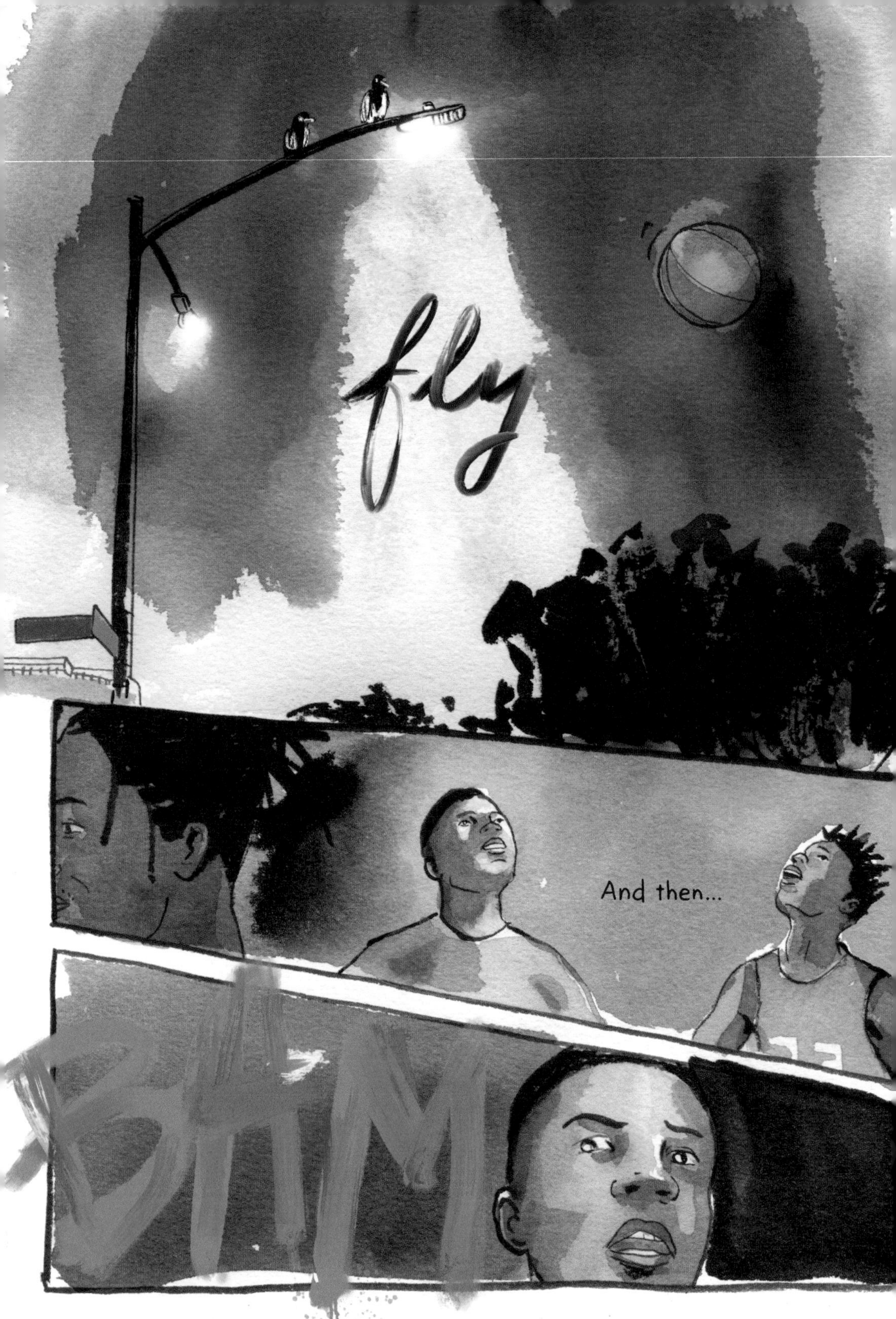
fly
And then...
BAM

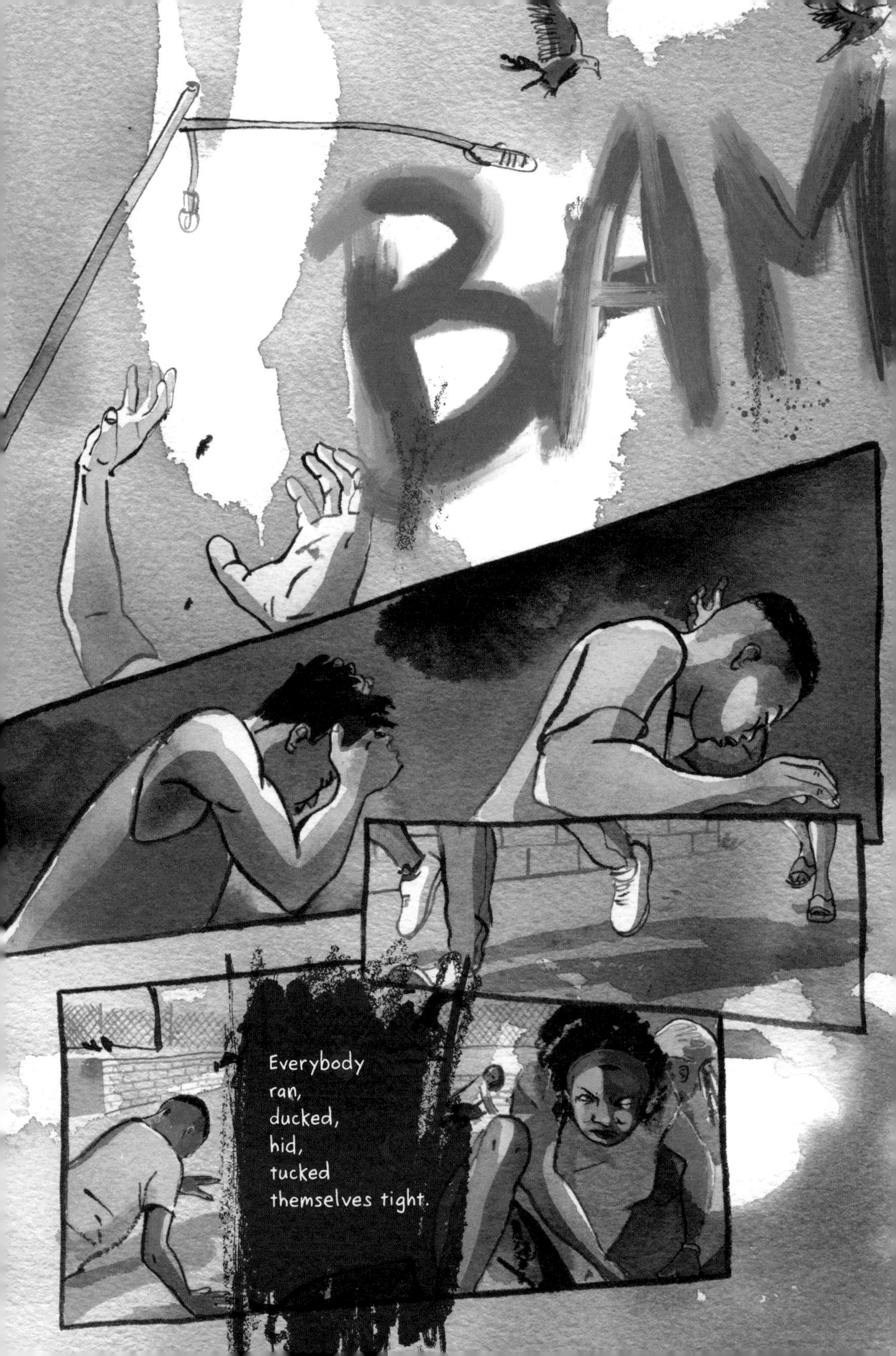
BAM
Everybody
ran,
ducked,
hid,
tucked
themselves tight.

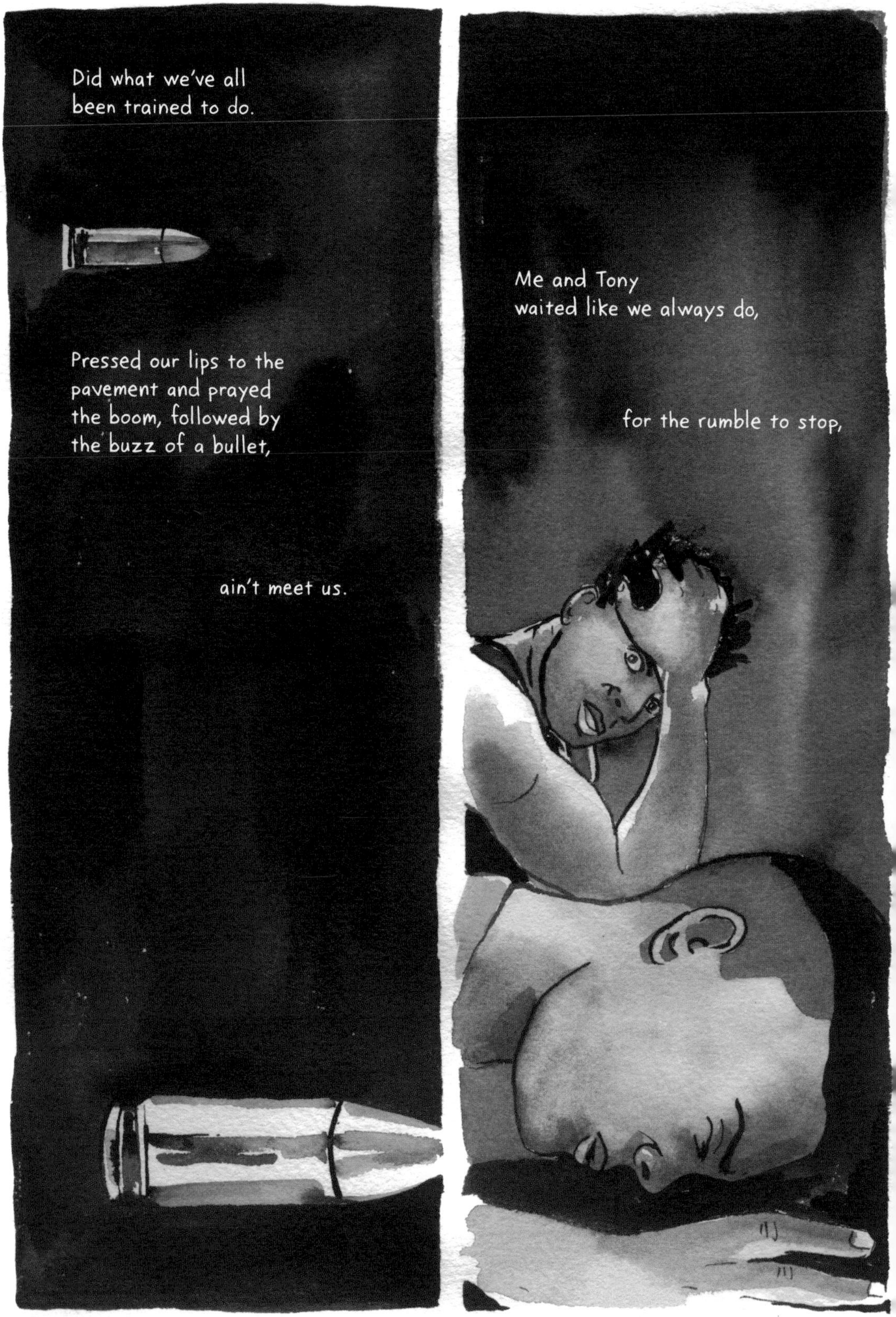
Did what we've all been trained to do.
Pressed our lips to the pavement and prayed the boom, followed by the buzz of a bullet,
ain't meet us.
Me and Tony waited like we always do,
for the rumble to stop,

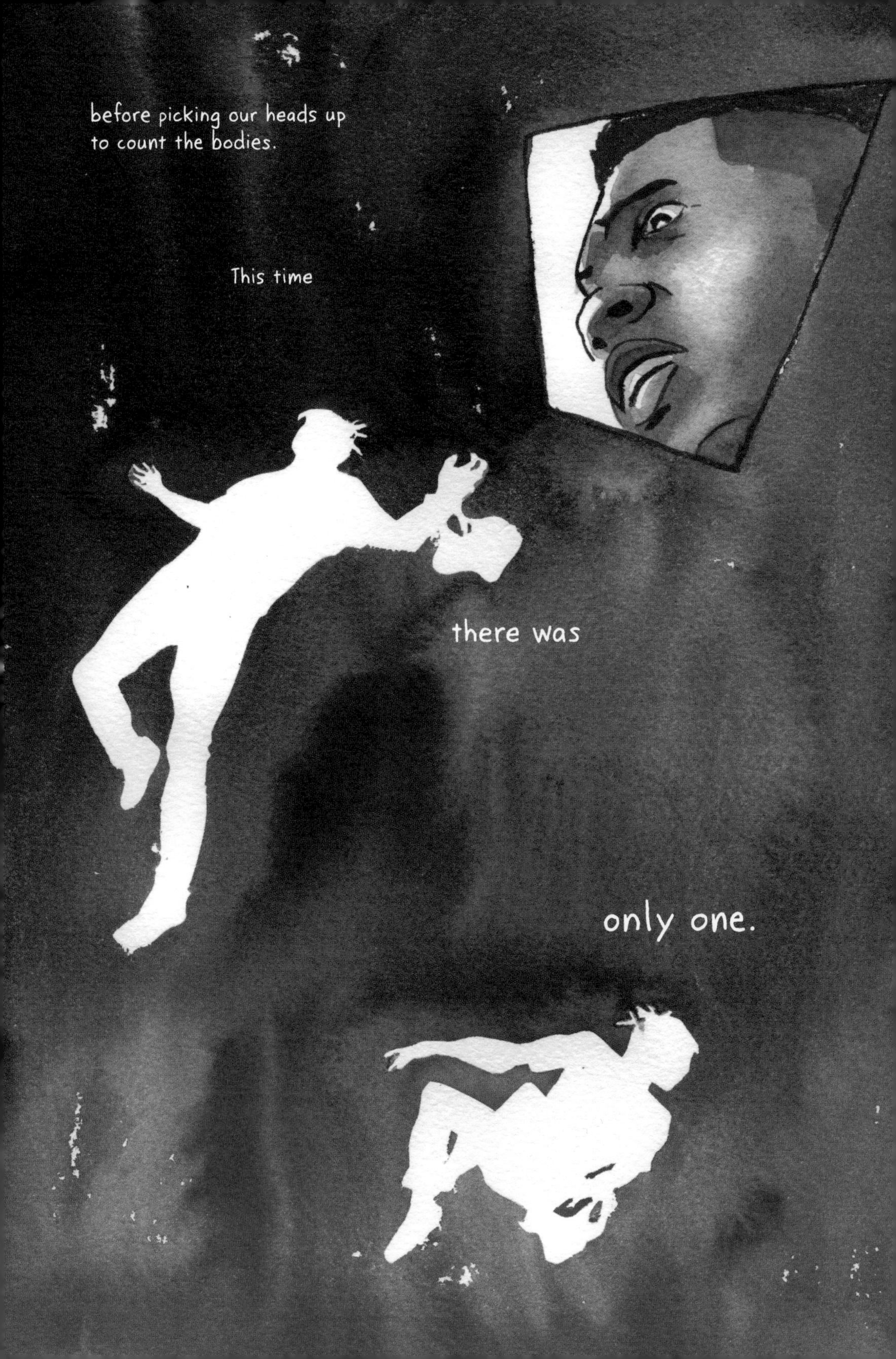
before picking our heads up
to count the bodies.
This time
there was
only one.

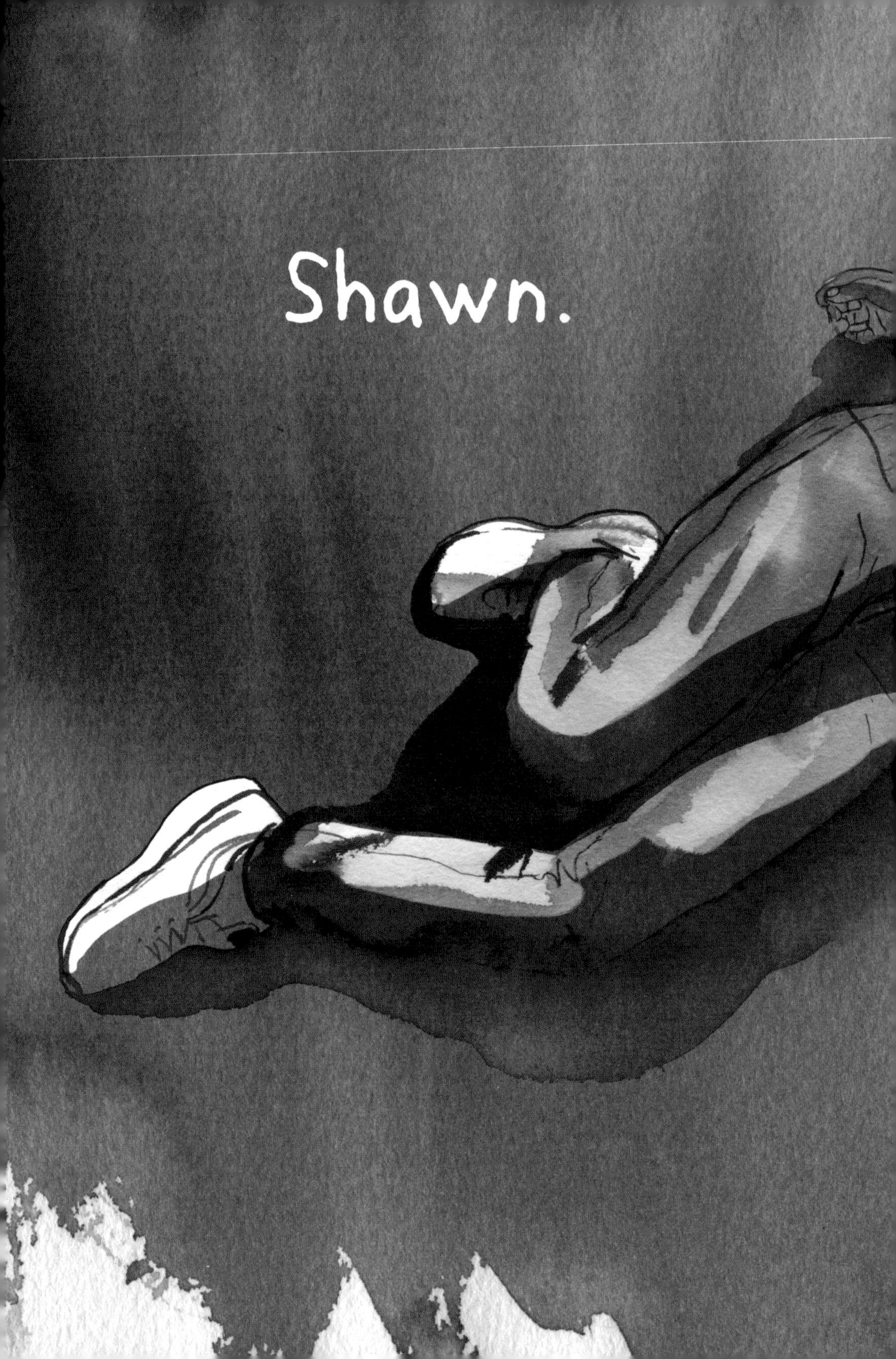
Shawn.

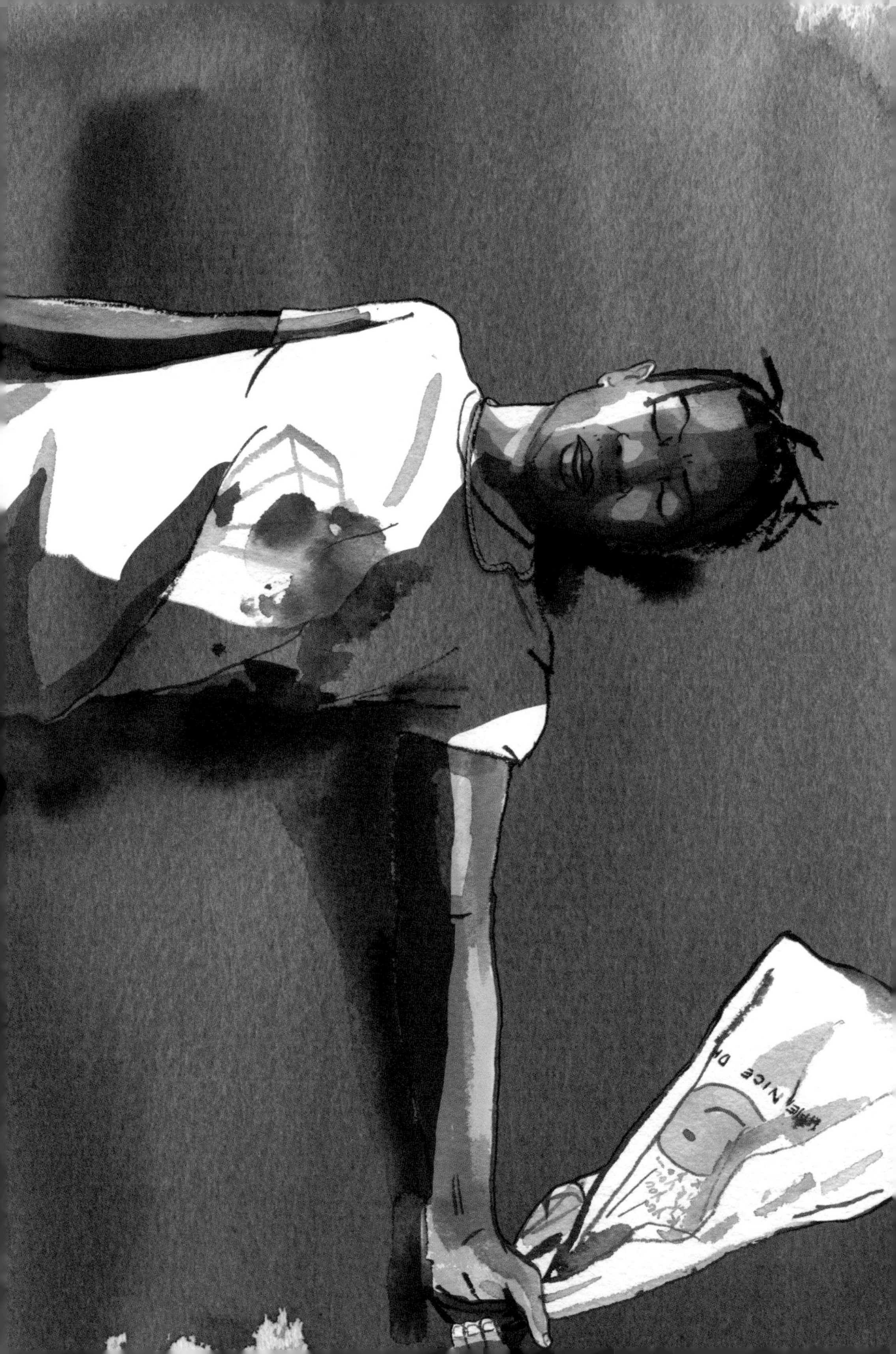

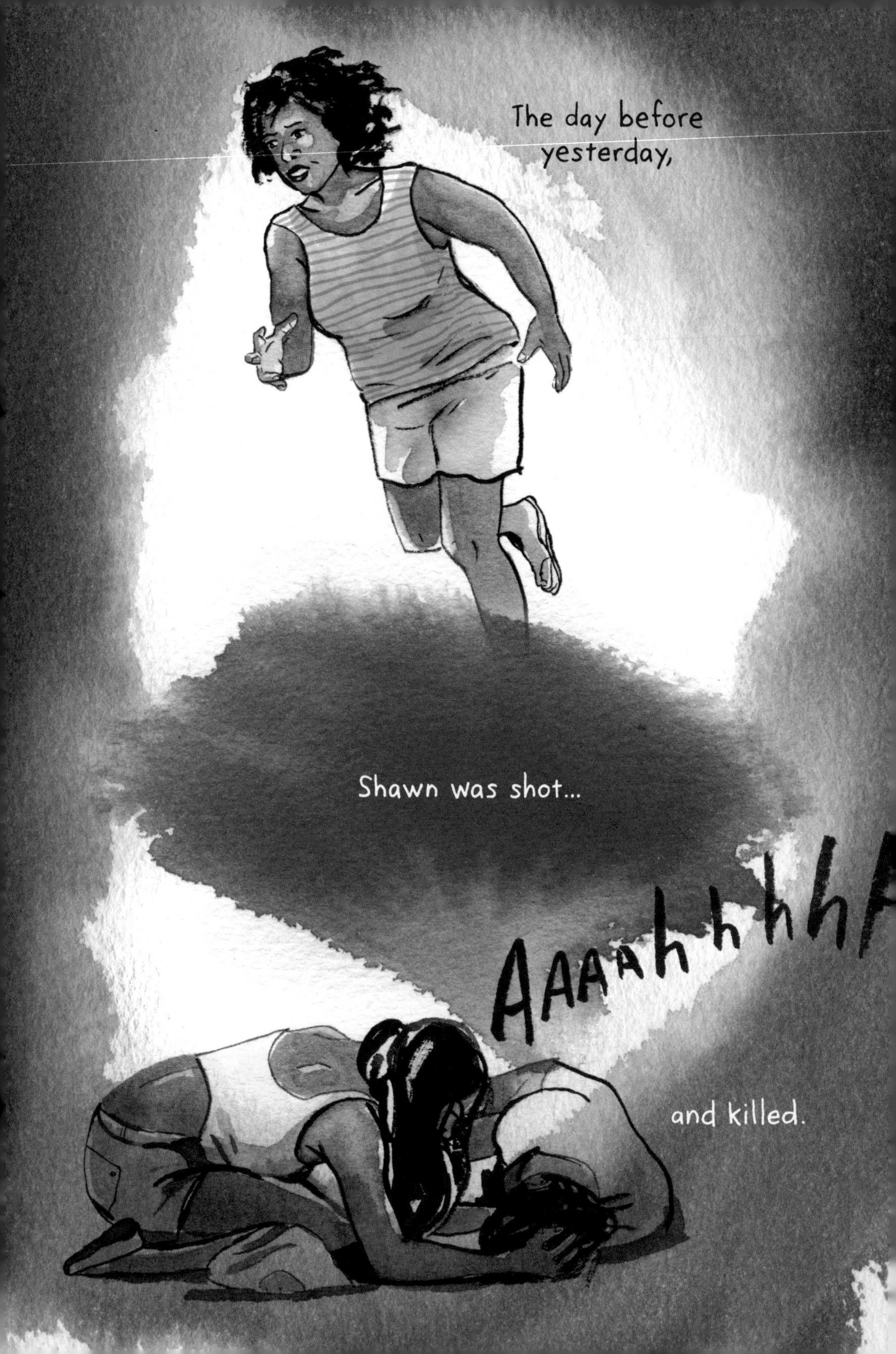
The day before yesterday,
Shawn was shot...
Aaaahhhhh
and killed.

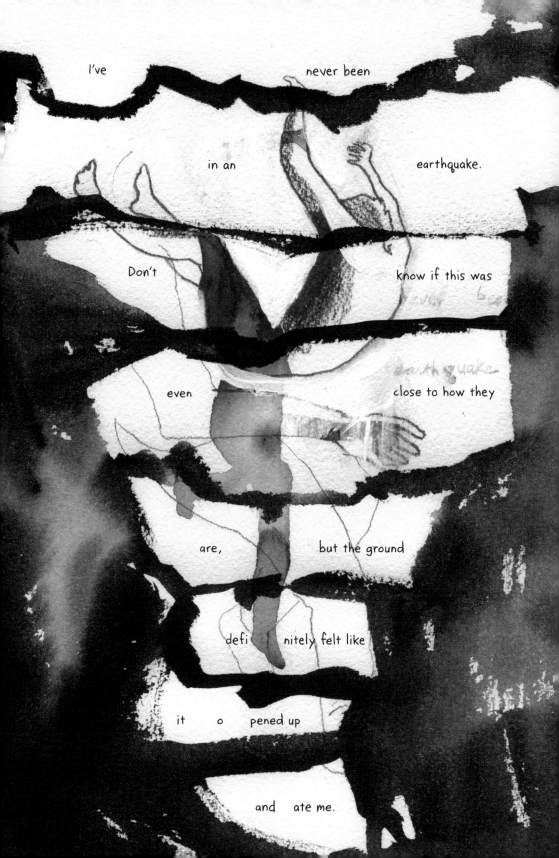

I've   never been

in an   earthquake.

Don't   know if this was

even   close to how they

are,   but the ground

defi   nitely felt like

it   o   pened up

and   ate me.

I don't know you,
don't know
your last name,

if you got
brothers
or sisters
or mothers
or fathers
or cousins
that be like

brothers
and sisters
or aunties
or uncles
that be like

mothers
and fathers,

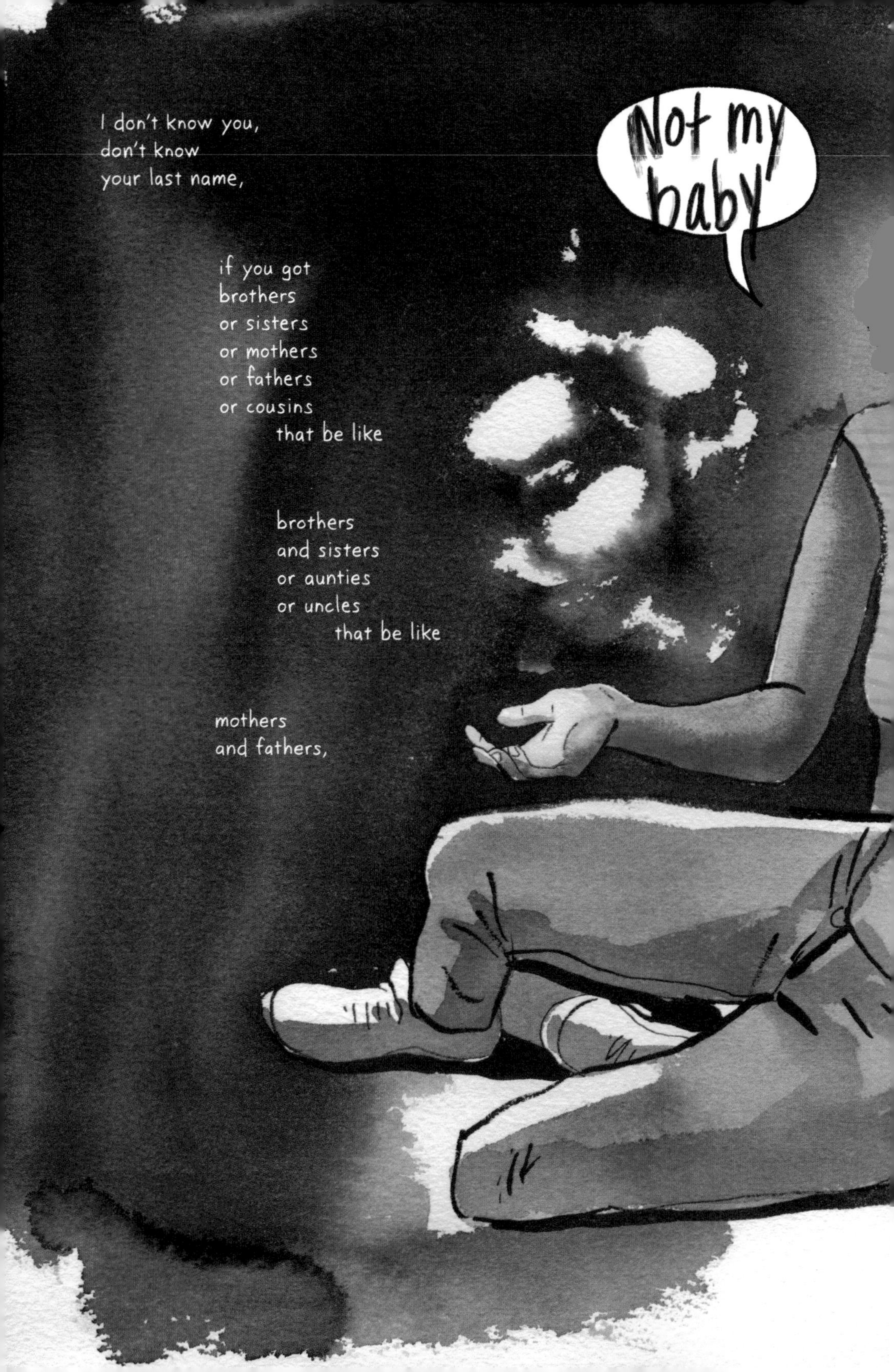
Not my baby

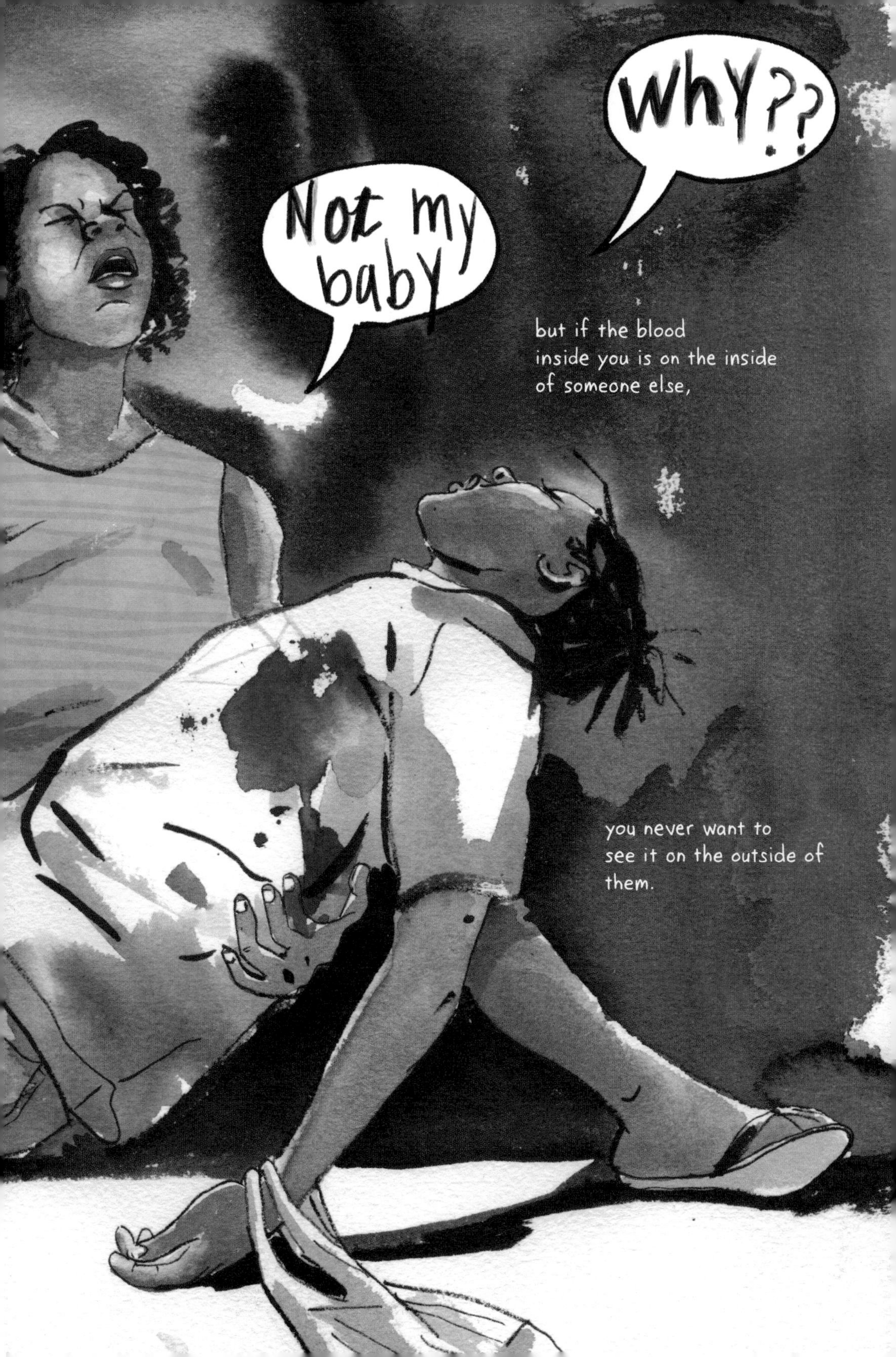
Not my baby
WHY??
but if the blood inside you is on the inside of someone else,
you never want to see it on the outside of them.

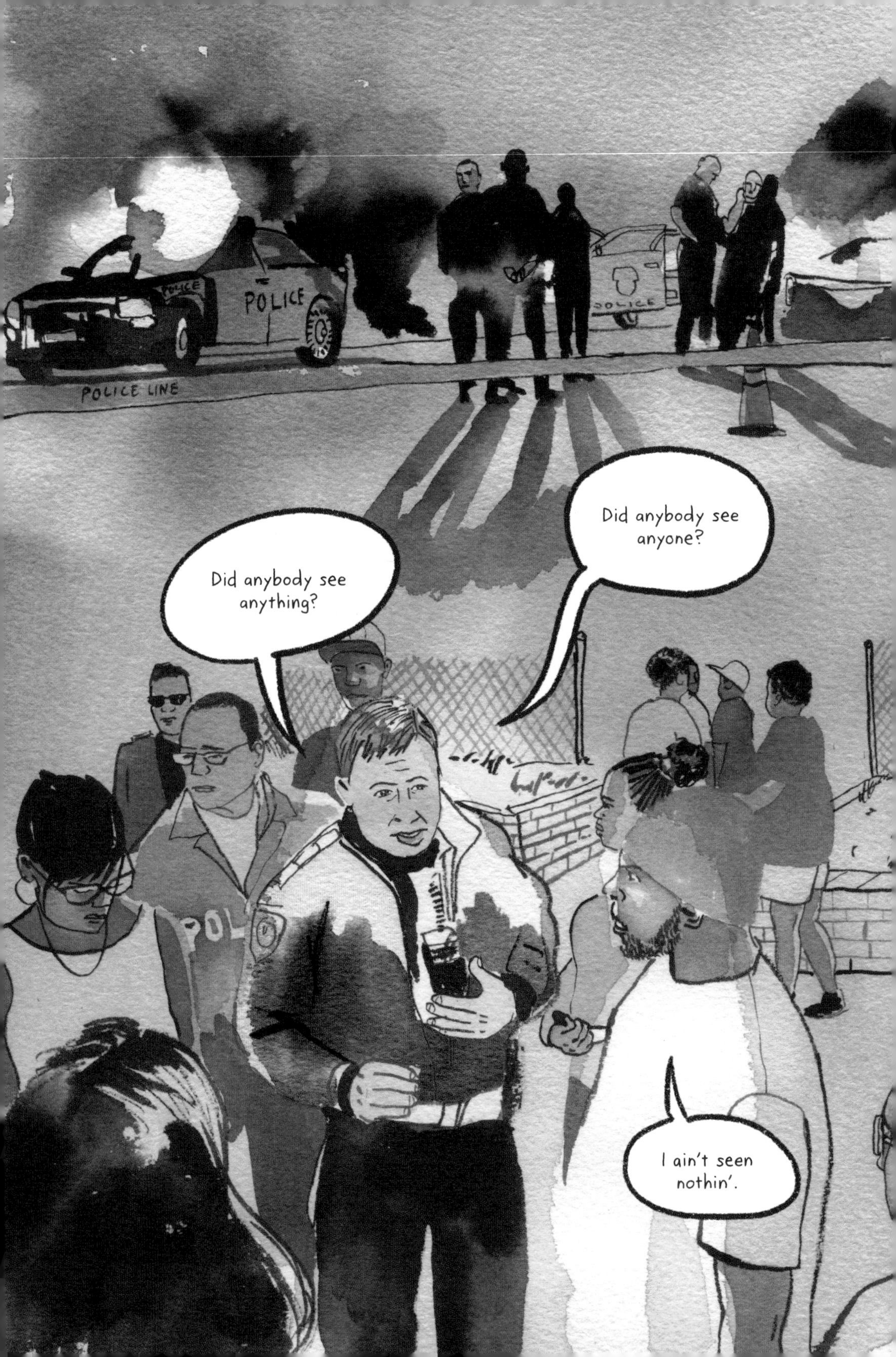
POLICE
POLICE
POLICE LINE
Did anybody see anything?
Did anybody see anyone?
I ain't seen nothin'.

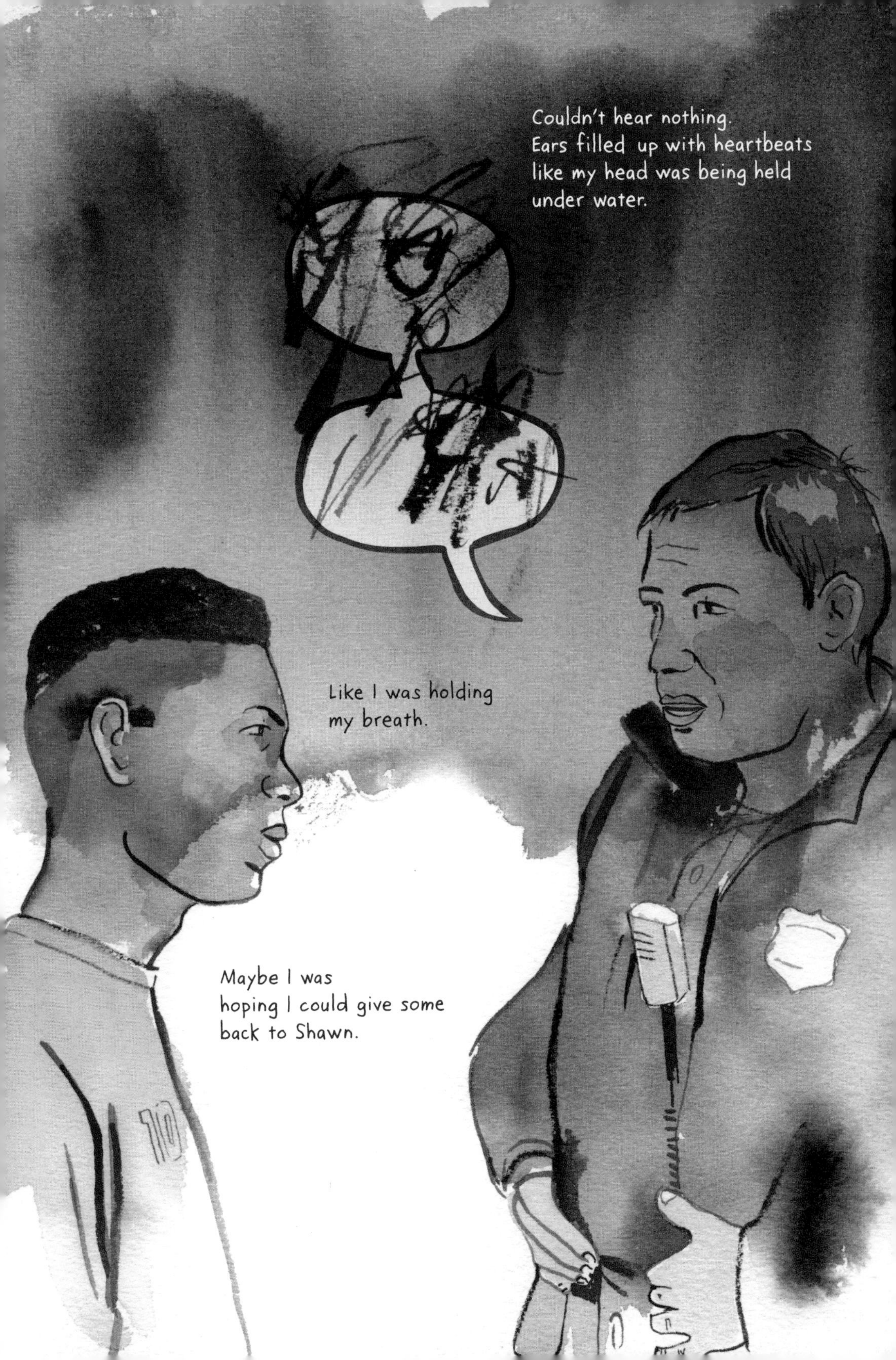
Couldn't hear nothing. Ears filled up with heartbeats like my head was being held under water.
Like I was holding my breath.
Maybe I was hoping I could give some back to Shawn.

Or maybe somehow

join him.

In that bag,
    special soap
        for my mother's eczema.

THANK YOU
THANK YOU
THANK YOU
THANK YOU

HAVE A NICE DAY

I've seen her scratch until it bleeds.

Curse the invisible thing trying to eat her.

Maybe there's something
    invisible
        trying to eat
            all of us as
                if we are beef.

THANK YOU
THANK YOU
THANK YOU
THANK YOU

HAVE A NICE D

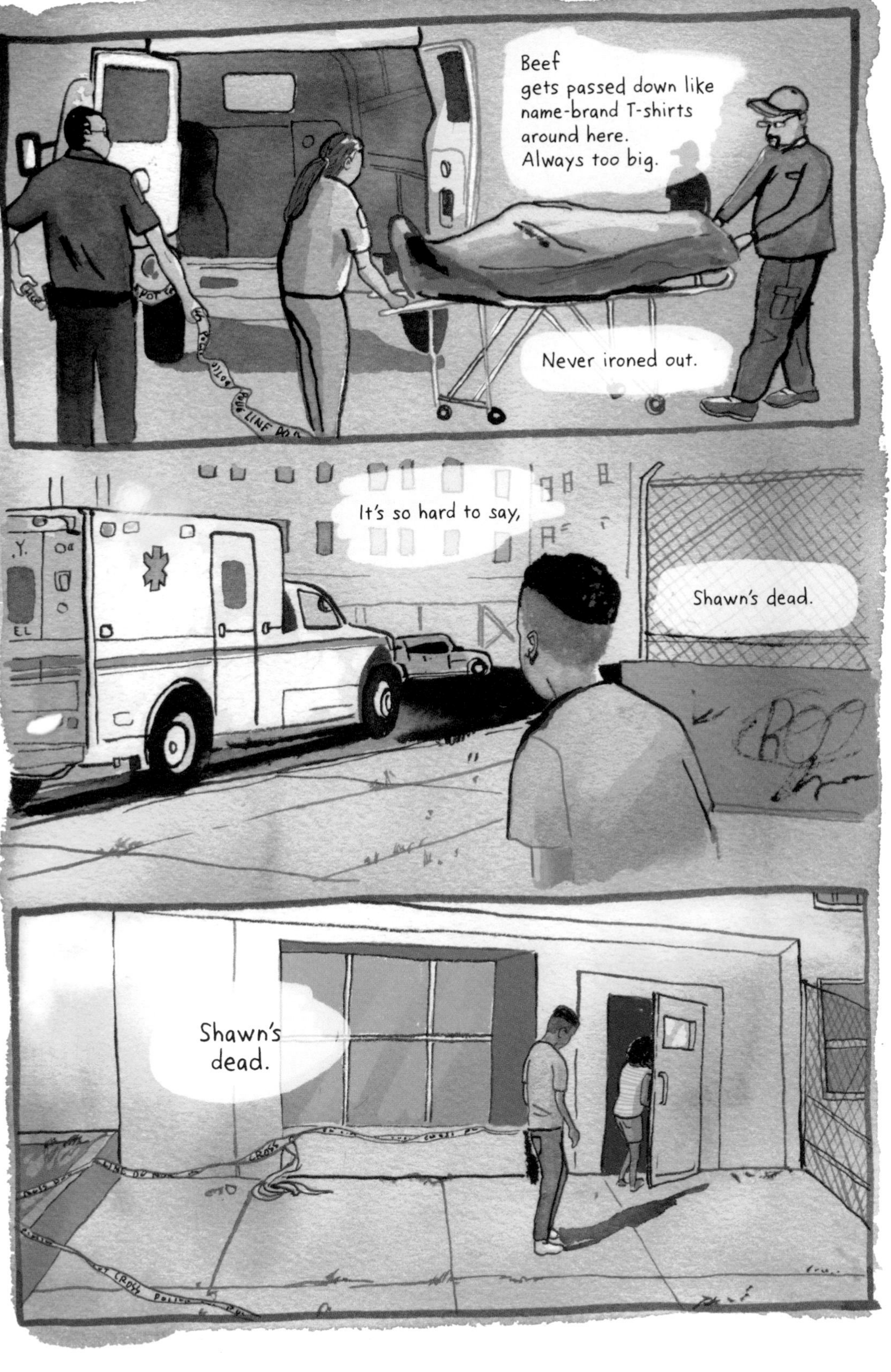

Beef
gets passed down like
name-brand T-shirts
around here.
Always too big.
Never ironed out.
It's so hard to say,
Shawn's dead.
Shawn's dead.

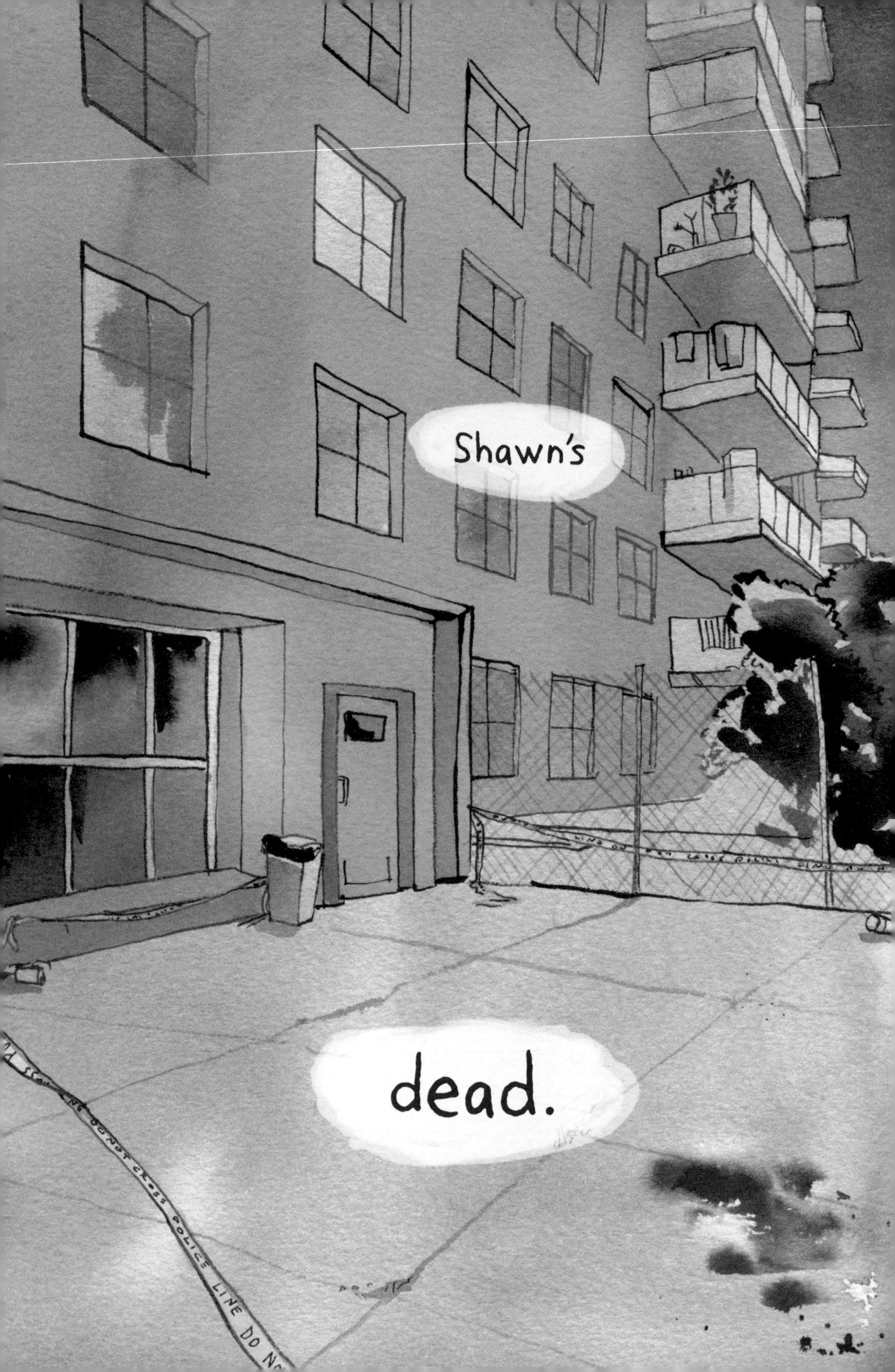
Shawn's
dead.
DO NOT CROSS POLICE LINE

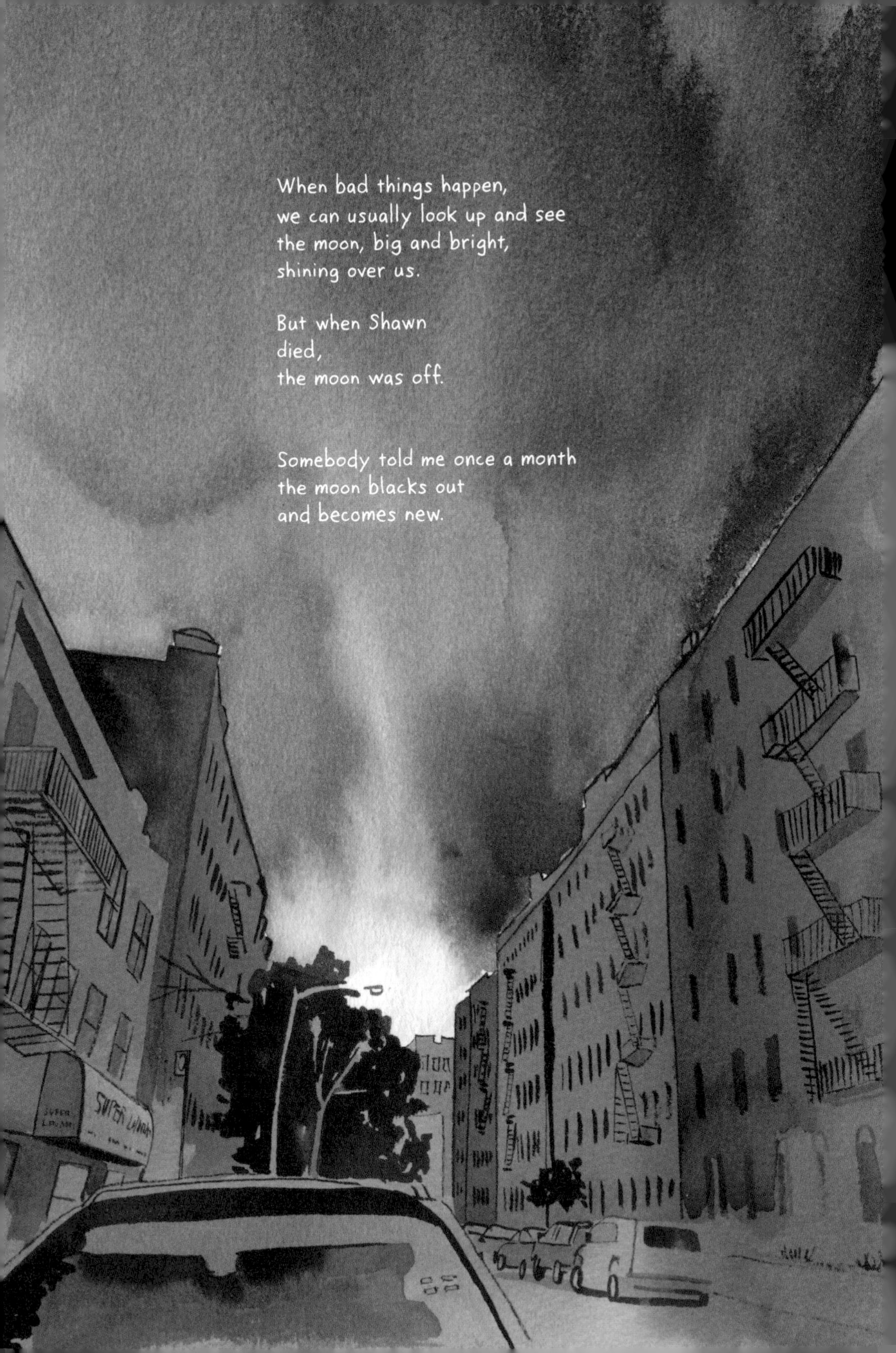
When bad things happen,
we can usually look up and see
the moon, big and bright,
shining over us.

But when Shawn
died,
the moon was off.

Somebody told me once a month
the moon blacks out
and becomes new.

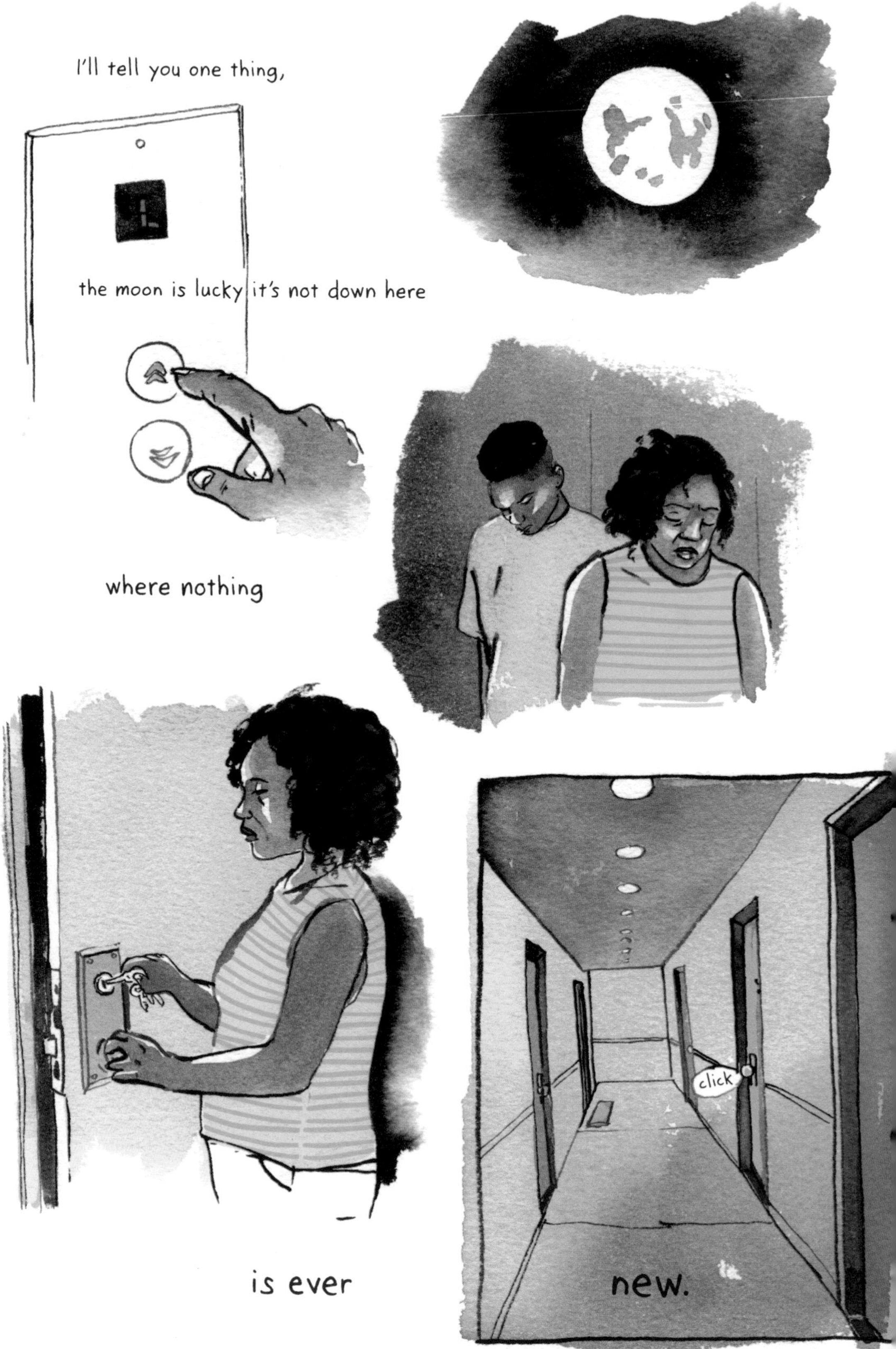
I'll tell you one thing,
the moon is lucky it's not down here
where nothing
is ever
click
new.

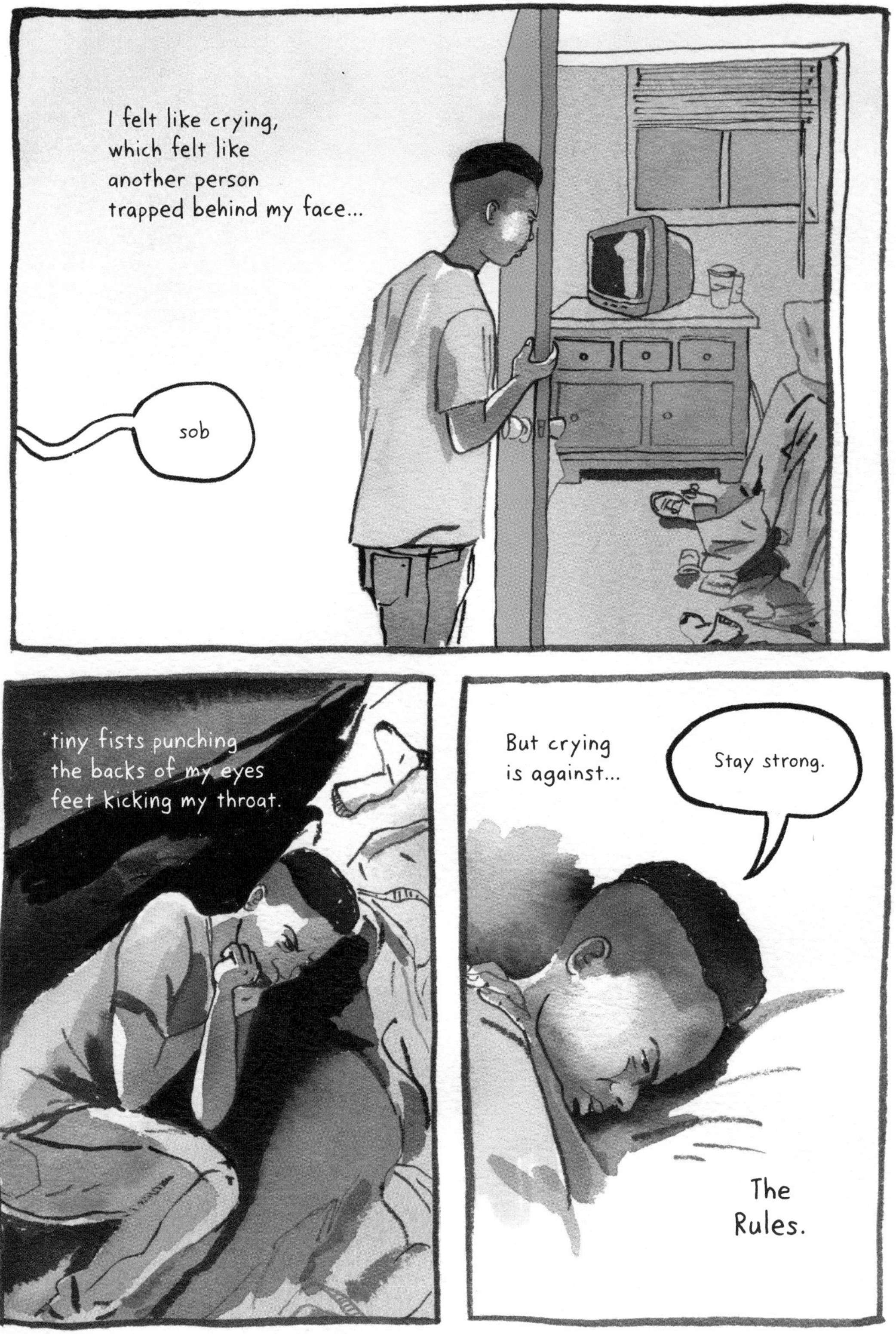
I felt like crying, which felt like another person trapped behind my face...
sob
tiny fists punching the backs of my eyes feet kicking my throat.
But crying is against...
Stay strong.
The Rules.

The Rules

No. 1: Crying

Don't.
No matter what.
Don't.

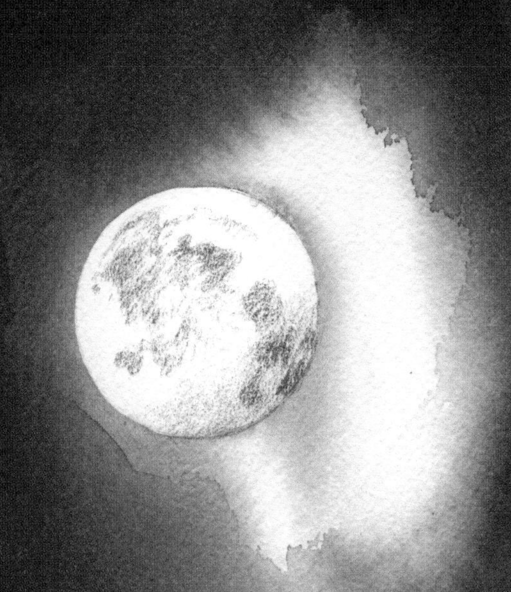

No.2: Snitching

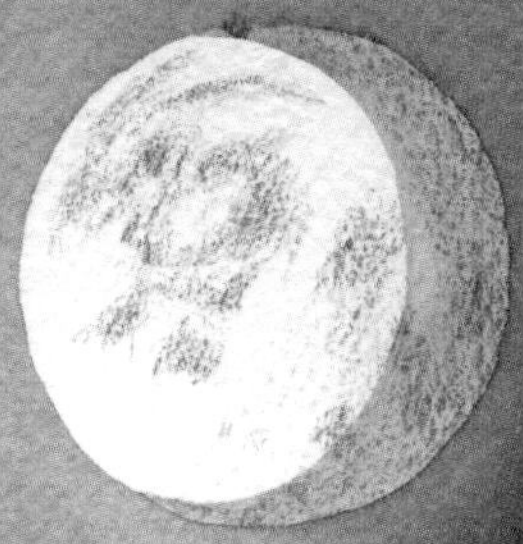

Don't.
No matter what.
Don't.

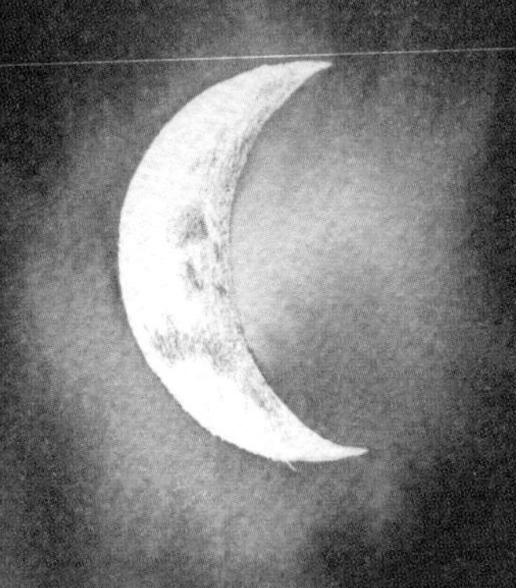

No.3: Revenge

If someone you love
gets killed,

find the person
who killed
them and...

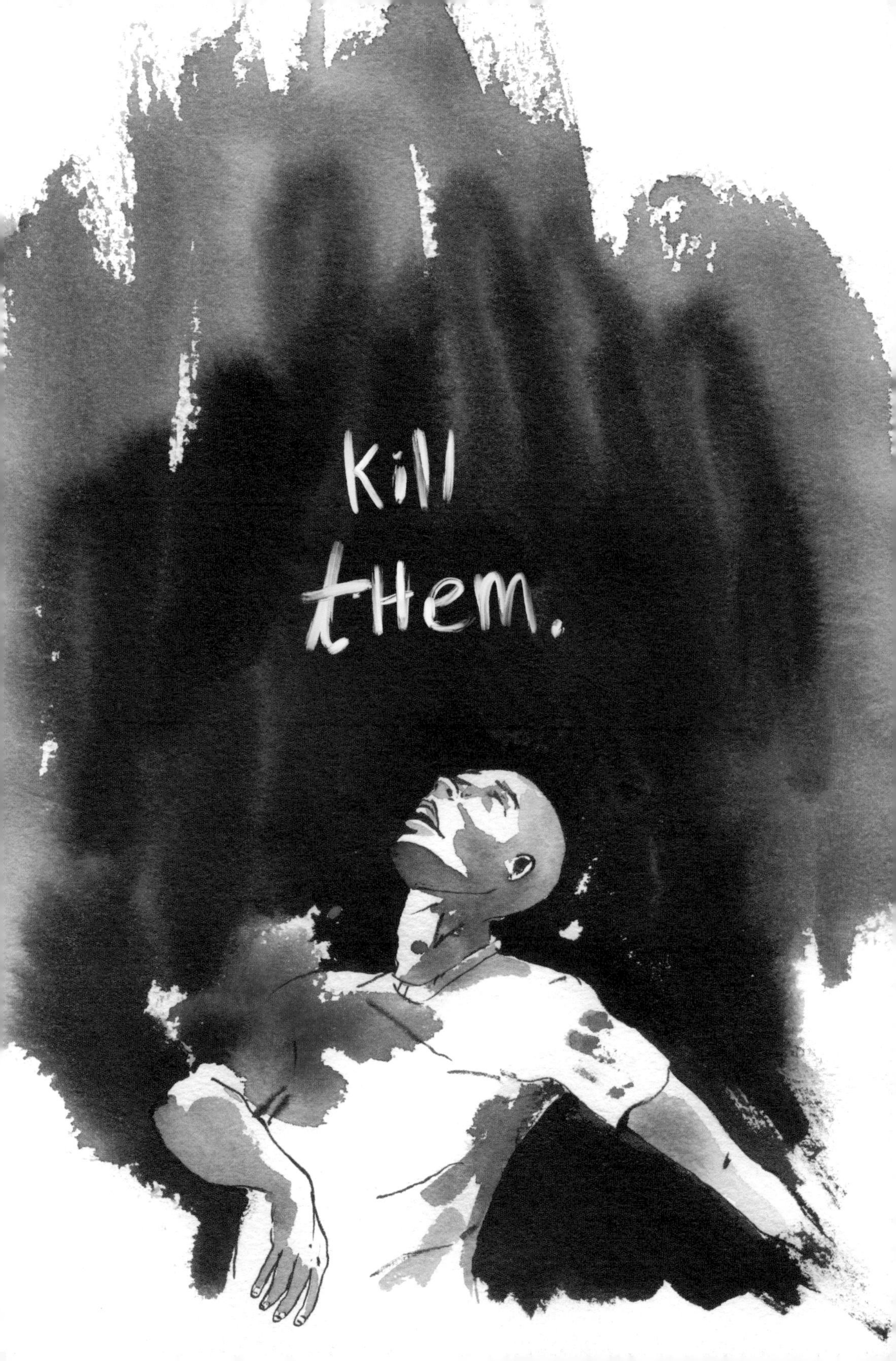
kill
them.

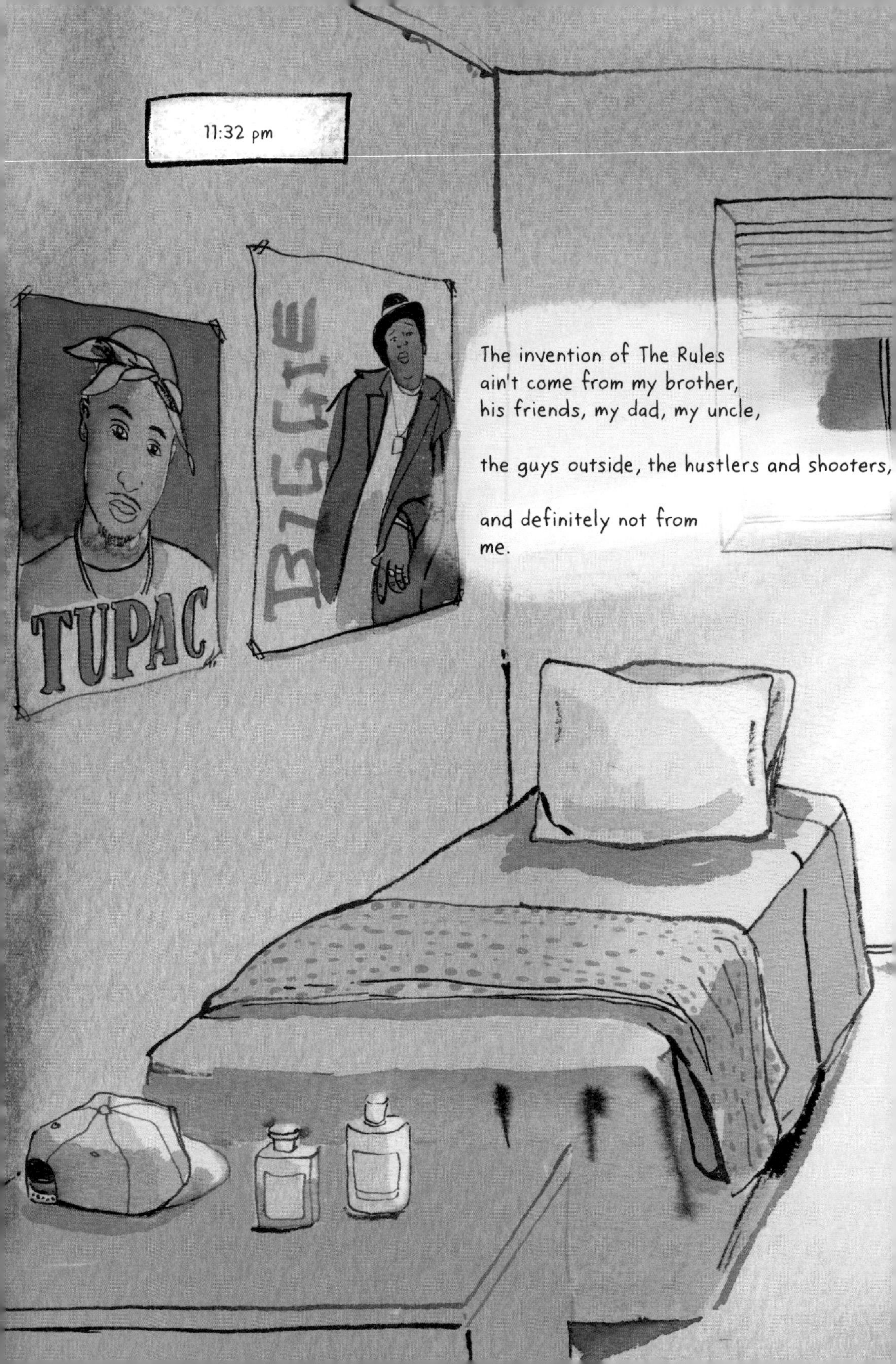
11:32 pm
TUPAC
BIGGIE
The invention of The Rules
ain't come from my brother,
his friends, my dad, my uncle,
the guys outside, the hustlers and shooters,
and definitely not from
me.

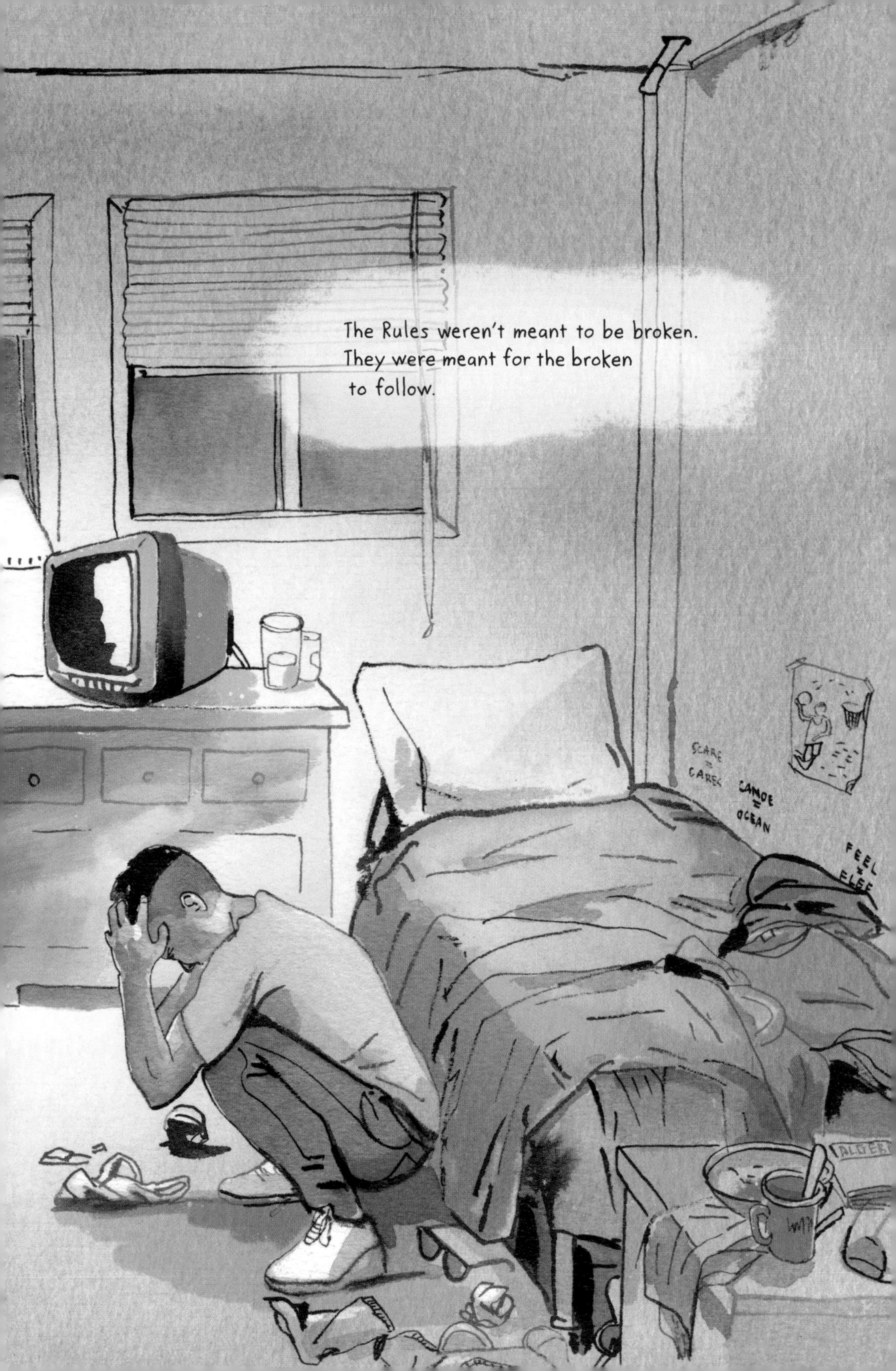

The Rules weren't meant to be broken.
They were meant for the broken
to follow.
CANOE = OCEAN

I won't pretend that Shawn
was the kind of guy
who was home before curfew.

After he turned eighteen,
our mother used to tell him,

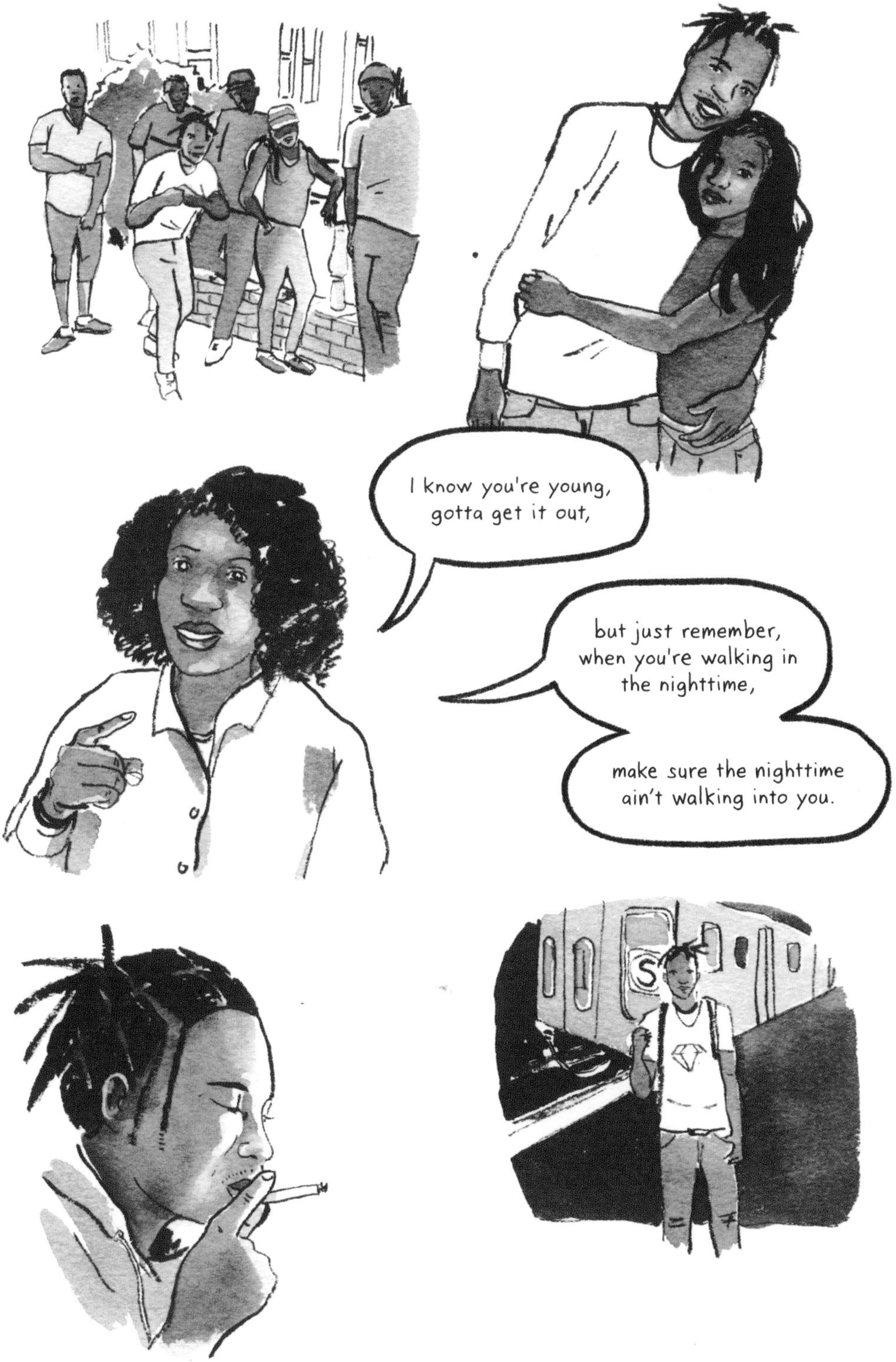
I know you're young, gotta get it out,
but just remember, when you're walking in the nighttime,
make sure the nighttime ain't walking into you.

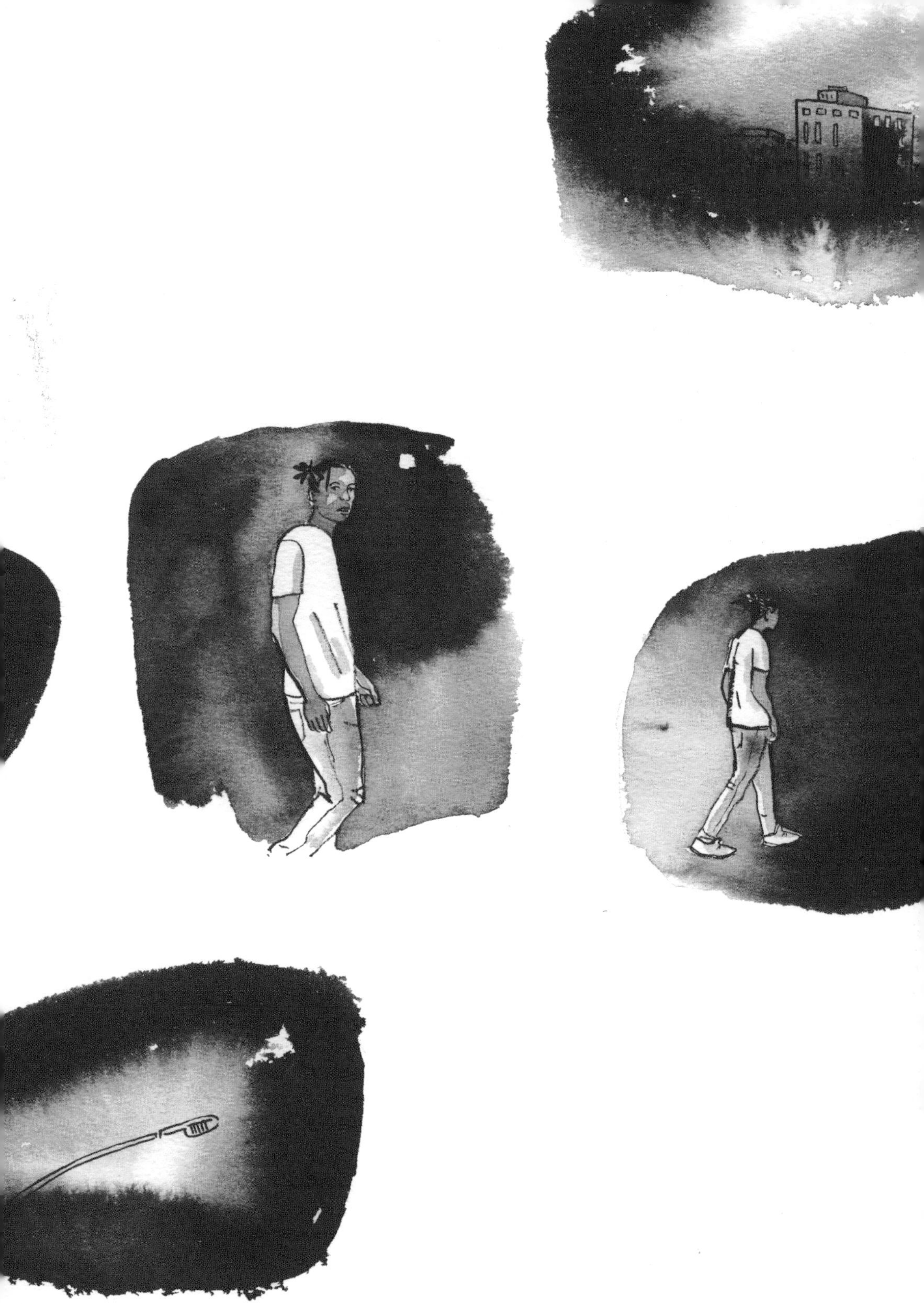

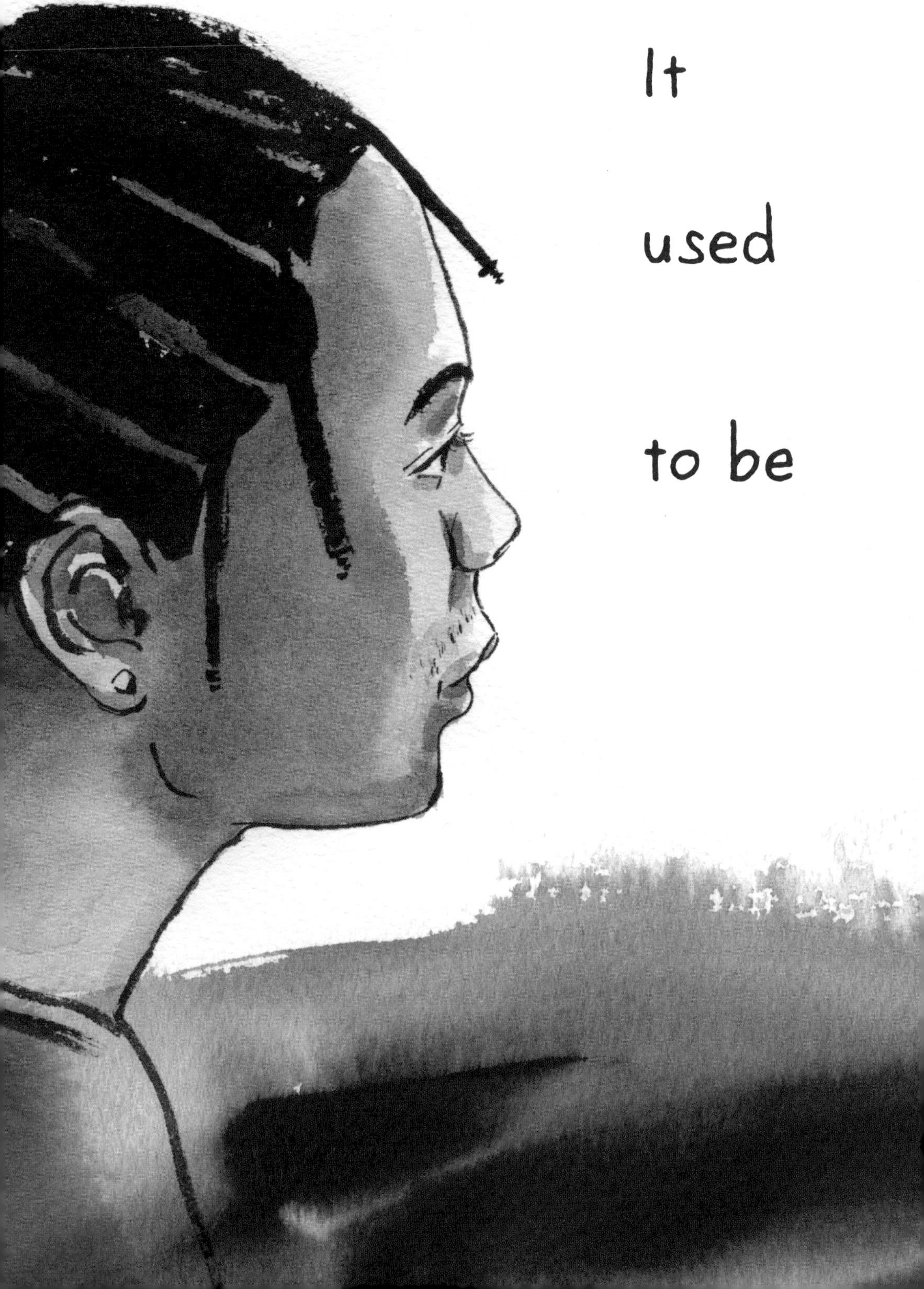

It

used

to be

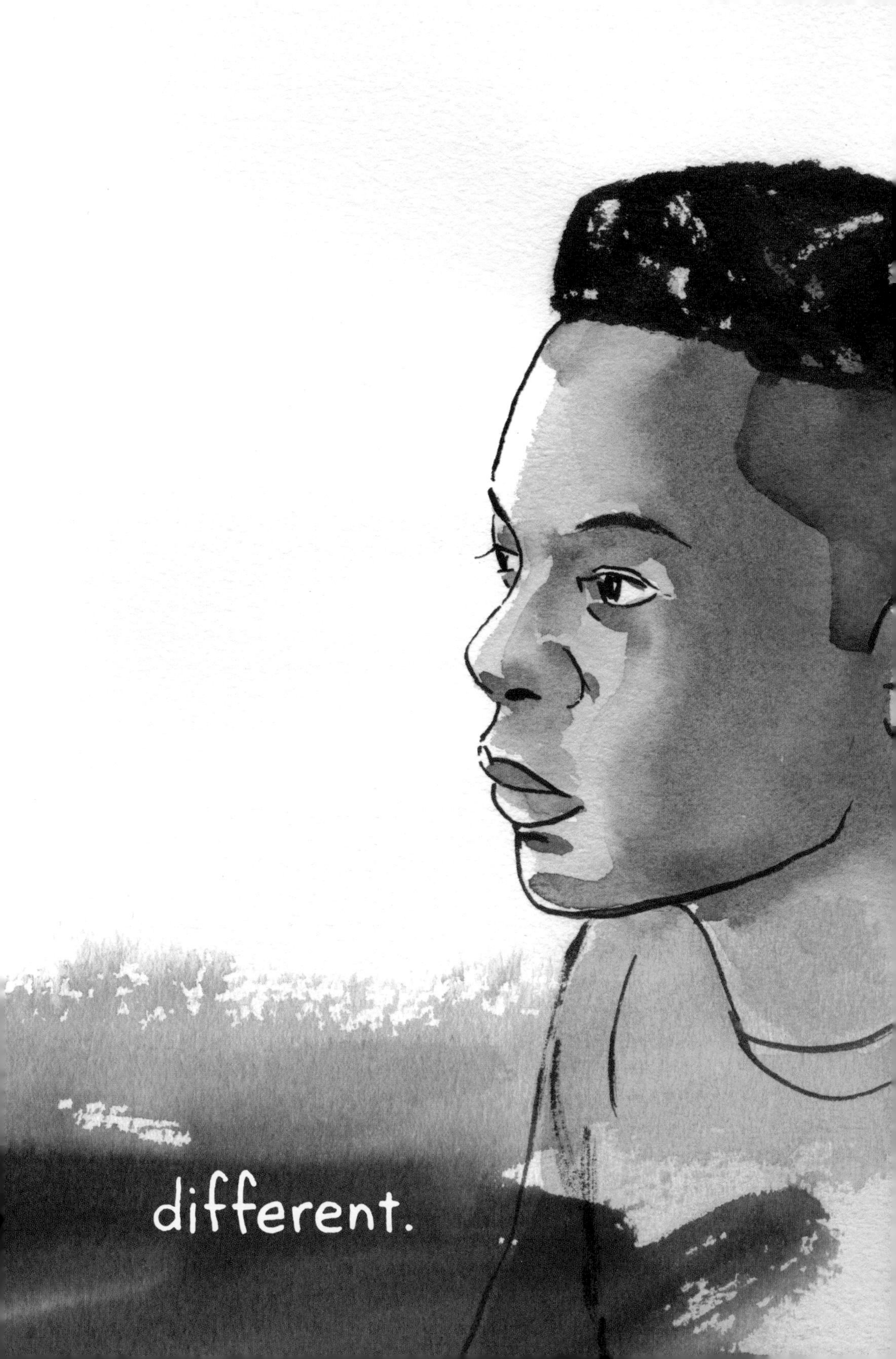
different.

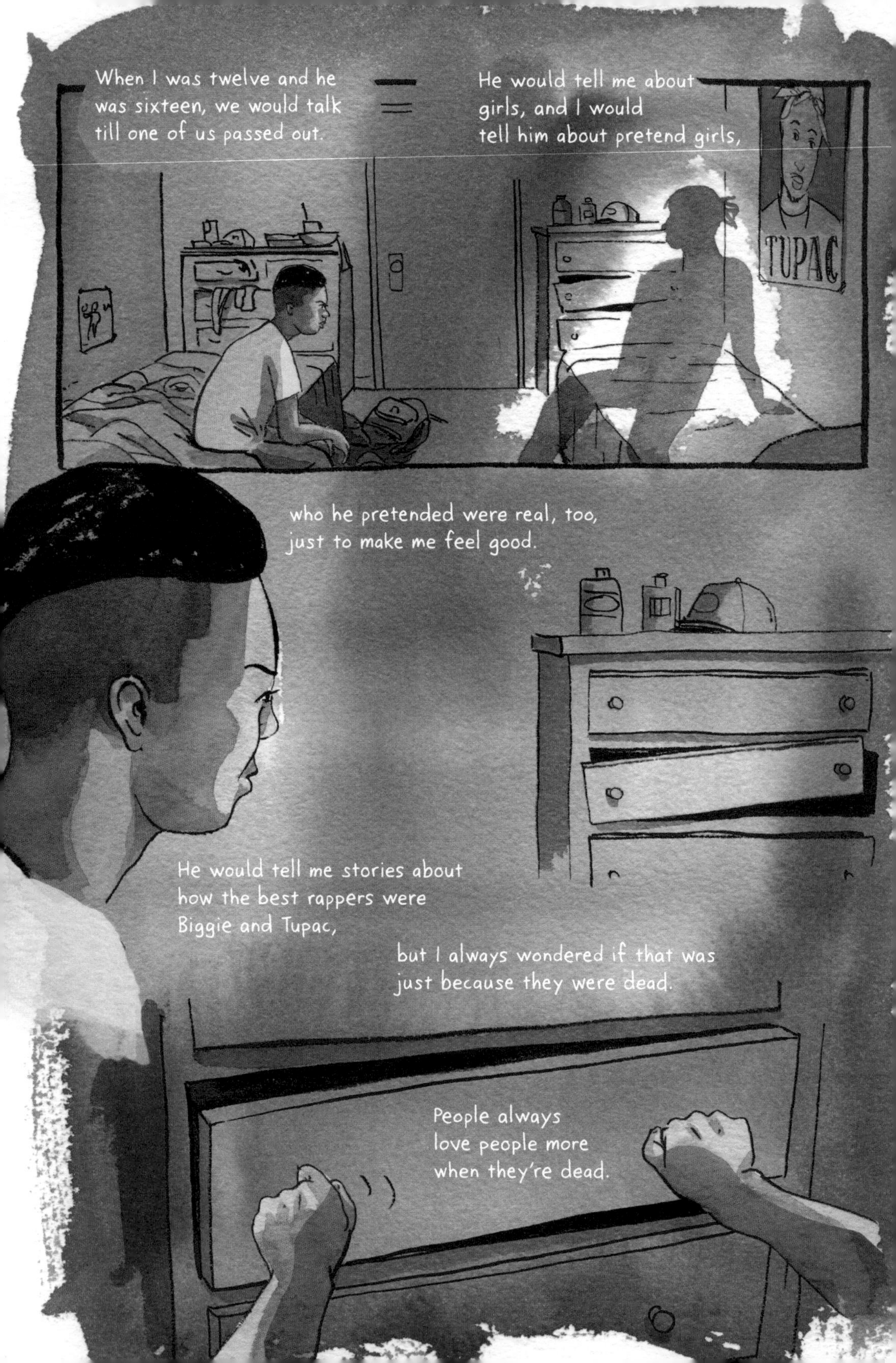
When I was twelve and he was sixteen, we would talk till one of us passed out.
He would tell me about girls, and I would tell him about pretend girls,
TUPAC
who he pretended were real, too, just to make me feel good.
He would tell me stories about how the best rappers were Biggie and Tupac,
but I always wondered if that was just because they were dead.
People always love people more when they're dead.

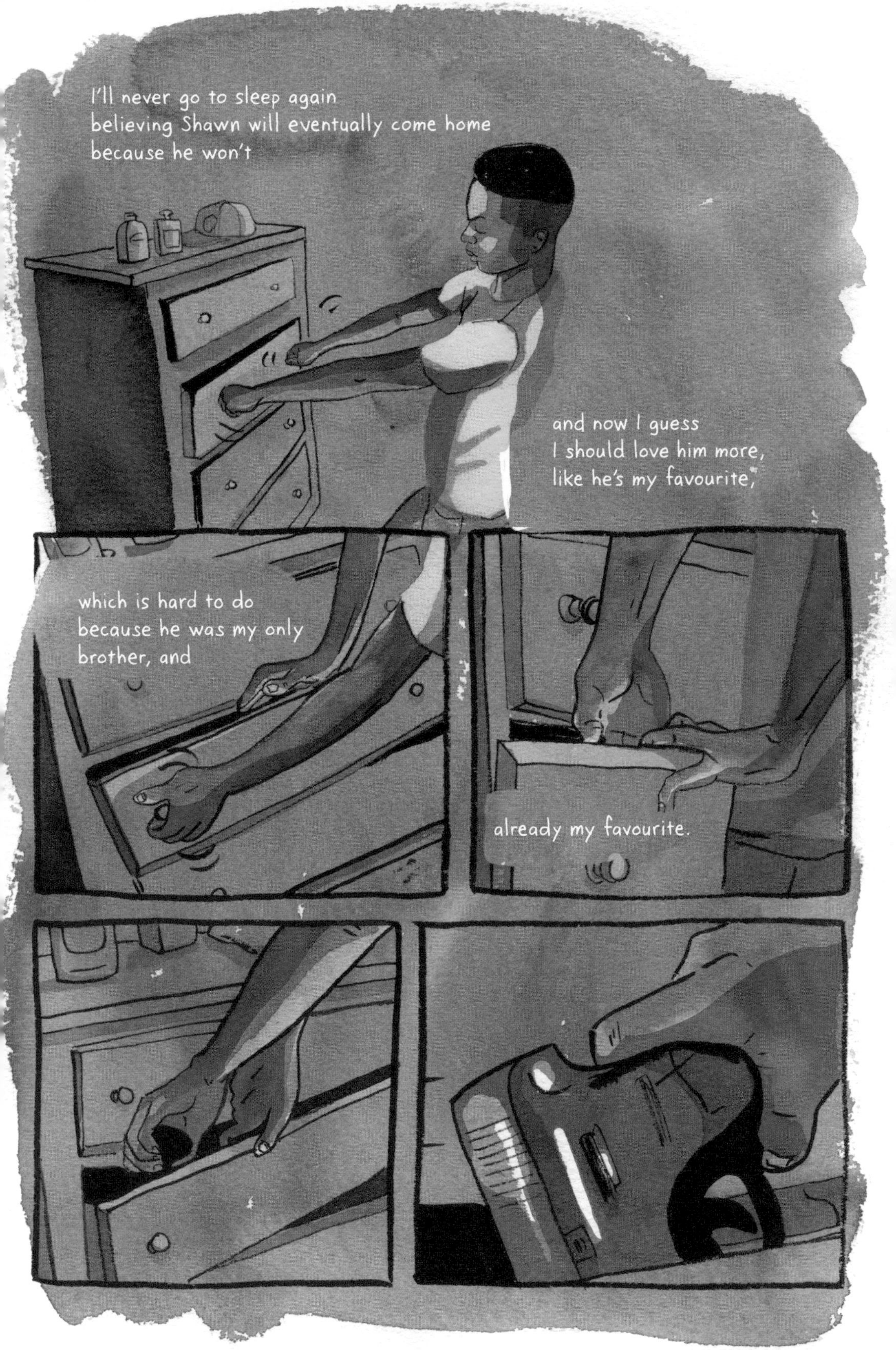
I'll never go to sleep again
believing Shawn will eventually come home
because he won't
and now I guess
I should love him more,
like he's my favourite,
which is hard to do
because he was my only
brother, and
already my favourite.

A cannon
A strap
A piece
A biscuit
A burner

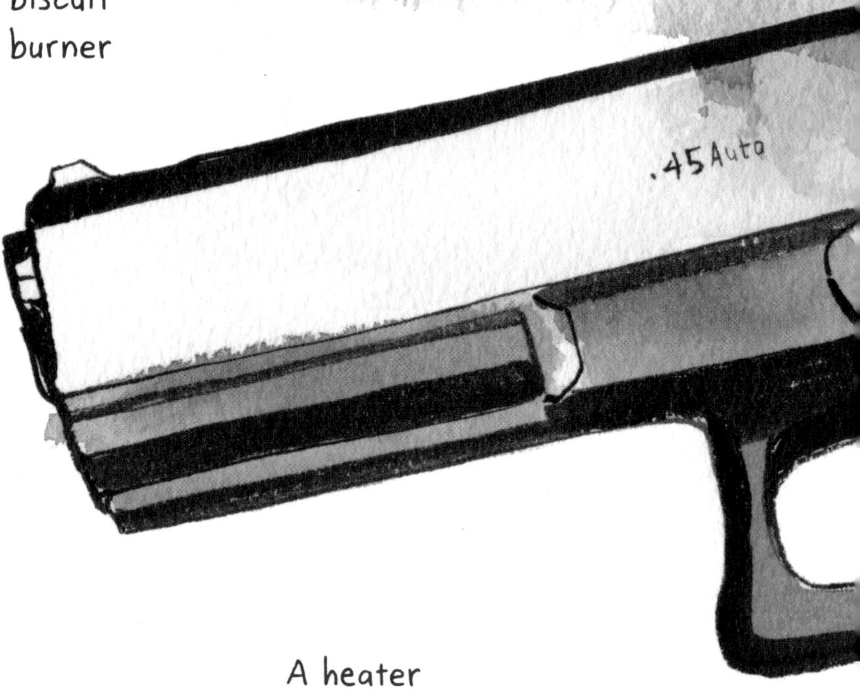
.45 Auto

A heater
A chopper
A gat
A hammer
A tool

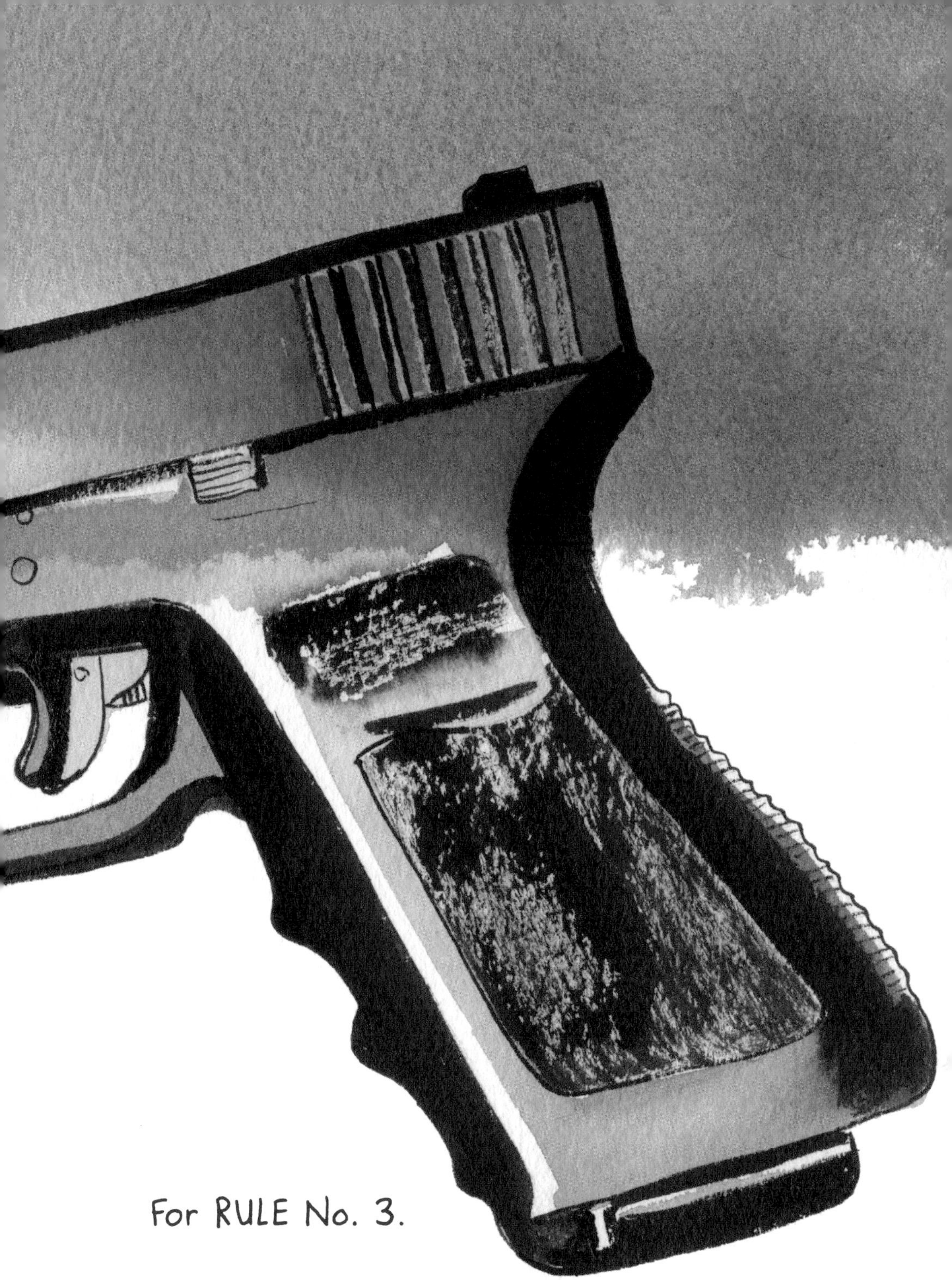

For RULE No. 3.

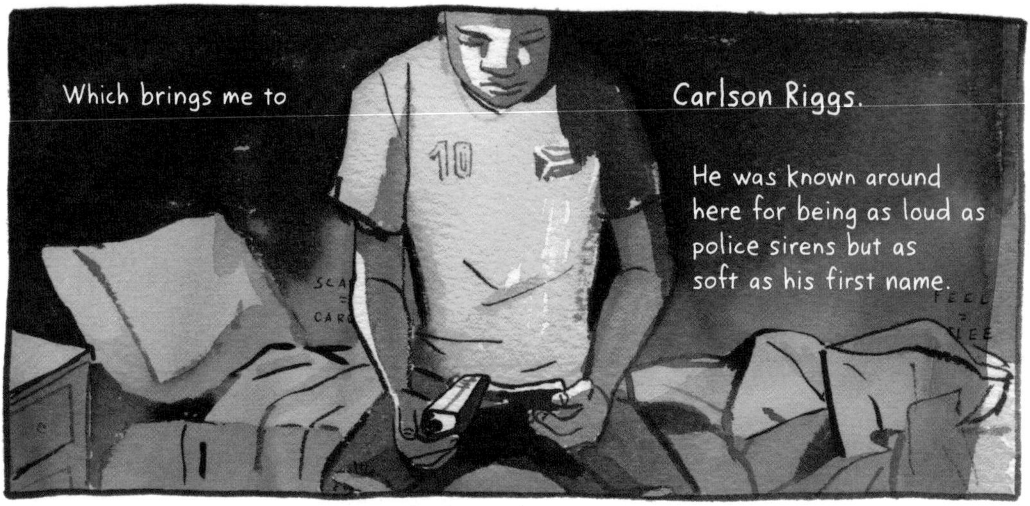
Which brings me to Carlson Riggs.
He was known around here for being as loud as police sirens but as soft as his first name.

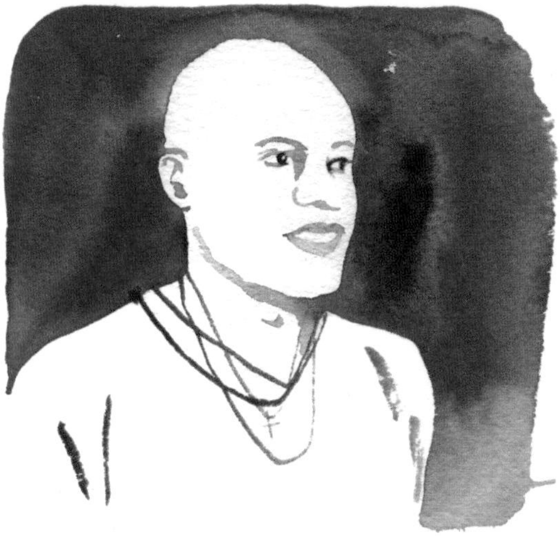

People said Riggs talked so much trash because he was short, but I think it was because his mom made him take gymnastics when he was a kid, and when you wear tights and know how to do cartwheels it might be a good idea to also know how to defend yourself.

Or at least talk like you can.

Riggs and Shawn were so-called friends.

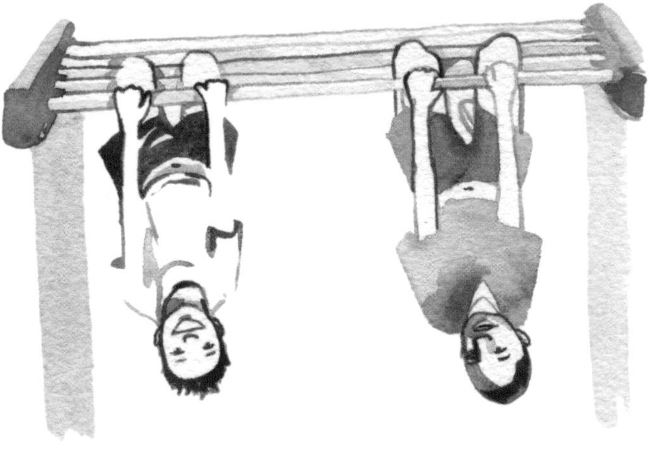

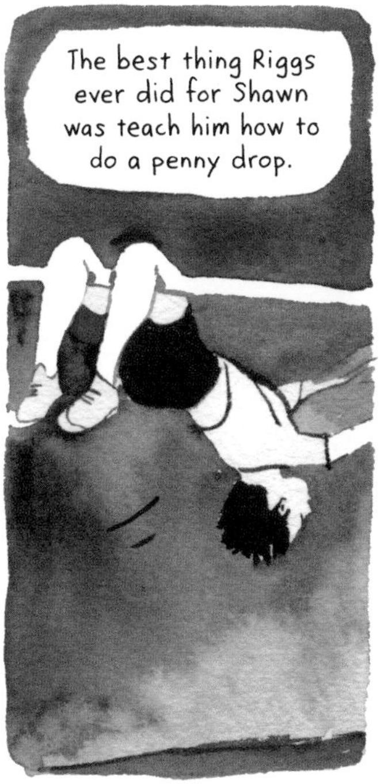
The best thing Riggs ever did for Shawn was teach him how to do a penny drop.

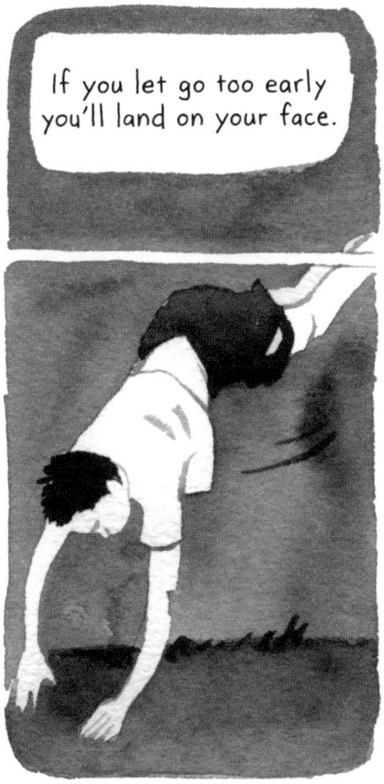
If you let go too early you'll land on your face.

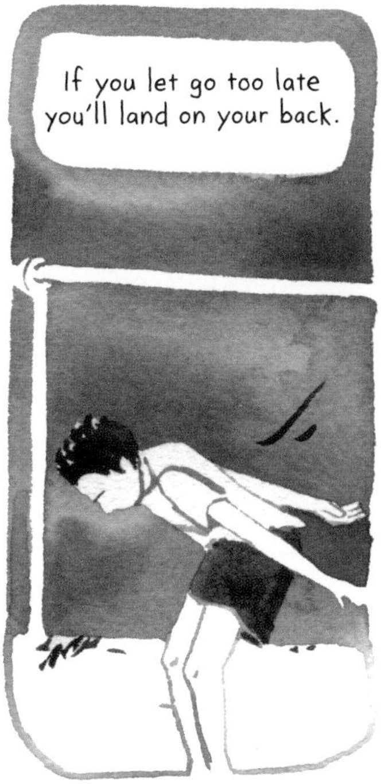
If you let go too late you'll land on your back.

To land on your feet, you gotta time it just right.

Shawn taught me how to time it perfectly.

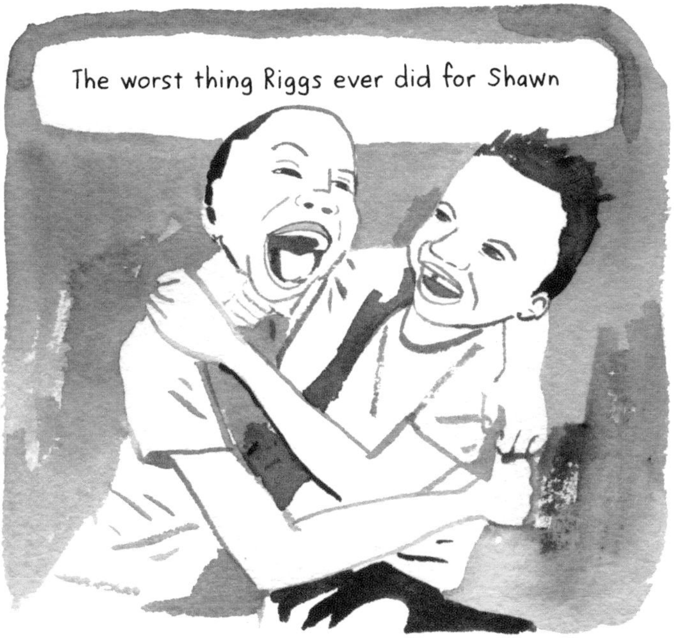
The worst thing Riggs ever did for Shawn

was shoot him.

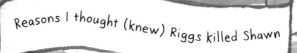

Reasons I thought (knew) Riggs killed Shawn

No. 1:
TURF

abandoned parking lot

JR playground

P.S. 92

Riggs moved to a different part of the hood where the Dark Suns hang and bang and be wild.

SuperLaundry

bus stop

our building

Tony's Pizza

He wanted to join so he could have a backbone built for him by the bite of his block boys who wait for anyone to cross the line into their territory,

Library

OJ's Fruit Market

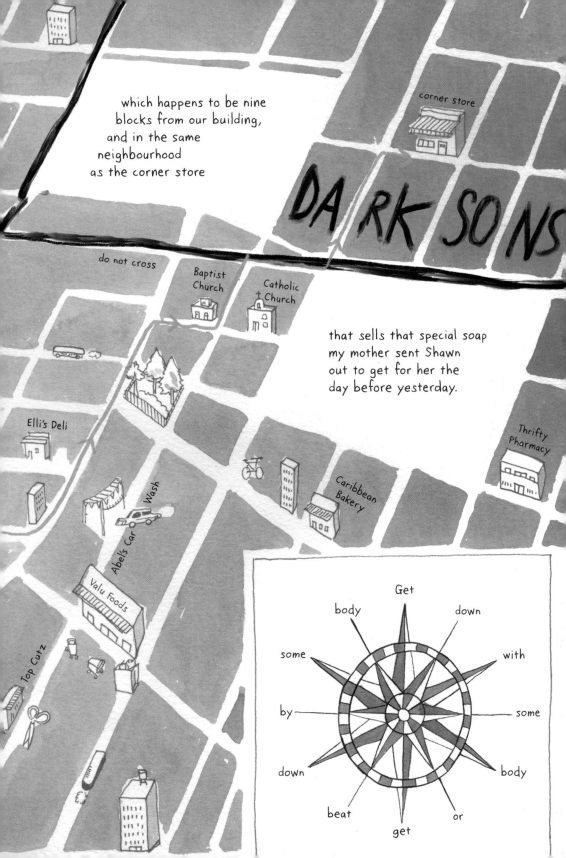

which happens to be nine
blocks from our building,
and in the same
neighbourhood
as the corner store

corner store

DARK SONS

do not cross

Baptist
Church

Catholic
Church

that sells that special soap
my mother sent Shawn
out to get for her the
day before yesterday.

Elli's Deli

Thrifty
Pharmacy

Caribbean
Bakery

Abel's Car Wash

Valu Foods

Top Cutz

Get

body   down

some   with

by   some

down   body

beat   or

get

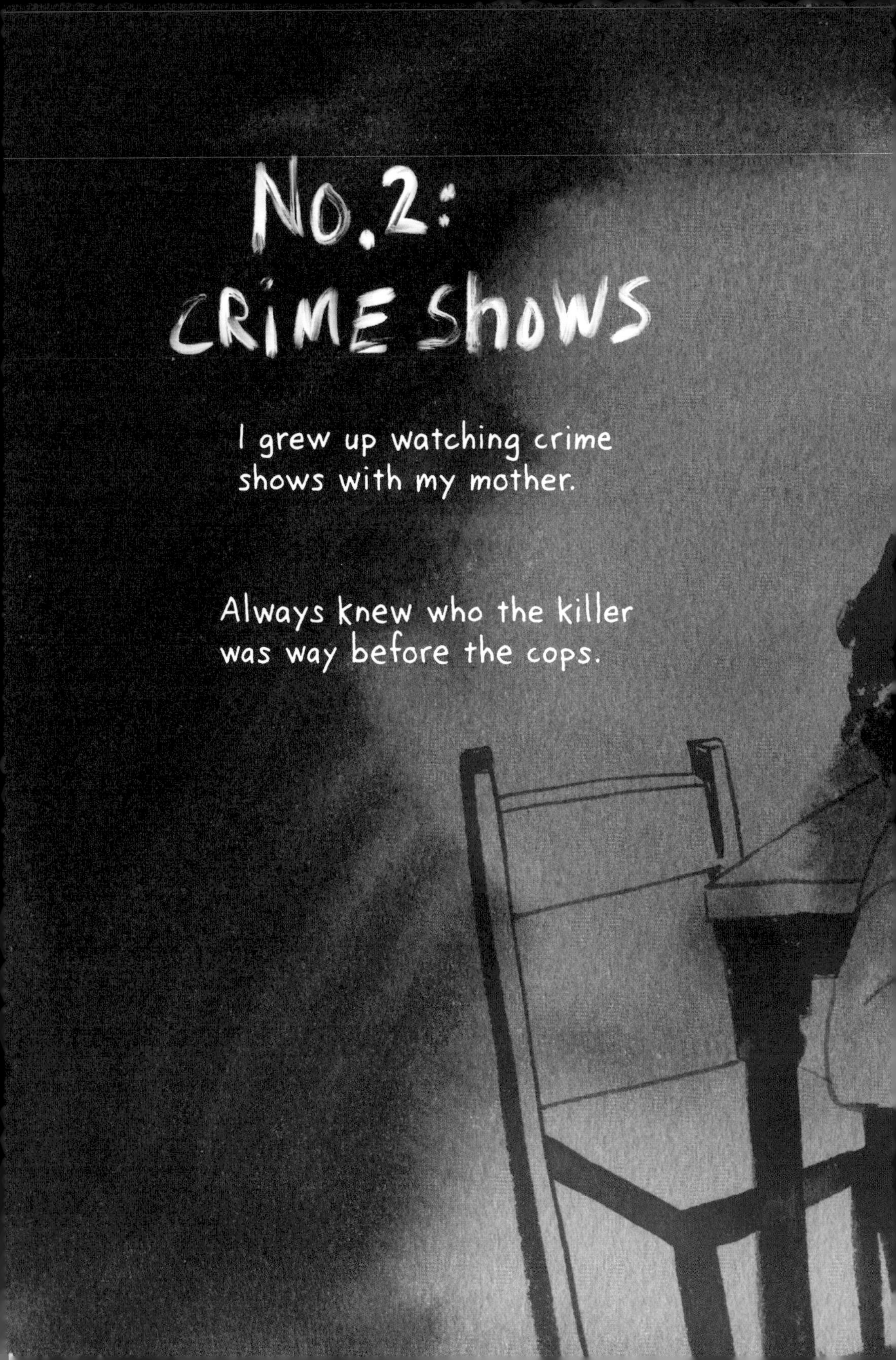
No.2:
CRIME SHOWS
I grew up watching crime shows with my mother.
Always knew who the killer was way before the cops.

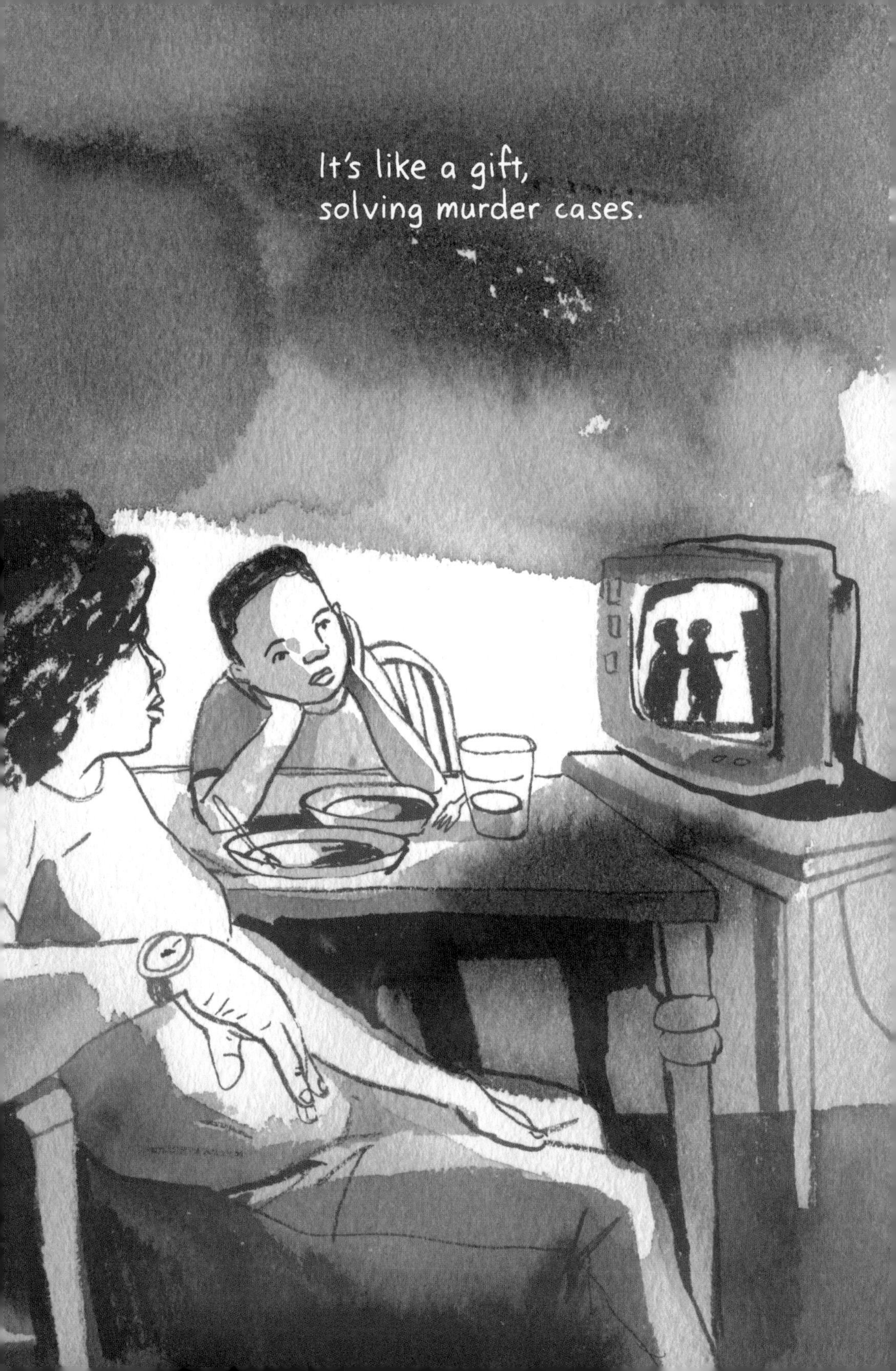
It's like a gift,
solving murder cases.

No.3:

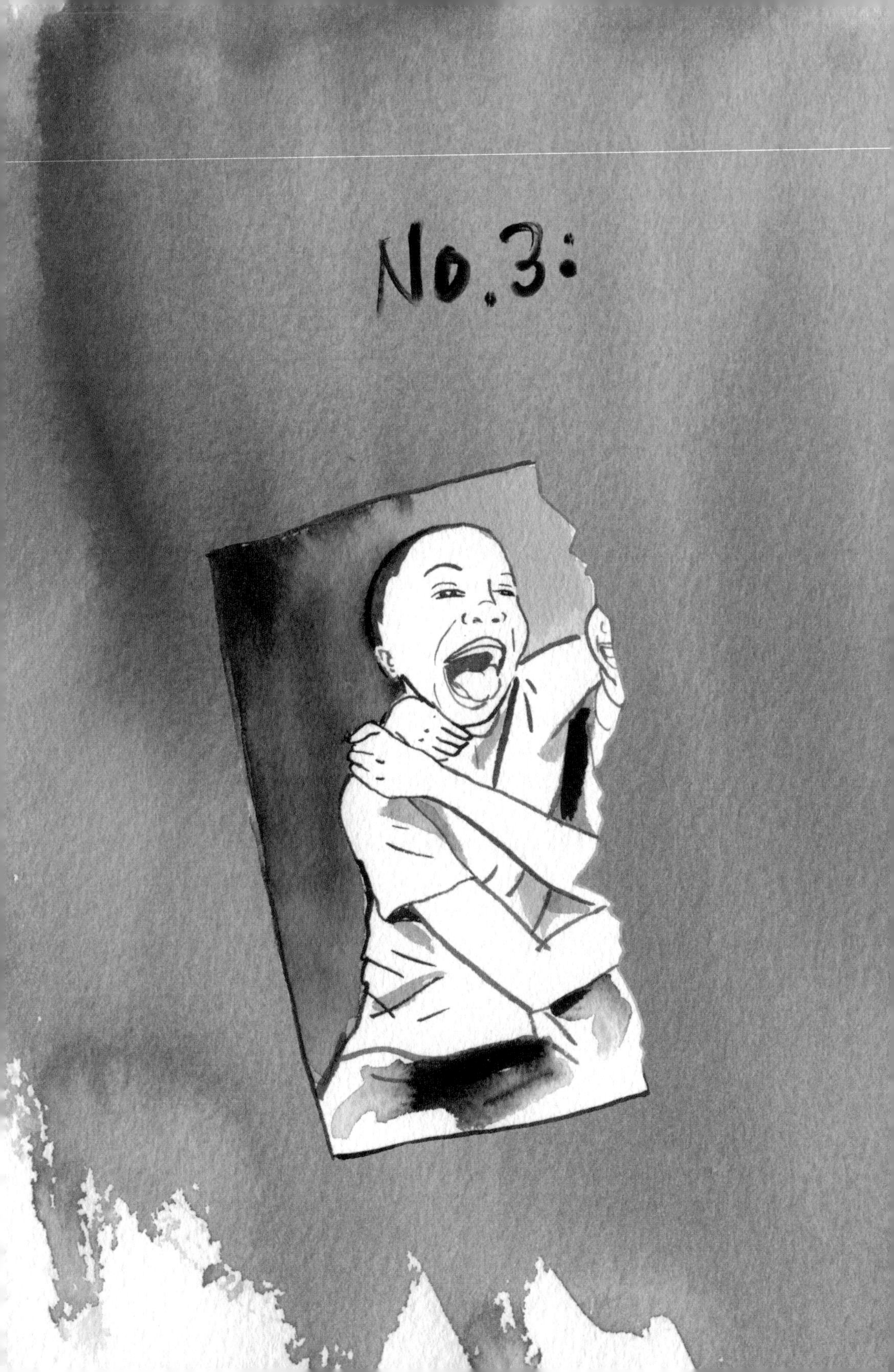

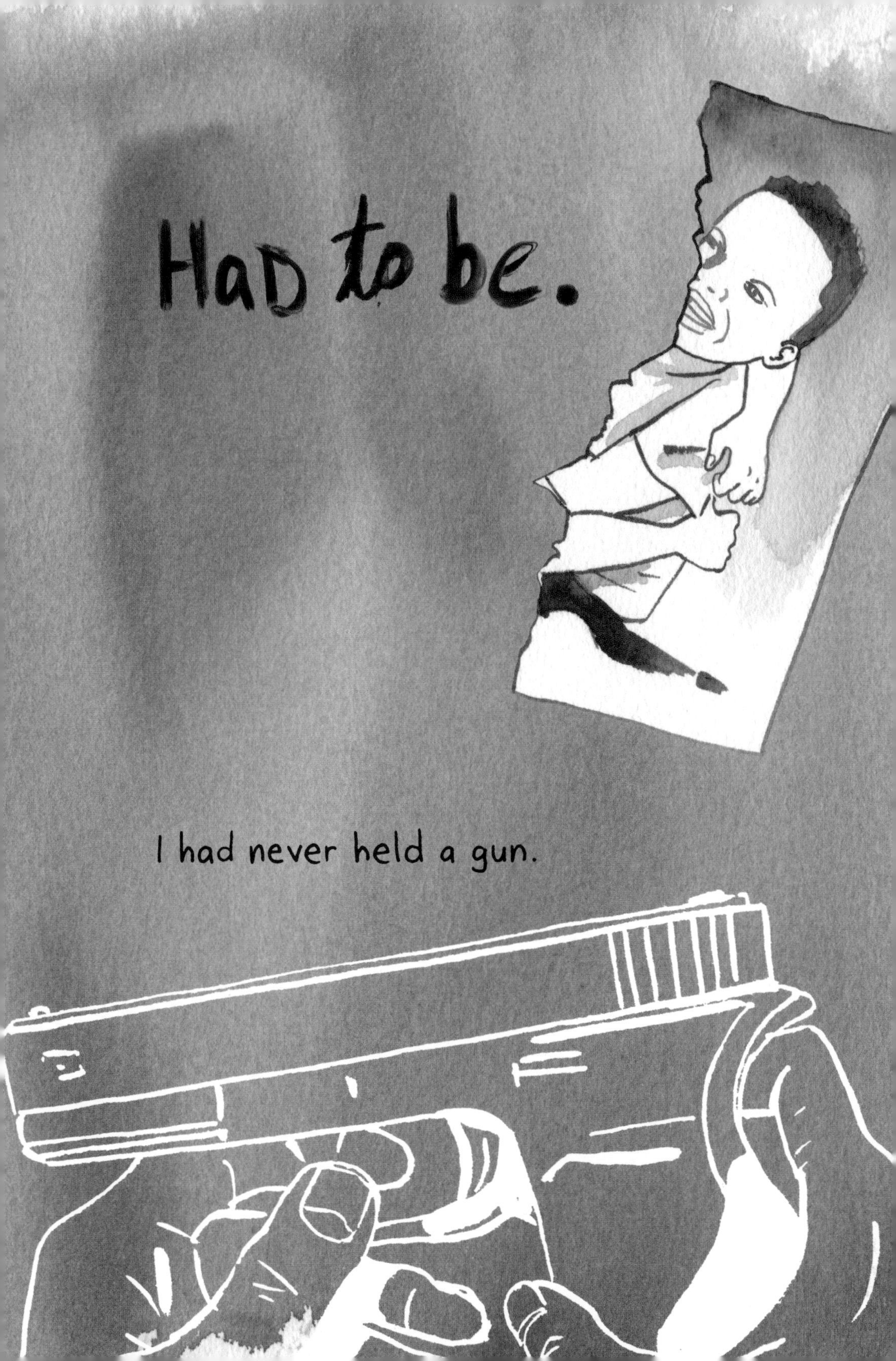
HaD to be.
I had never held a gun.

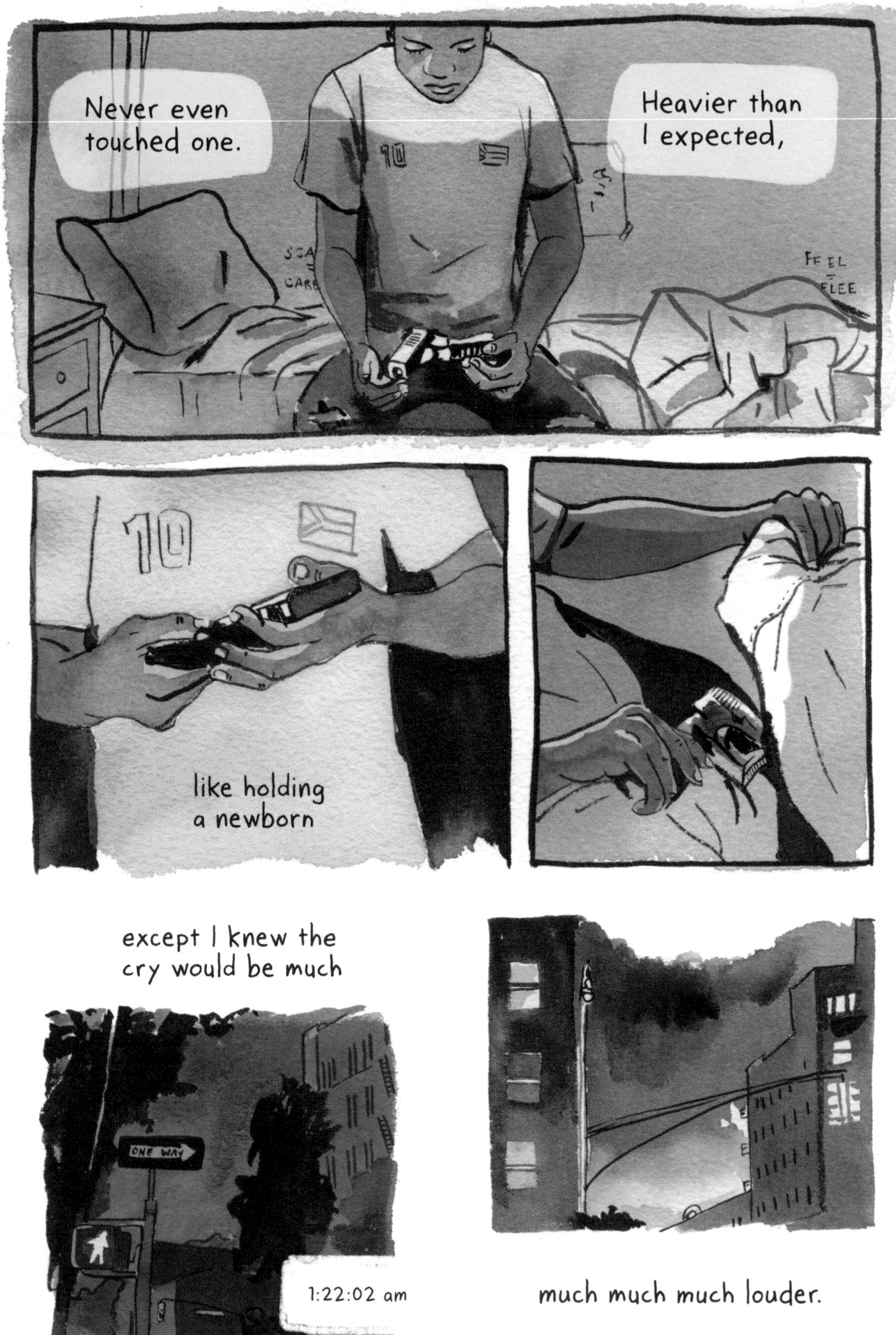
Never even touched one.
Heavier than I expected,
like holding a newborn
except I knew the cry would be much
ONE WAY
1:22:02 am
much much much louder.

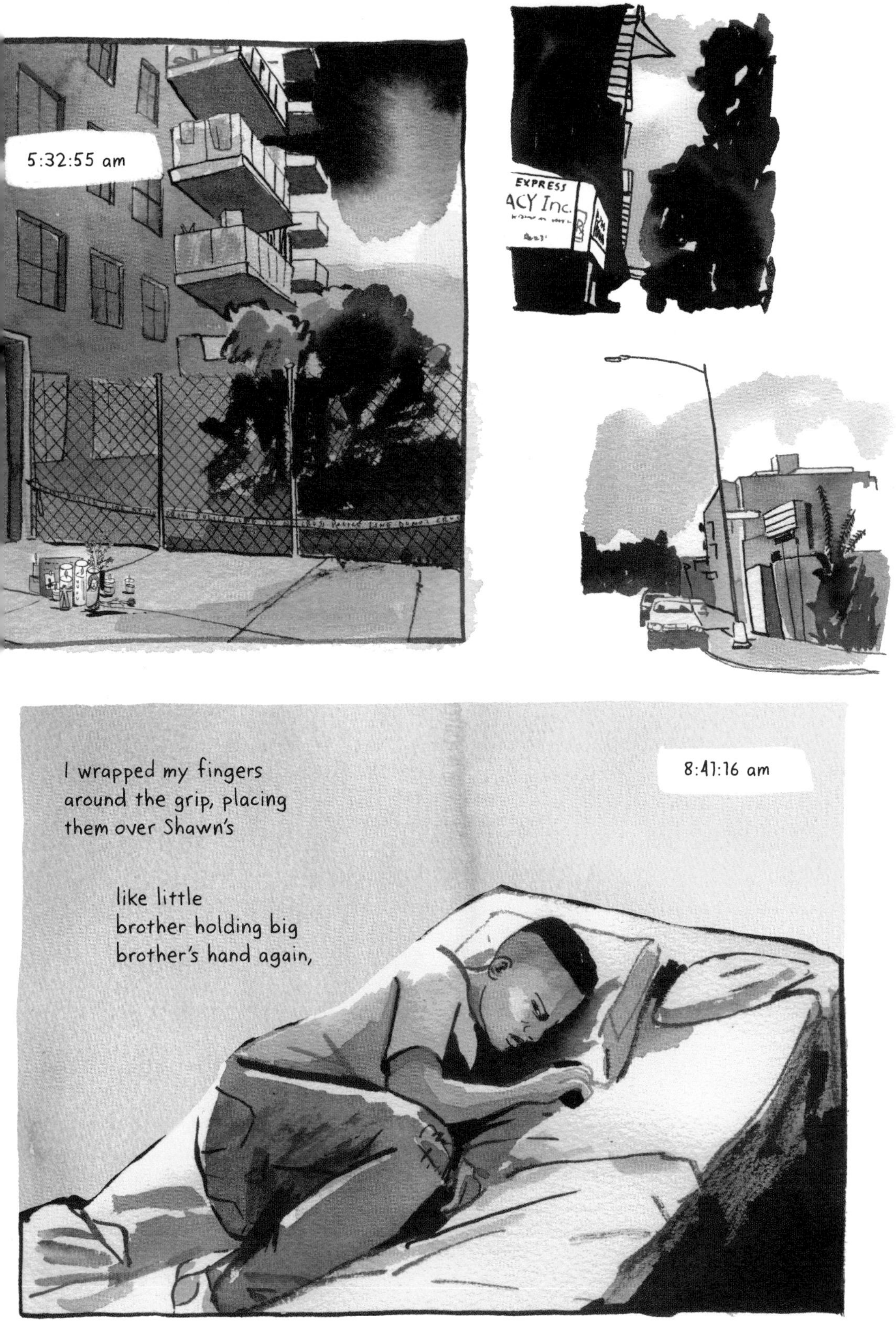
5:32:55 am
EXPRESS
ACY Inc.
I wrapped my fingers
around the grip, placing
them over Shawn's
8:41:16 am
like little
brother holding big
brother's hand again,

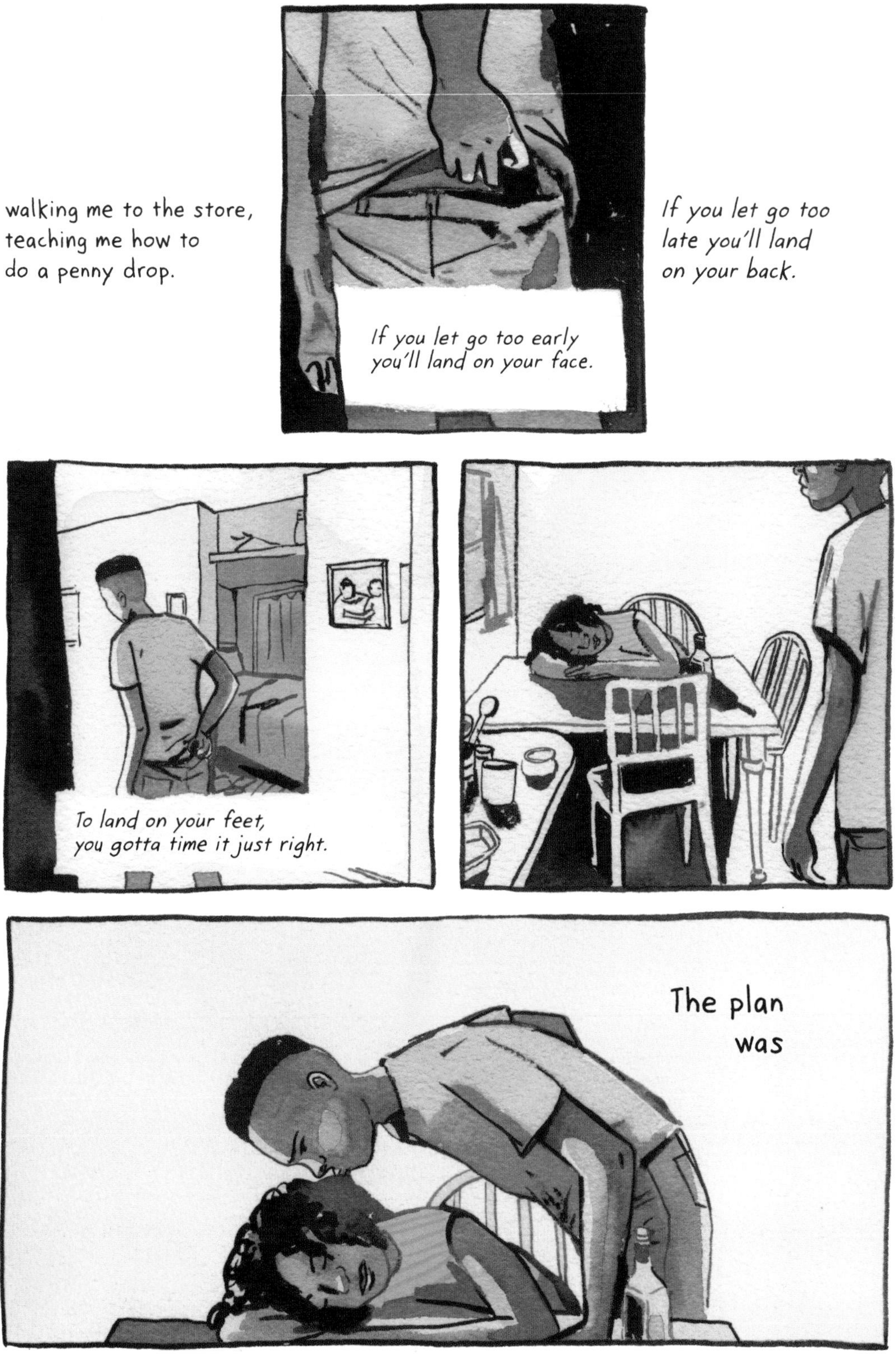
walking me to the store, teaching me how to do a penny drop.
If you let go too early you'll land on your face.
If you let go too late you'll land on your back.
To land on your feet, you gotta time it just right.
The plan was

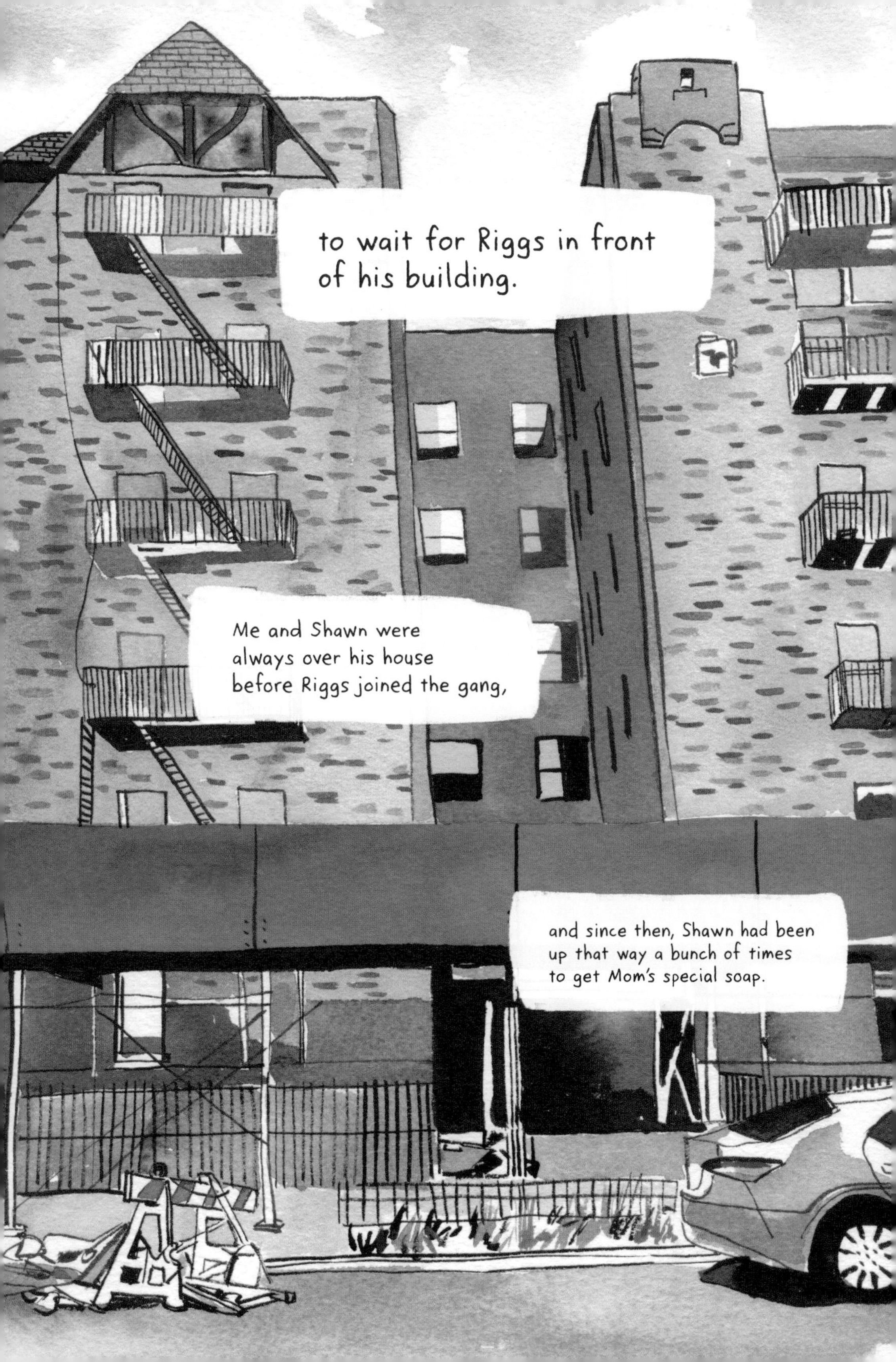
to wait for Riggs in front of his building.
Me and Shawn were always over his house before Riggs joined the gang,
and since then, Shawn had been up that way a bunch of times to get Mom's special soap.

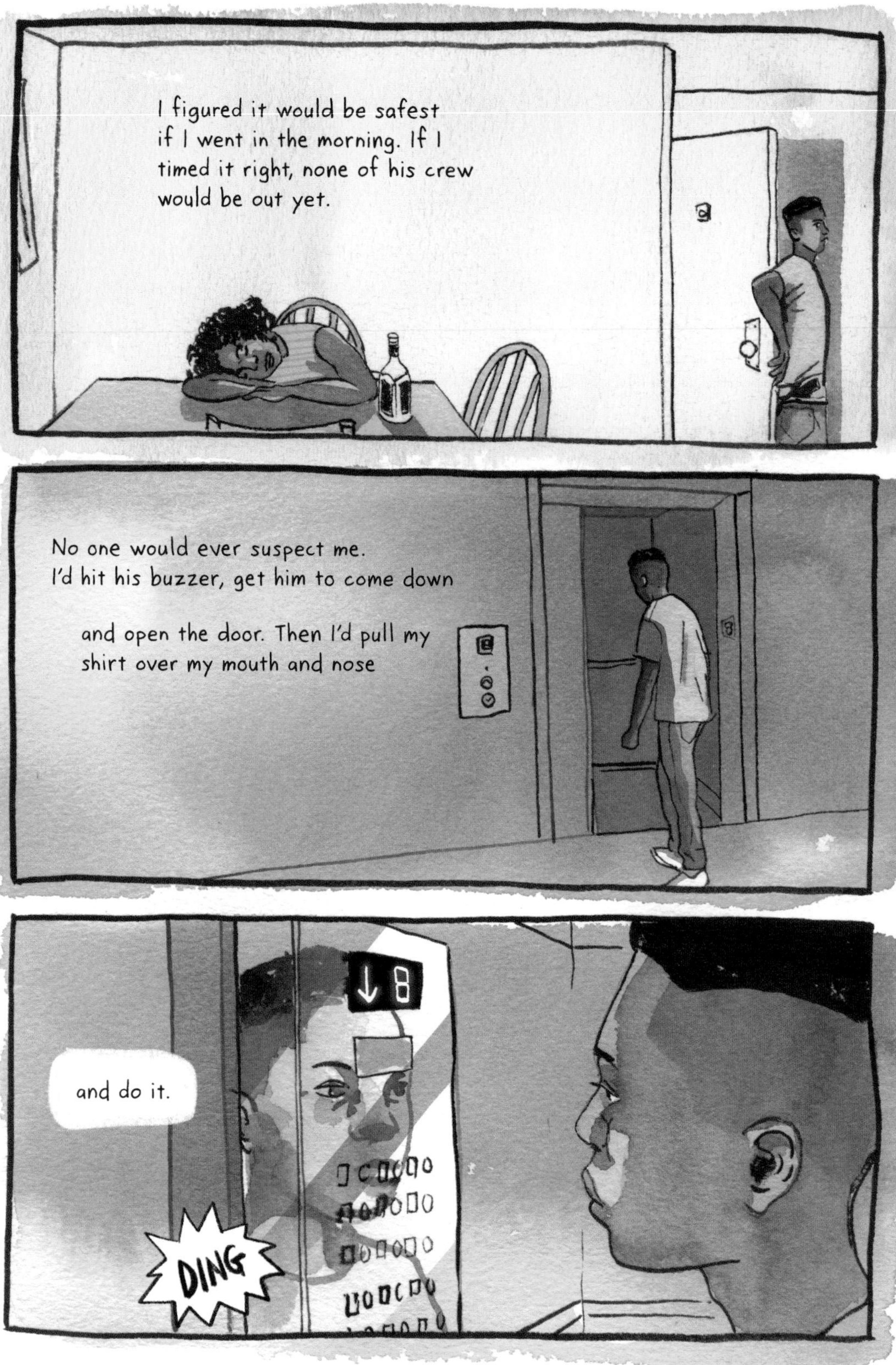
I figured it would be safest if I went in the morning. If I timed it right, none of his crew would be out yet.
No one would ever suspect me. I'd hit his buzzer, get him to come down
and open the door. Then I'd pull my shirt over my mouth and nose
8
and do it.
DING

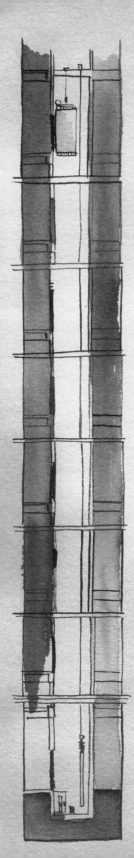

NO SMOKING

CAPACITY 2000 LBS

CITY ID NO. 3P577Q

09:08:02 am
RIP BUCK
You'll be missed
4-EVA
It's uncomfortable when you feel like someone is looking at you but only when you not looking.
Do I know you?
You don't recognise me?
Nah. Not really.

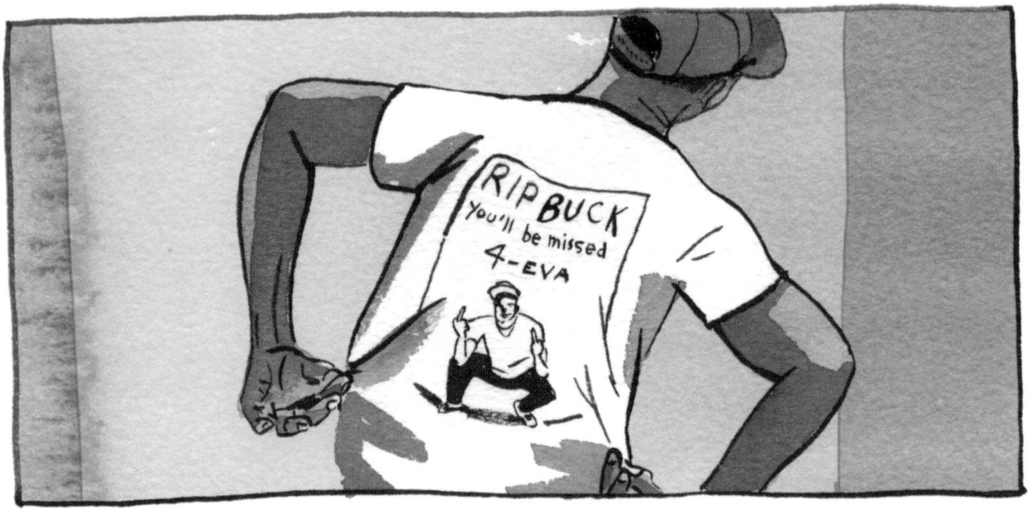
RIP BUCK
You'll be missed
4-EVA

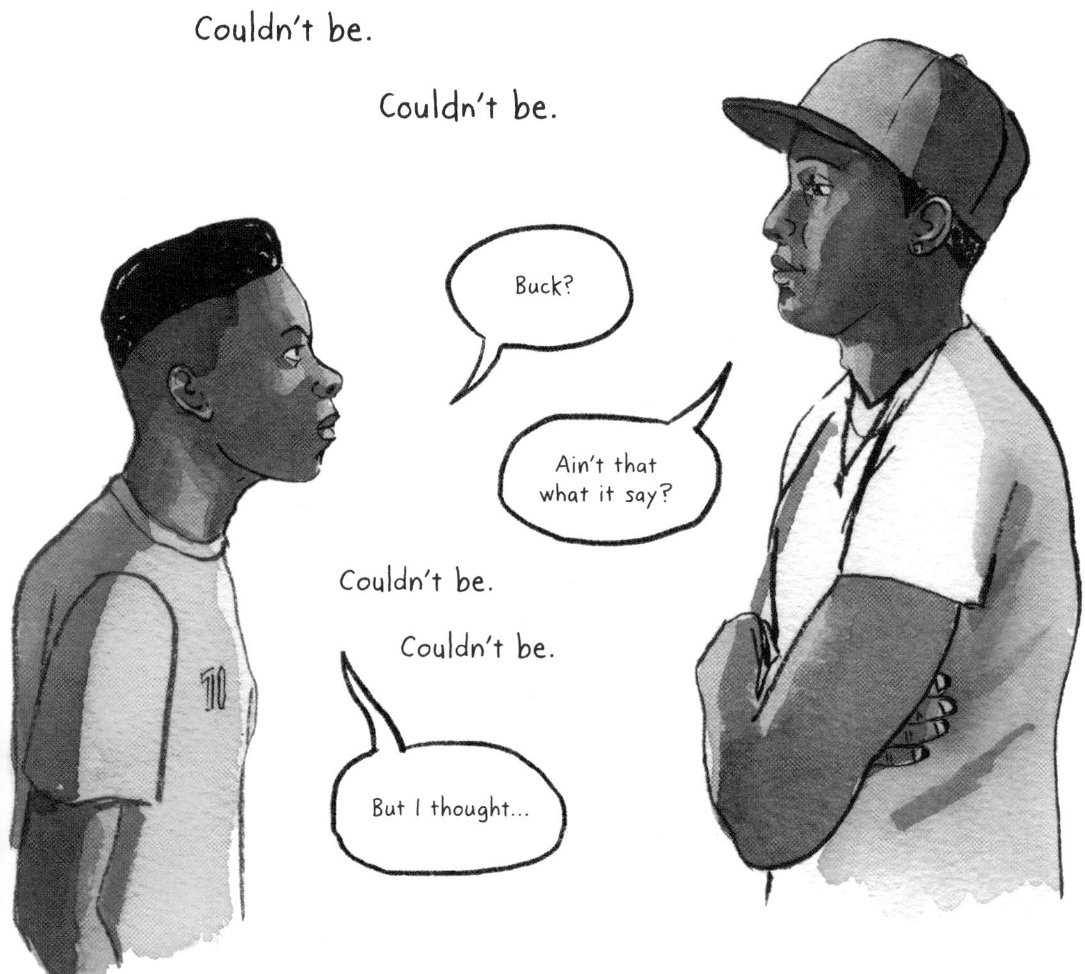
Couldn't be.
Couldn't be.
Buck?
Ain't that what it say?
Couldn't be.
Couldn't be.
But I thought...

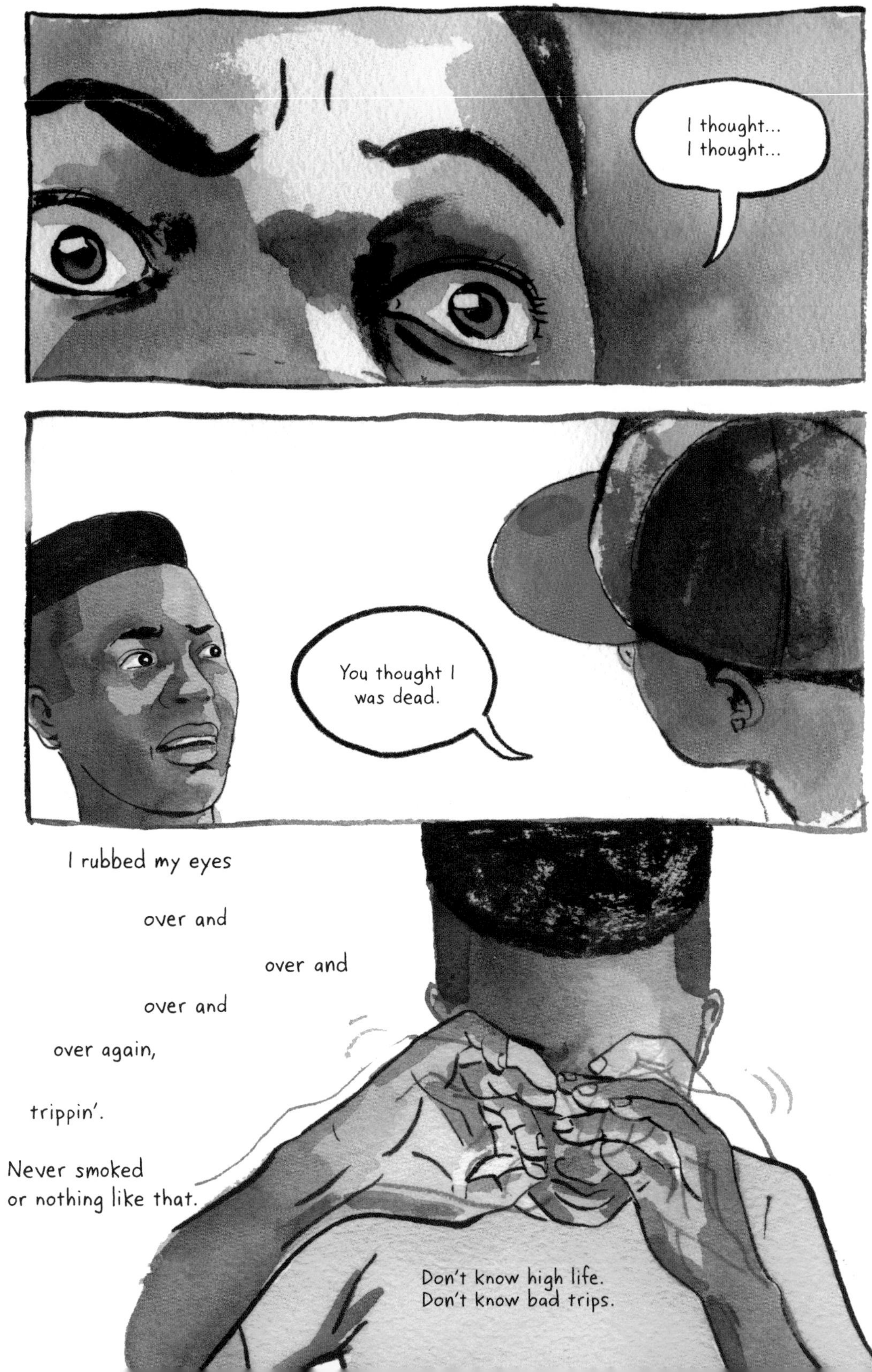

I thought...
I thought...
You thought I was dead.
I rubbed my eyes
over and
over and
over and
over again,
trippin'.
Never smoked
or nothing like that.
Don't know high life.
Don't know bad trips.

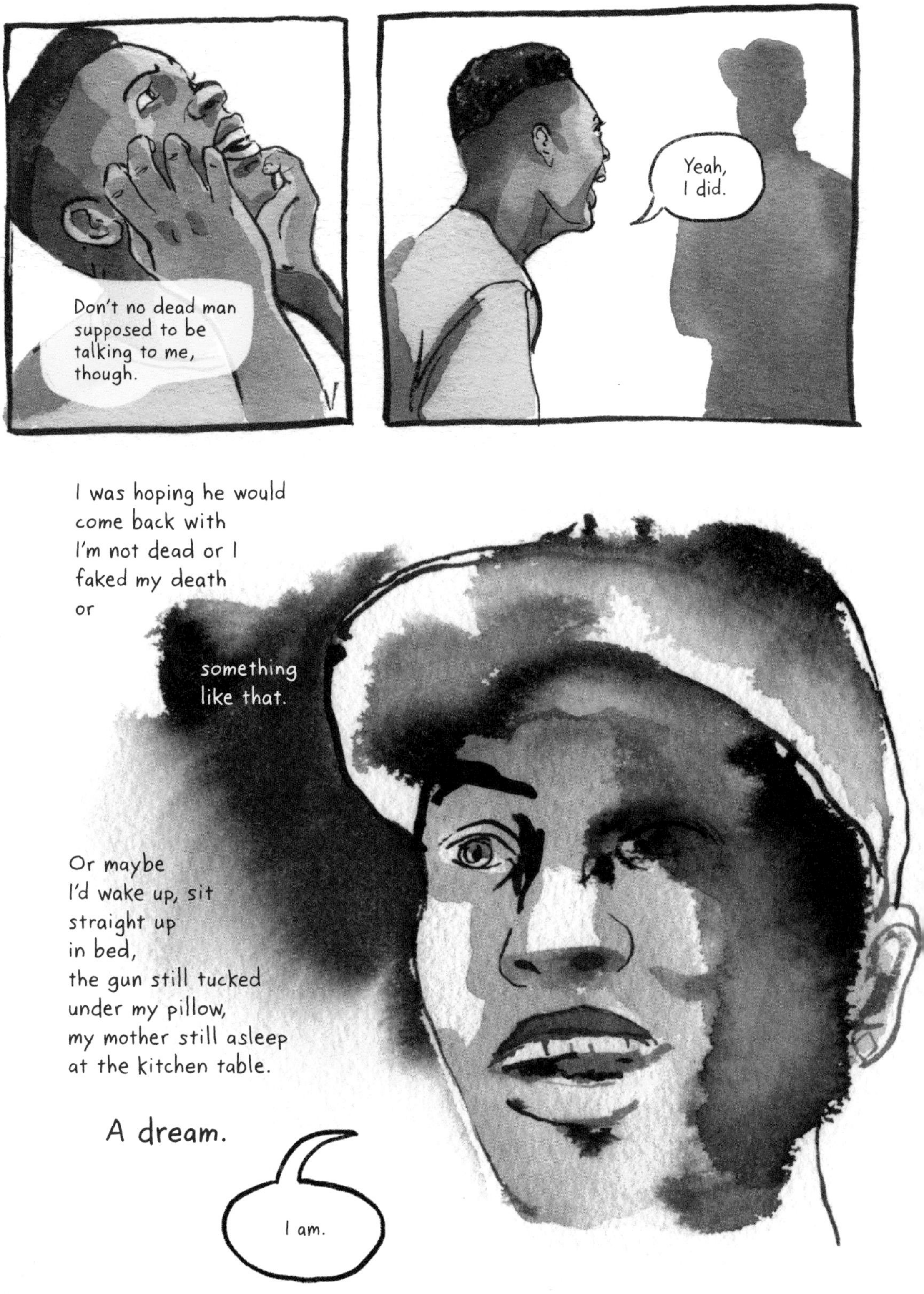
Don't no dead man supposed to be talking to me, though.
Yeah, I did.
I was hoping he would come back with I'm not dead or I faked my death or
something like that.
Or maybe I'd wake up, sit straight up in bed, the gun still tucked under my pillow, my mother still asleep at the kitchen table.
A dream.
I am.

I did all the wake-up tricks.

Pinched the meat
in my armpit,
slapped myself
in the face,
even tried to
blink myself
awake.

Blink

blink

blink

but

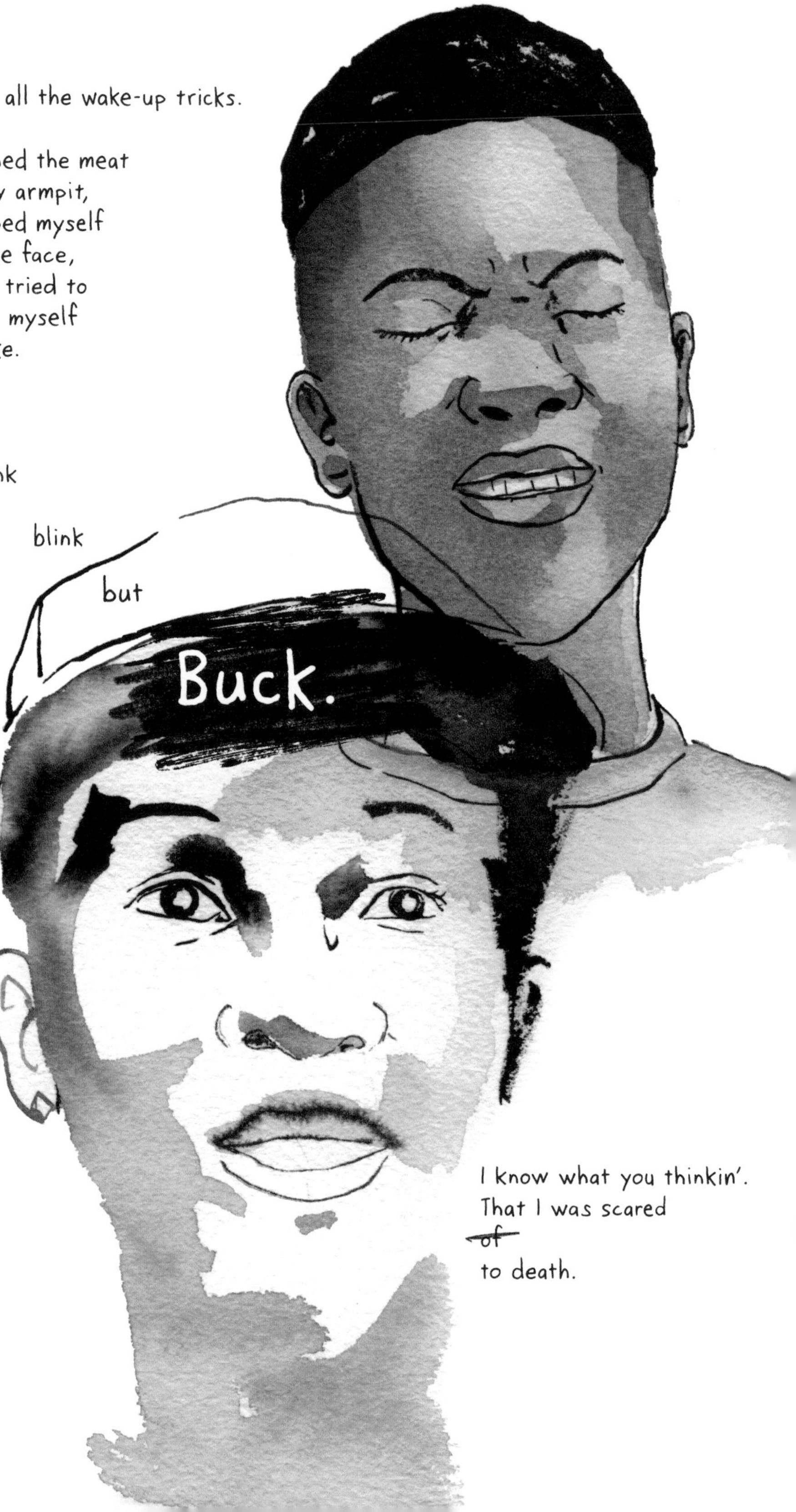

Buck.

I know what you thinkin'.
That I was scared
~~of~~
to death.

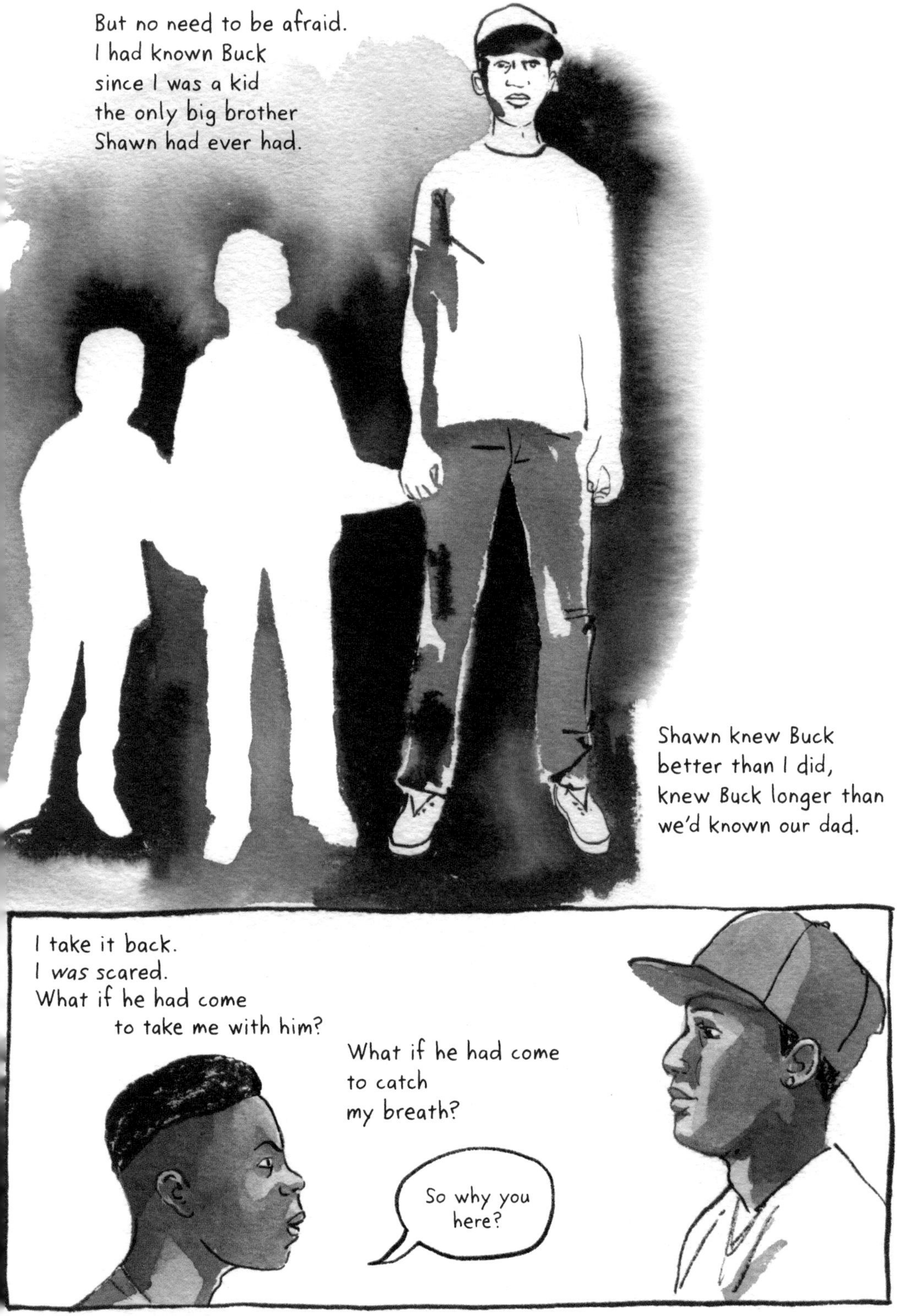
But no need to be afraid.
I had known Buck
since I was a kid
the only big brother
Shawn had ever had.
Shawn knew Buck
better than I did,
knew Buck longer than
we'd known our dad.
I take it back.
I *was* scared.
What if he had come
to take me with him?
What if he had come
to catch
my breath?
So why you
here?

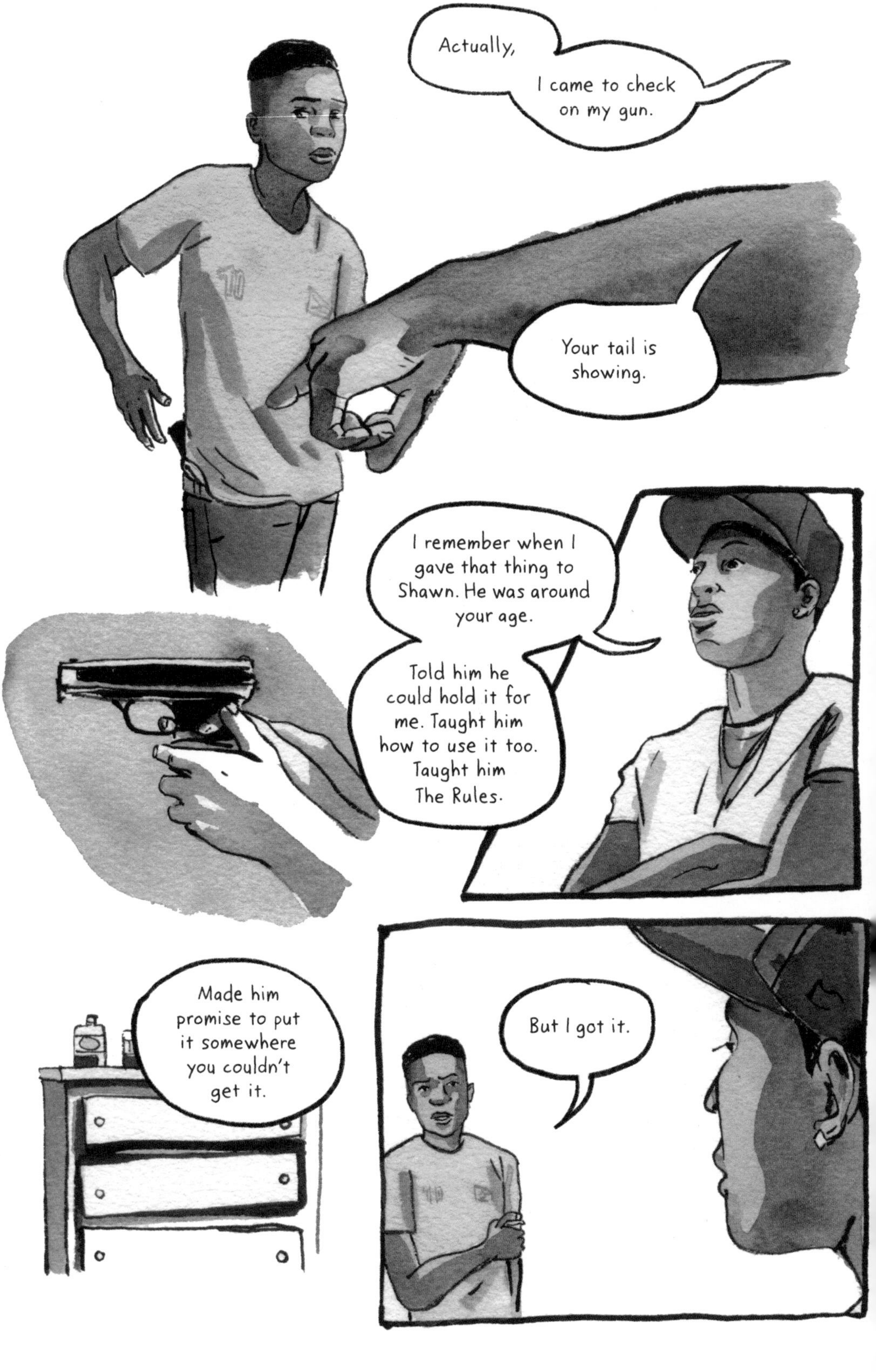
Actually, I came to check on my gun.
Your tail is showing.
I remember when I gave that thing to Shawn. He was around your age.
Told him he could hold it for me. Taught him how to use it too. Taught him The Rules.
Made him promise to put it somewhere you couldn't get it.
But I got it.

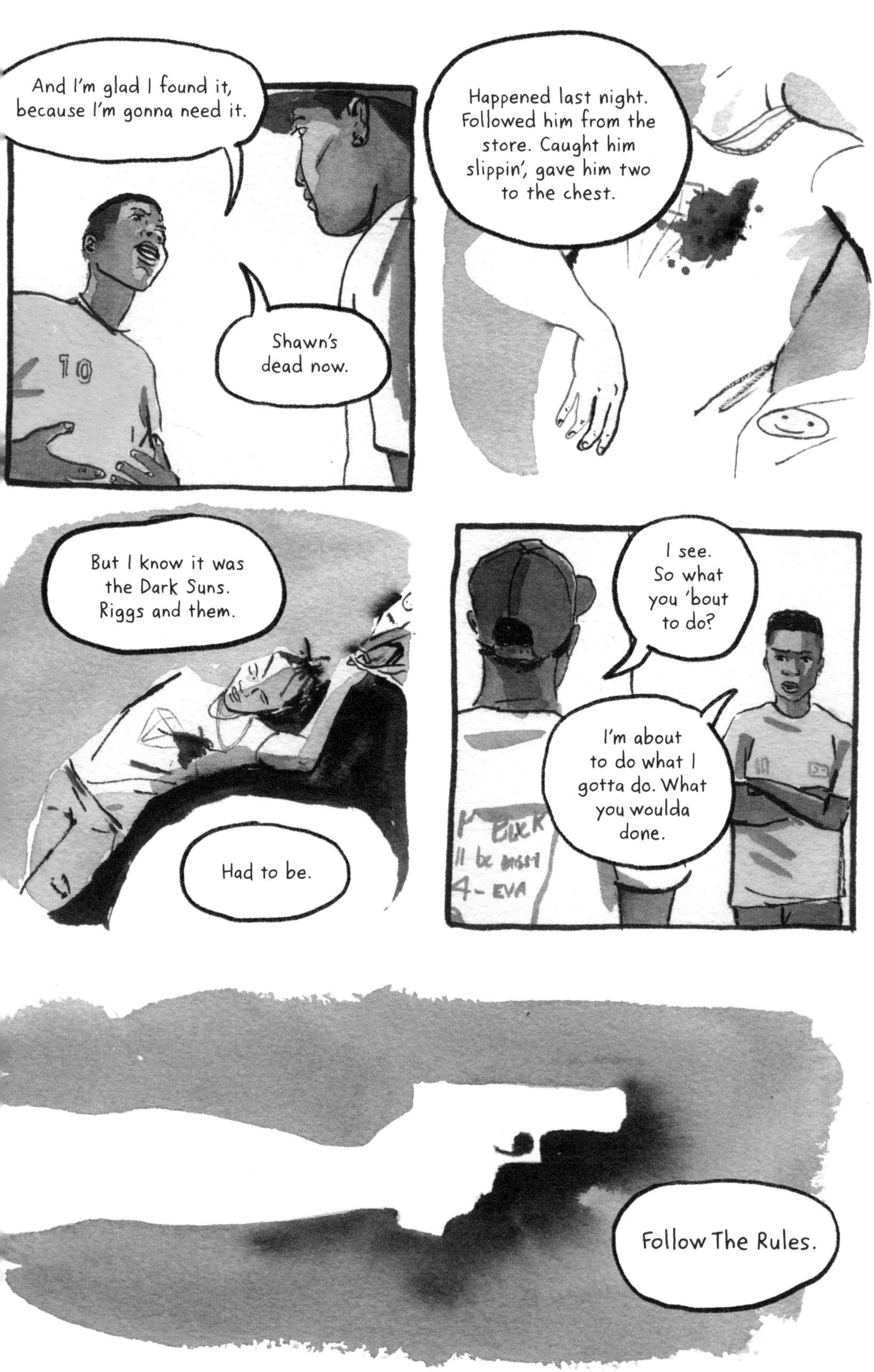
And I'm glad I found it, because I'm gonna need it.
Shawn's dead now.
Happened last night. Followed him from the store. Caught him slippin', gave him two to the chest.
But I know it was the Dark Suns. Riggs and them.
Had to be.
I see. So what you 'bout to do?
I'm about to do what I gotta do. What you woulda done.
Follow The Rules.

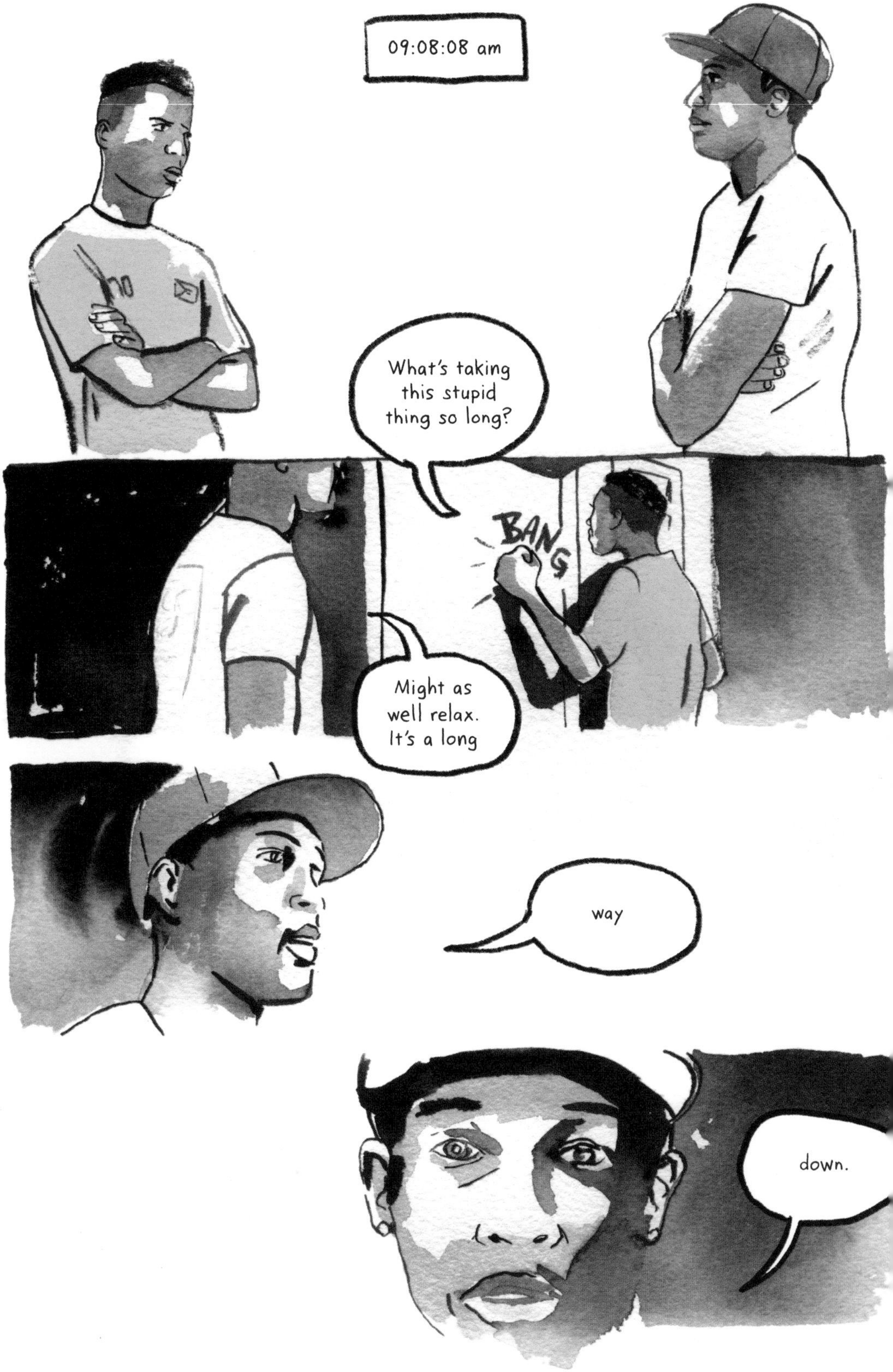
09:08:08 am
What's taking this stupid thing so long?
BANG
Might as well relax. It's a long
way
down.

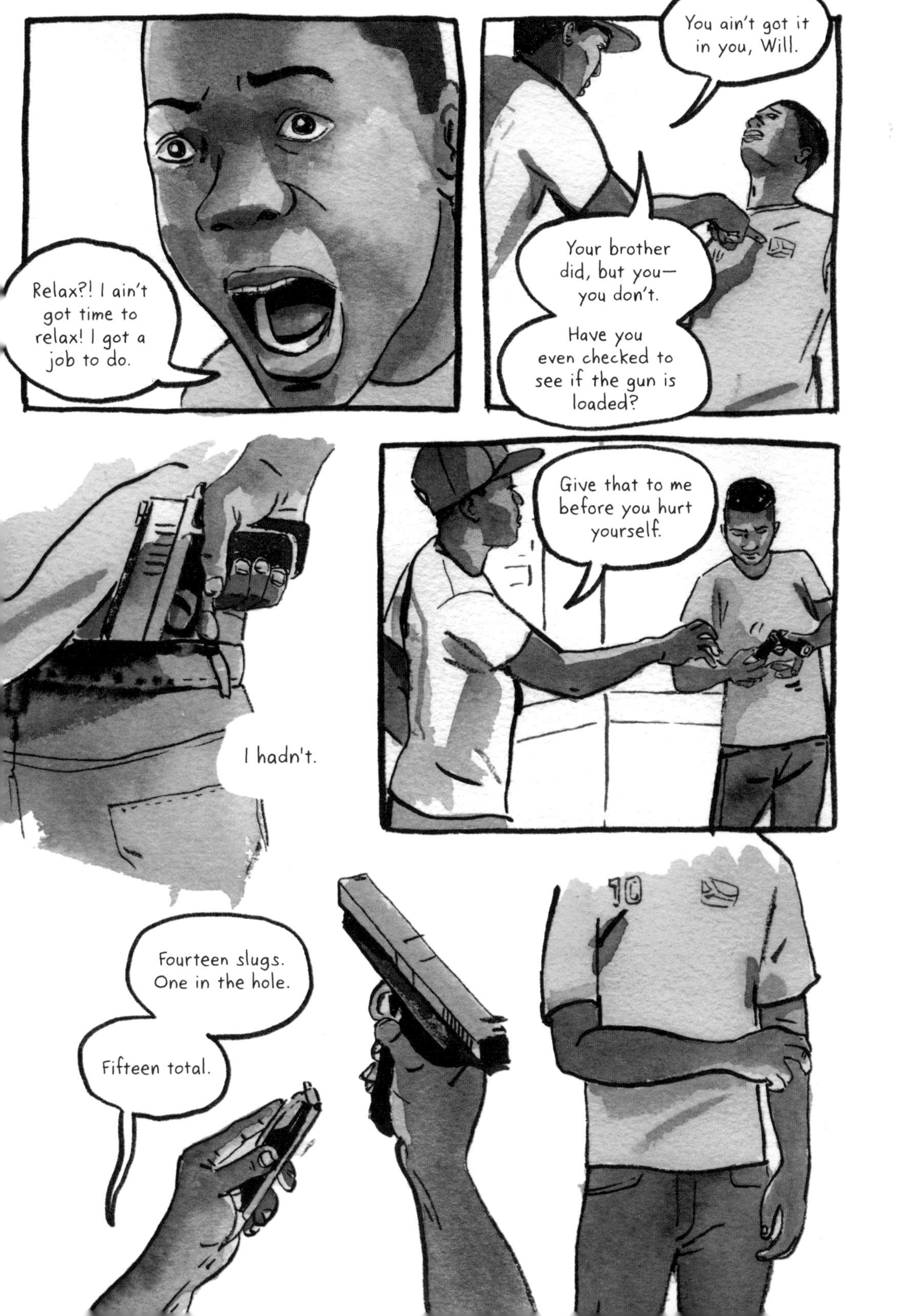
Relax?! I ain't got time to relax! I got a job to do.
You ain't got it in you, Will.
Your brother did, but you— you don't.
Have you even checked to see if the gun is loaded?
I hadn't.
Give that to me before you hurt yourself.
Fourteen slugs. One in the hole.
Fifteen total.

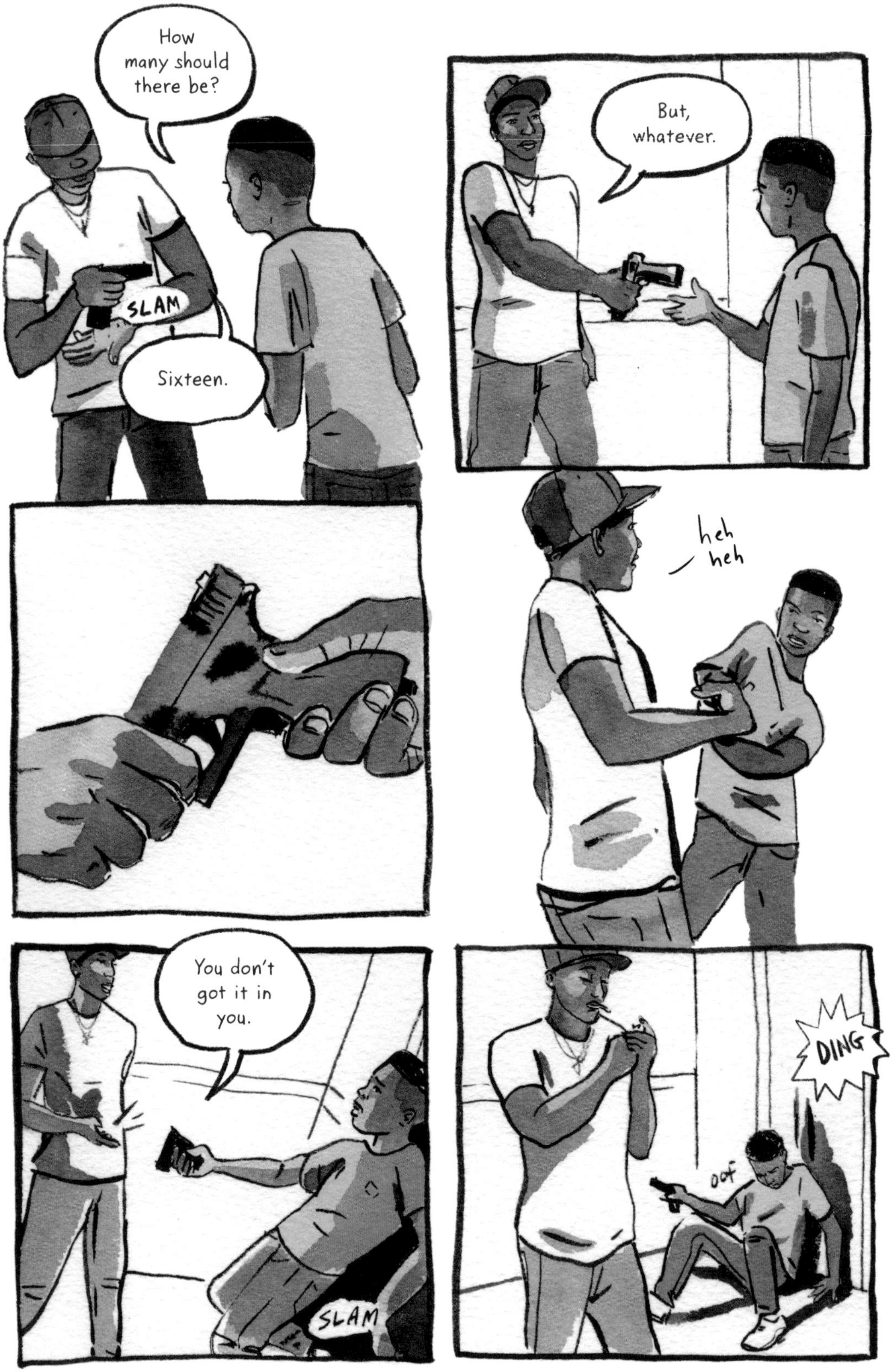
How many should there be?
SLAM
Sixteen.
But, whatever.
heh heh
You don't got it in you.
SLAM
DING
oof

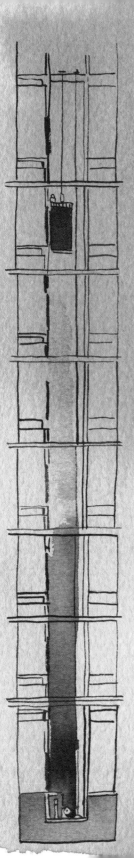

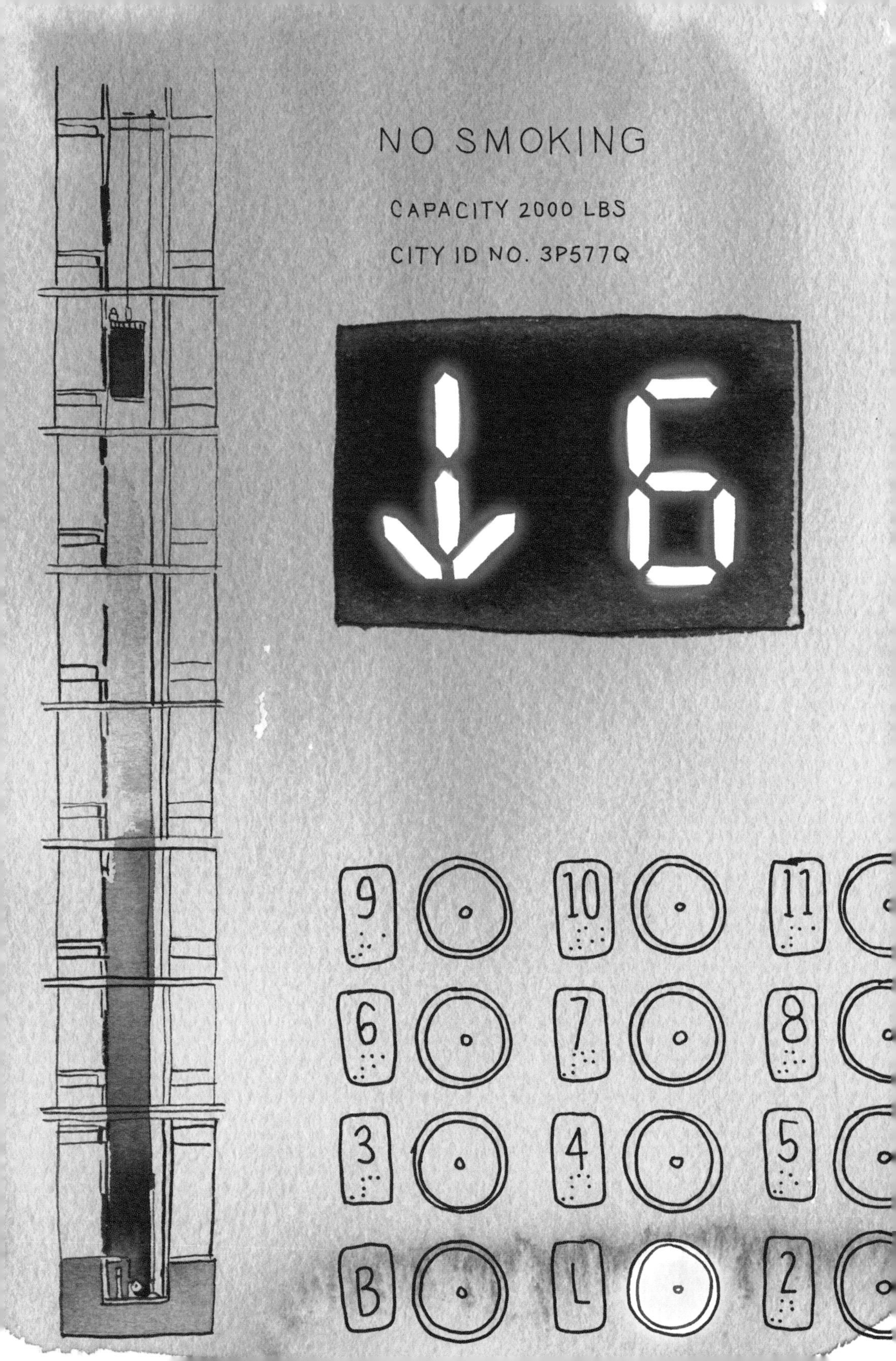

NO SMOKING

CAPACITY 2000 LBS

CITY ID NO. 3P577Q

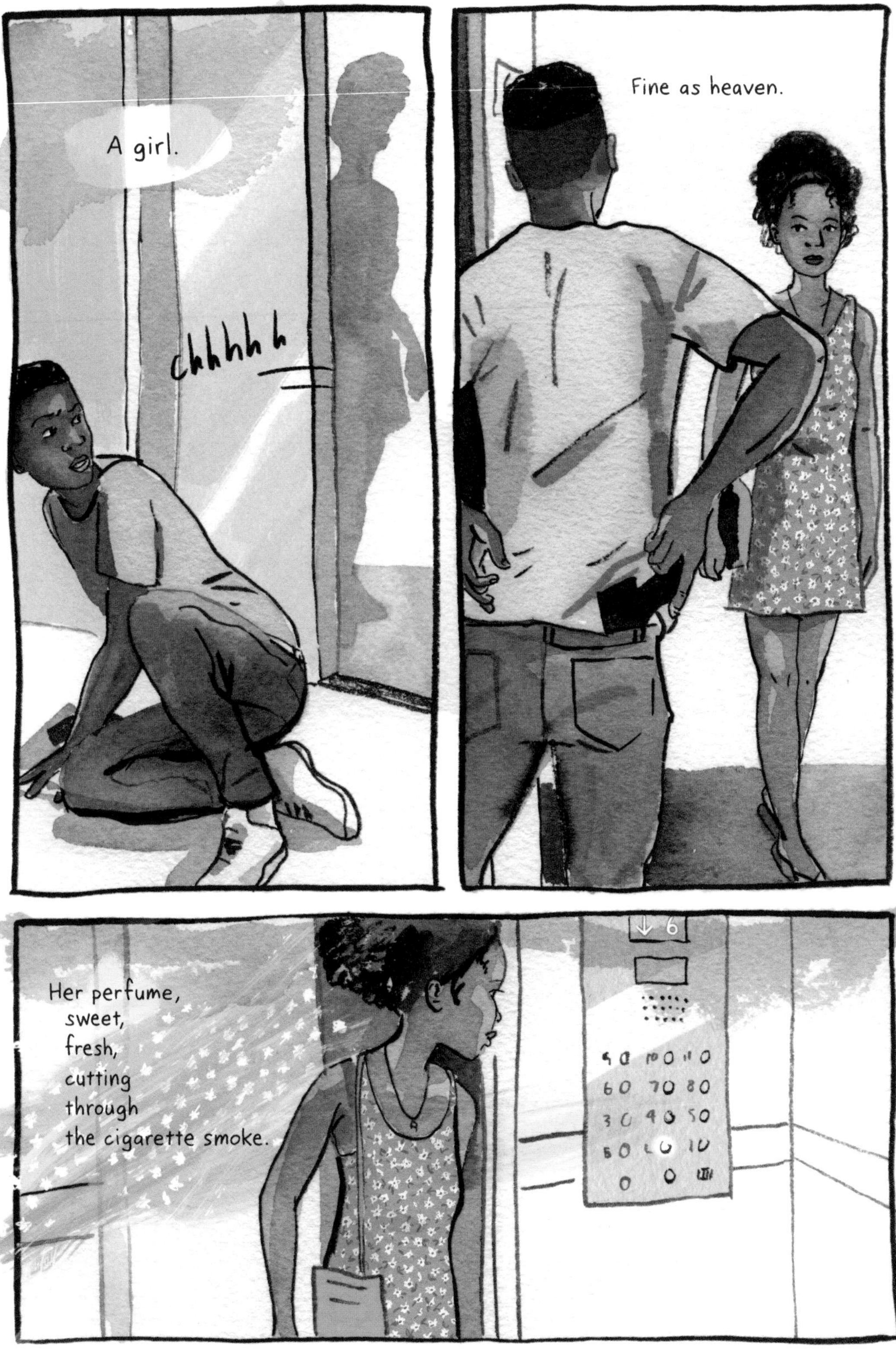
A girl.
chhhhh
Fine as heaven.
Her perfume,
sweet,
fresh,
cutting
through
the cigarette smoke.

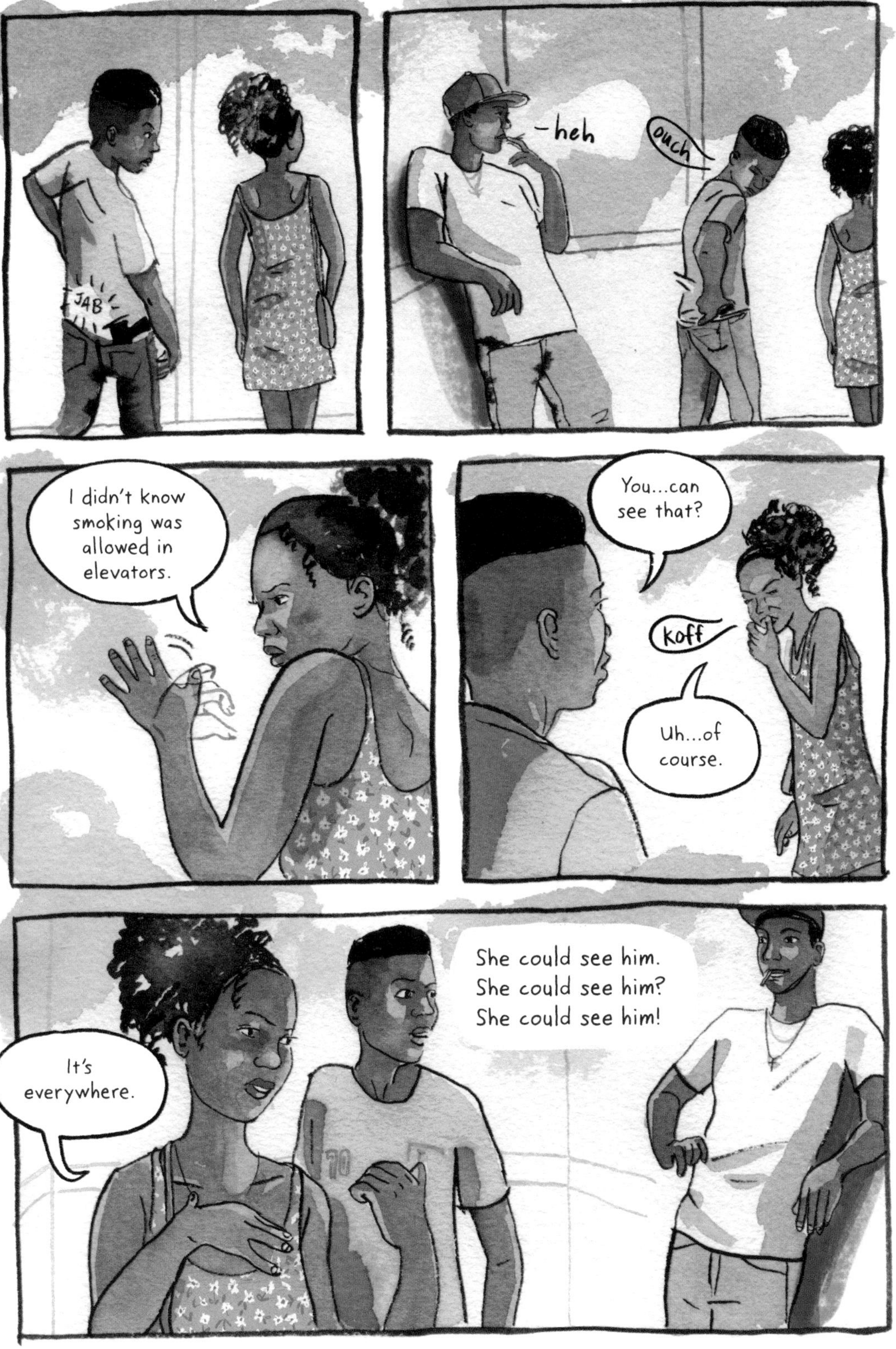
JAB
-heh
ouch
I didn't know smoking was allowed in elevators.
You...can see that?
koff
Uh...of course.
It's everywhere.
She could see him.
She could see him?
She could see him!

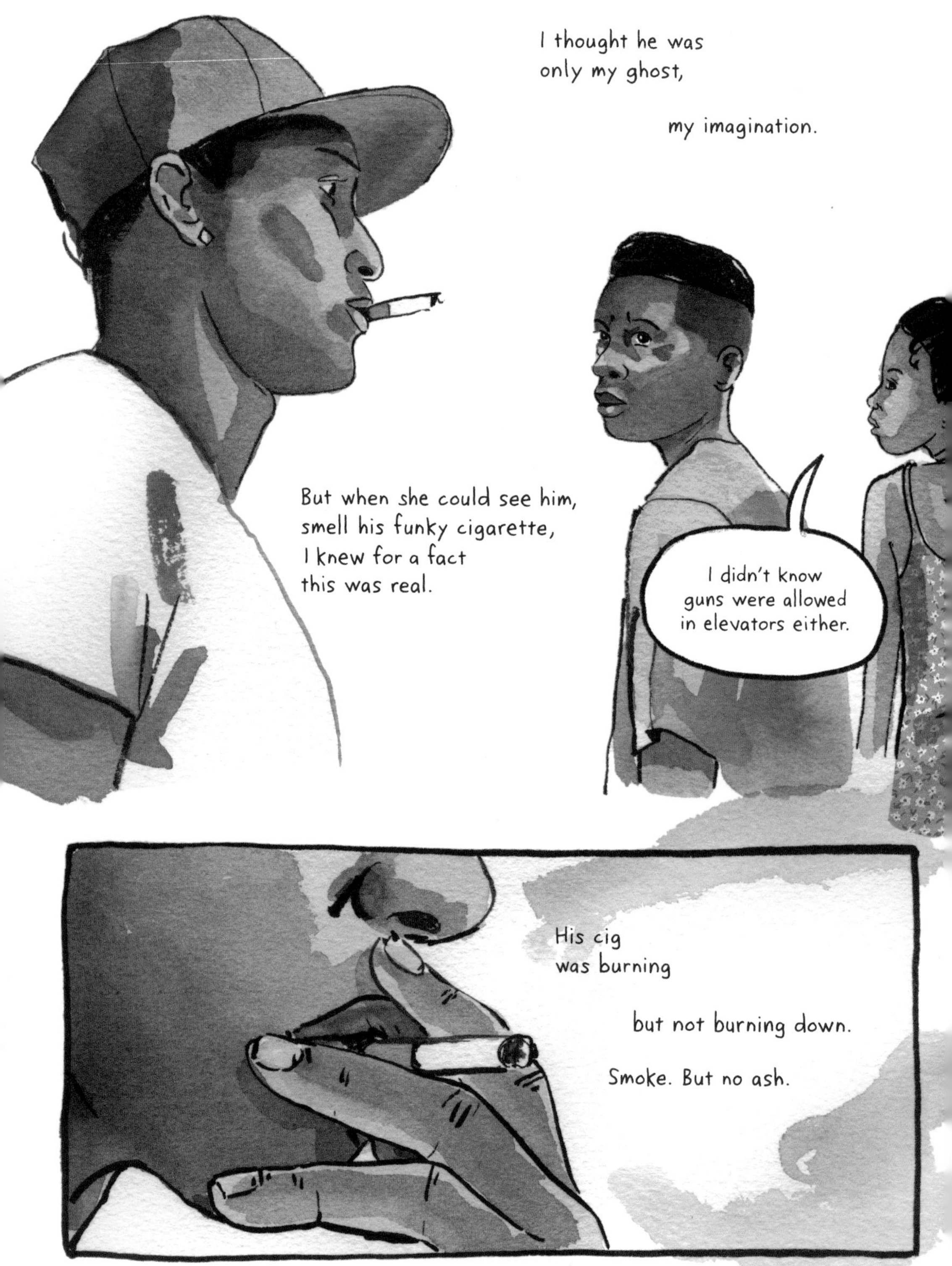
I thought he was
only my ghost,
my imagination.
But when she could see him,
smell his funky cigarette,
I knew for a fact
this was real.
I didn't know
guns were allowed
in elevators either.
His cig
was burning
but not burning down.
Smoke. But no ash.

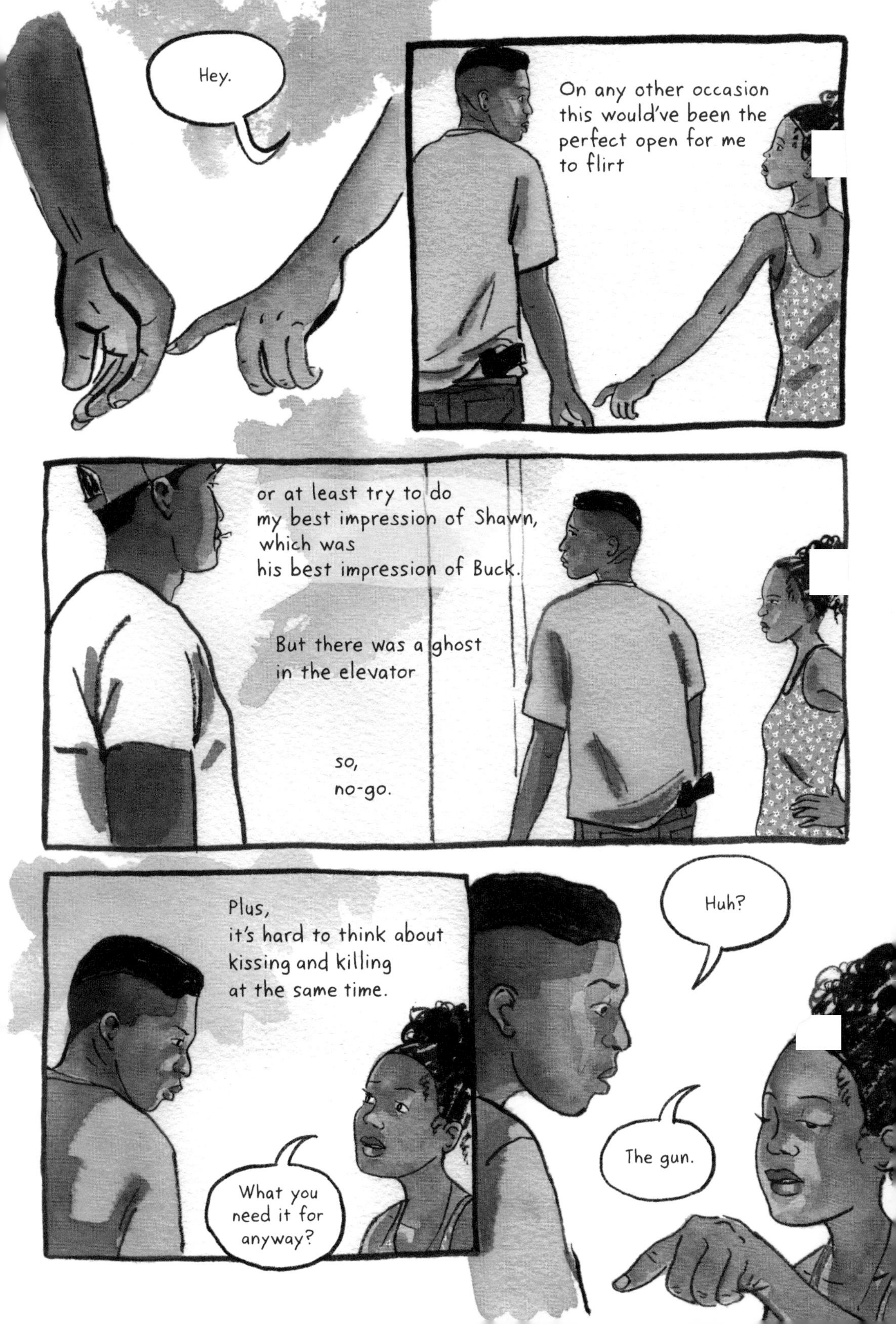
Hey.
On any other occasion this would've been the perfect open for me to flirt
or at least try to do my best impression of Shawn, which was his best impression of Buck.
But there was a ghost in the elevator
so, no-go.
Plus, it's hard to think about kissing and killing at the same time.
What you need it for anyway?
Huh?
The gun.

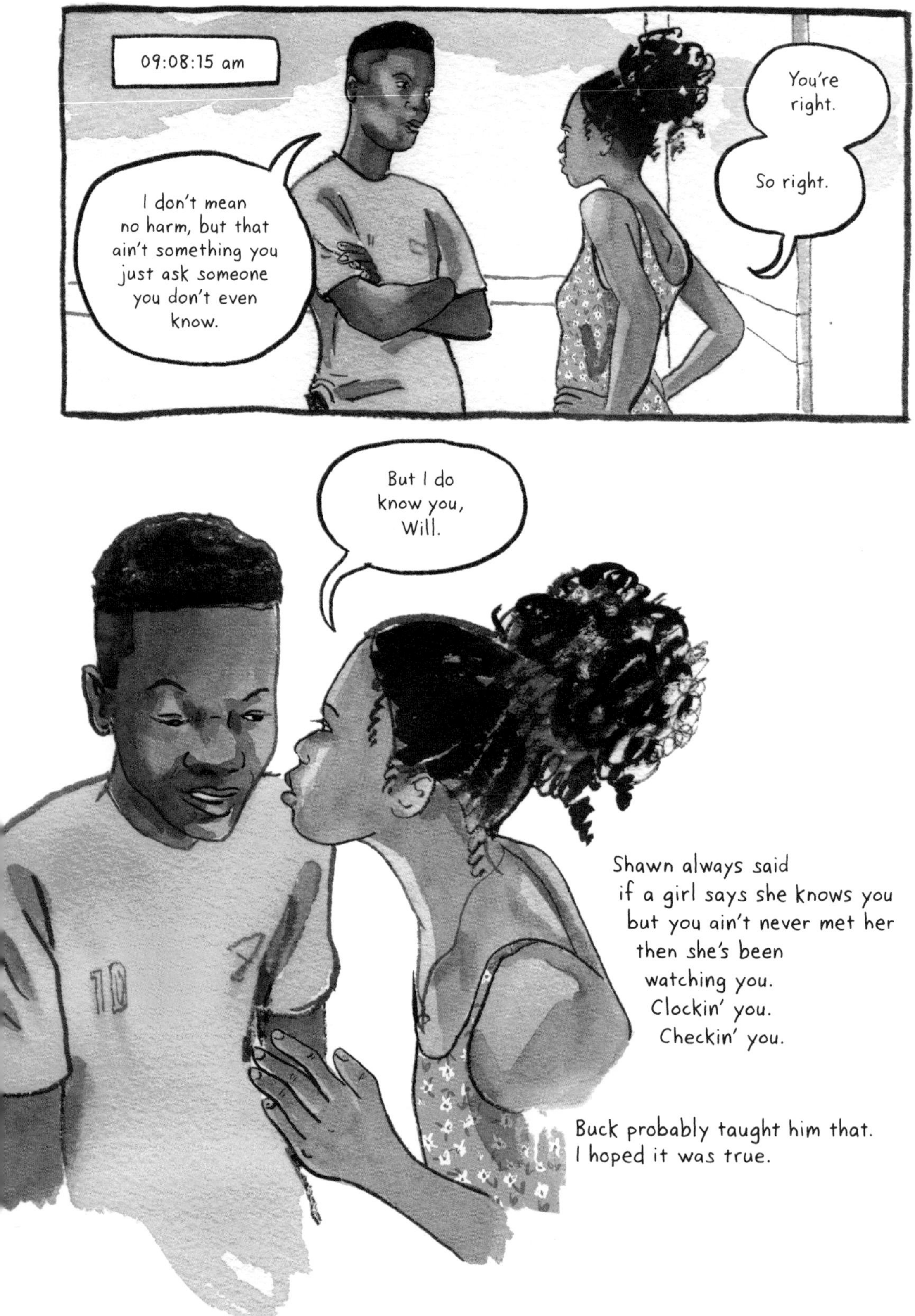
09:08:15 am
I don't mean no harm, but that ain't something you just ask someone you don't even know.
You're right.
So right.
But I do know you, Will.
Shawn always said
if a girl says she knows you
but you ain't never met her
then she's been
watching you.
Clockin' you.
Checkin' you.
Buck probably taught him that.
I hoped it was true.

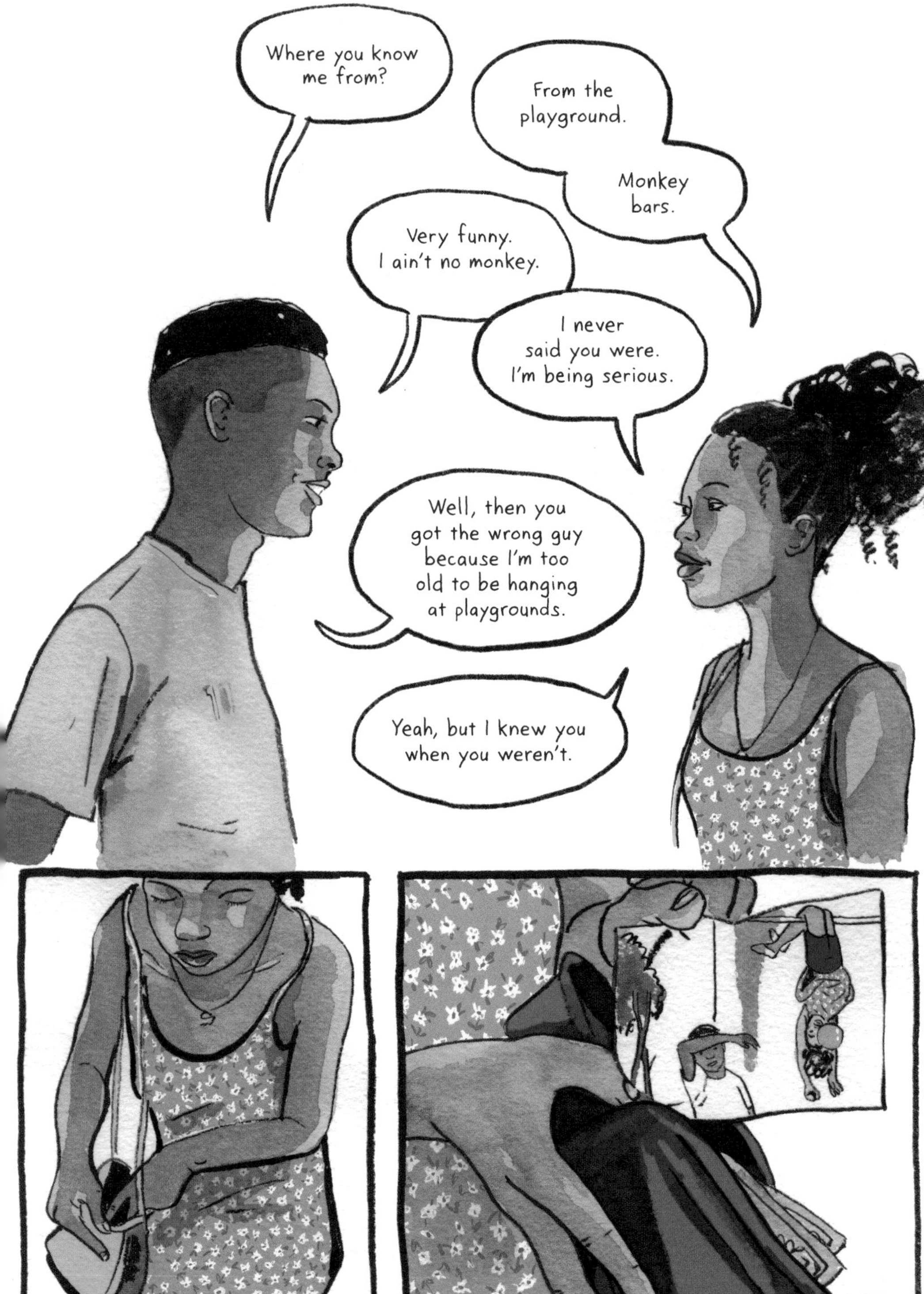
Where you know me from?
From the playground.
Monkey bars.
Very funny. I ain't no monkey.
I never said you were. I'm being serious.
Well, then you got the wrong guy because I'm too old to be hanging at playgrounds.
Yeah, but I knew you when you weren't.

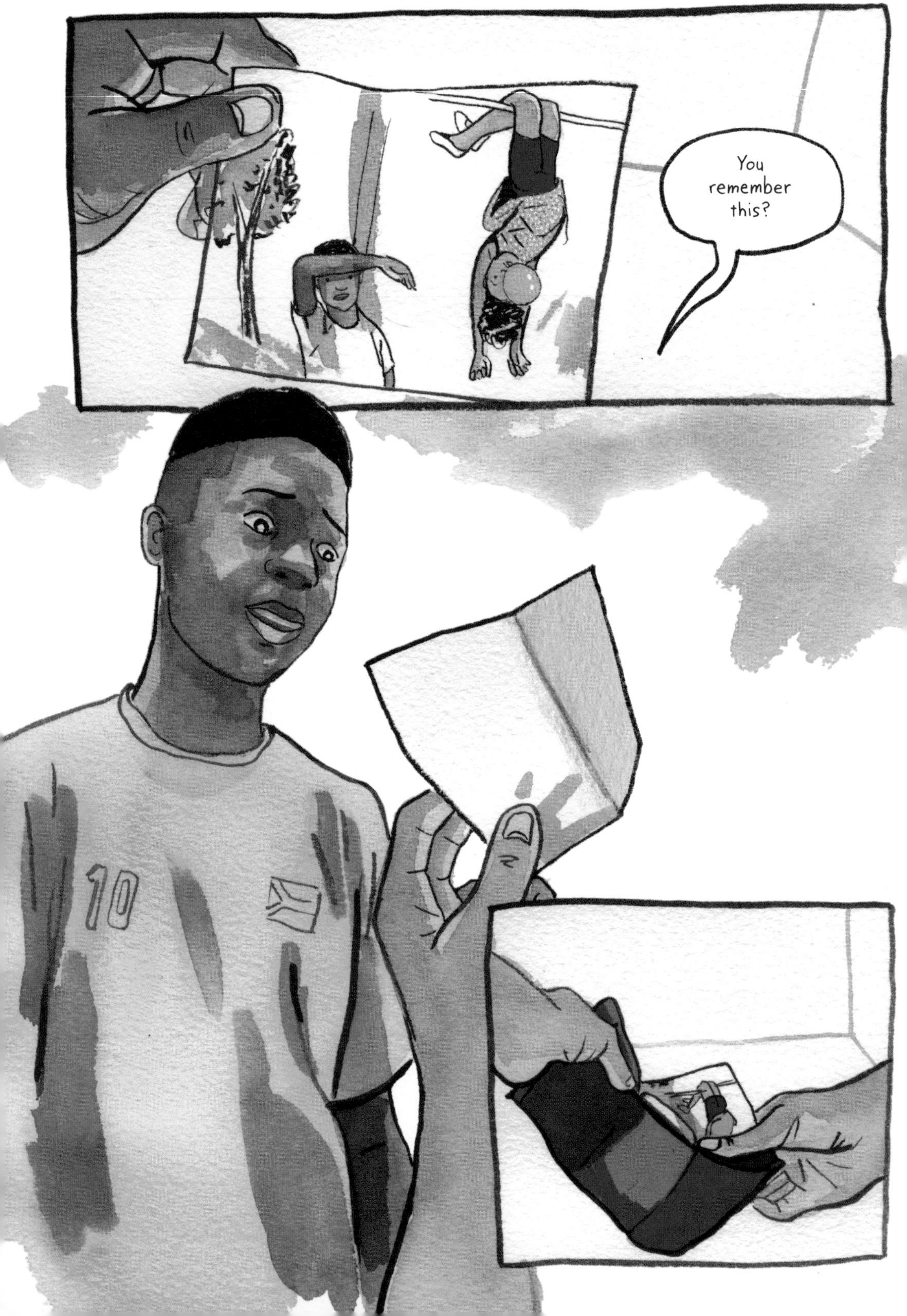
You remember this?
10

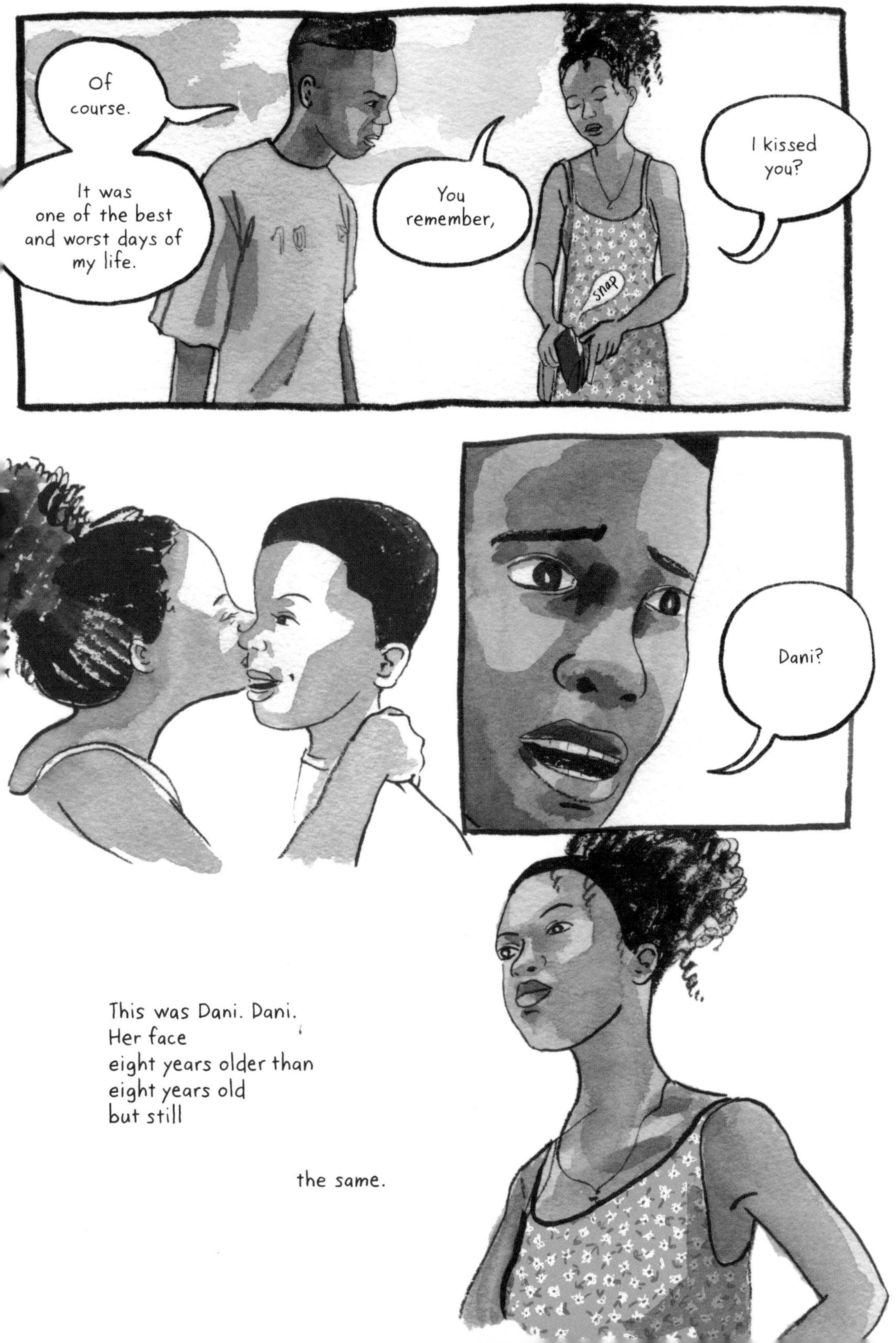

Of course.
It was one of the best and worst days of my life.
You remember,
I kissed you?
snap
Dani?
This was Dani. Dani. Her face eight years older than eight years old but still
the same.

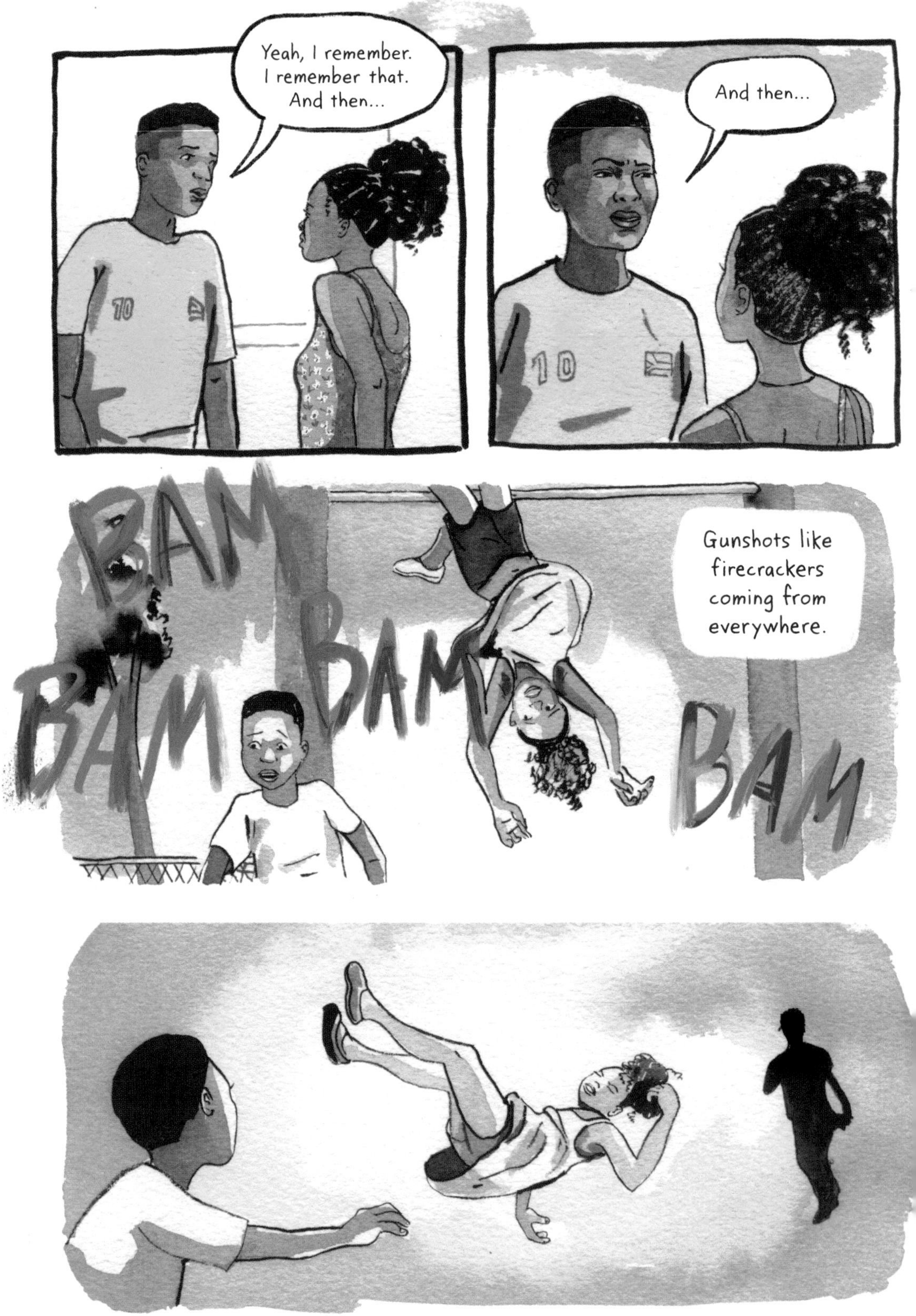
Yeah, I remember.
I remember that.
And then...
And then...
BAM
BAM
BAM
BAM
BAM
Gunshots like firecrackers coming from everywhere.

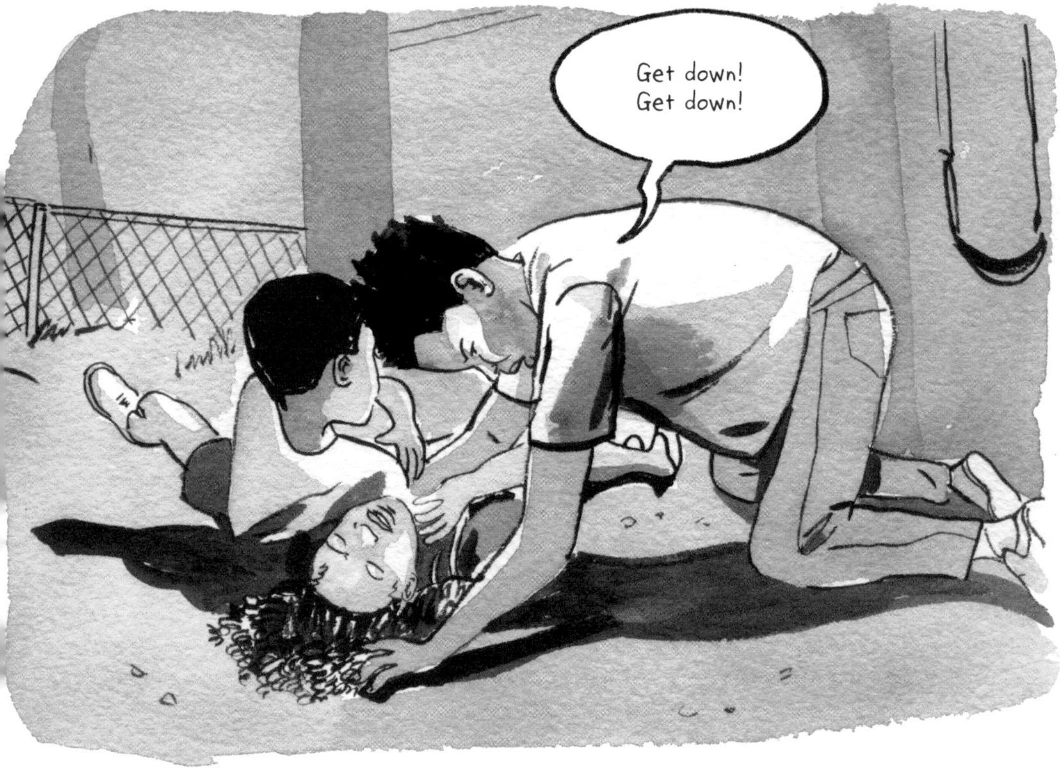
Get down!
Get down!

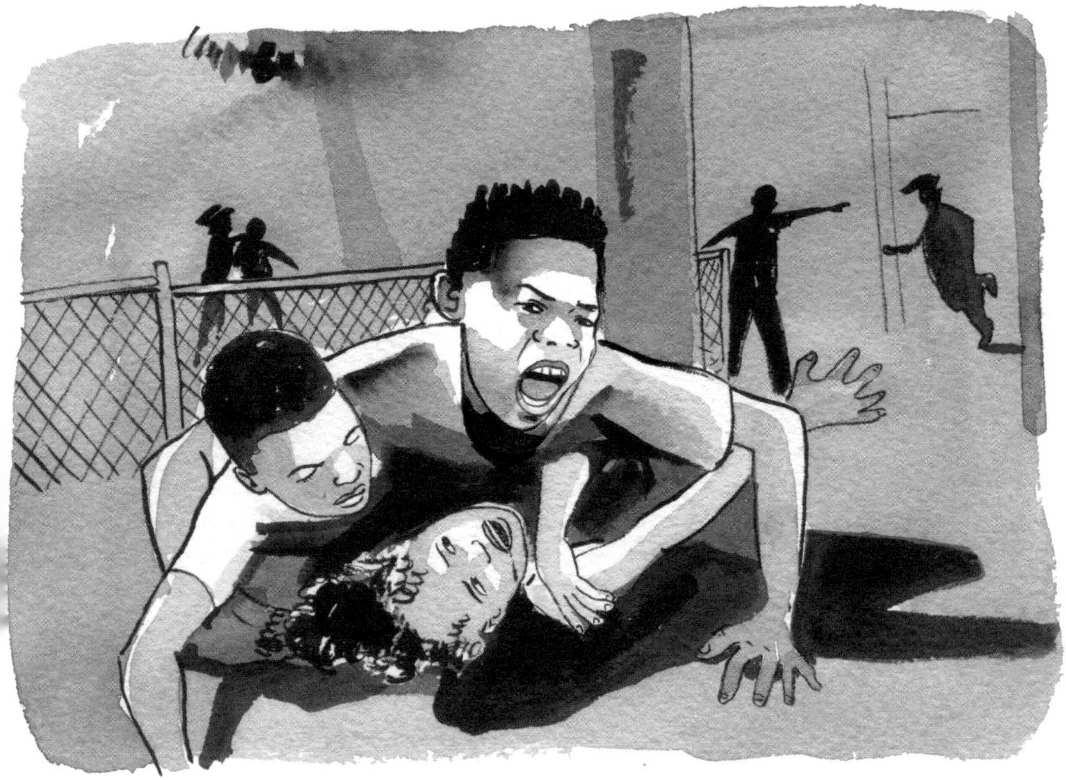

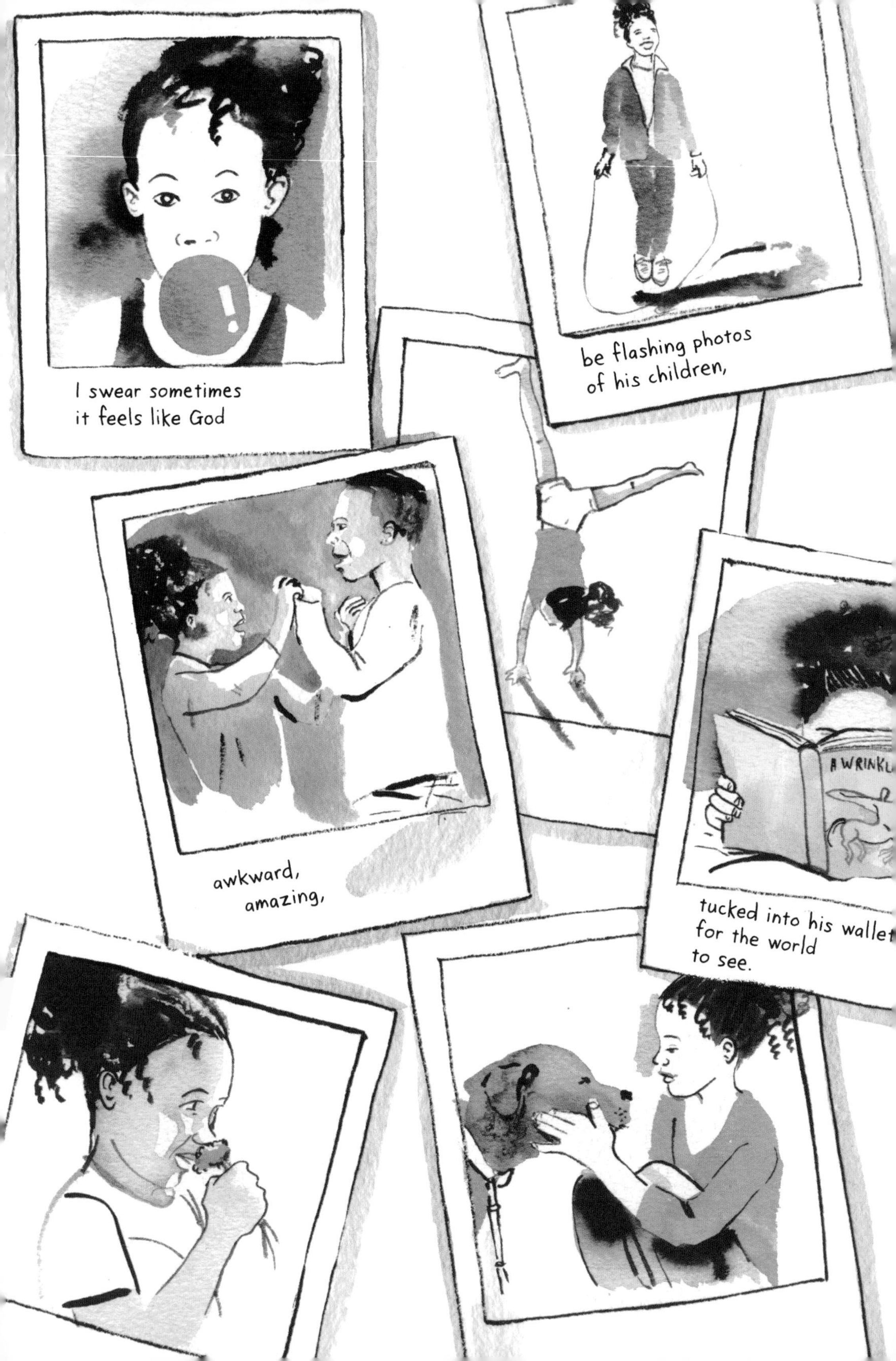
I swear sometimes
it feels like God
be flashing photos
of his children,
awkward,
amazing,
tucked into his wallet
for the world
to see.

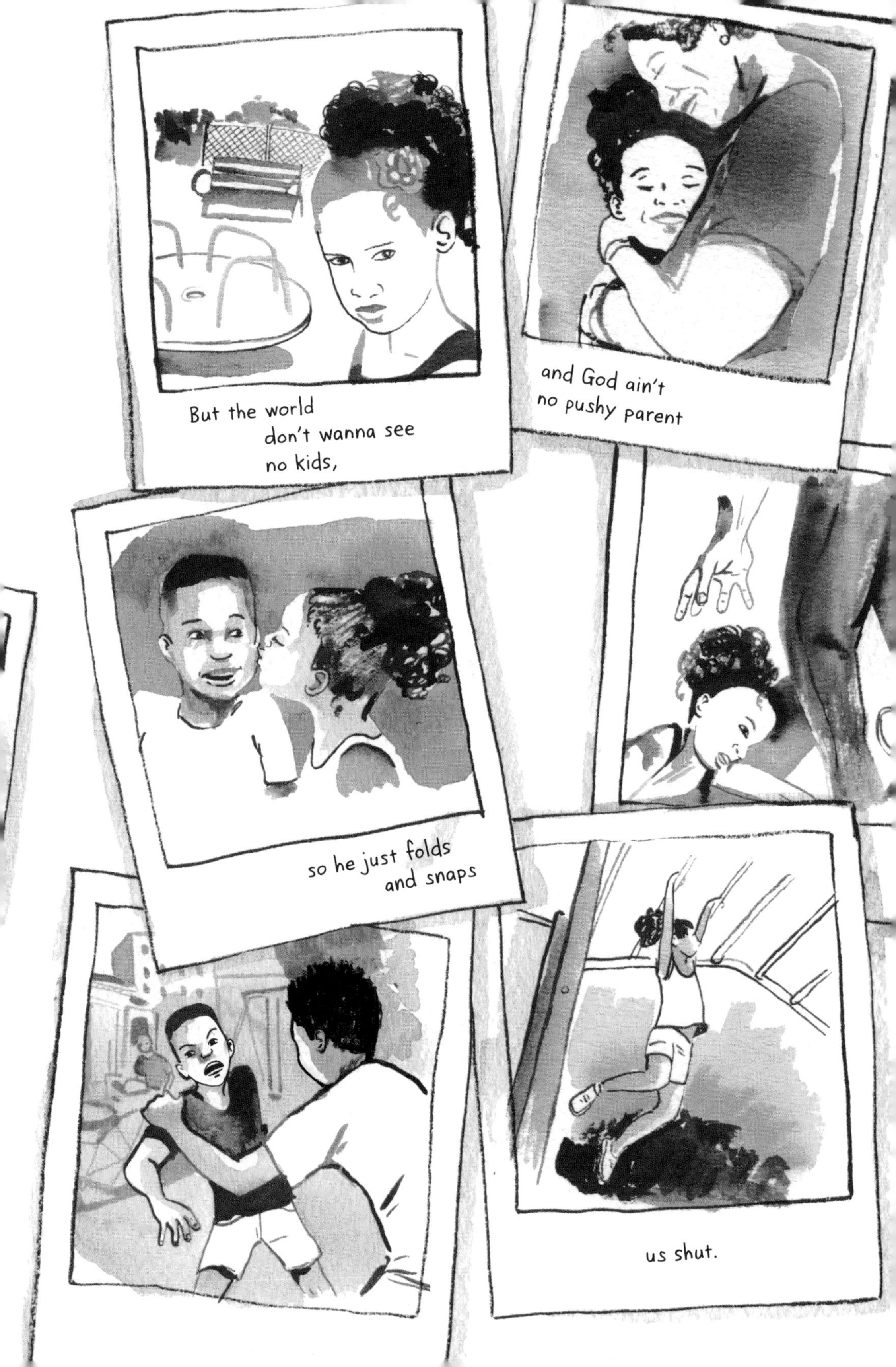

But the world
don't wanna see
no kids,
and God ain't
no pushy parent
so he just folds
and snaps
us shut.

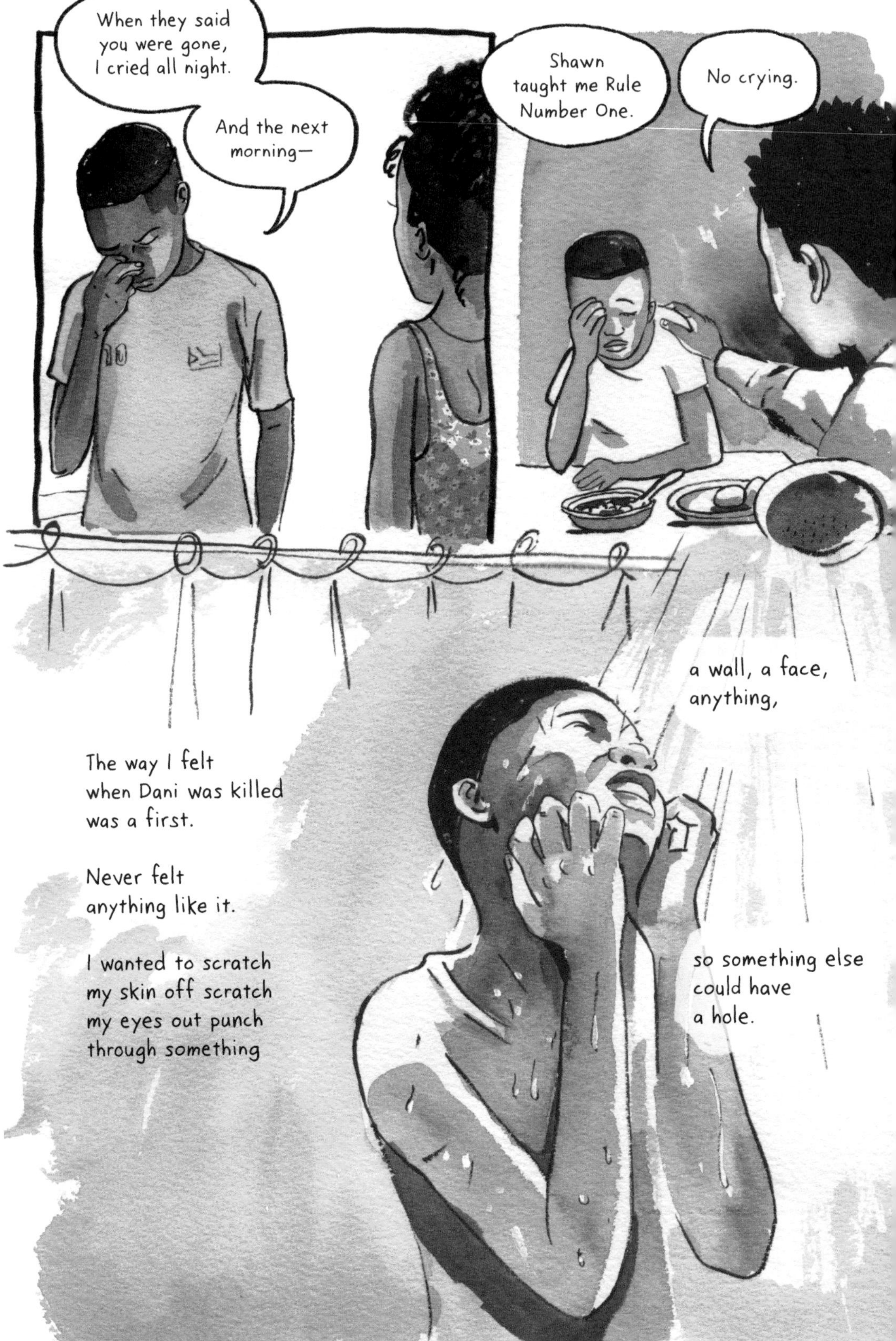
When they said you were gone, I cried all night.
And the next morning—
Shawn taught me Rule Number One.
No crying.
a wall, a face, anything,
The way I felt when Dani was killed was a first.
Never felt anything like it.
I wanted to scratch my skin off scratch my eyes out punch through something
so something else could have a hole.

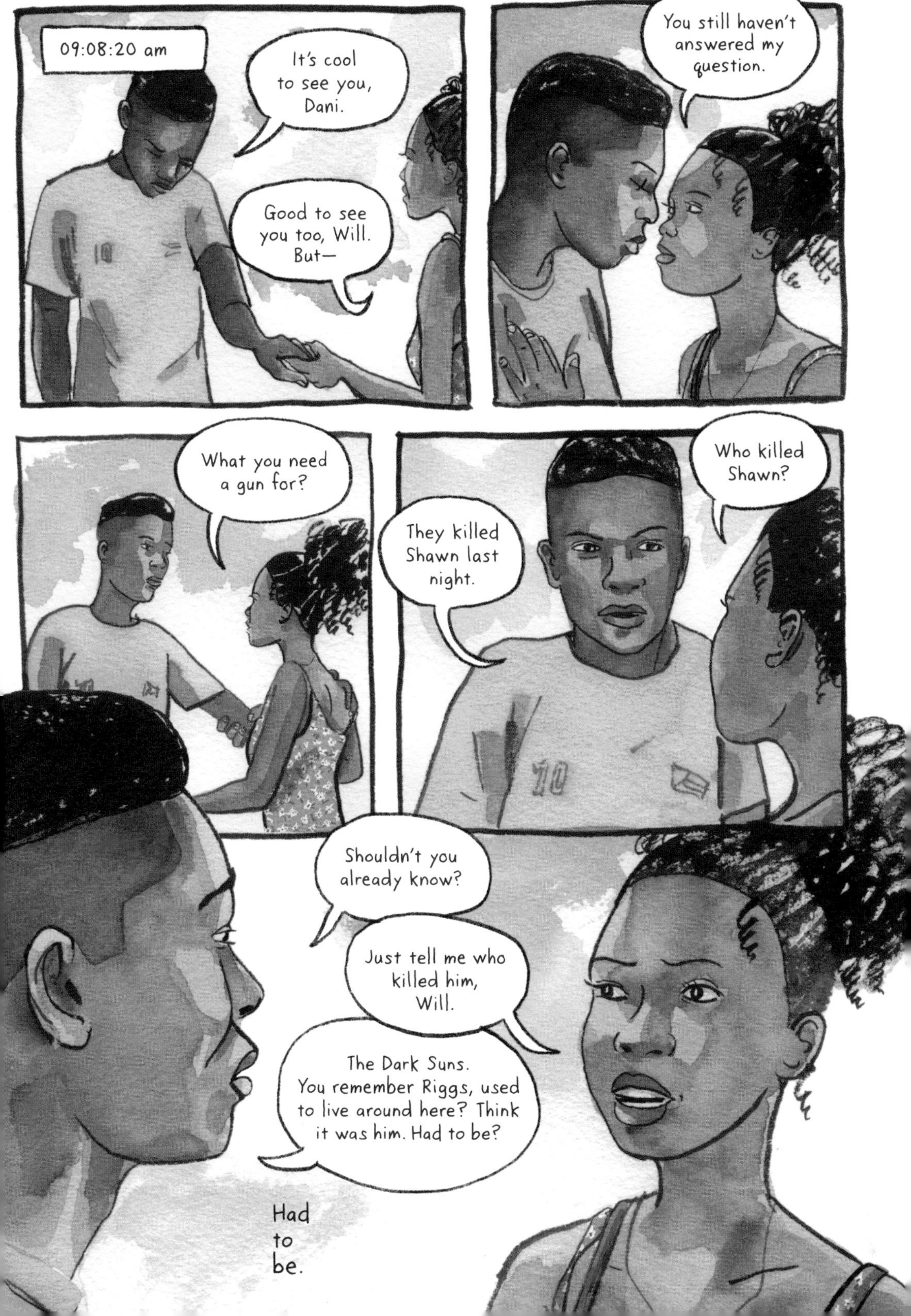

09:08:20 am
It's cool to see you, Dani.
Good to see you too, Will. But—
You still haven't answered my question.
What you need a gun for?
They killed Shawn last night.
Who killed Shawn?
Shouldn't you already know?
Just tell me who killed him, Will.
The Dark Suns. You remember Riggs, used to live around here? Think it was him. Had to be?
Had to be.

Dani was killed
before she ever learned
The Rules.

So I explained them to
her so she wouldn't think
less of me for following
them

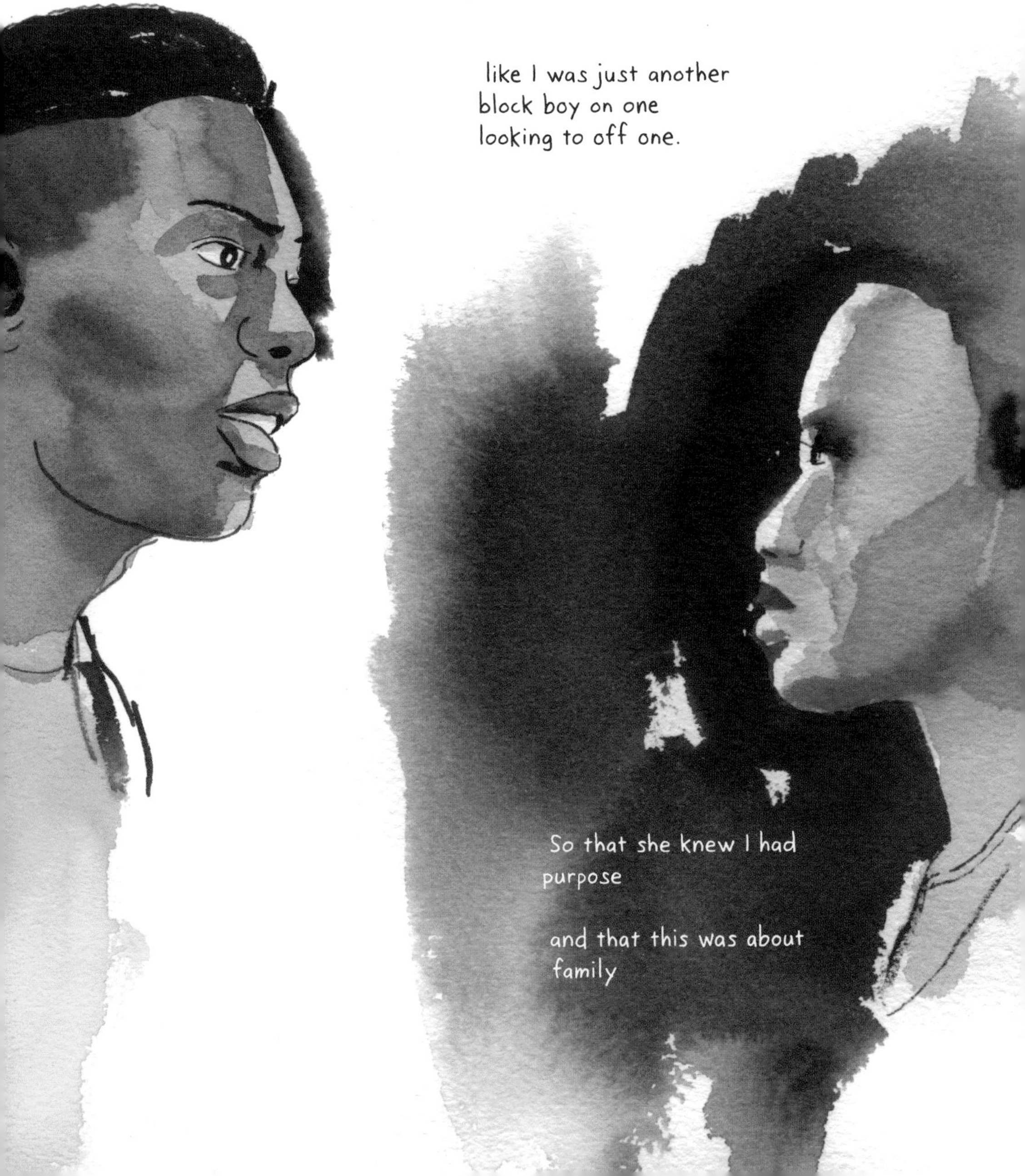
like I was just another
block boy on one
looking to off one.
So that she knew I had
purpose
and that this was about
family

and had I known
The Rules when we
were kids I would've
done the same thing

for her.

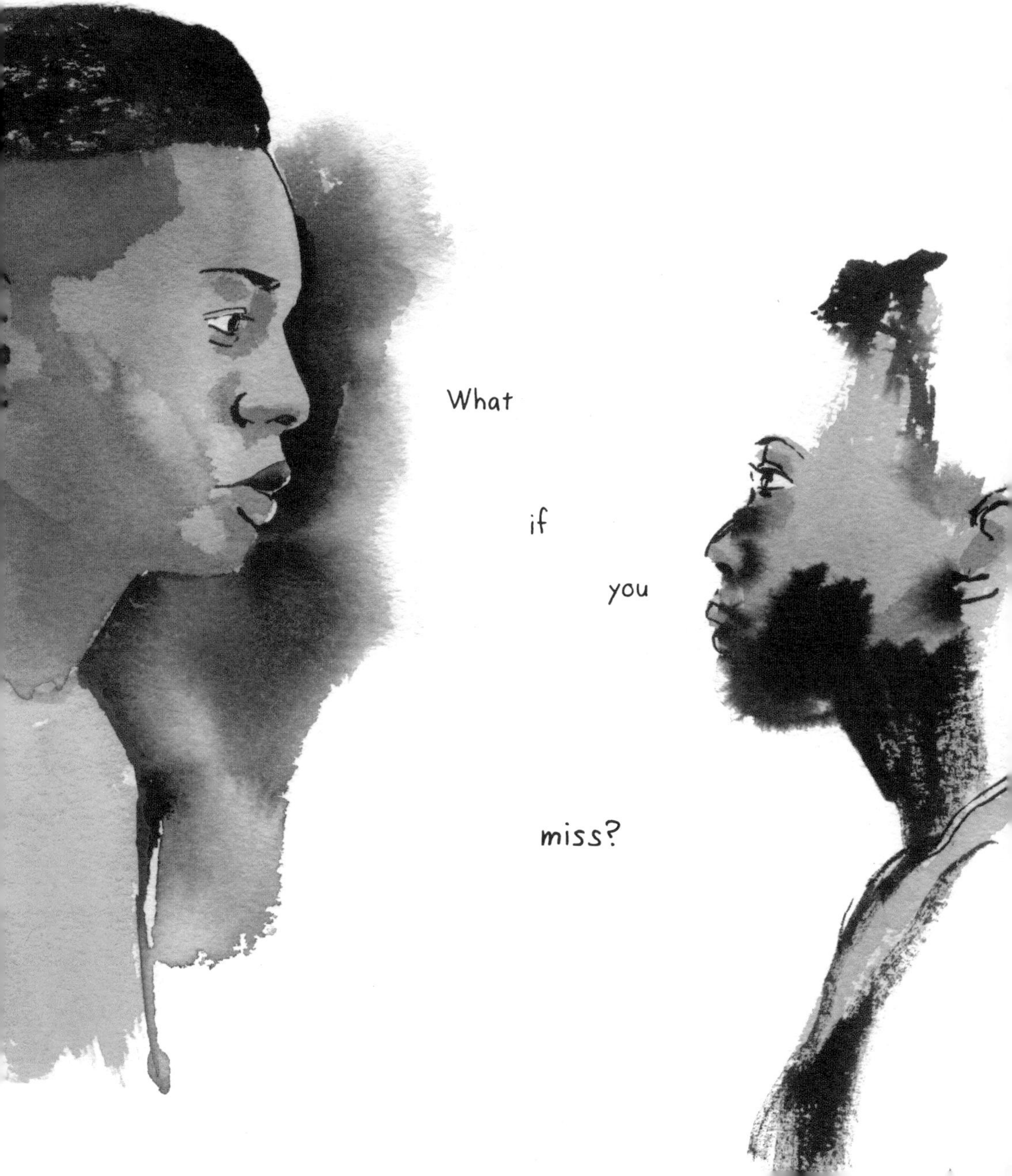
What
if
you
miss?

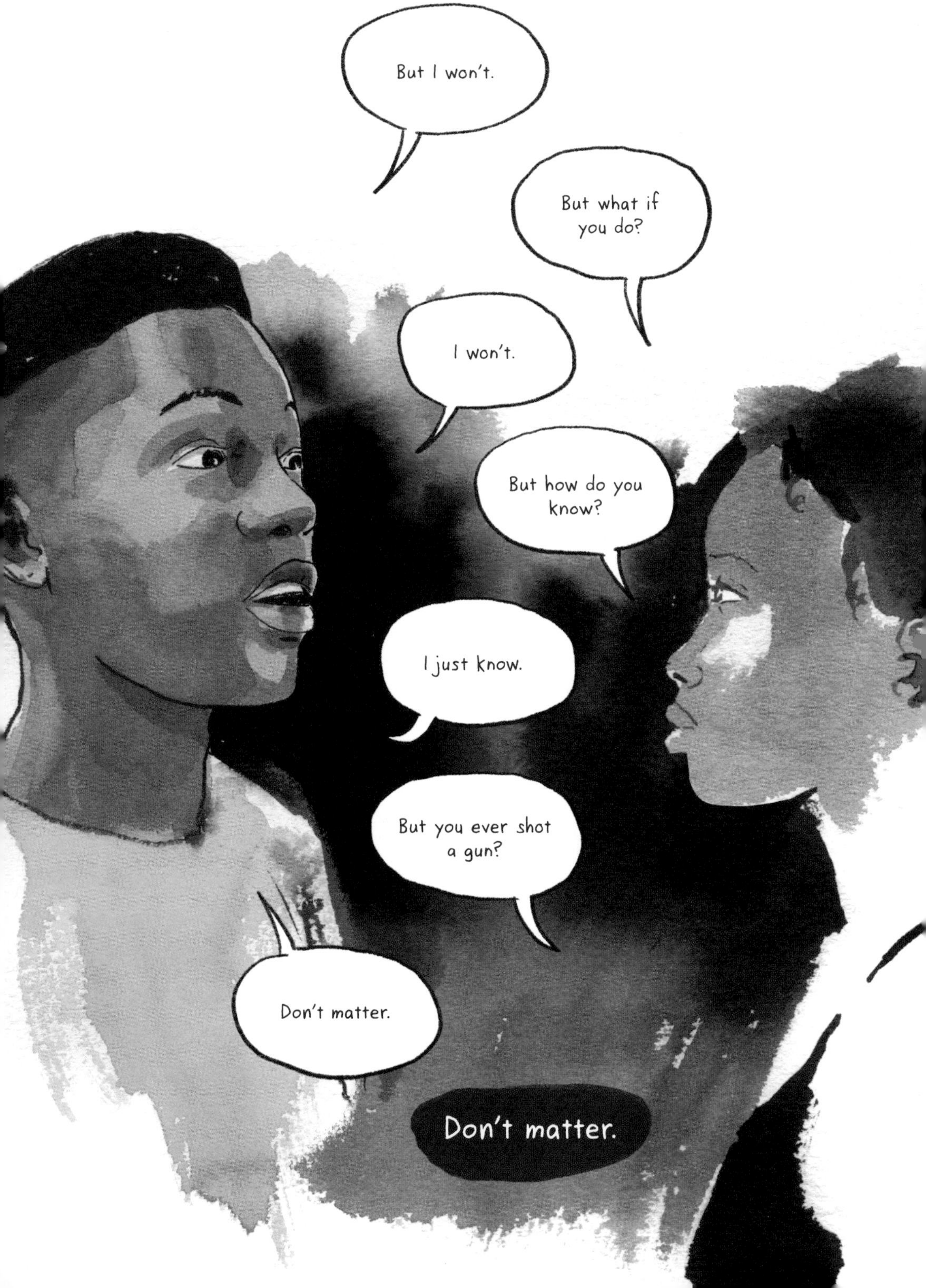
But I won't.
But what if you do?
I won't.
But how do you know?
I just know.
But you ever shot a gun?
Don't matter.
Don't matter.

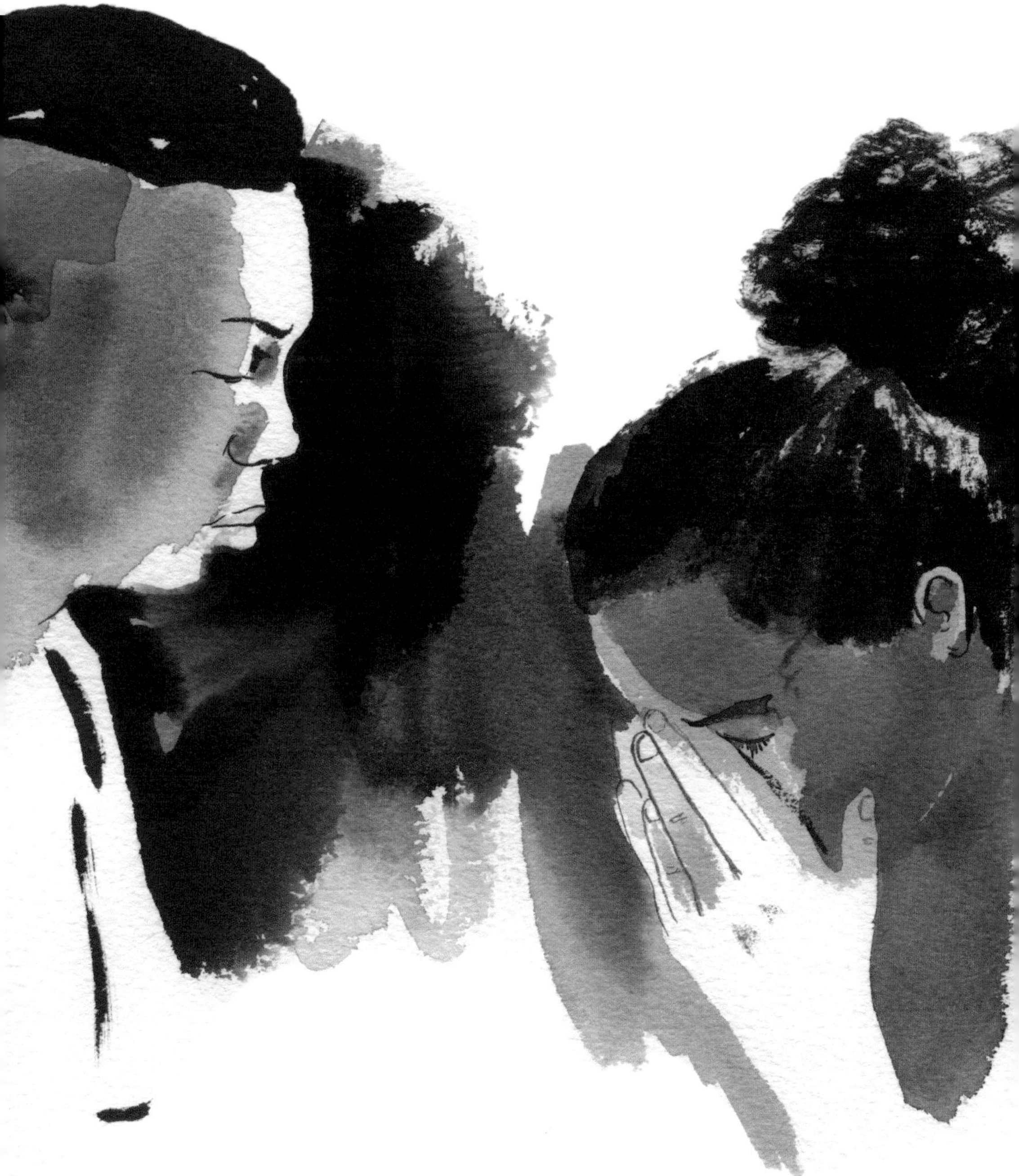

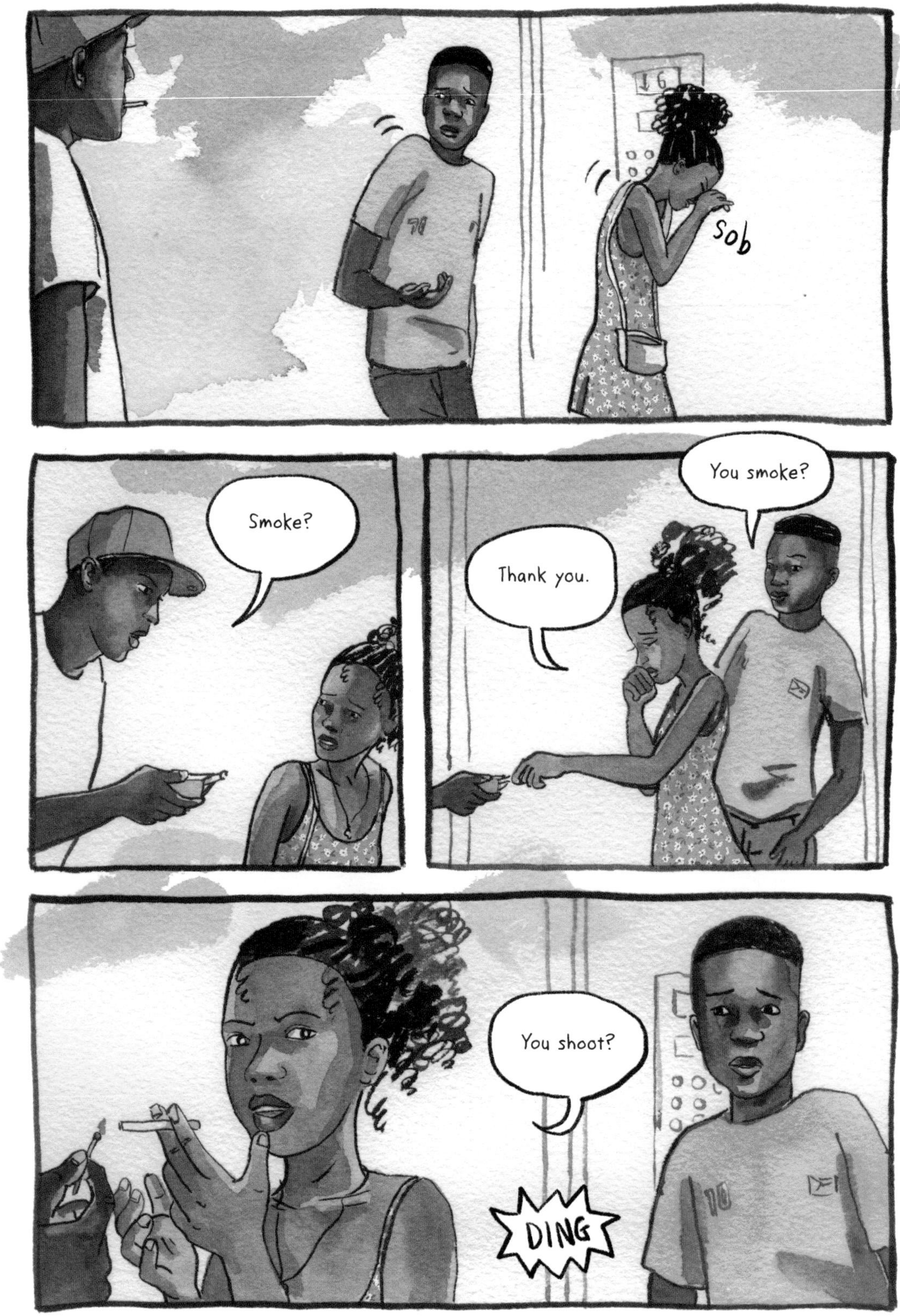
Sob
Smoke?
You smoke?
Thank you.
You shoot?
DING

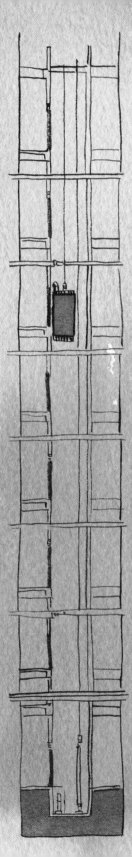

NO SMOKING

CAPACITY 2000 LBS
CITY ID NO. 3P577Q

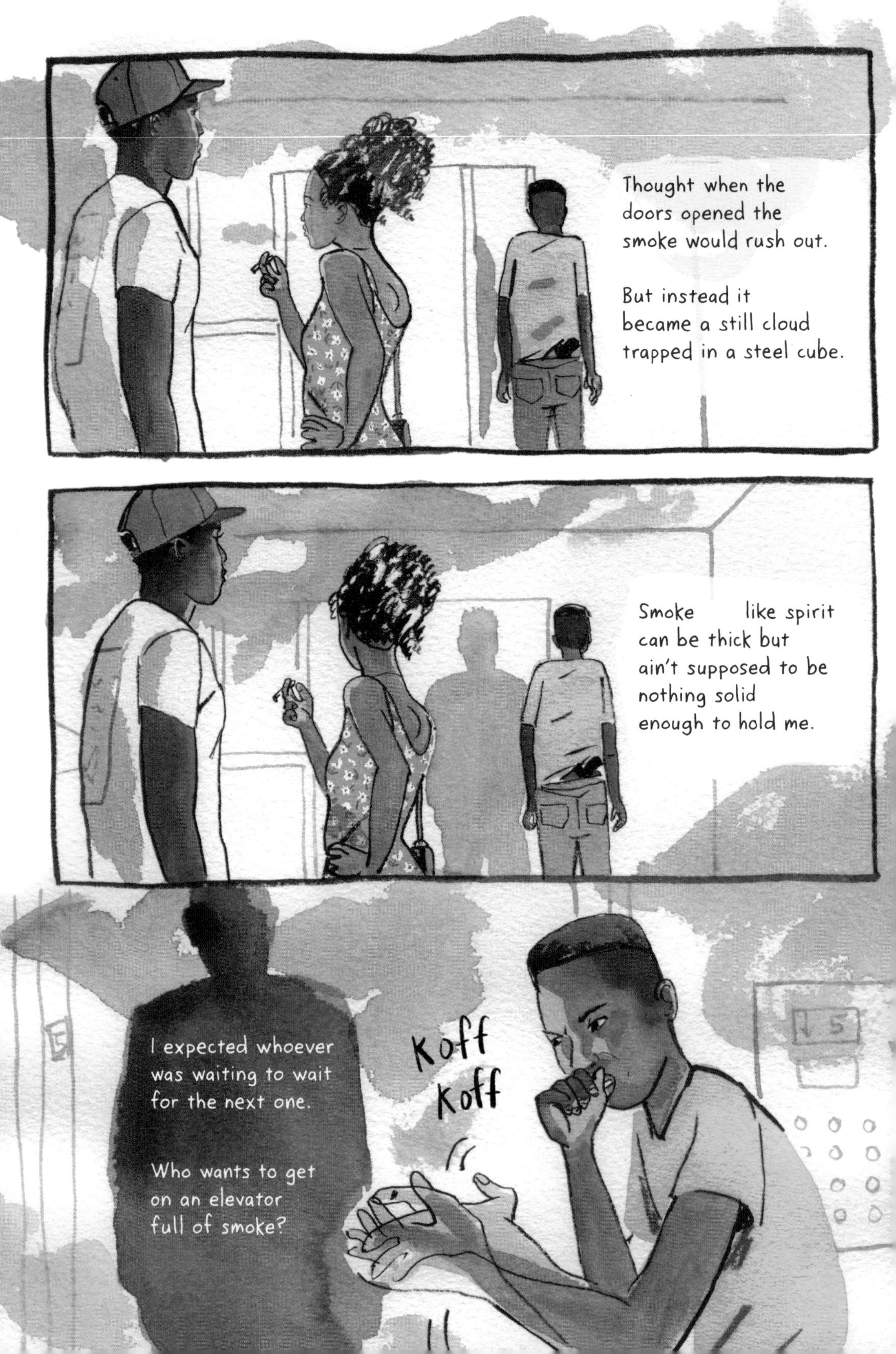
Thought when the doors opened the smoke would rush out.
But instead it became a still cloud trapped in a steel cube.
Smoke like spirit can be thick but ain't supposed to be nothing solid enough to hold me.
I expected whoever was waiting to wait for the next one.
Who wants to get on an elevator full of smoke?
Koff Koff

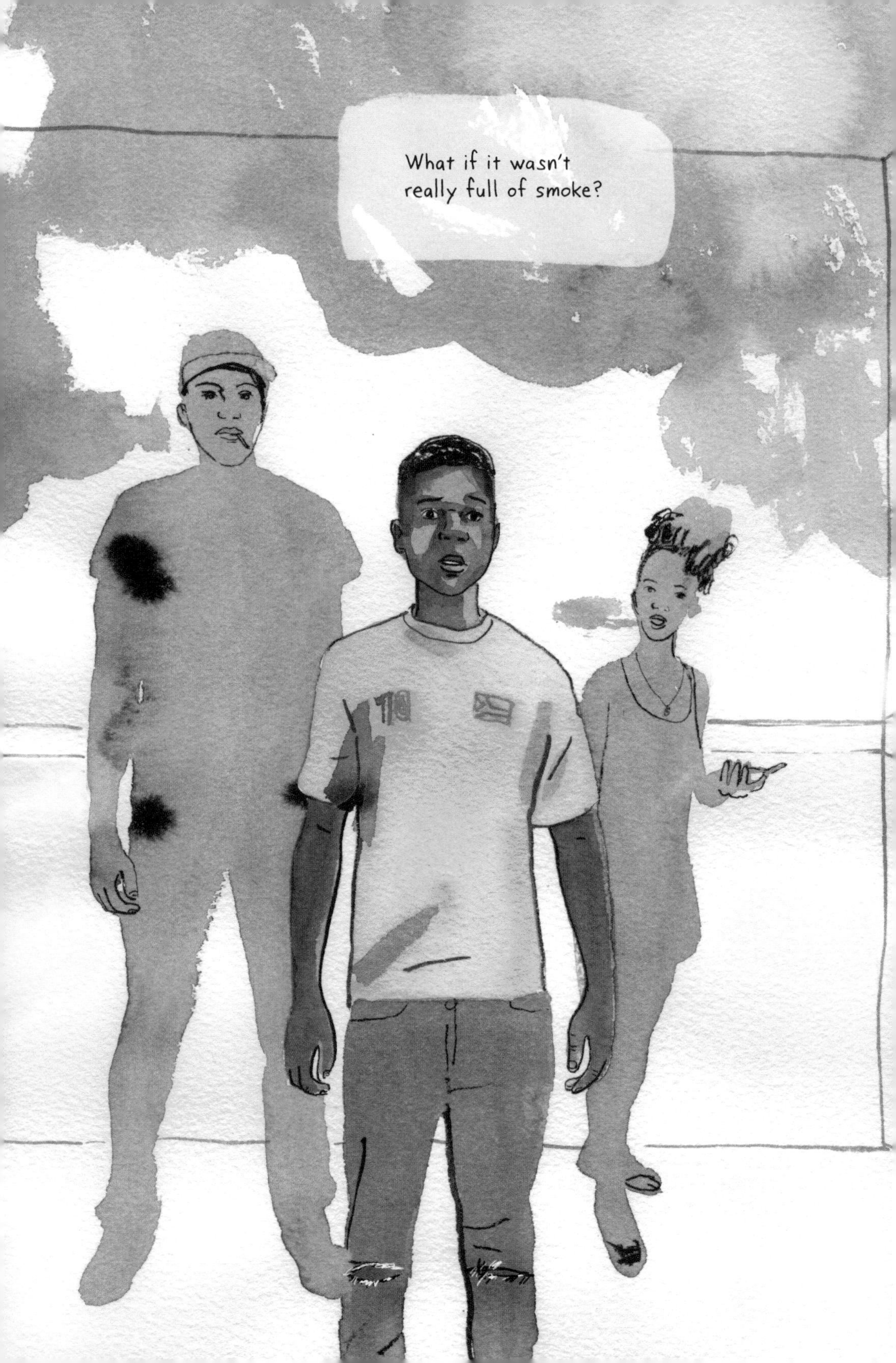
What if it wasn't really full of smoke?

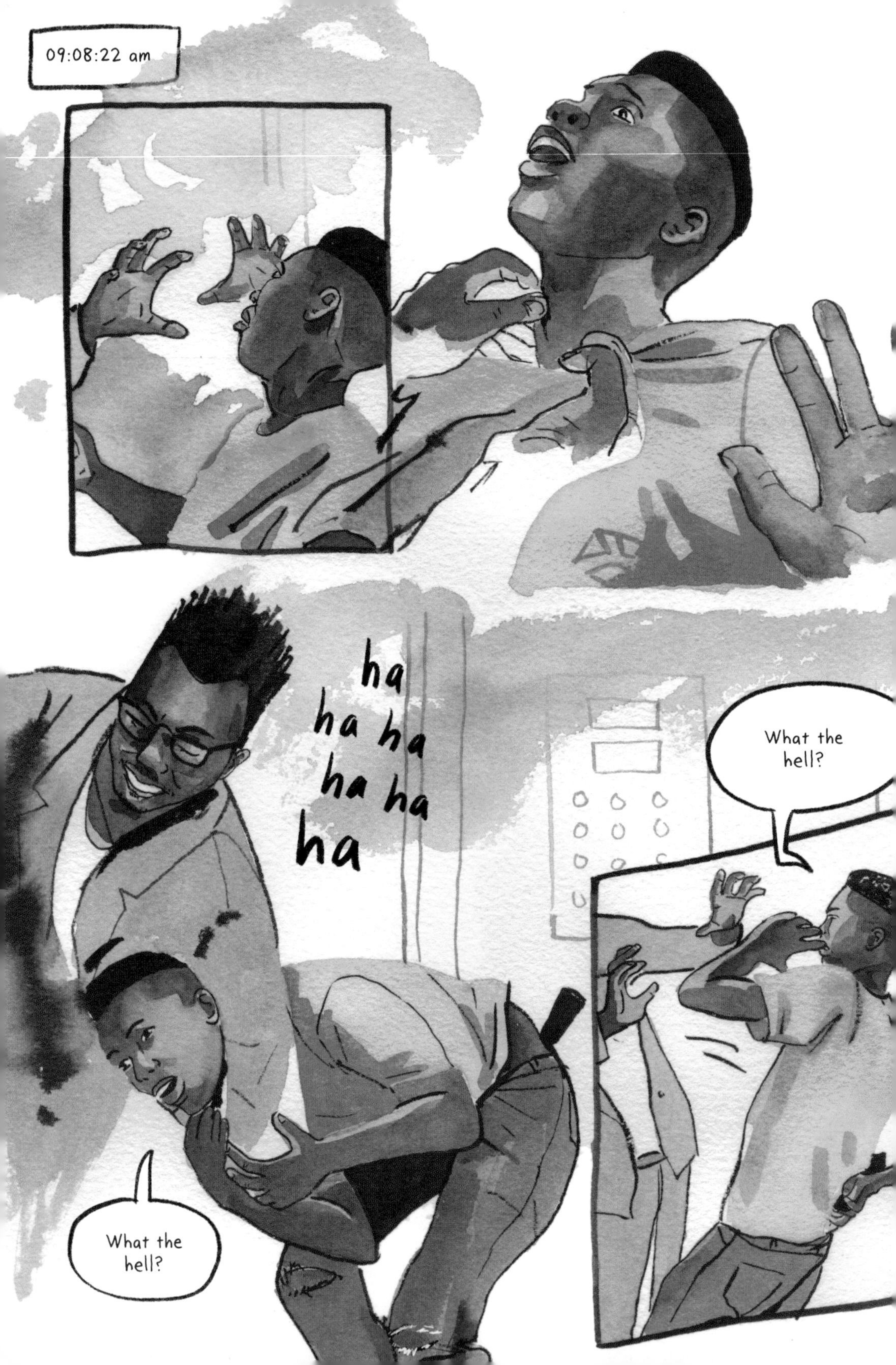
09:08:22 am
ha
ha ha
ha ha
ha
What the hell?
What the hell?

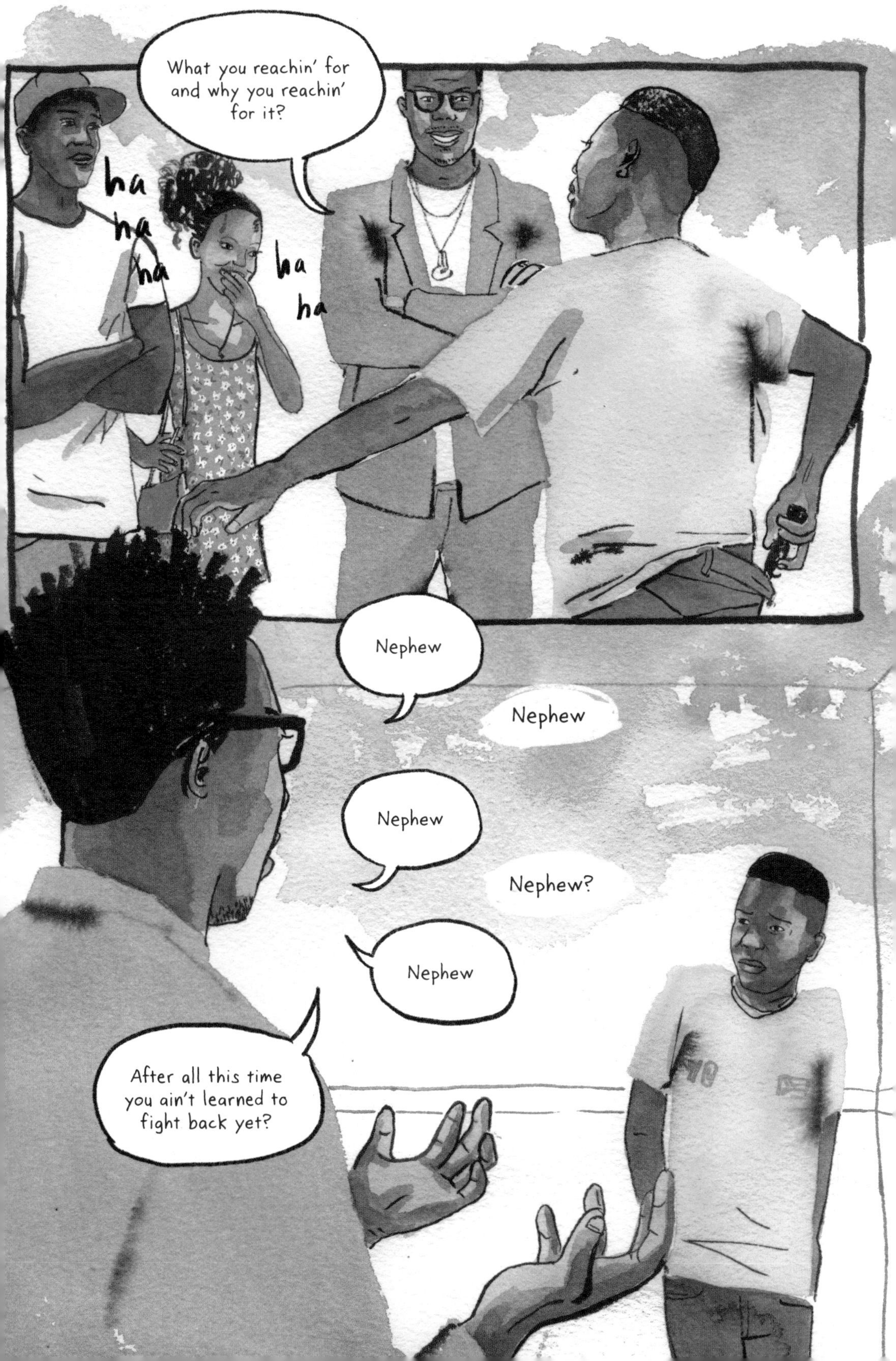
ha ha ha
What you reachin' for and why you reachin' for it?
ha ha
Nephew
Nephew
Nephew
Nephew?
Nephew
After all this time you ain't learned to fight back yet?

There are
so many pictures
of Uncle Mark in
our house.

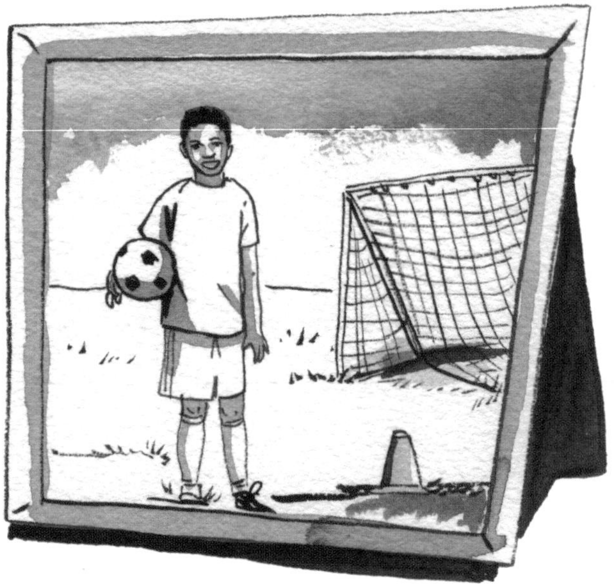

Posing with my father, his shorter
younger brother.

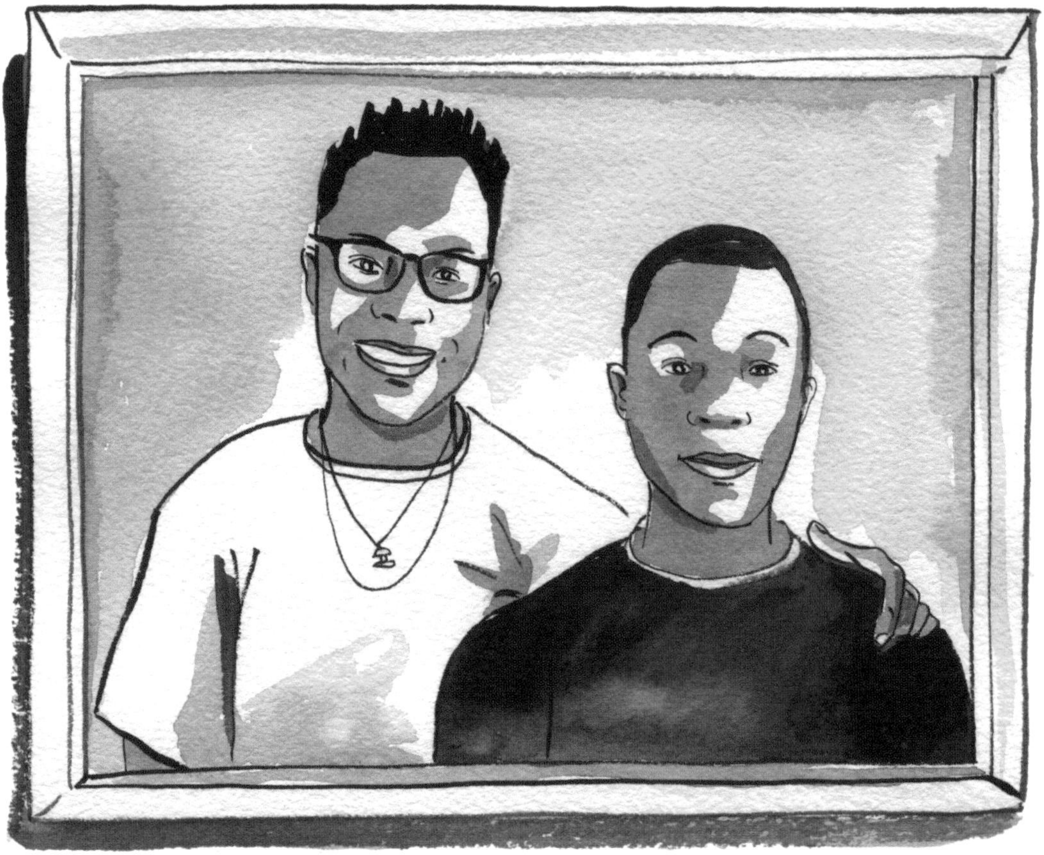

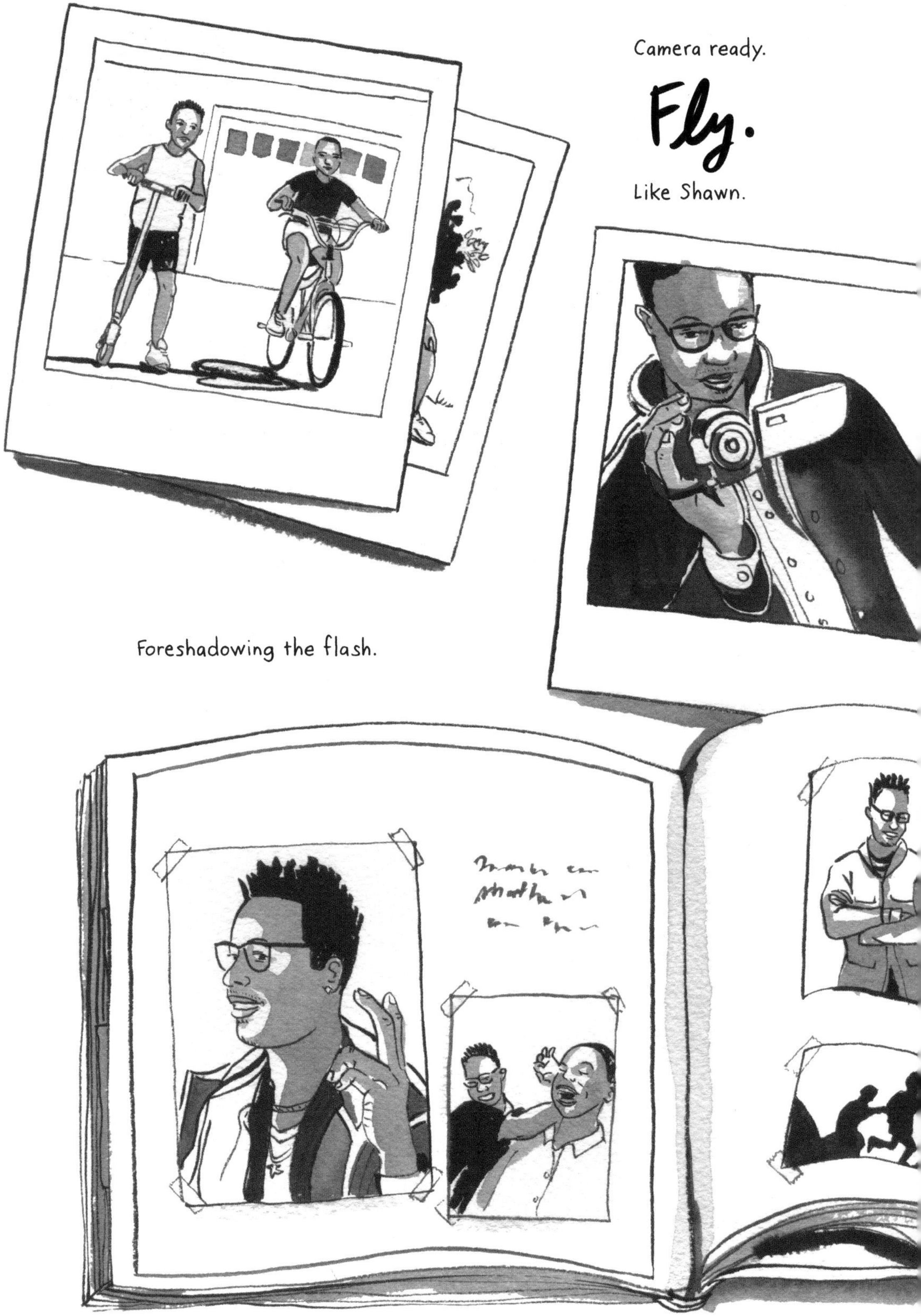
Camera ready.
Fly.
Like Shawn.
Foreshadowing the flash.

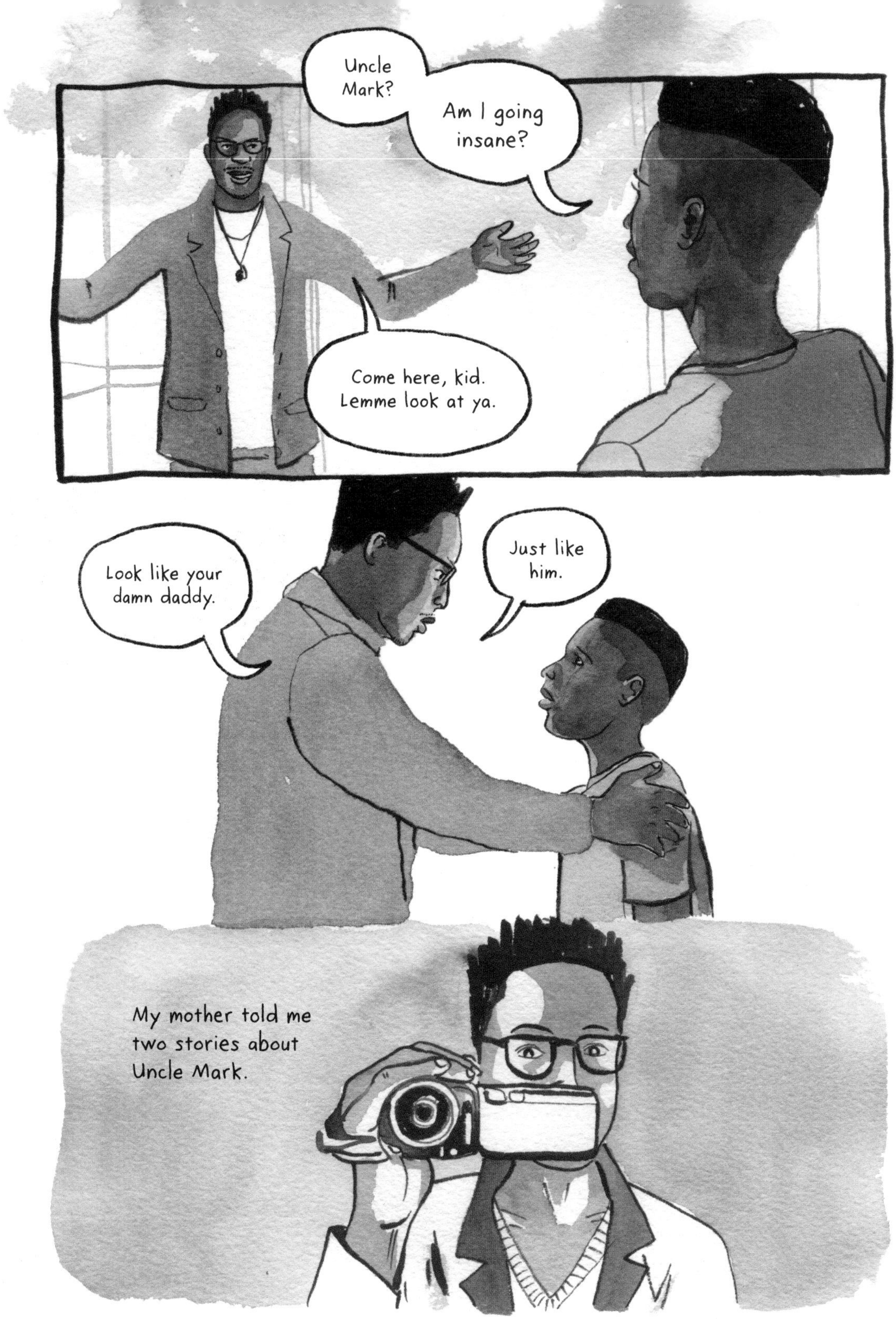
Uncle Mark?
Am I going insane?
Come here, kid. Lemme look at ya.
Look like your damn daddy.
Just like him.
My mother told me two stories about Uncle Mark.

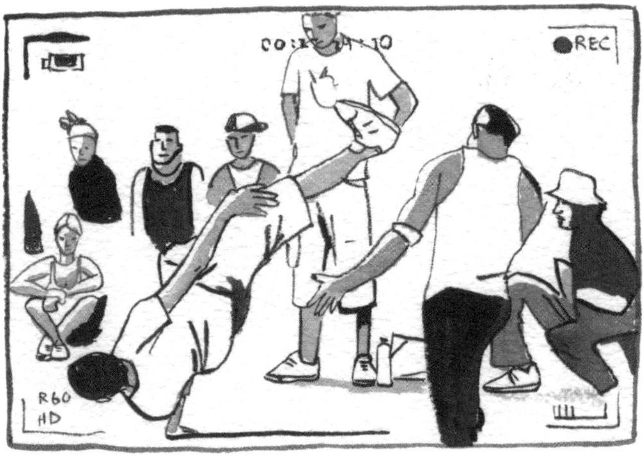
REC
R60
HD

Story No.1

ABOUT UNCLE MARK

He videotaped everything with a camera his mother, my grandmother, bought him

for his eighteenth birthday.

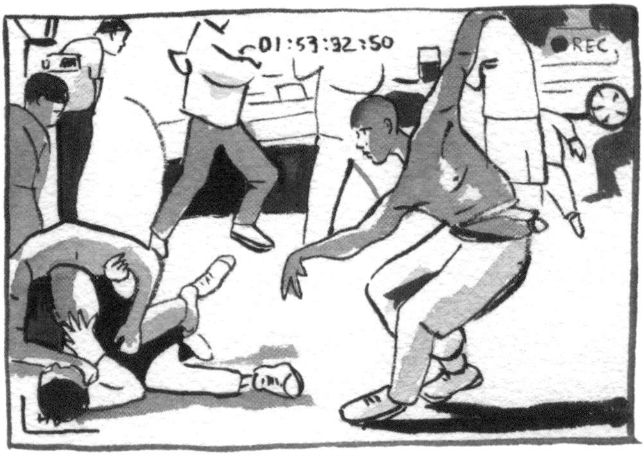
01:53:32:50
REC

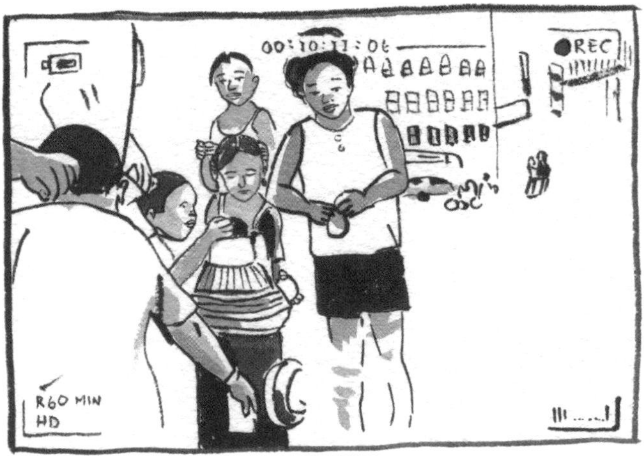
00:10:11:06
REC
R60 MIN
HD

But he dreamed of making a movie.

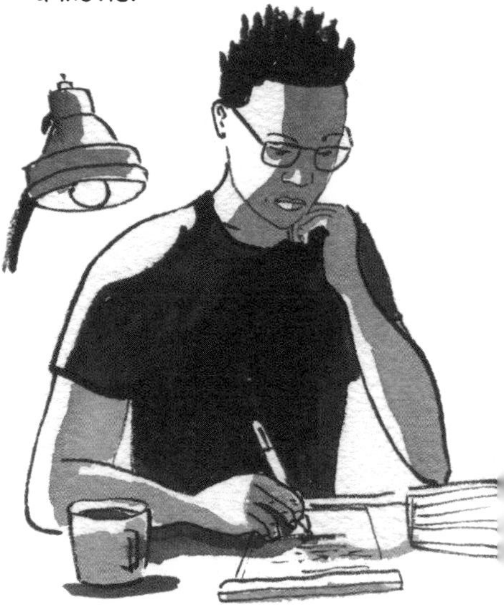

Script idea:

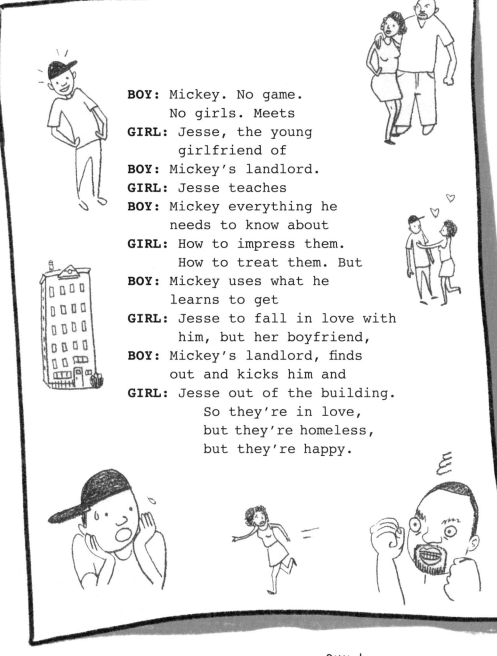

BOY: Mickey. No game.
No girls. Meets
GIRL: Jesse, the young
girlfriend of
BOY: Mickey's landlord.
GIRL: Jesse teaches
BOY: Mickey everything he
needs to know about
GIRL: How to impress them.
How to treat them. But
BOY: Mickey uses what he
learns to get
GIRL: Jesse to fall in love with
him, but her boyfriend,
BOY: Mickey's landlord, finds
out and kicks him and
GIRL: Jesse out of the building.
So they're in love,
but they're homeless,
but they're happy.

Riiiight.

CASTING OF THE WORST, STUPIDEST MOVIE EVER:

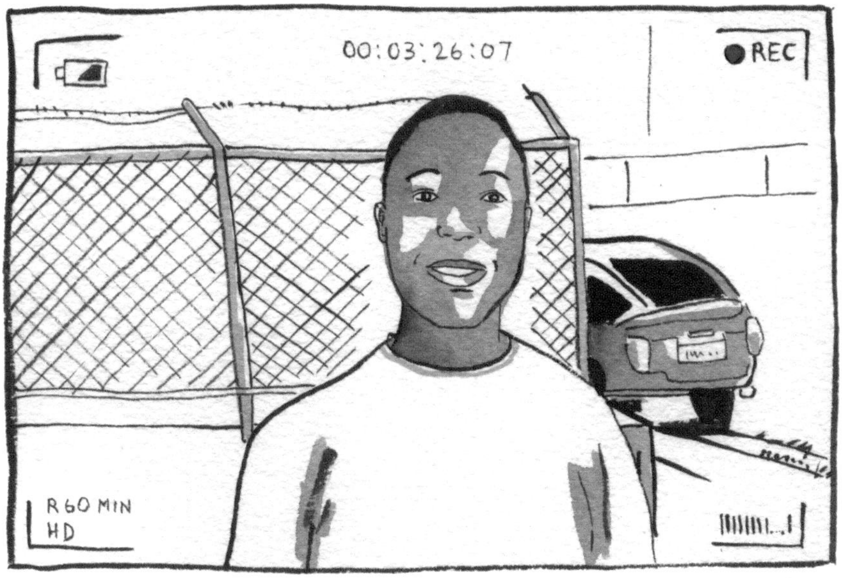
00:03:26:07
REC
R60 MIN
HD

BOY: Mickey
to be played by Uncle Mark's little brother, my father, Mikey.

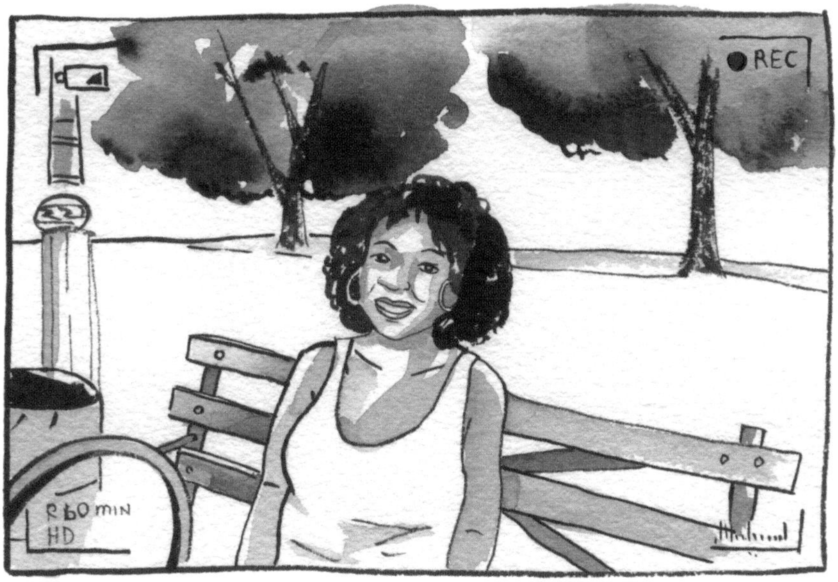
REC
R60 MIN
HD

GIRL: Jesse
to be played by the younger sister of a girl
Uncle Mark used to date, Shari, my mother.

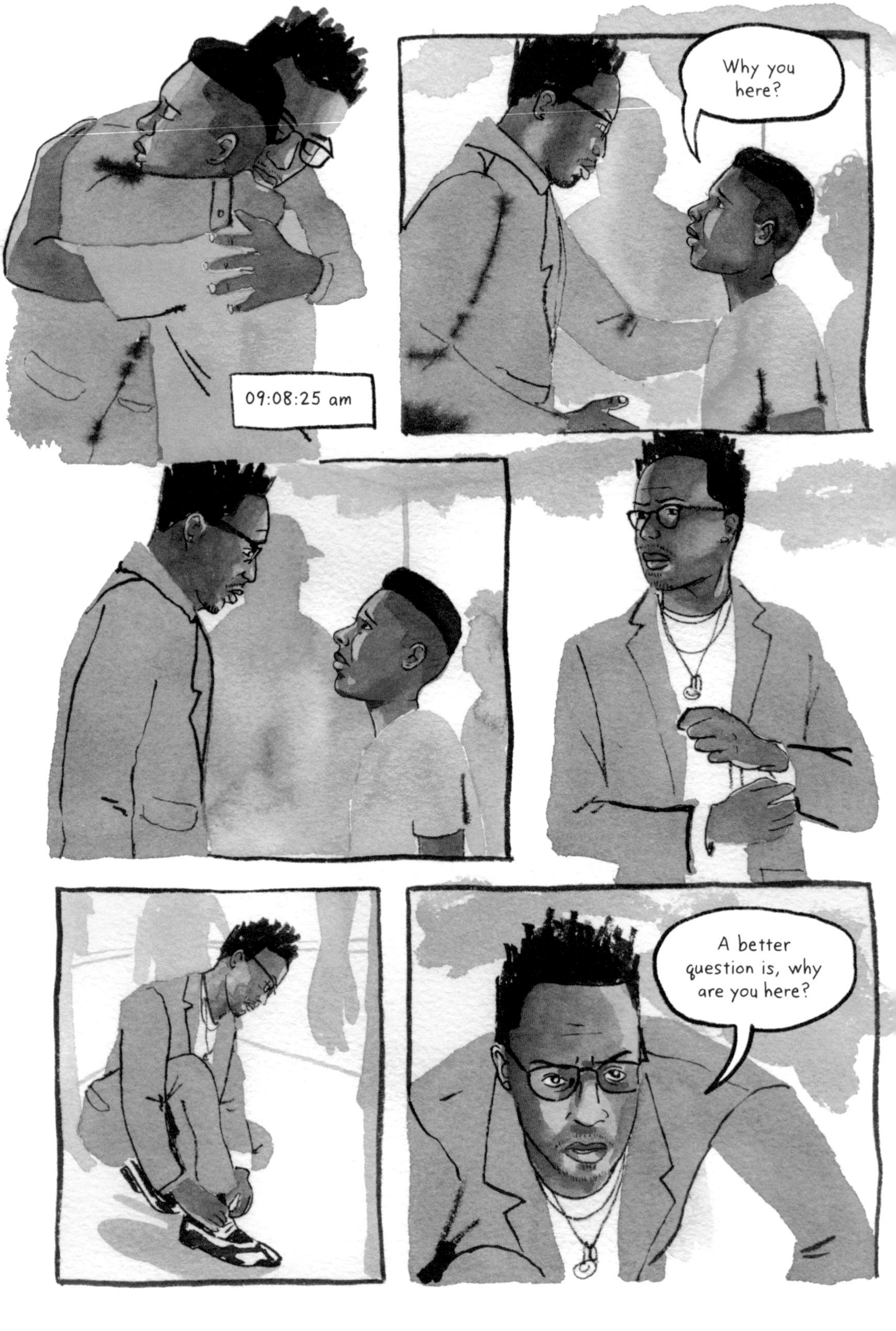
09:08:25 am
Why you here?
A better question is, why are you here?

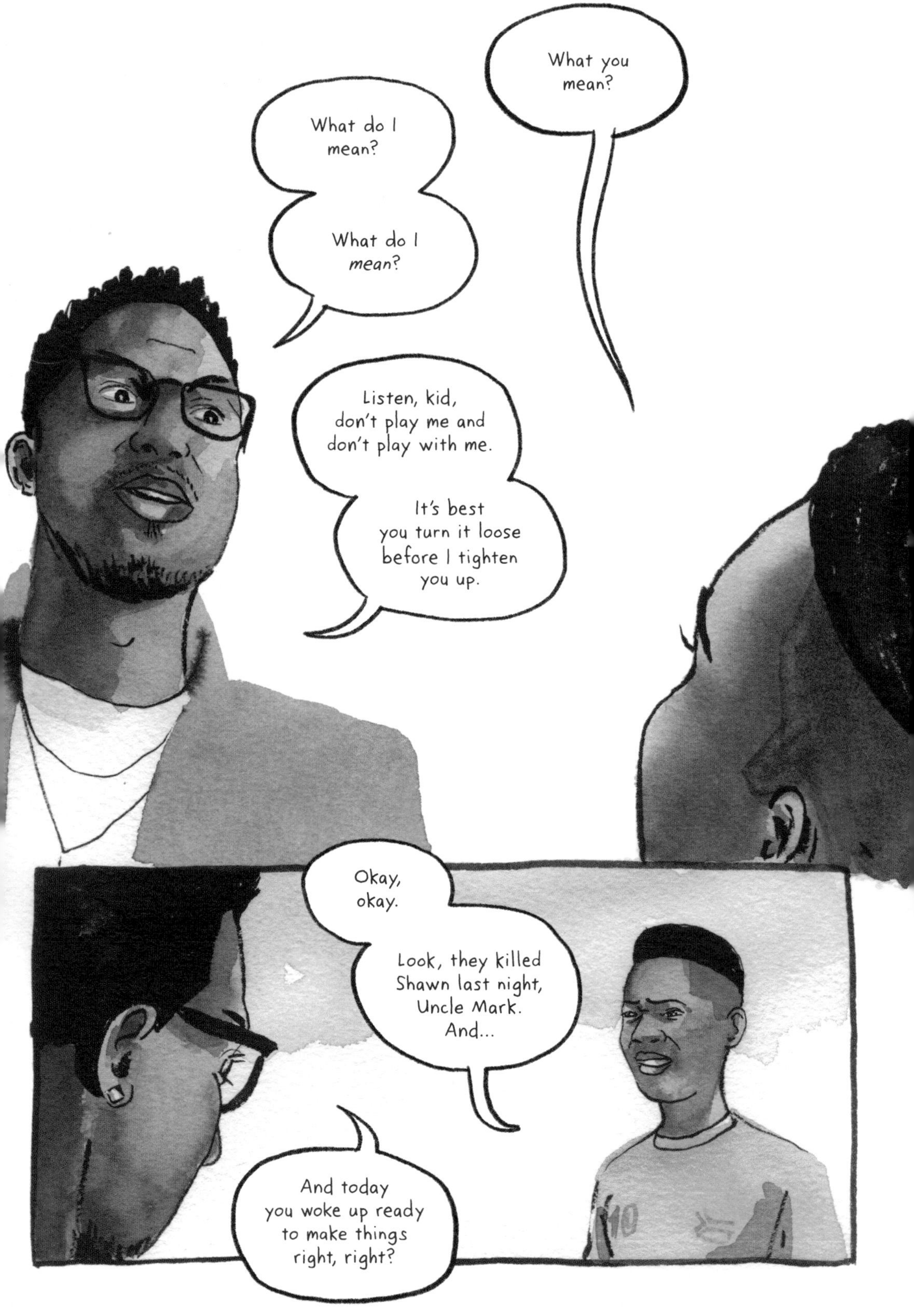
What you mean?
What do I mean?
What do I *mean*?
Listen, kid, don't play me and don't play with me.
It's best you turn it loose before I tighten you up.
Okay, okay.
Look, they killed Shawn last night, Uncle Mark. And...
And today you woke up ready to make things right, right?

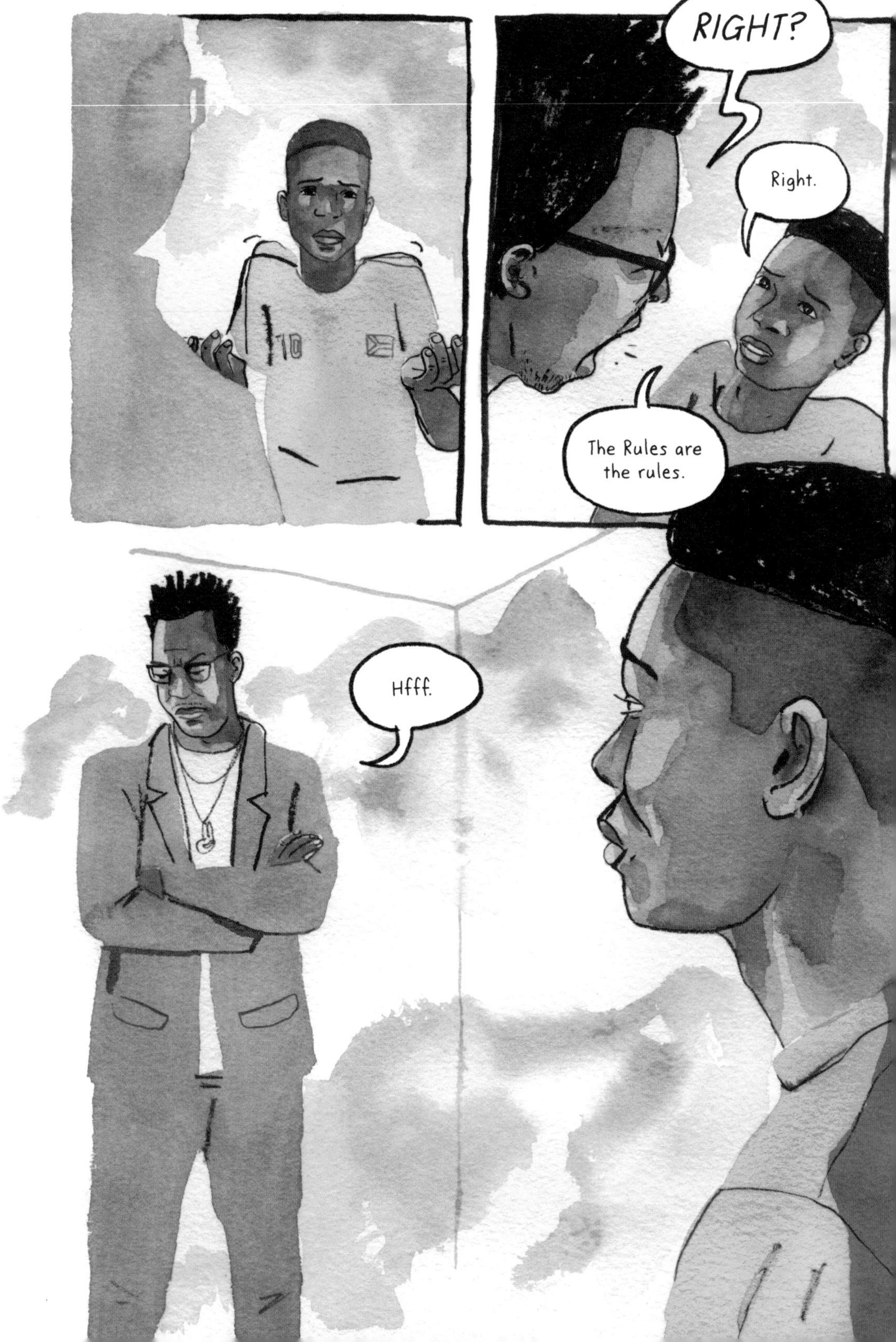
RIGHT?
Right.
The Rules are the rules.
Hfff.

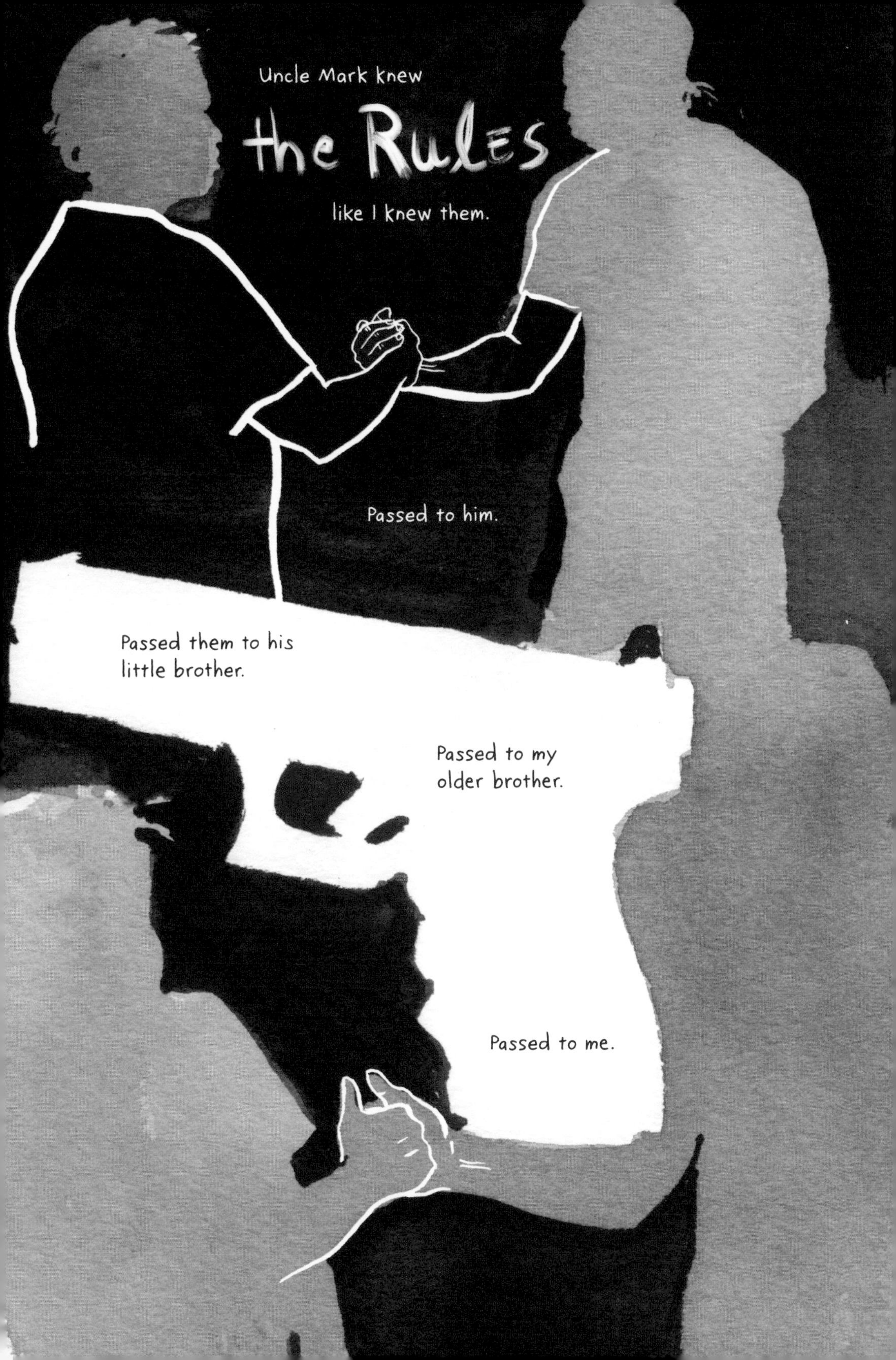
Uncle Mark knew
the Rules
like I knew them.
Passed to him.
Passed them to his little brother.
Passed to my older brother.
Passed to me.

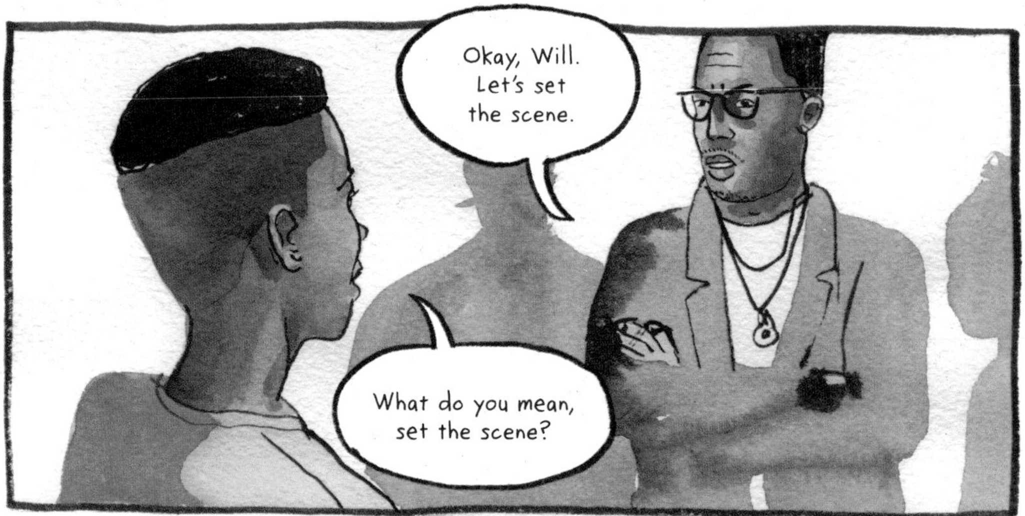
Okay, Will. Let's set the scene.
What do you mean, set the scene?

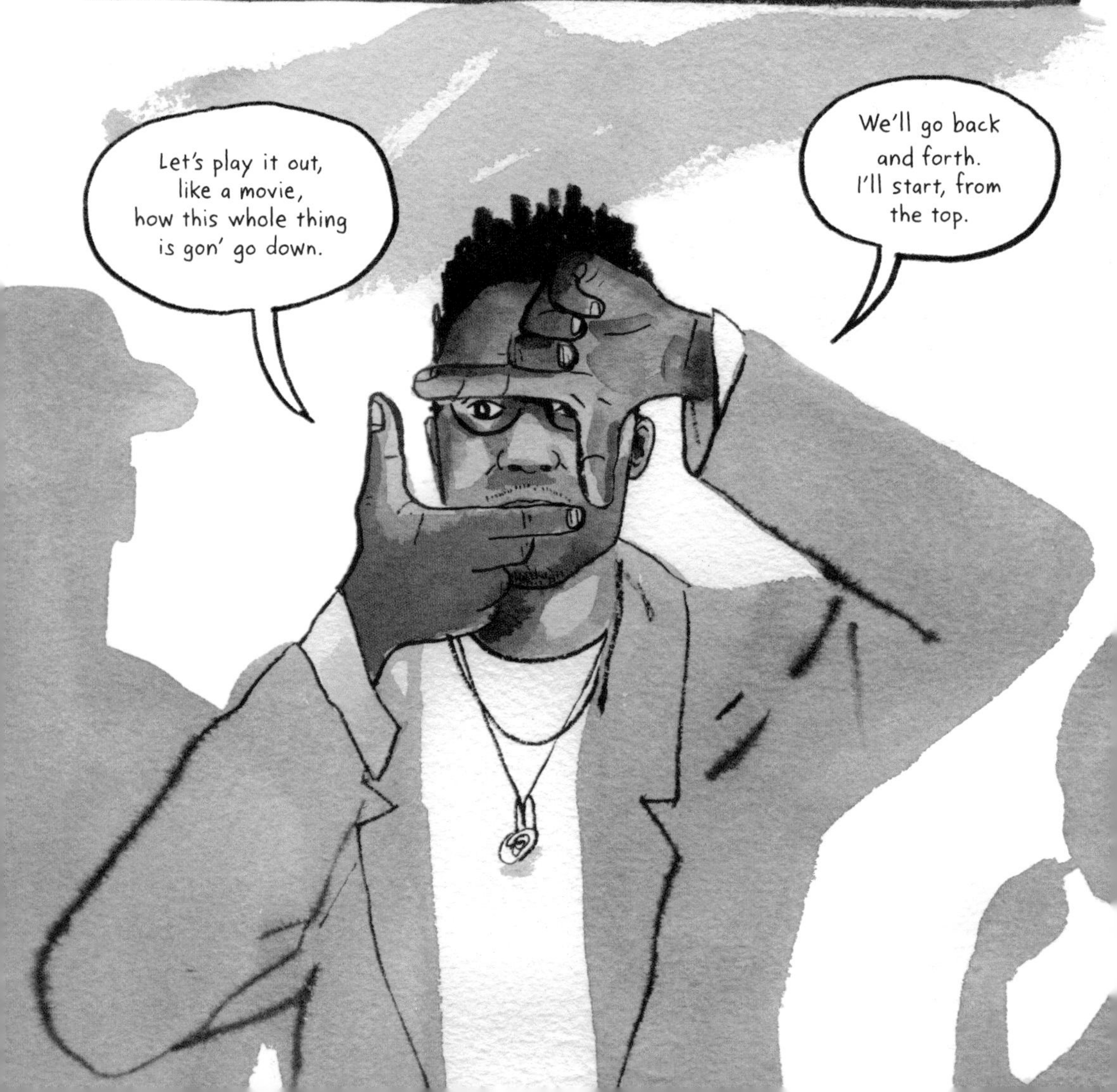
Let's play it out, like a movie, how this whole thing is gon' go down.
We'll go back and forth. I'll start, from the top.

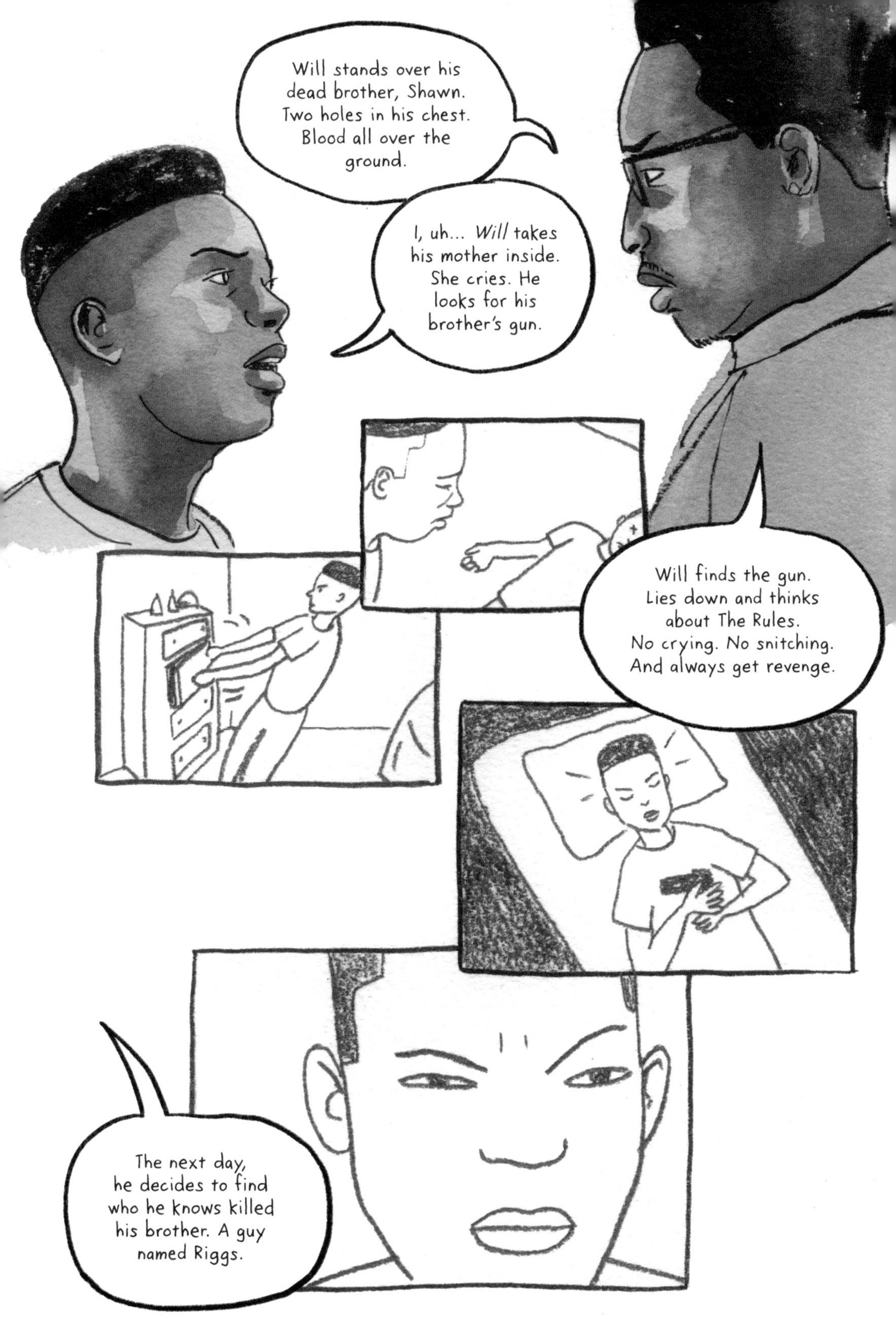
Will stands over his dead brother, Shawn. Two holes in his chest. Blood all over the ground.
I, uh... *Will* takes his mother inside. She cries. He looks for his brother's gun.
Will finds the gun. Lies down and thinks about The Rules. No crying. No snitching. And always get revenge.
The next day, he decides to find who he knows killed his brother. A guy named Riggs.

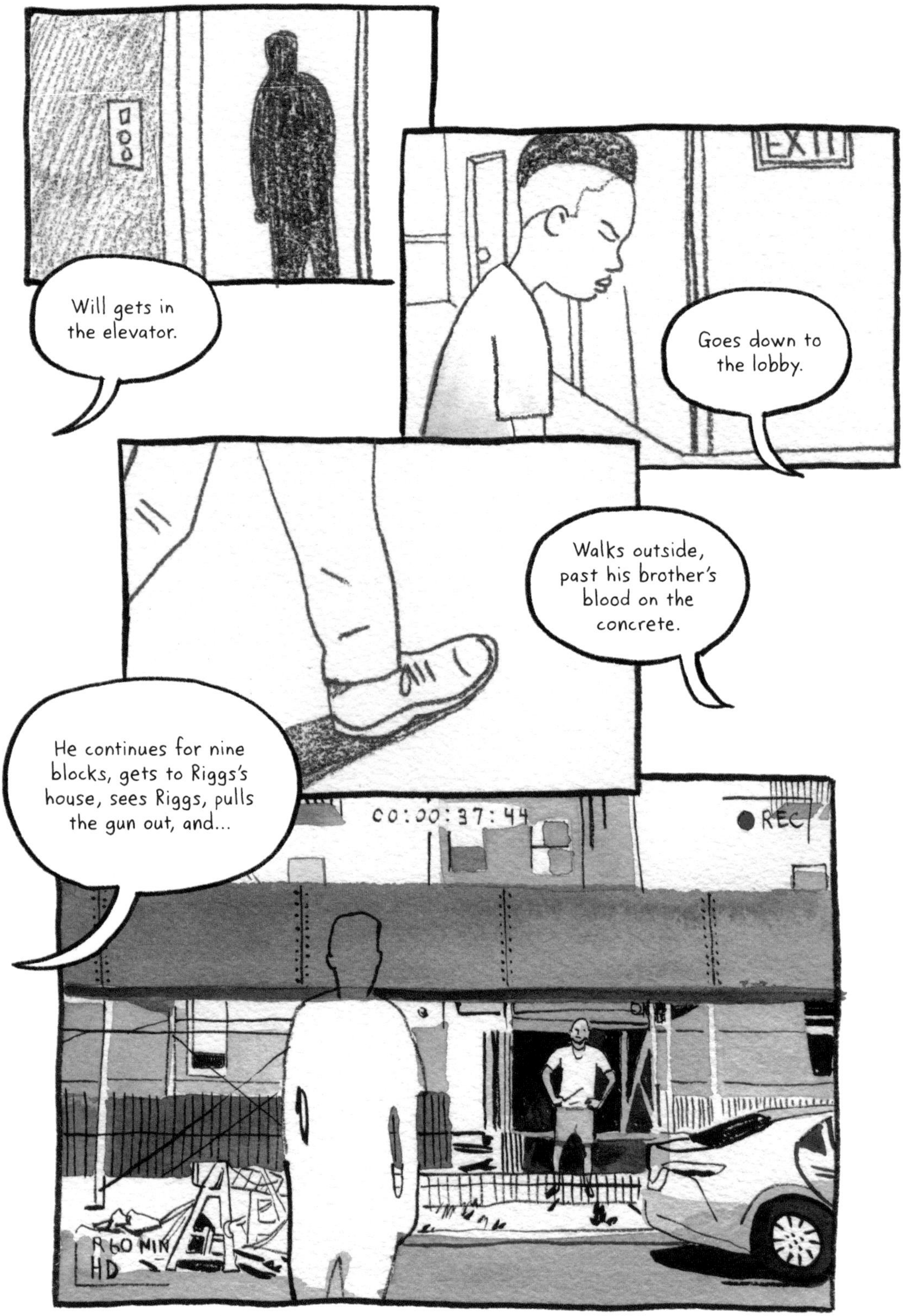
Will gets in the elevator.
EXIT
Goes down to the lobby.
Walks outside, past his brother's blood on the concrete.
He continues for nine blocks, gets to Riggs's house, sees Riggs, pulls the gun out, and...
00:00:37:44
REC

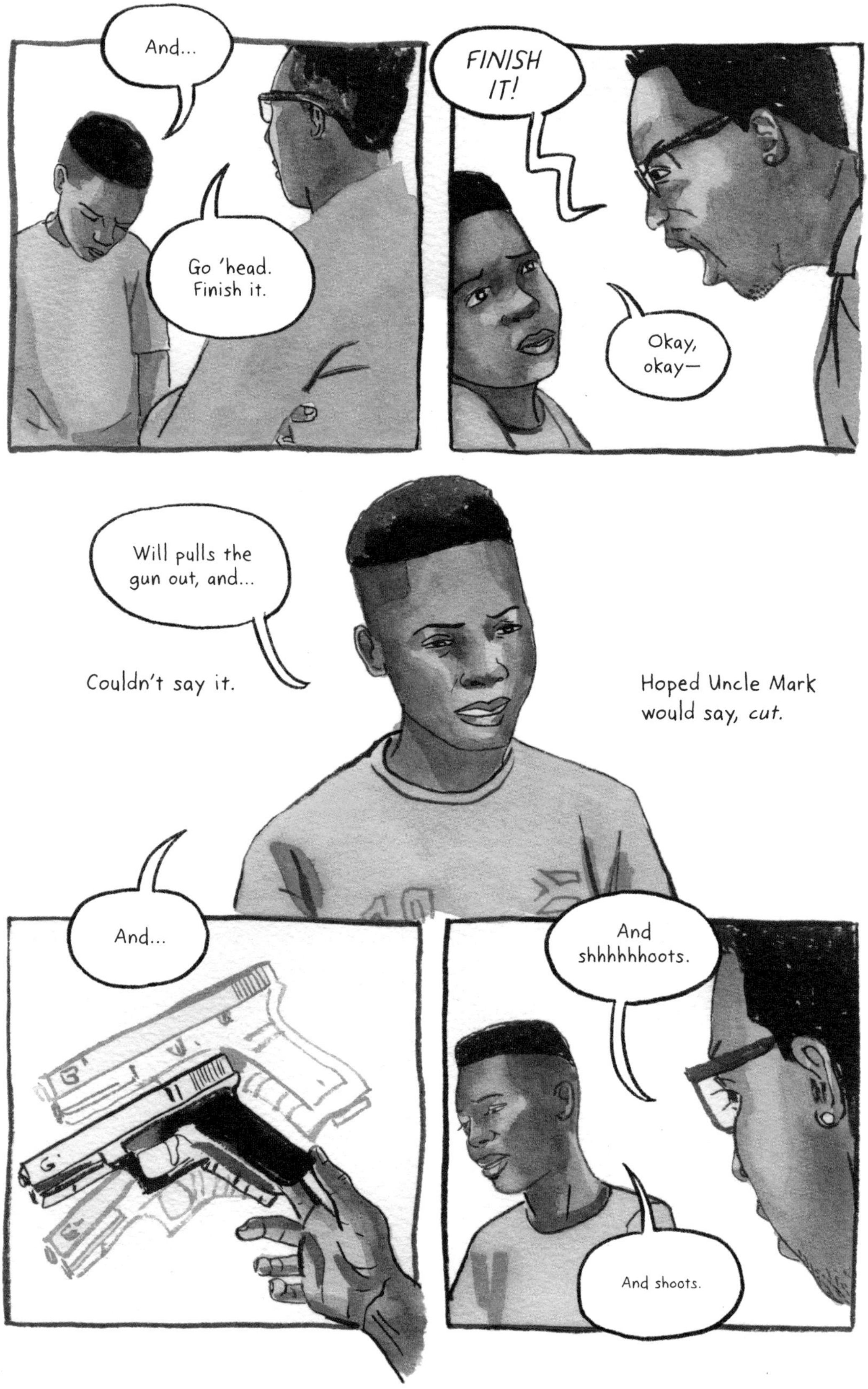
And...
Go 'head. Finish it.
FINISH IT!
Okay, okay—
Will pulls the gun out, and...
Couldn't say it.
Hoped Uncle Mark would say, *cut*.
And...
And shhhhhhoots.
And shoots.

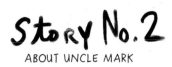

Story No. 2

ABOUT UNCLE MARK

Uncle Mark lost the camera his mother got him. Couldn't afford another one.

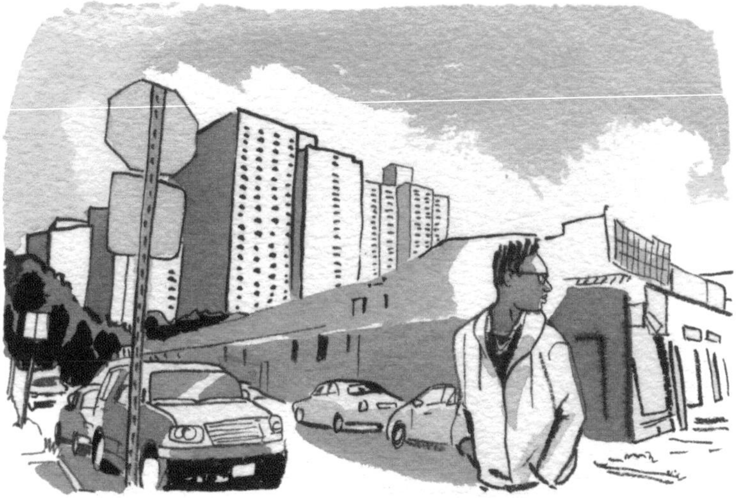

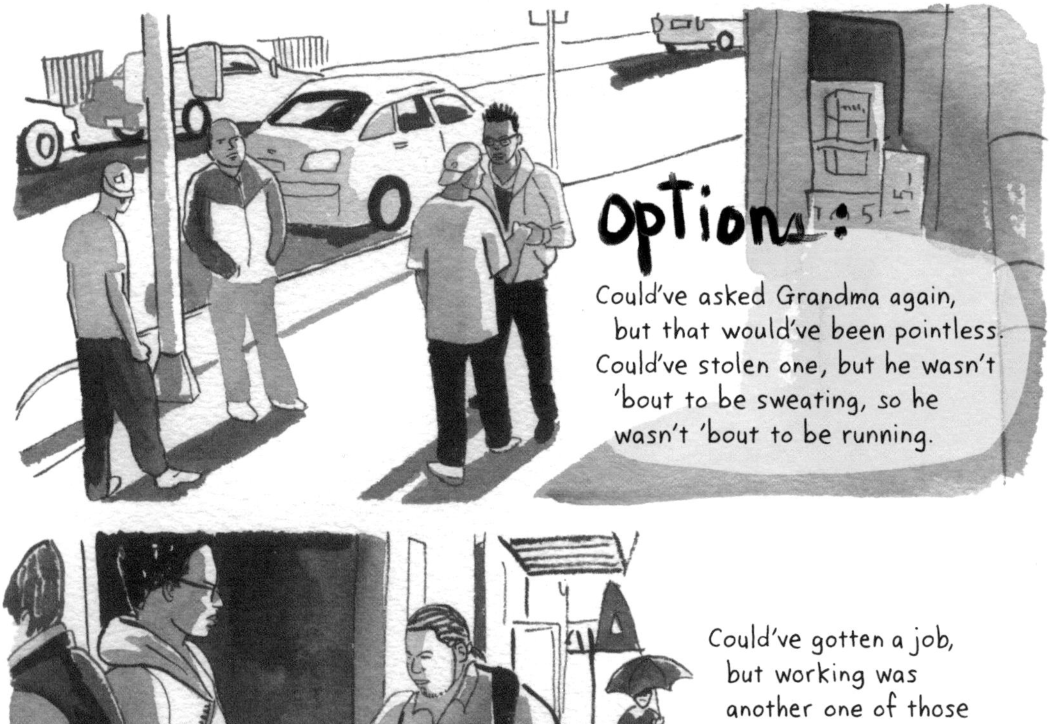
Options:
Could've asked Grandma again, but that would've been pointless.
Could've stolen one, but he wasn't 'bout to be sweating, so he wasn't 'bout to be running.

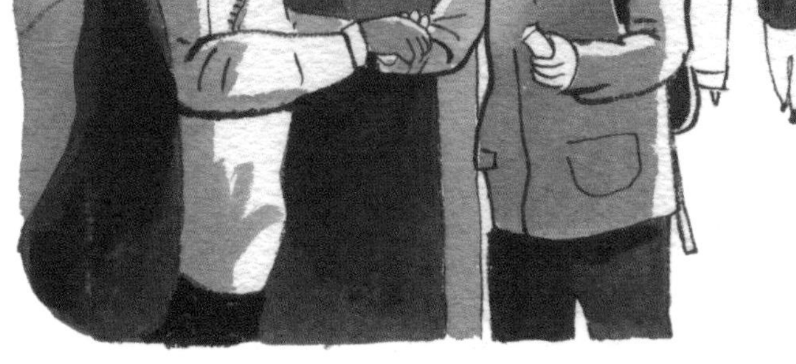

Could've gotten a job, but working was another one of those things Uncle Mark just wasn't 'bout to be doing.
So he did what a lot of people do around here.

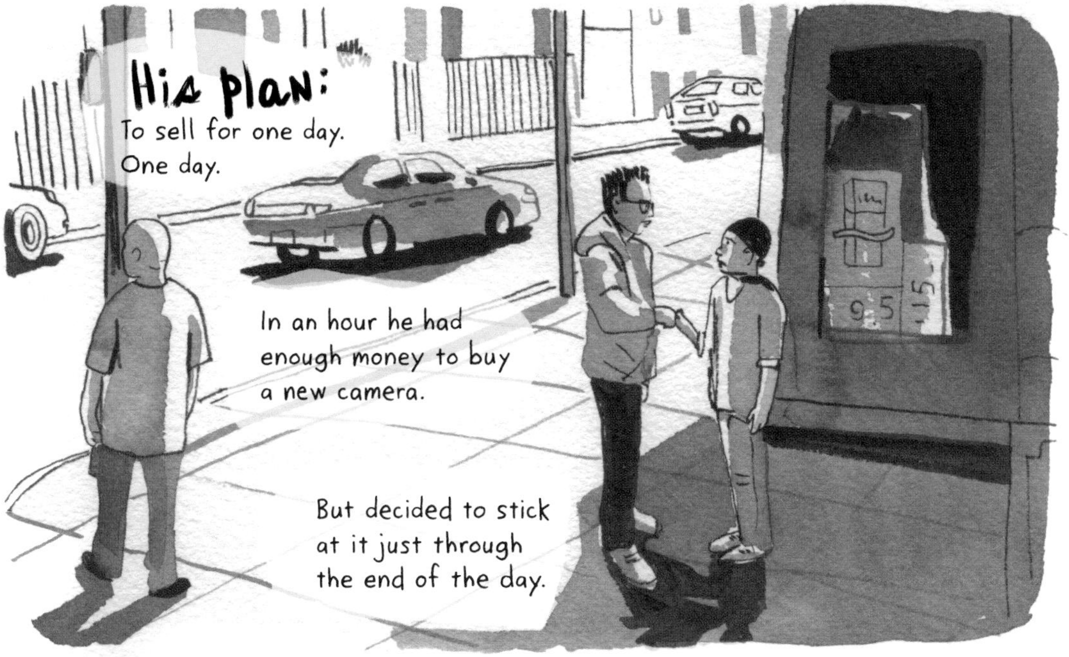
His plan:
To sell for one day.
One day.
In an hour he had
enough money to buy
a new camera.
But decided to stick
at it just through
the end of the day.
9.5
15

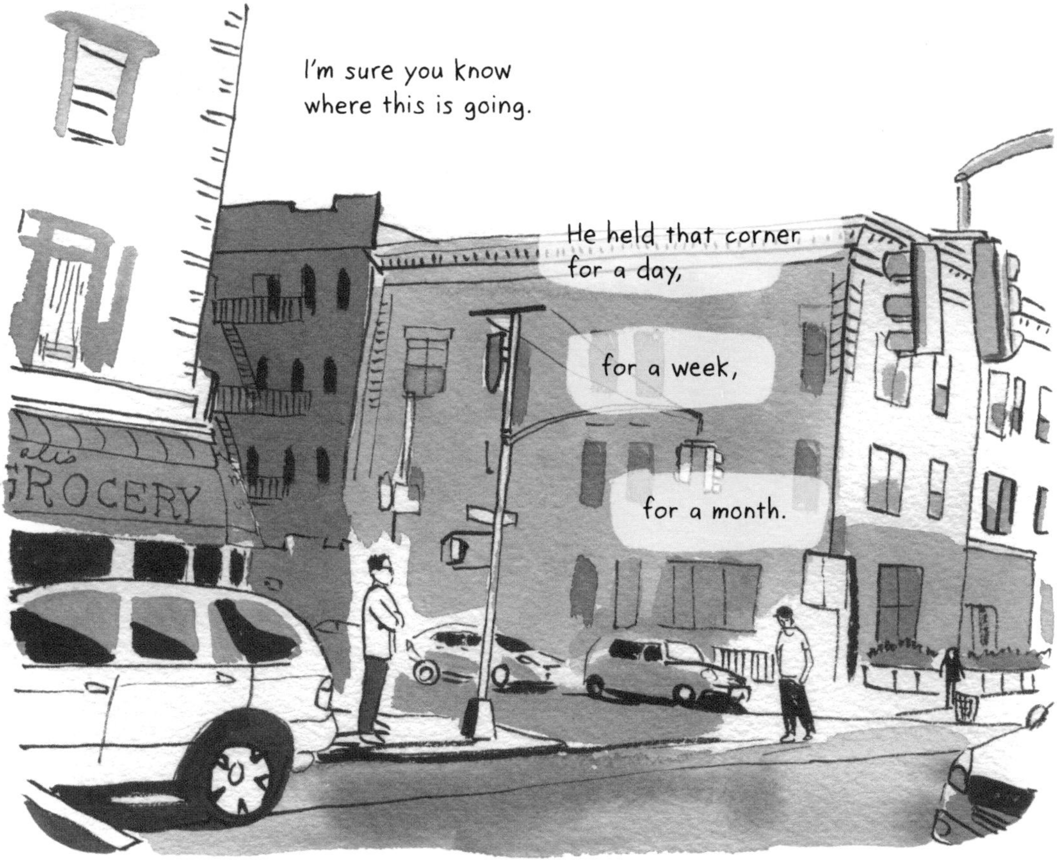
I'm sure you know
where this is going.
He held that corner
for a day,
for a week,
for a month.
GROCERY

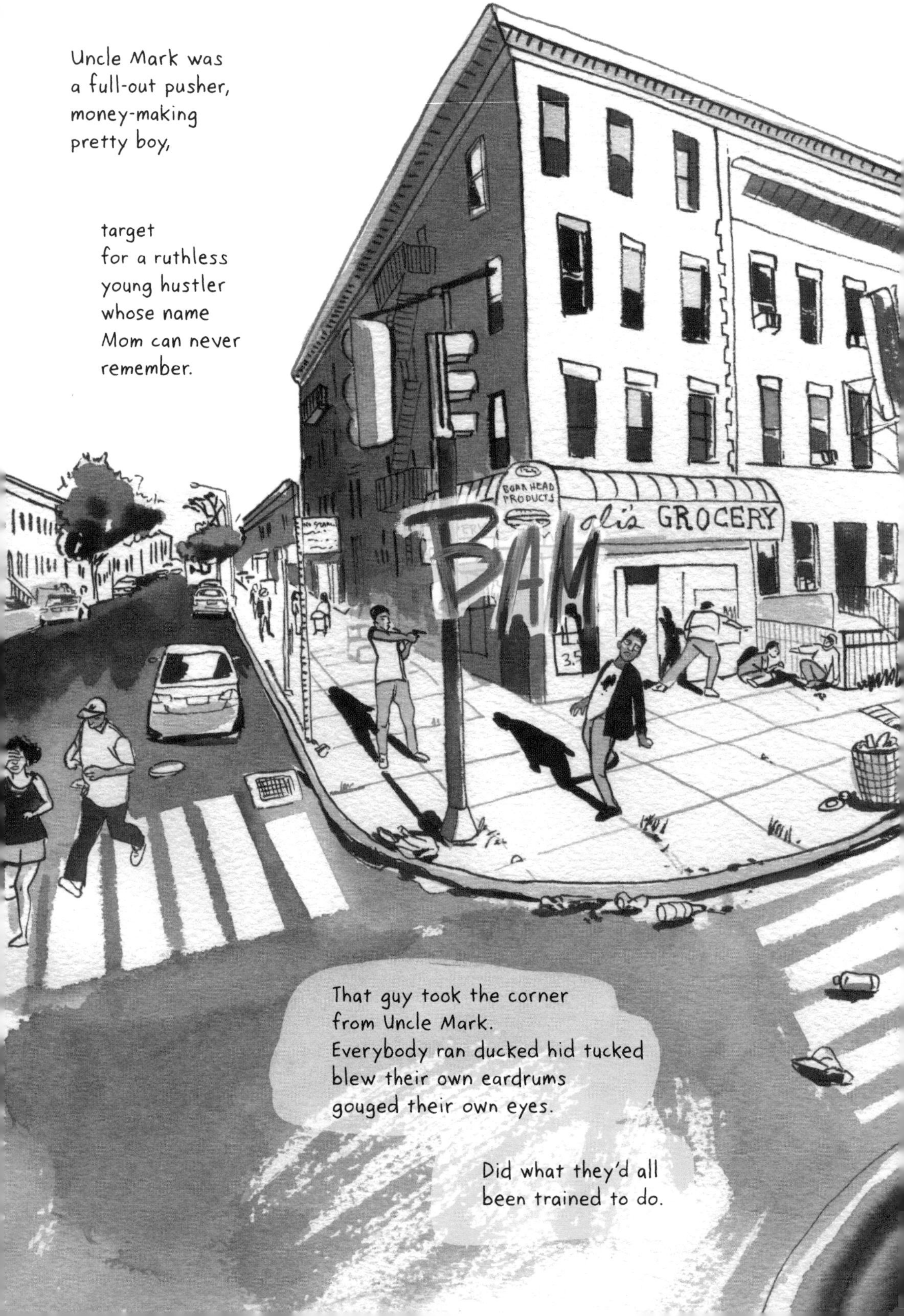
Uncle Mark was
a full-out pusher,
money-making
pretty boy,
target
for a ruthless
young hustler
whose name
Mom can never
remember.
BOAR HEAD
PRODUCTS
GROCERY
BAM
That guy took the corner
from Uncle Mark.
Everybody ran ducked hid tucked
blew their own eardrums
gouged their own eyes.
Did what they'd all
been trained to do.

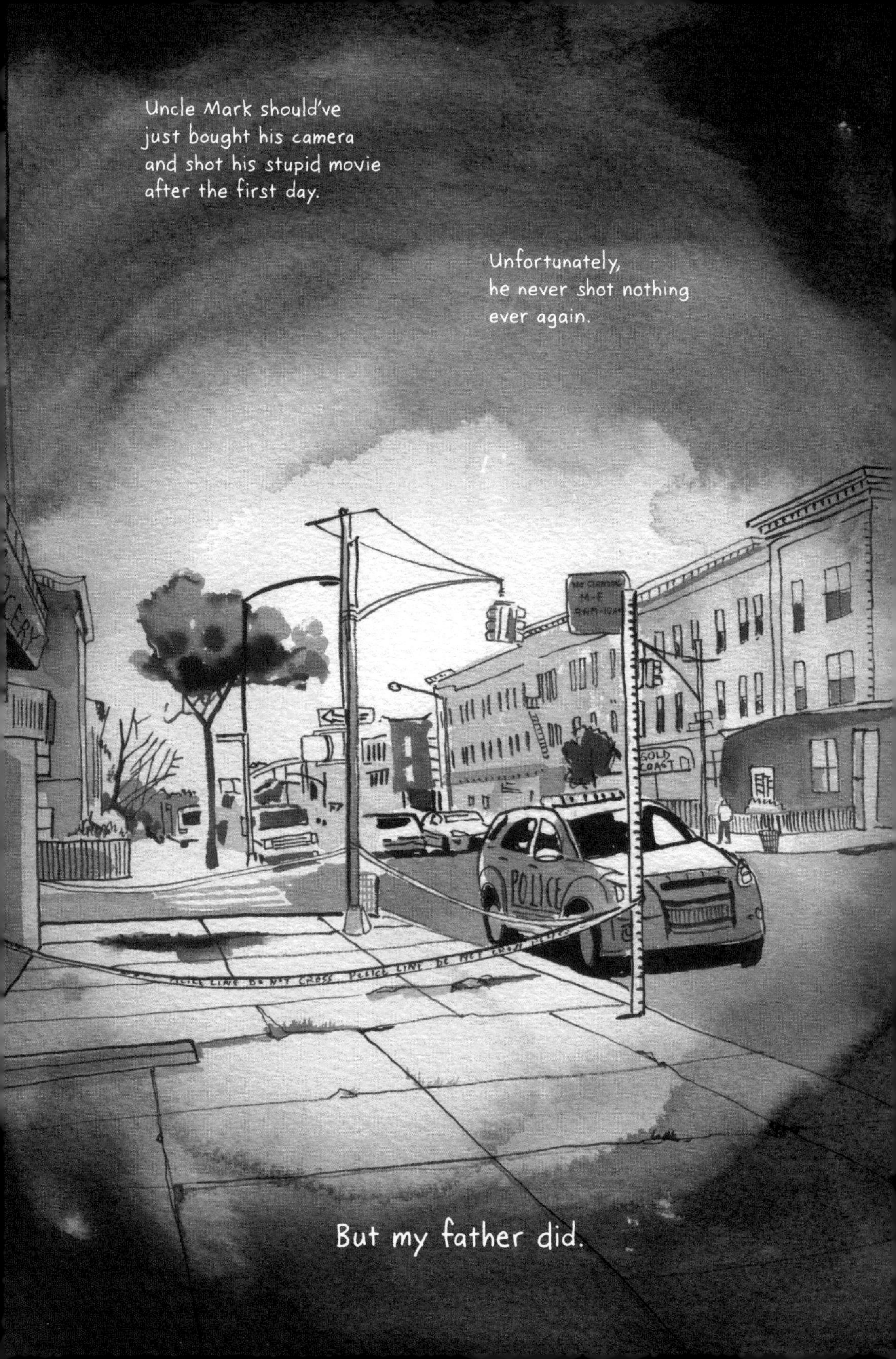
Uncle Mark should've just bought his camera and shot his stupid movie after the first day.
Unfortunately, he never shot nothing ever again.
GOLD COAST
POLICE
POLICE LINE DO NOT CROSS
But my father did.

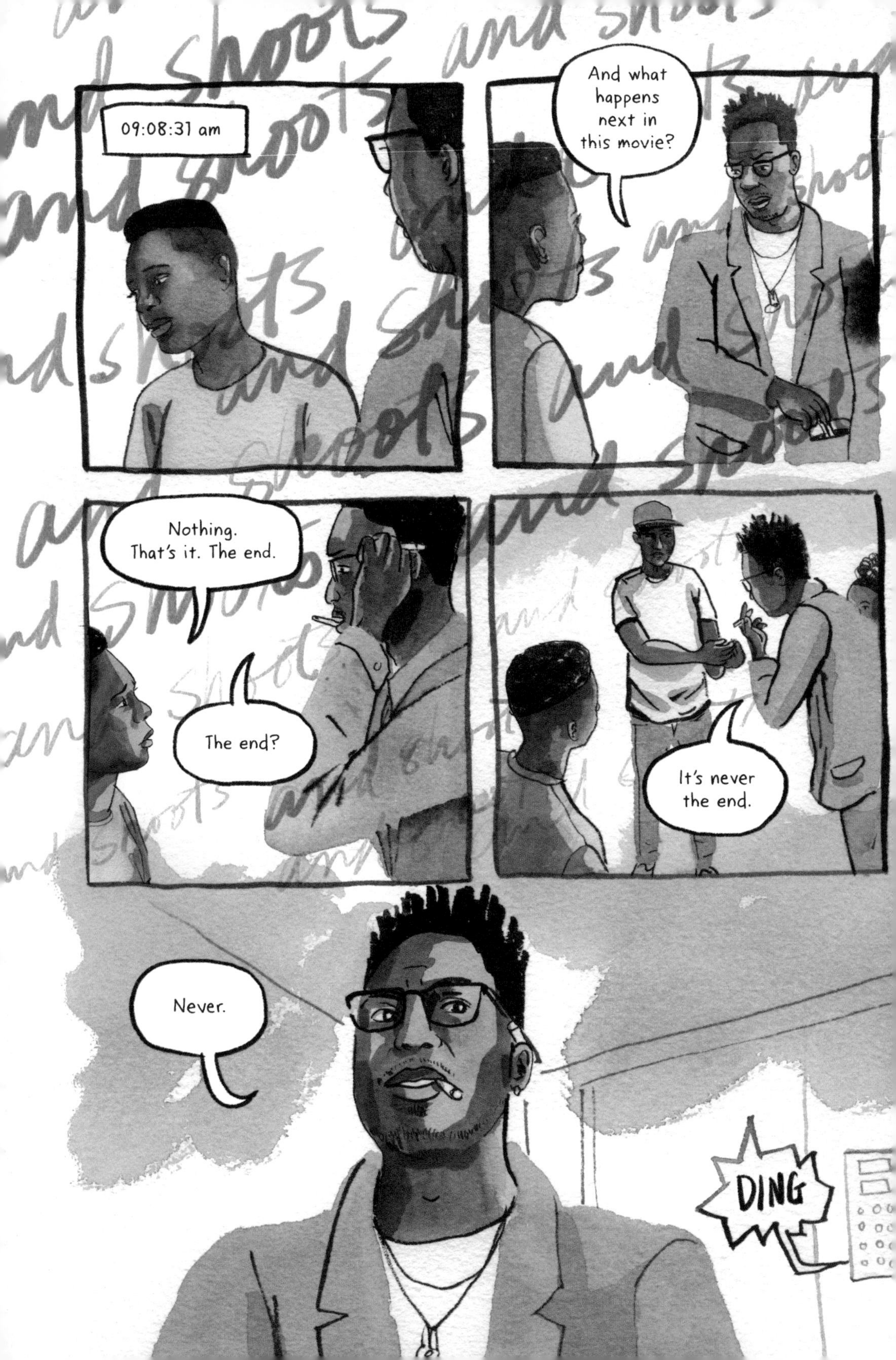
09:08:31 am
And what happens next in this movie?
Nothing. That's it. The end.
The end?
It's never the end.
Never.
DING

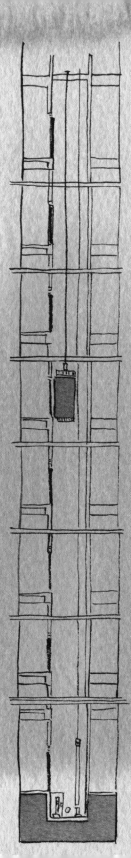

NO SMOKING

CAPACITY 2000 LBS

CITY ID NO. 3P577Q

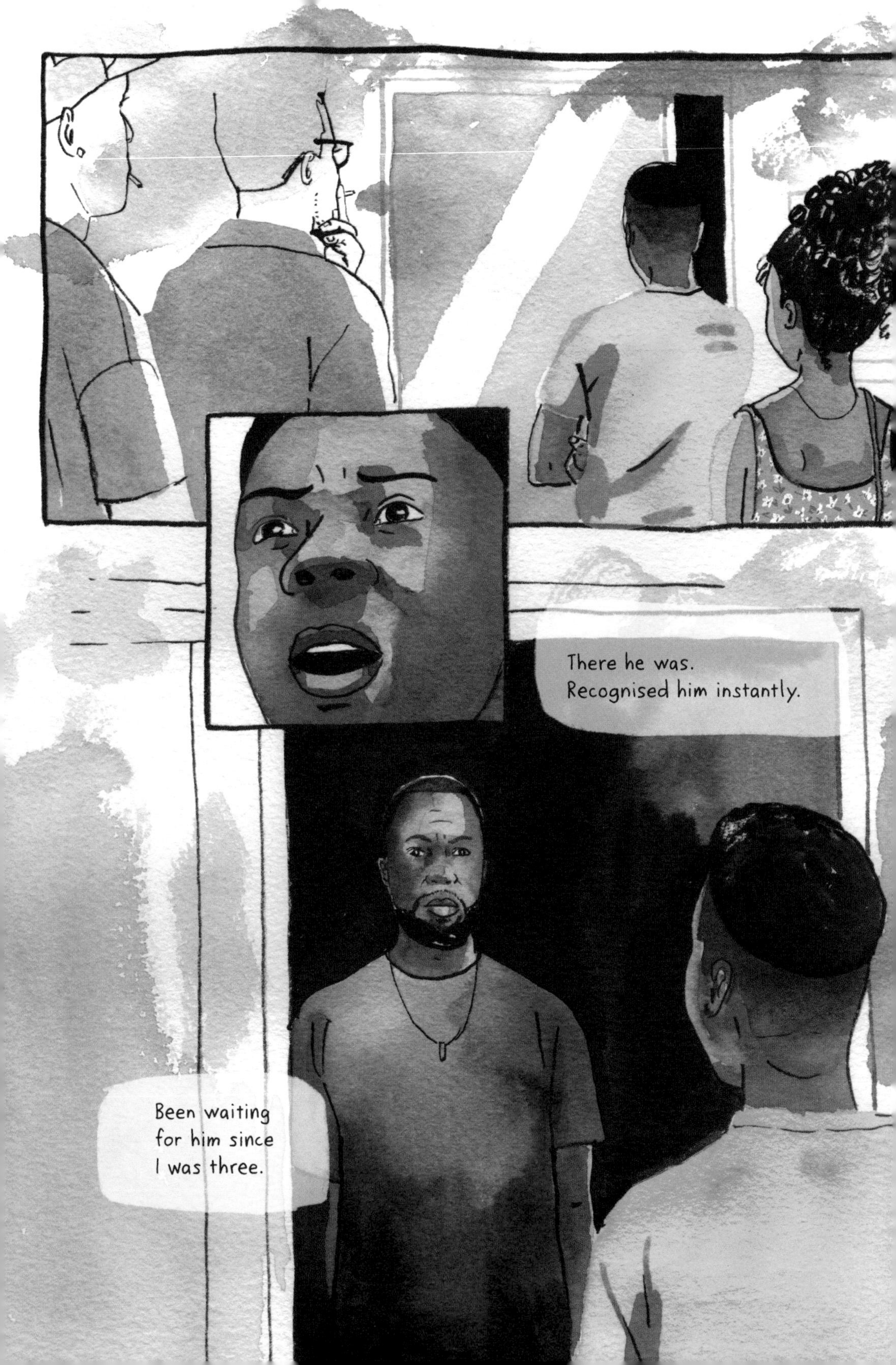
There he was.
Recognised him instantly.
Been waiting
for him since
I was three.

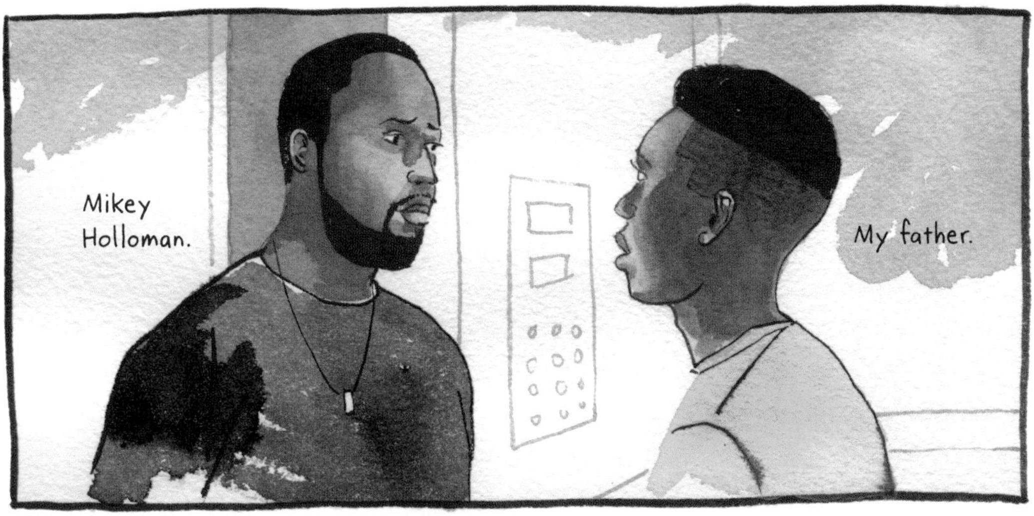
Mikey
Holloman.
My father.

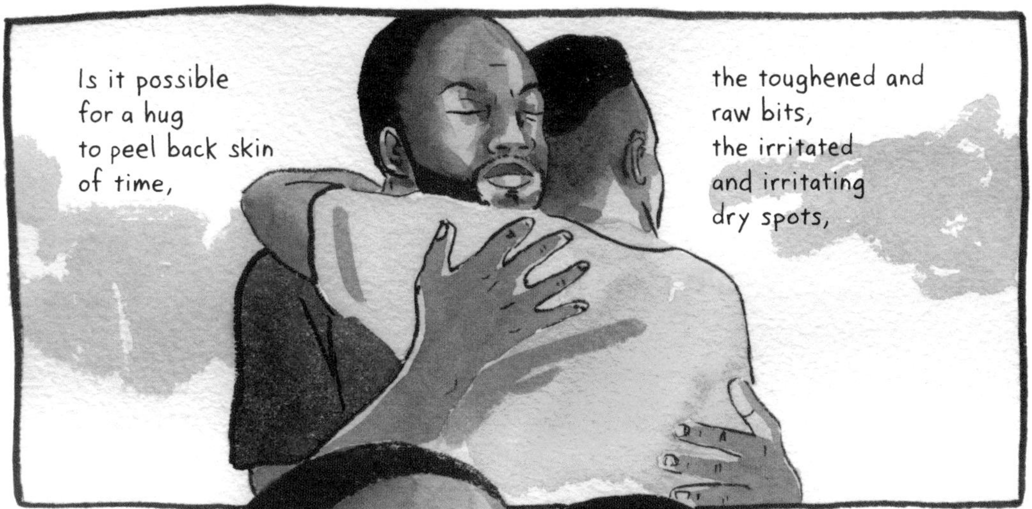
Is it possible
for a hug
to peel back skin
of time,
the toughened and
raw bits,
the irritated
and irritating
dry spots,

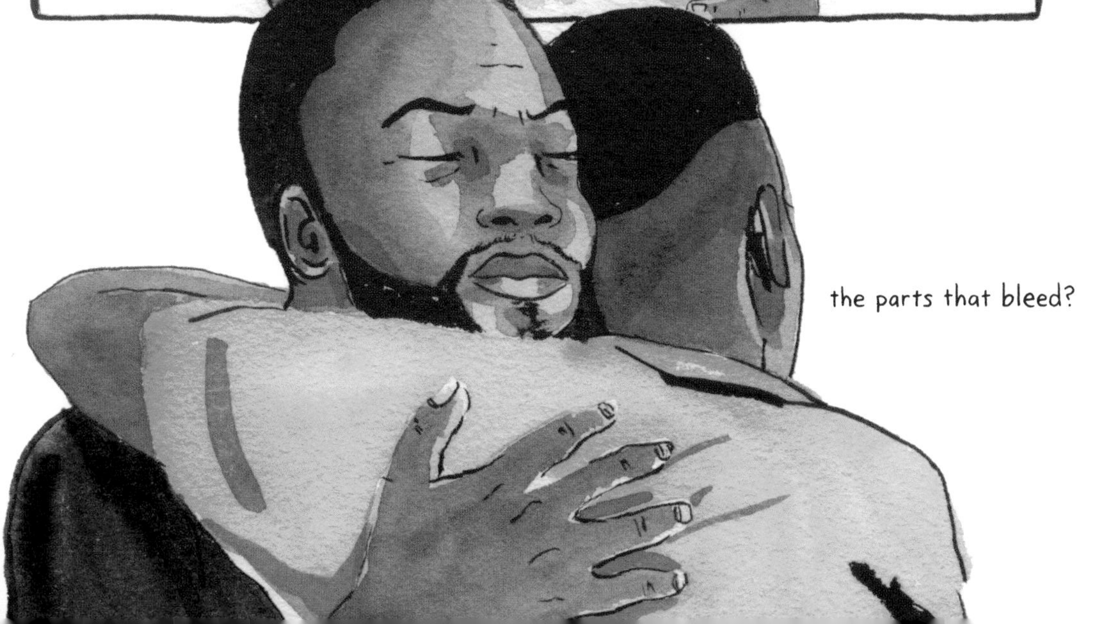
the parts that bleed?

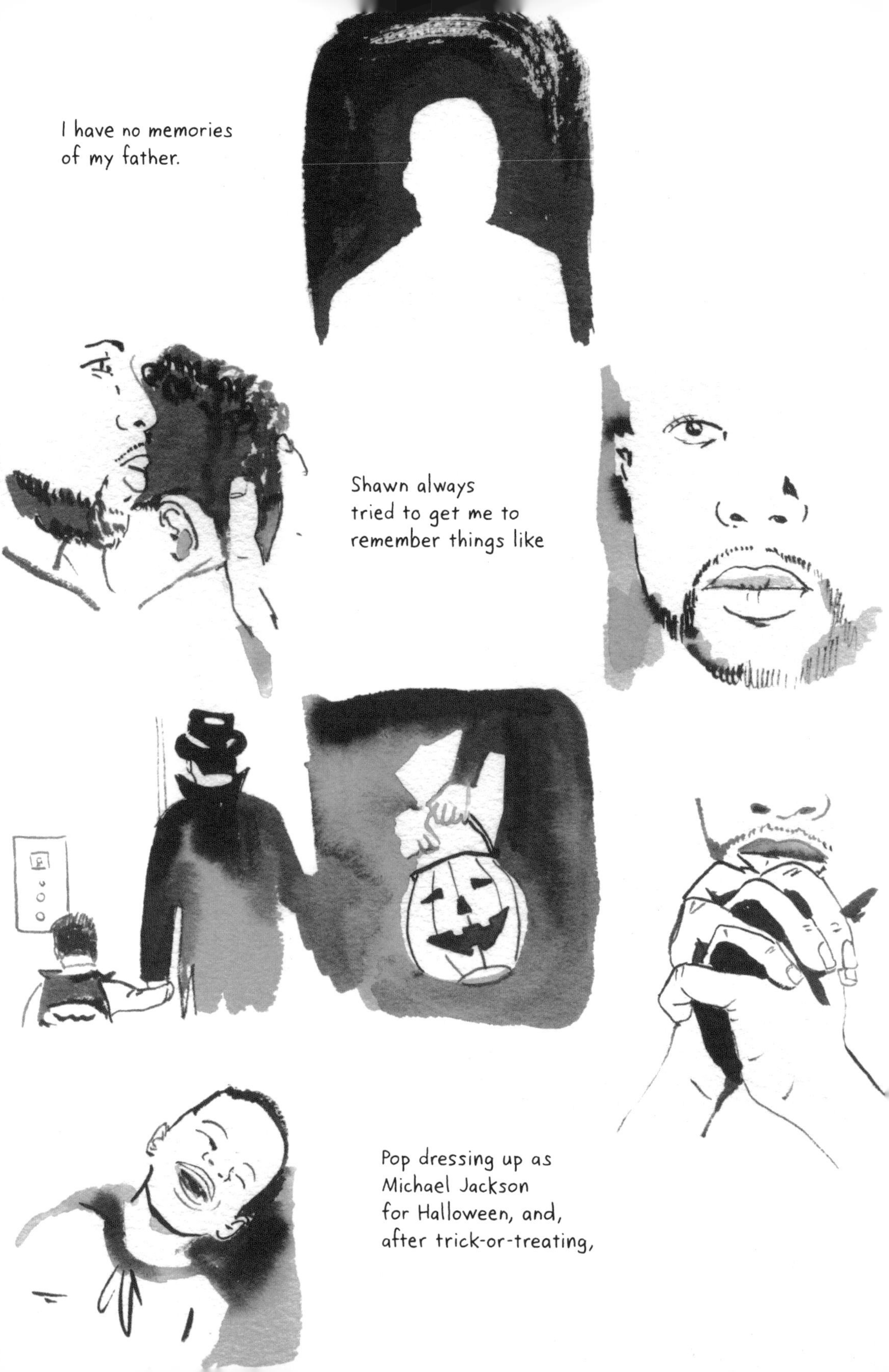
I have no memories of my father.
Shawn always tried to get me to remember things like
Pop dressing up as Michael Jackson for Halloween, and,
after trick-or-treating,

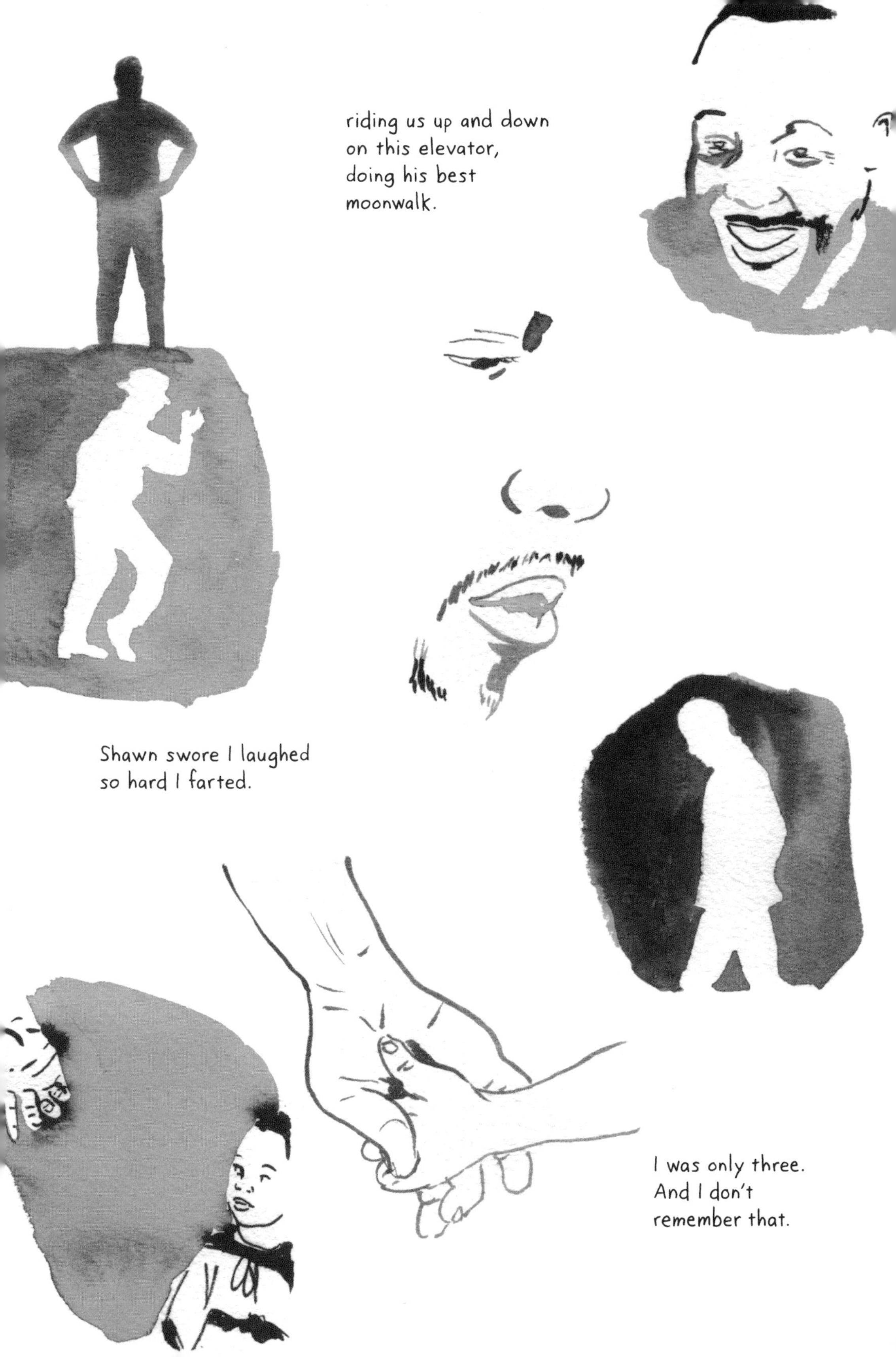
riding us up and down on this elevator, doing his best moonwalk.
Shawn swore I laughed so hard I farted.
I was only three. And I don't remember that.

A broken heart
killed my dad.
That's what my mother
always said.

As a kid
I always figured
his heart
was forreal broken

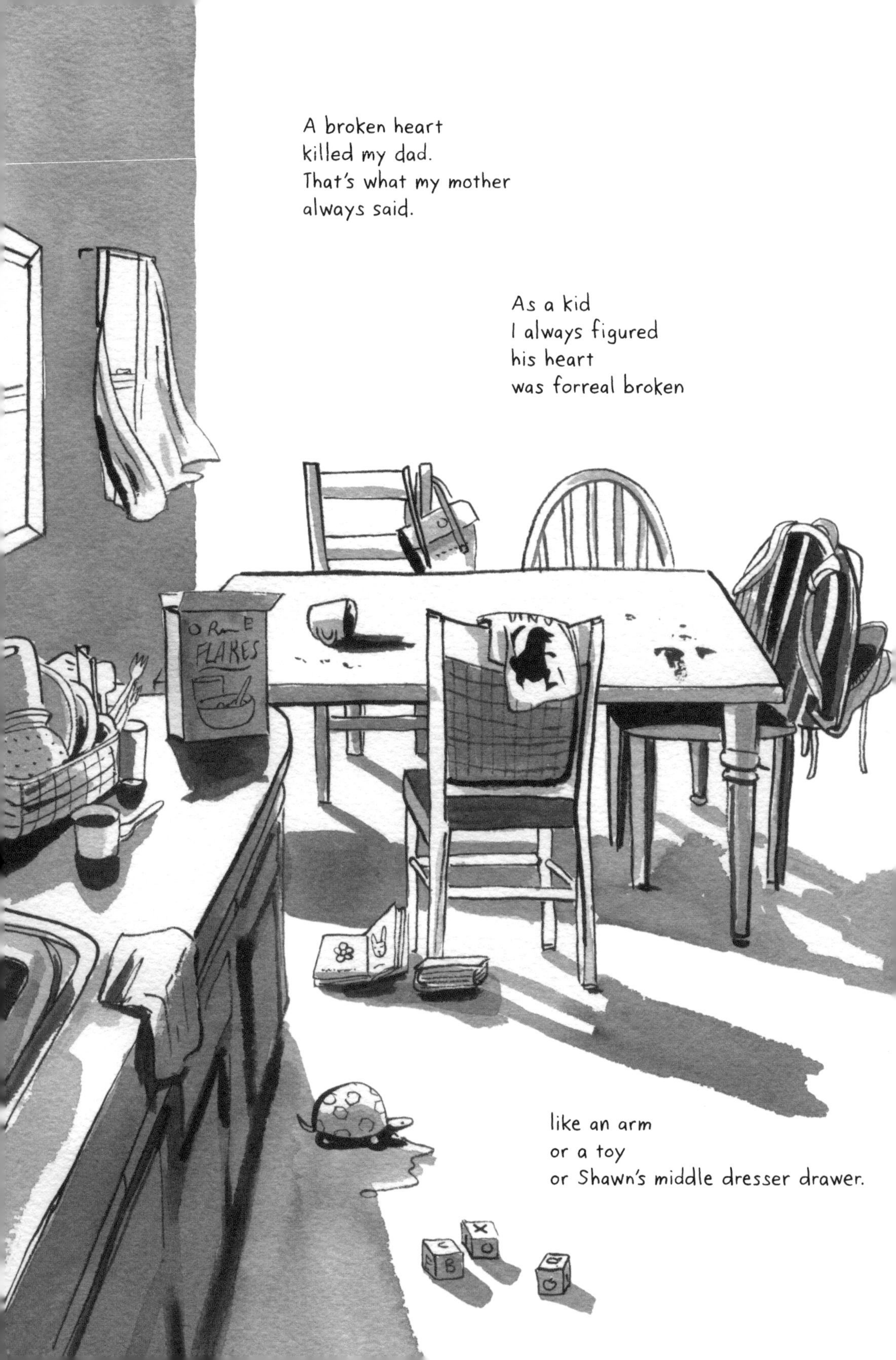
FLAKES

like an arm
or a toy
or Shawn's middle dresser drawer.

But that's not what Shawn said.

Shawn always said
our dad was killed
for killing the man
who killed our uncle.

Said he was at a pay
phone, probably talking
to Mom, when a guy
walked up on him,

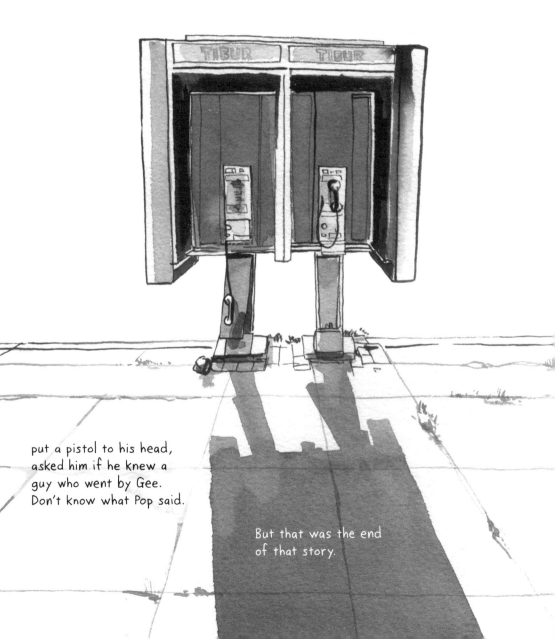

put a pistol to his head,
asked him if he knew a
guy who went by Gee.
Don't know what Pop said.

But that was the end
of that story.

I always used to ask Shawn how he knew that.
He said Buck told him. Said that was Buck's corner.
It was then that Buck started looking out for Shawn, who at the time was only seven.
JACKIE ROBINSON PLAYGROUND
Buck was sixteen.

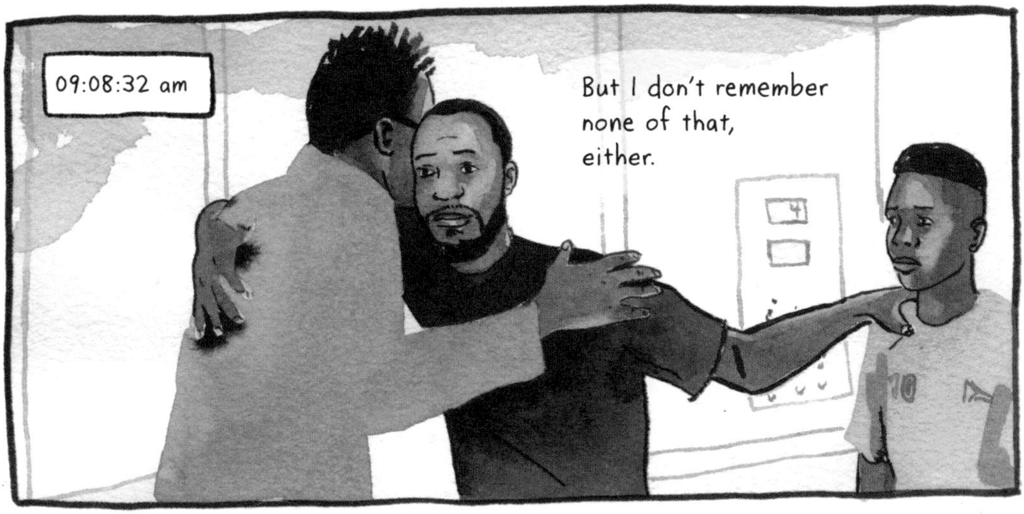
09:08:32 am
But I don't remember none of that, either.

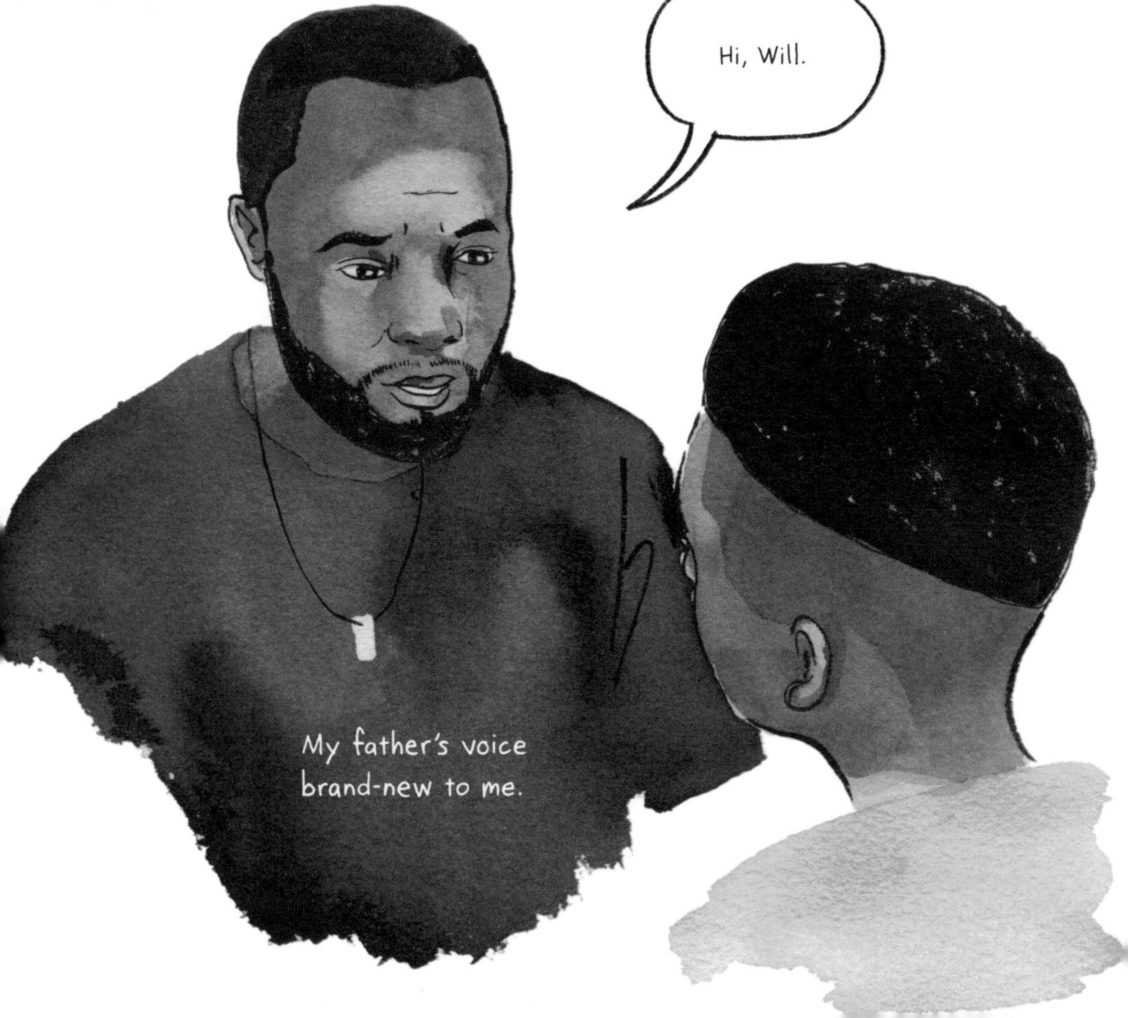
Hi, Will.
My father's voice brand-new to me.

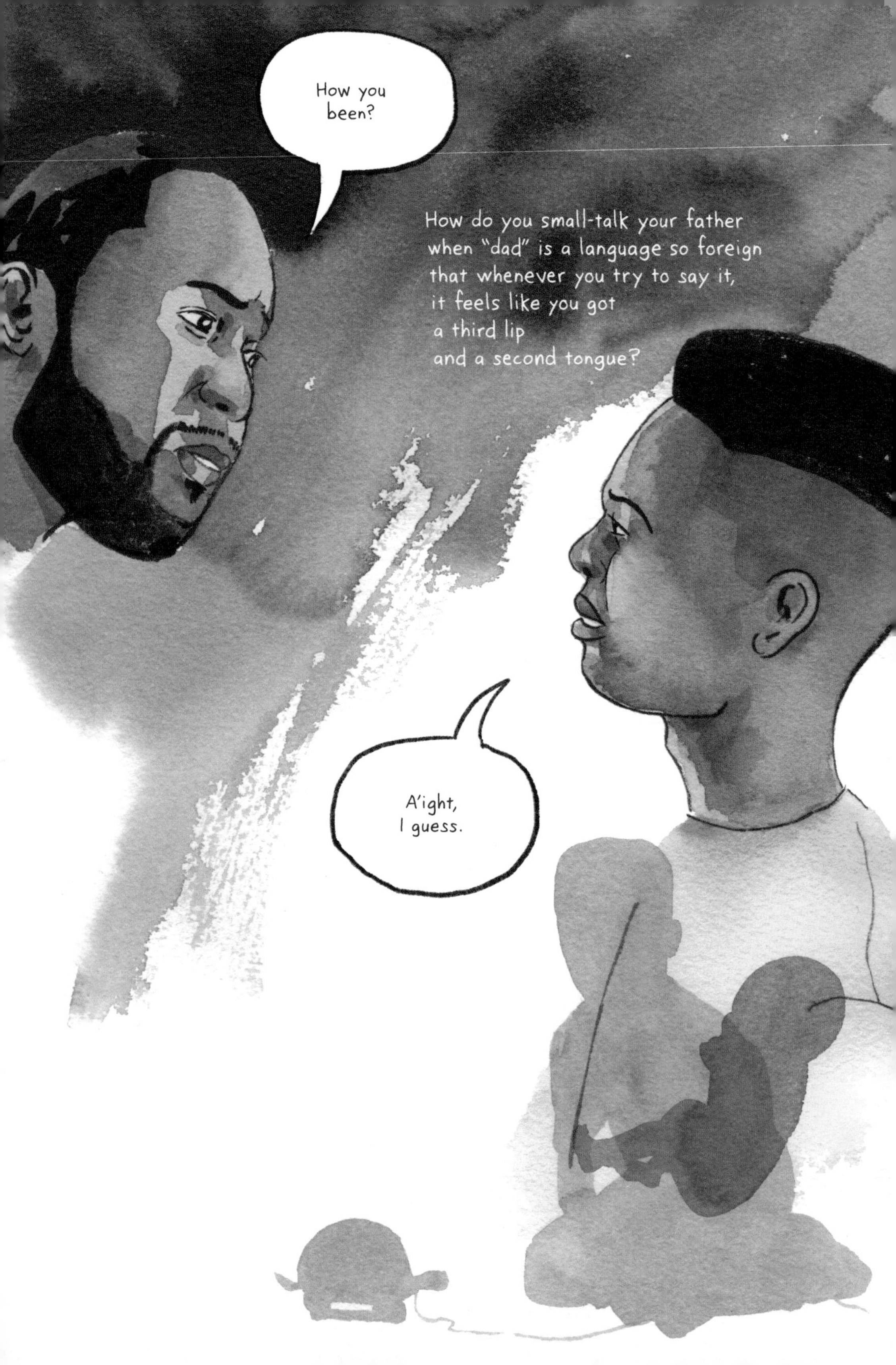
How you been?
How do you small-talk your father
when "dad" is a language so foreign
that whenever you try to say it,
it feels like you got
a third lip
and a second tongue?
A'ight, I guess.

I wanted to unload,
just tell him about Shawn,
and how Mom cried and drank
and scratched herself to sleep,
how I was feeling,
The Rules,

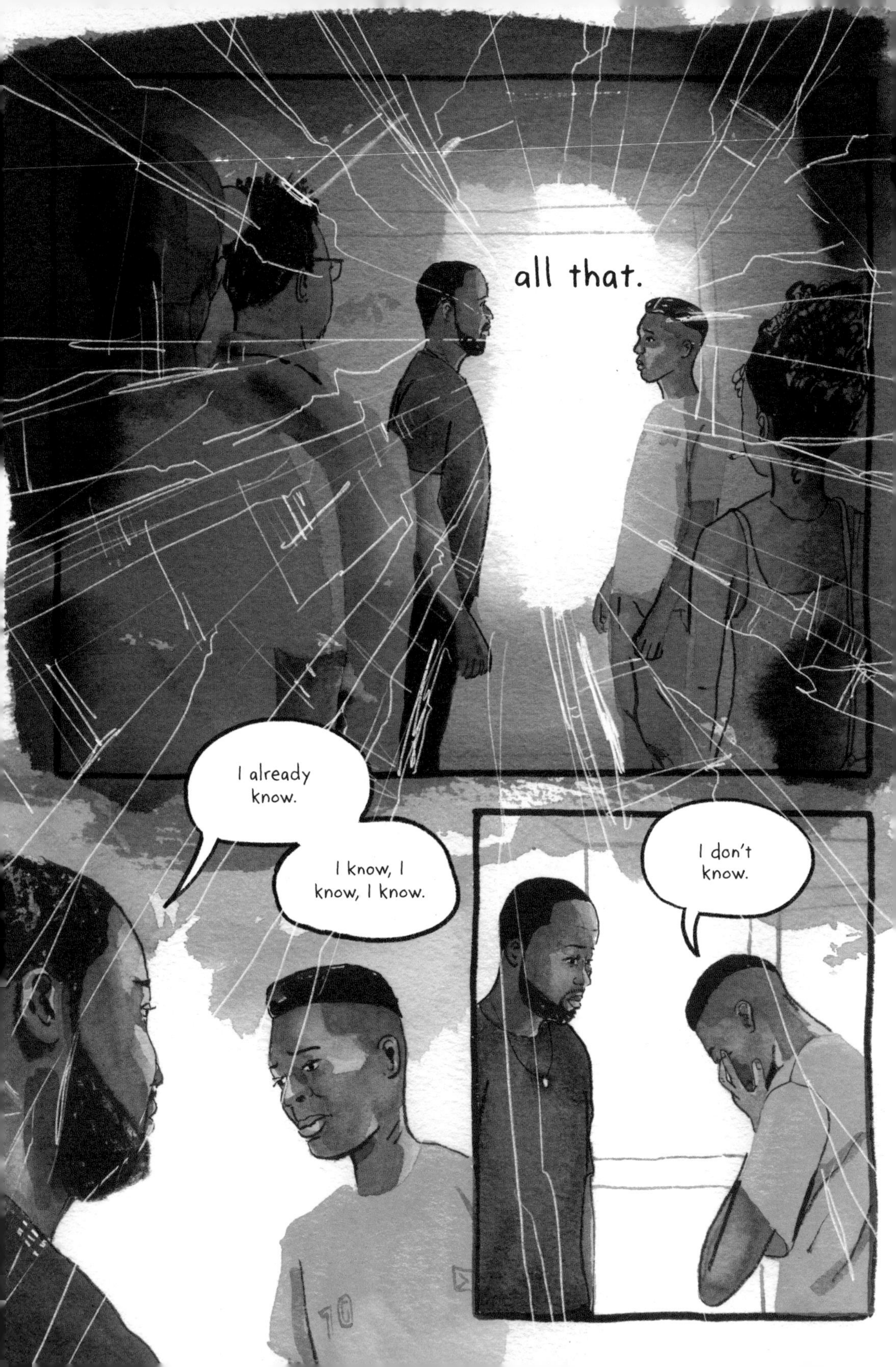
all that.
I already know.
I know, I know, I know.
I don't know.

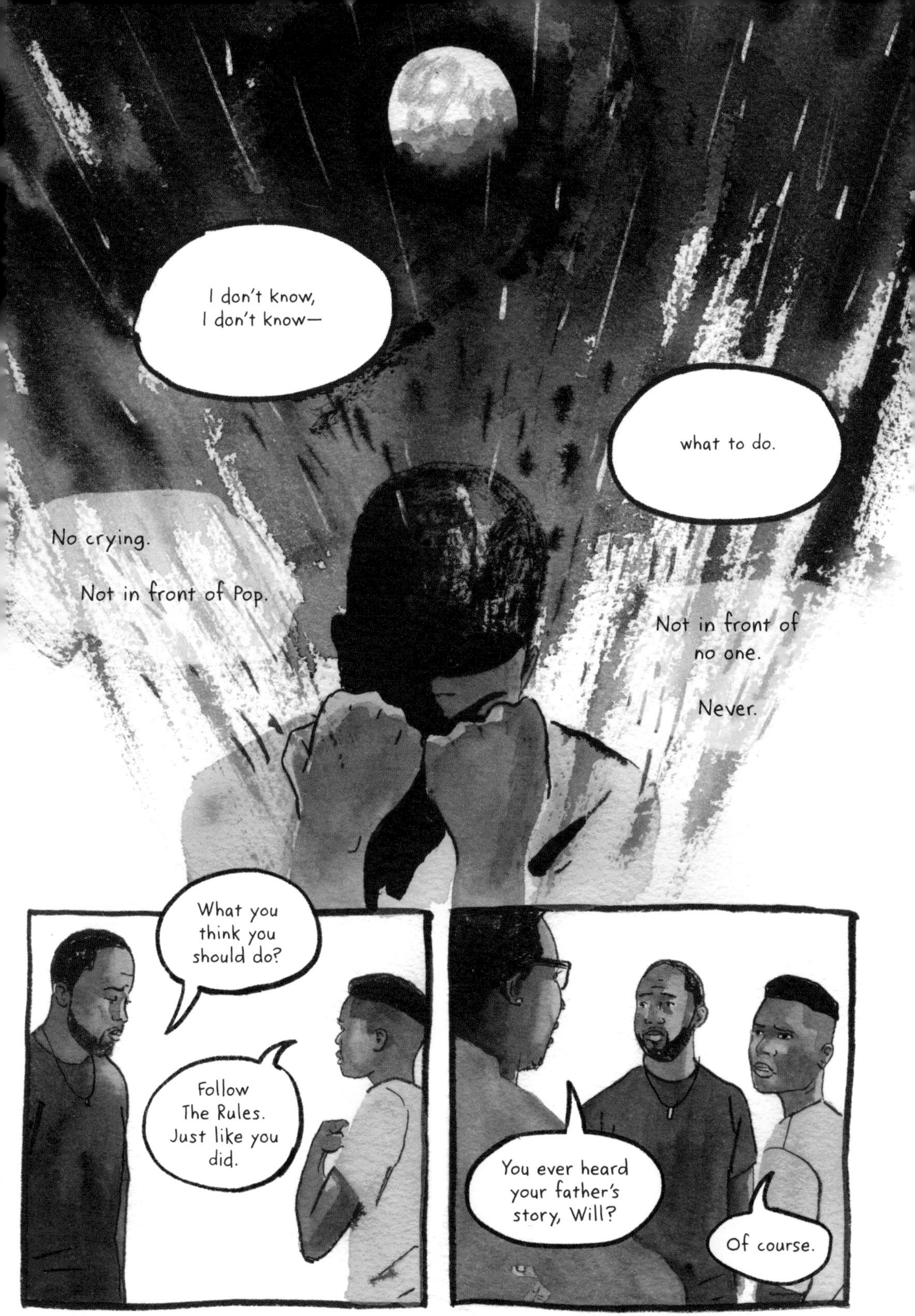
I don't know,
I don't know—
what to do.
No crying.
Not in front of Pop.
Not in front of no one.
Never.
What you think you should do?
Follow The Rules. Just like you did.
You ever heard your father's story, Will?
Of course.

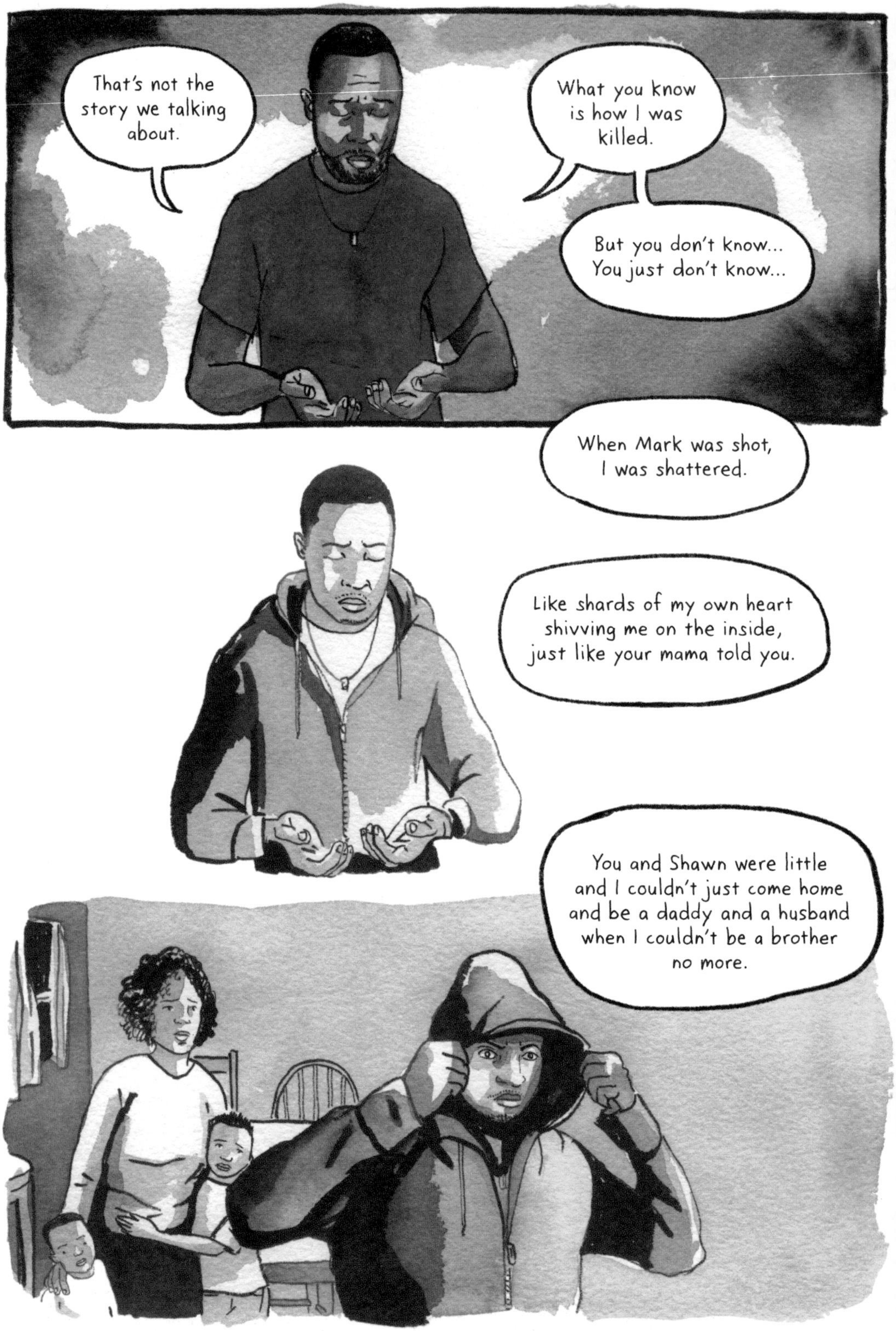
That's not the story we talking about.
What you know is how I was killed.
But you don't know... You just don't know...
When Mark was shot, I was shattered.
Like shards of my own heart shivving me on the inside, just like your mama told you.
You and Shawn were little and I couldn't just come home and be a daddy and a husband when I couldn't be a brother no more.

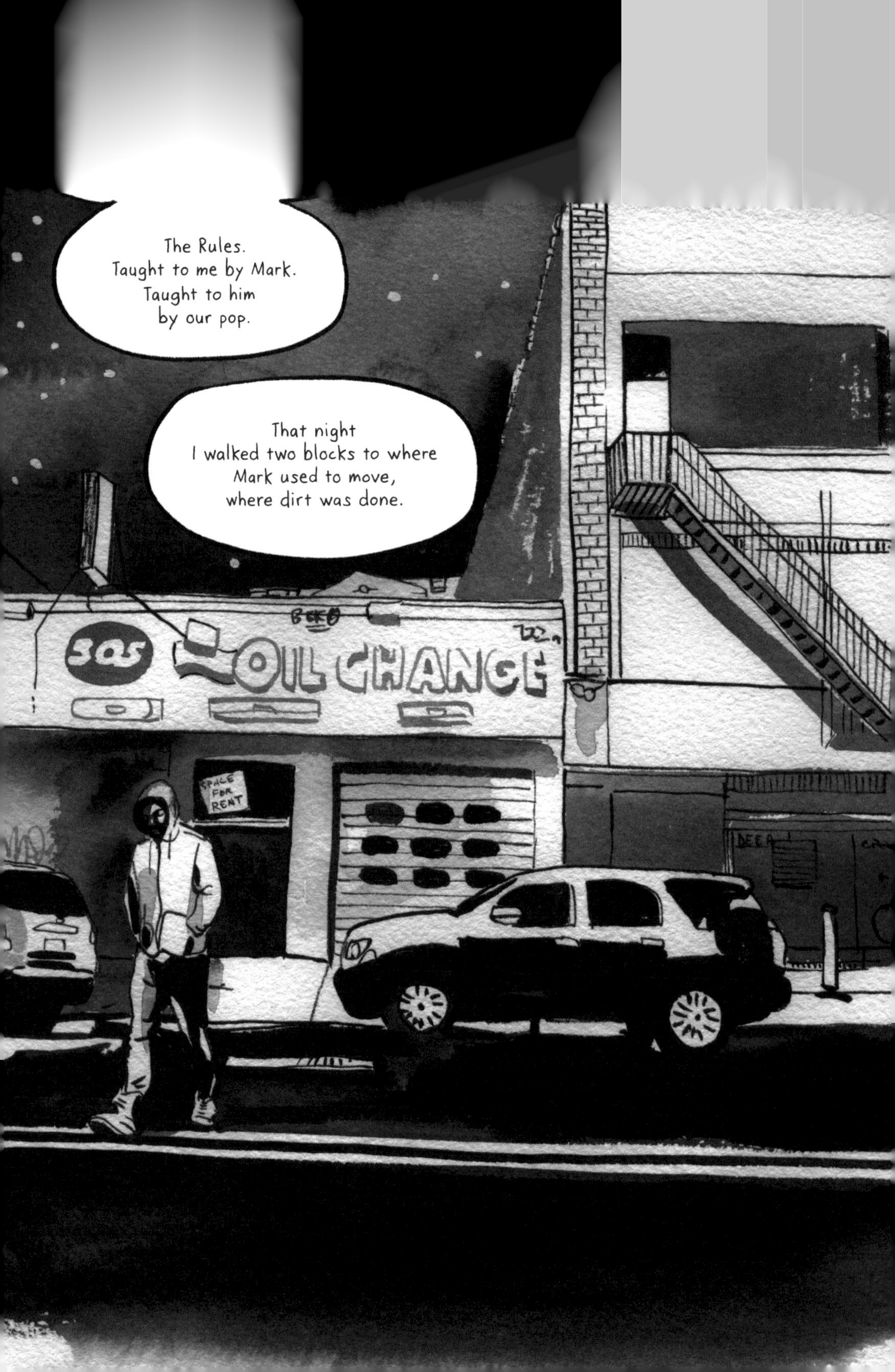
The Rules.
Taught to me by Mark.
Taught to him
by our pop.
That night
I walked two blocks to where
Mark used to move,
where dirt was done.
SOS
OIL CHANGE
SPACE FOR RENT

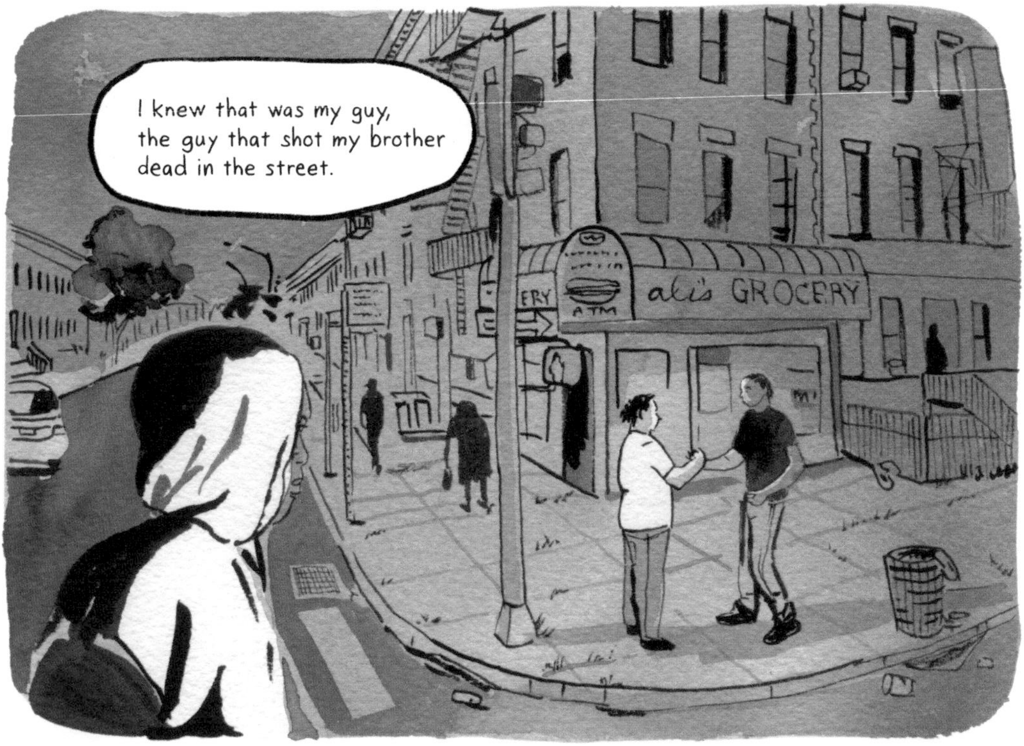
I knew that was my guy, the guy that shot my brother dead in the street.
ali's GROCERY
ATM

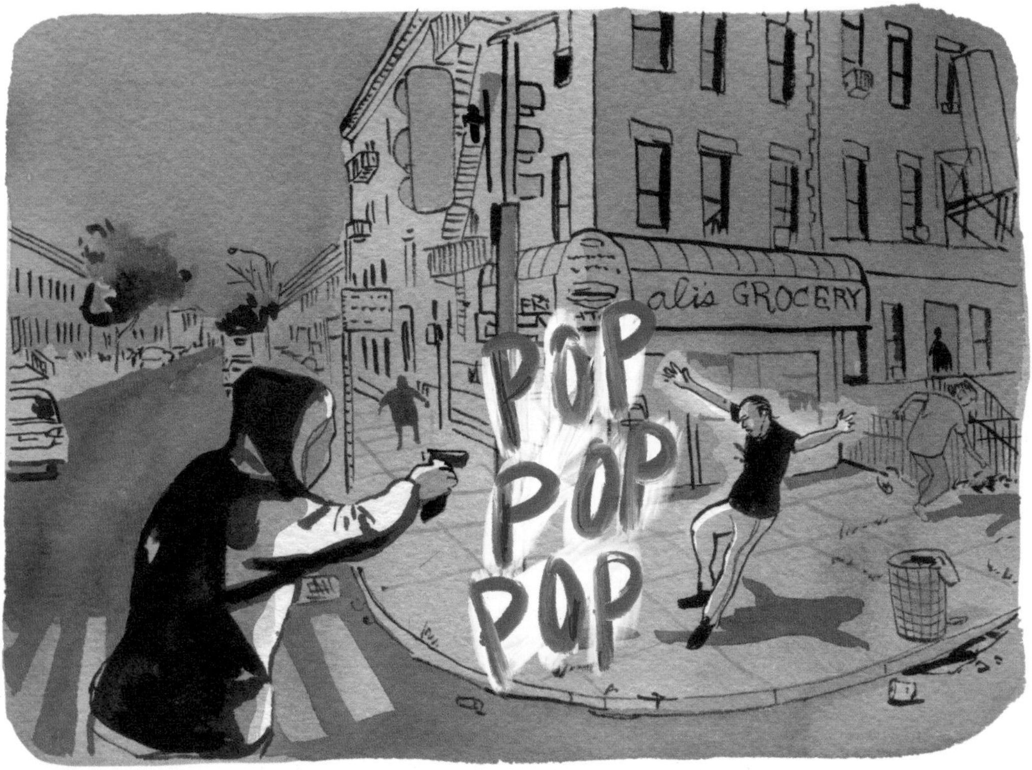
ali's GROCERY
POP
POP
POP

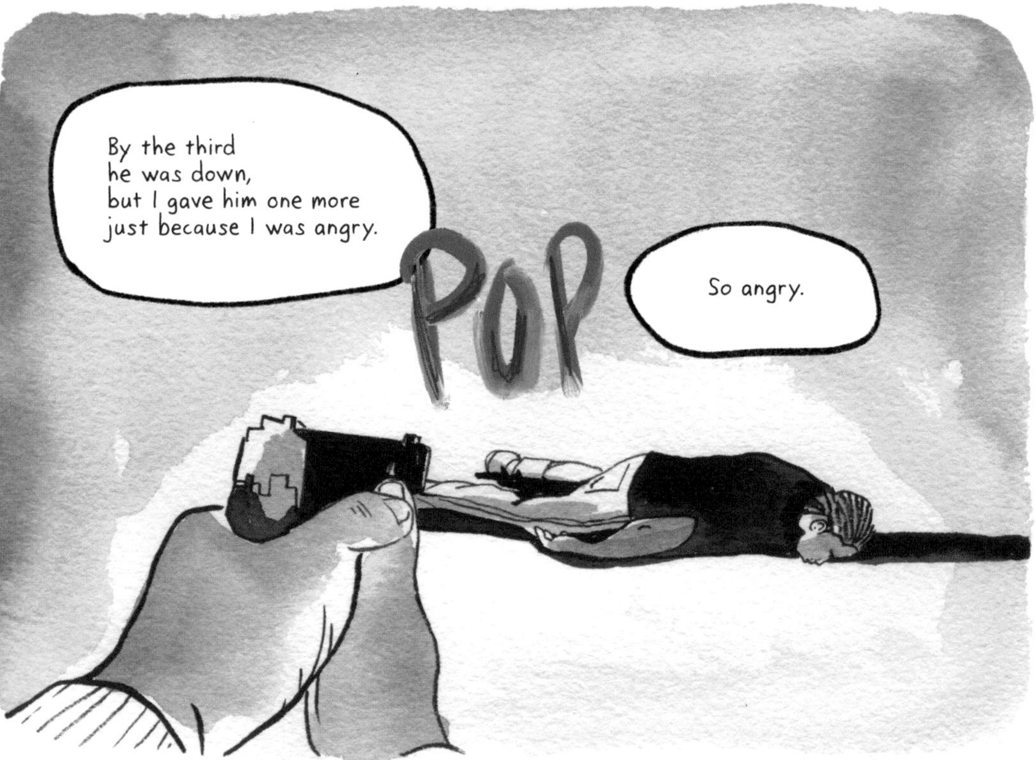
By the third he was down, but I gave him one more just because I was angry.
POP
So angry.

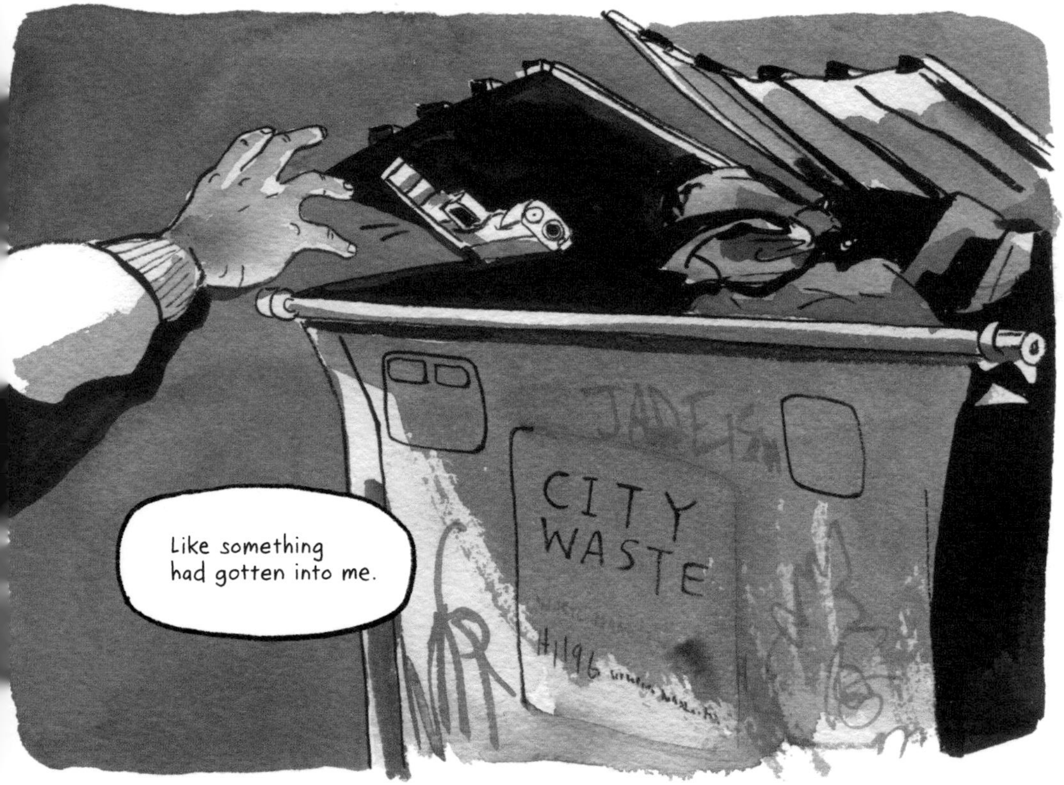
CITY WASTE
Like something had gotten into me.

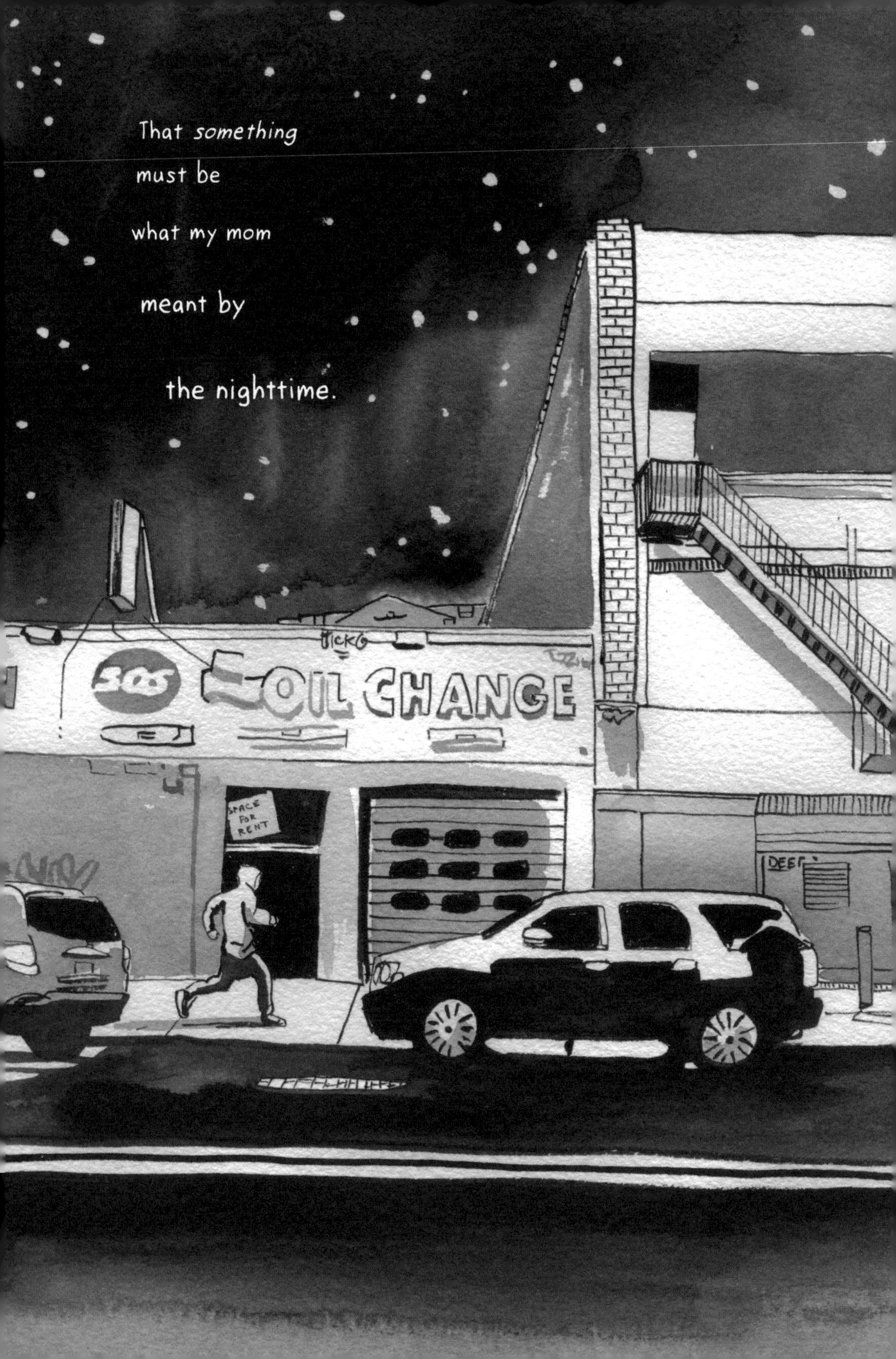
That *something* must be what my mom meant by the nighttime.
OIL CHANGE
SPACE FOR RENT

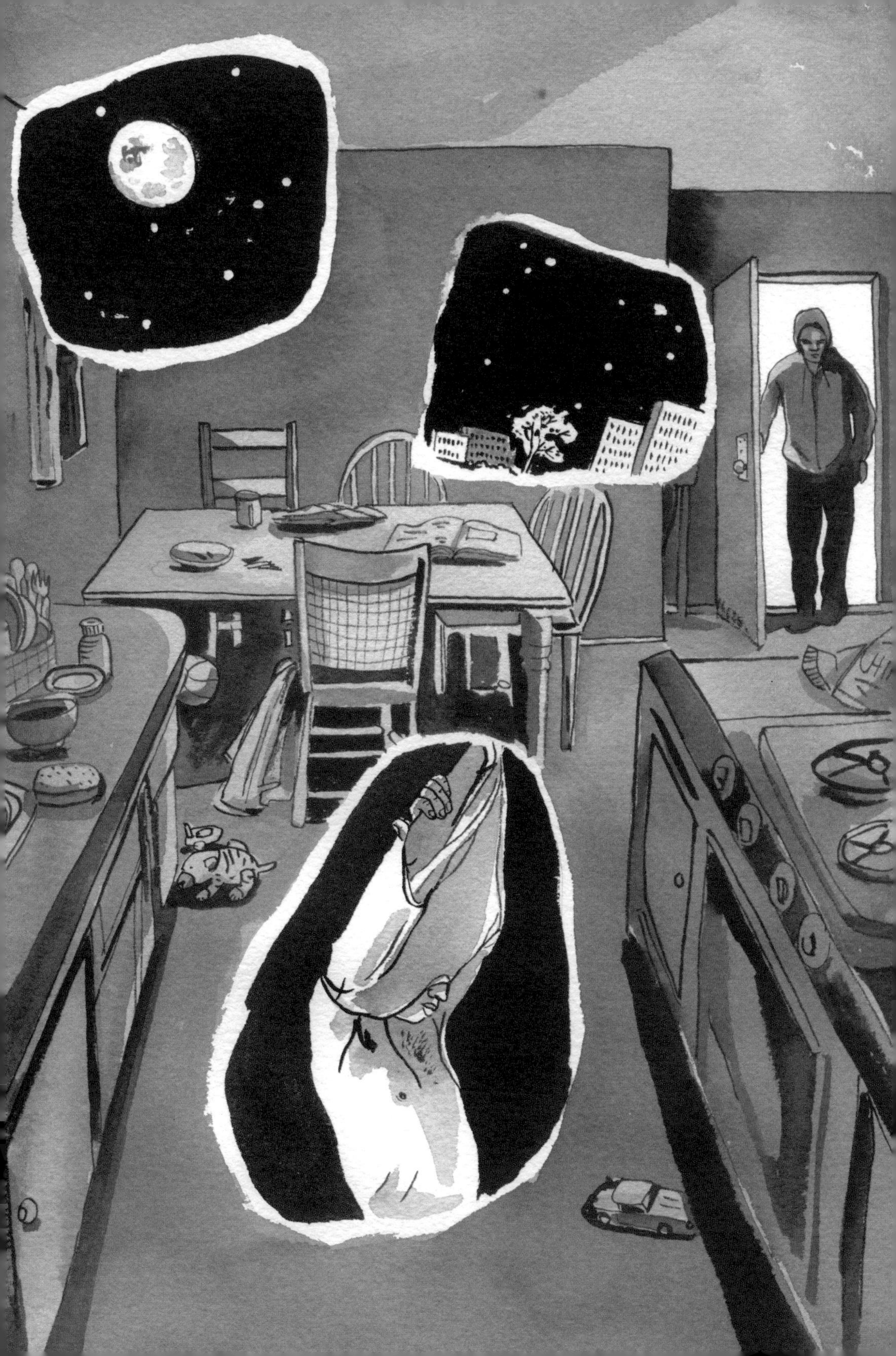

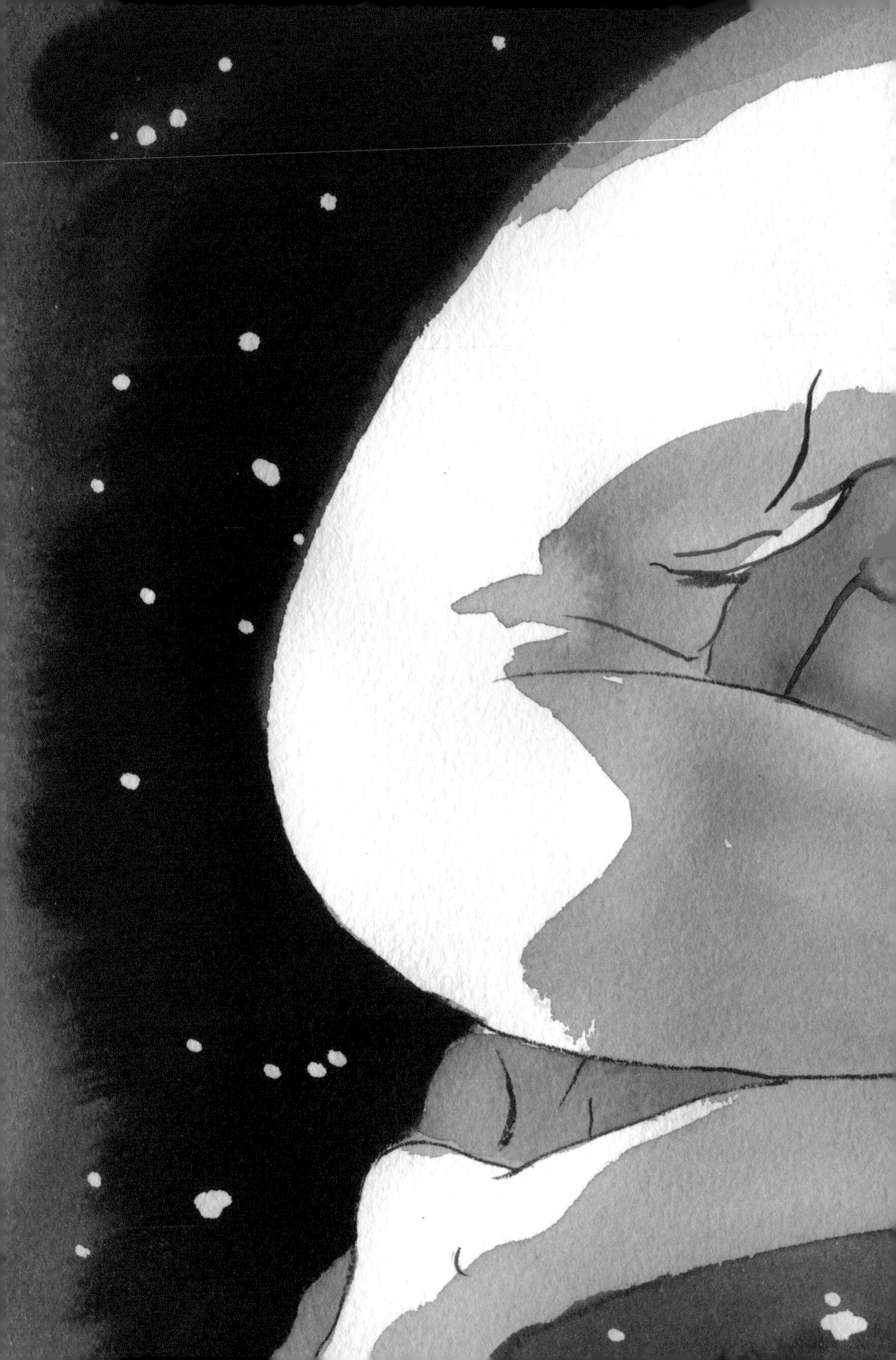

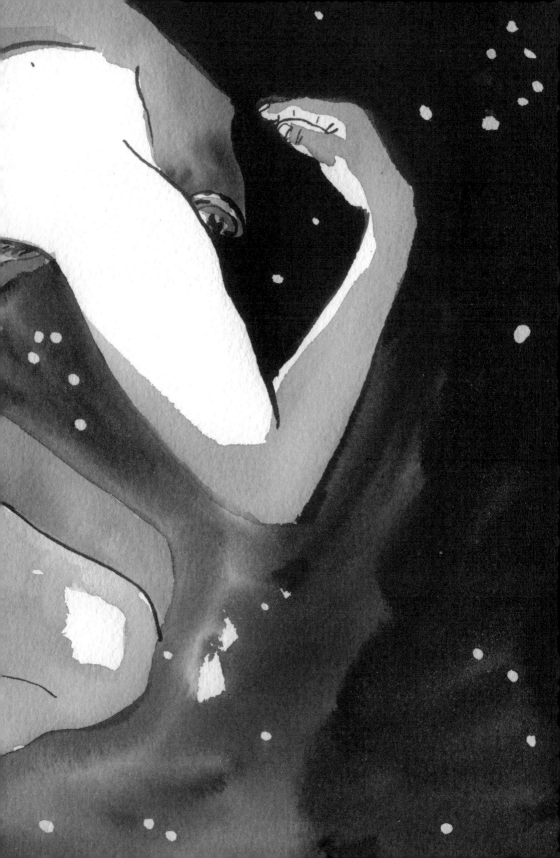

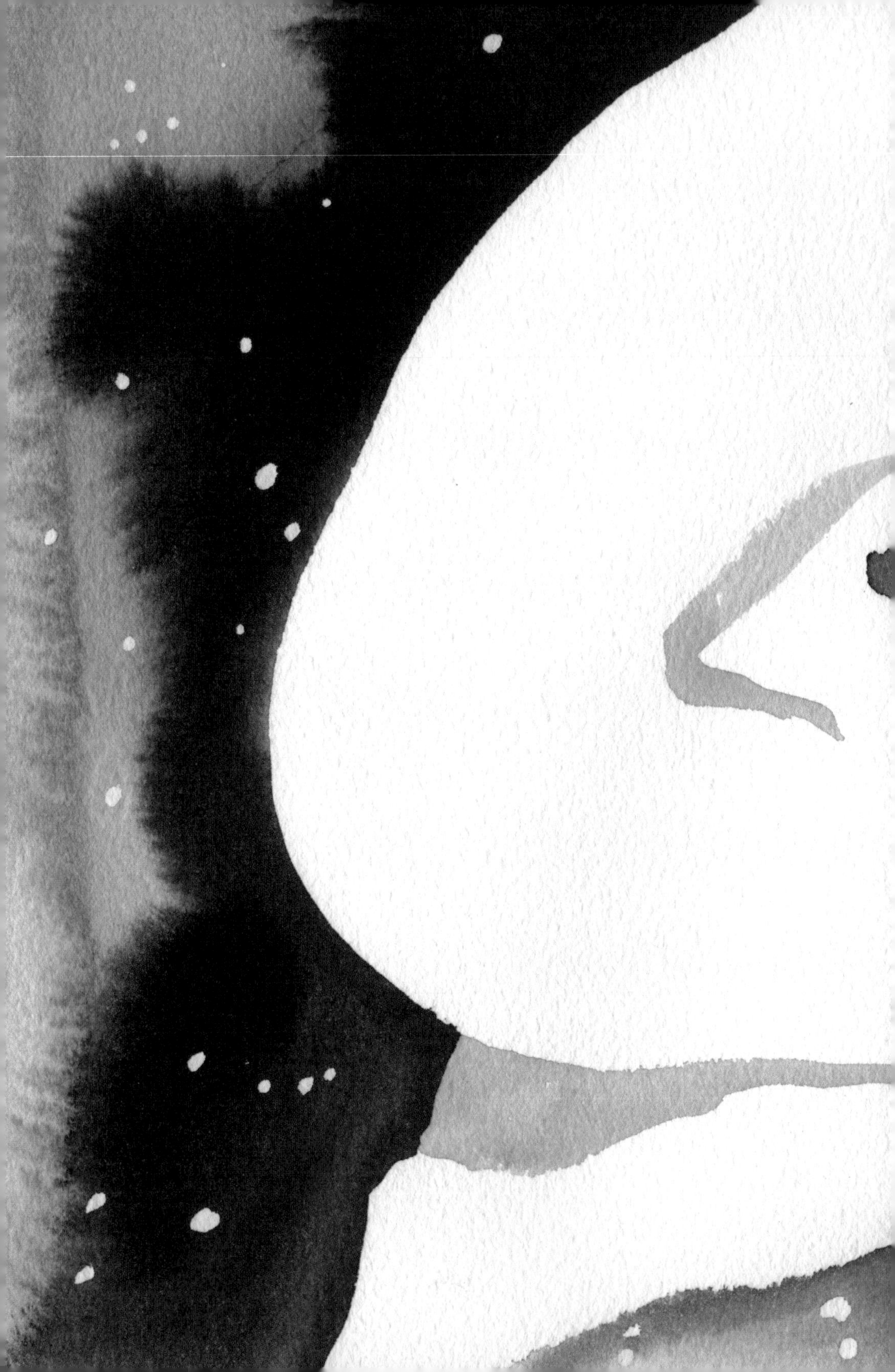

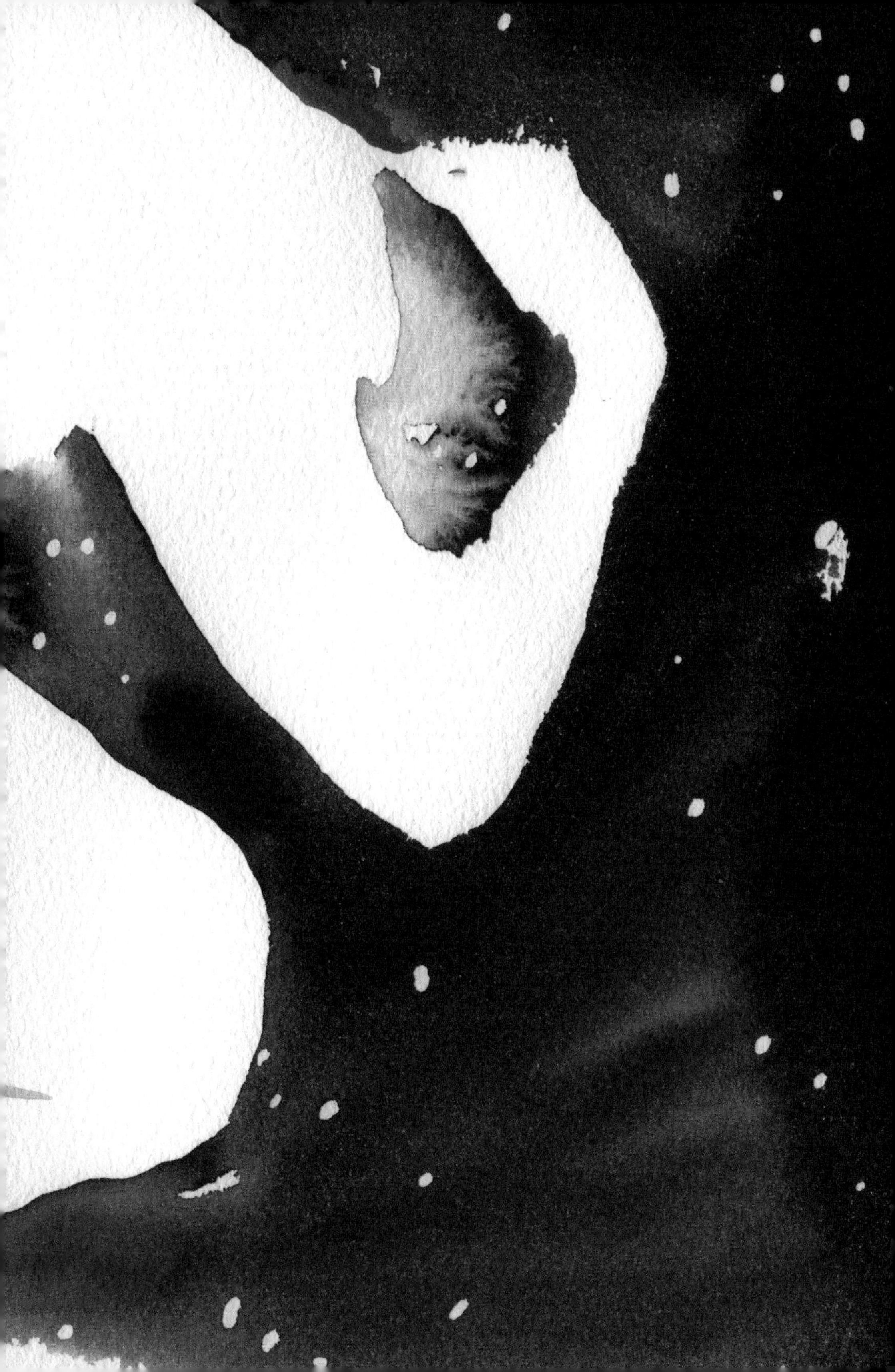

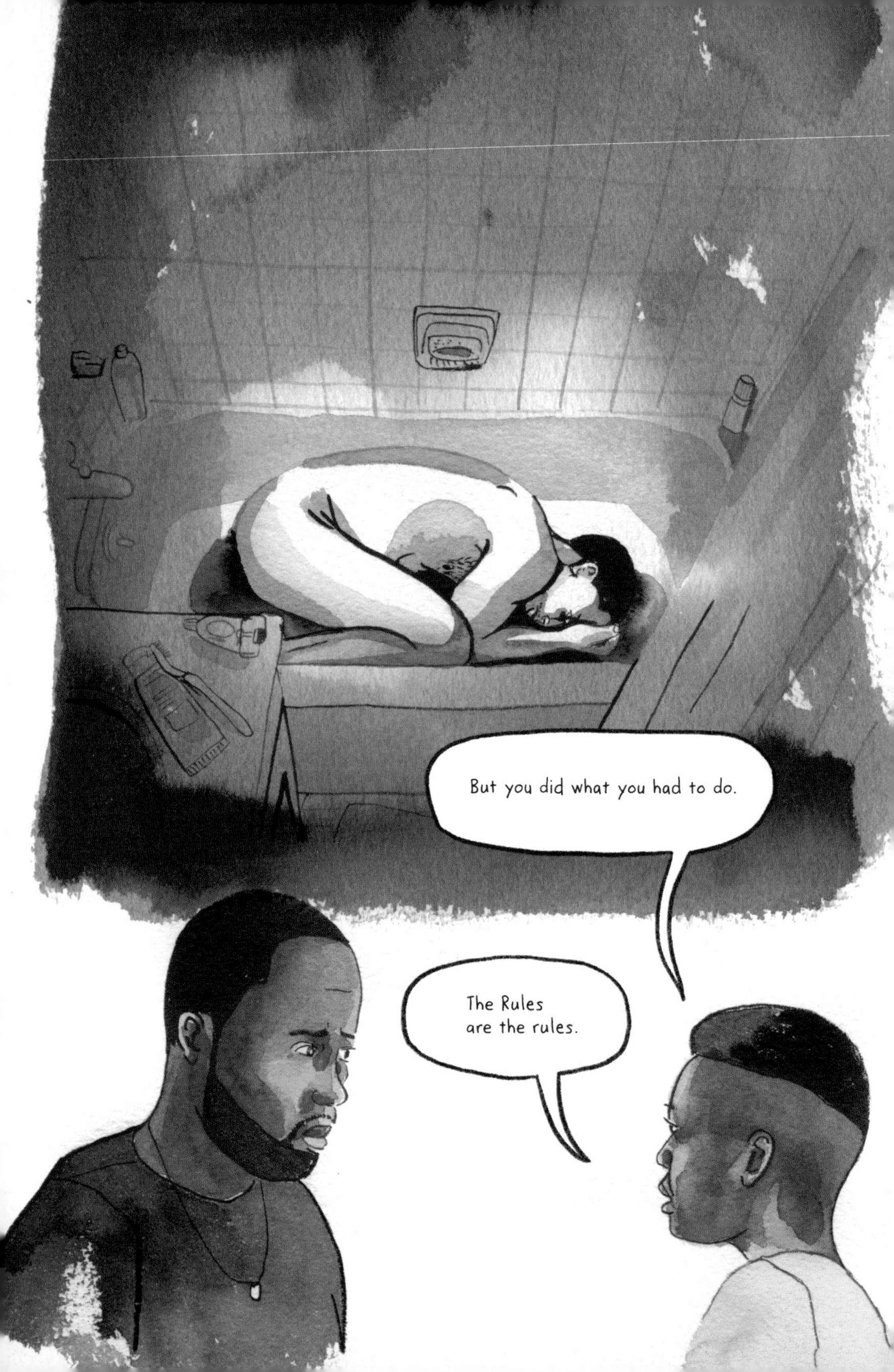
But you did what you had to do.
The Rules are the rules.

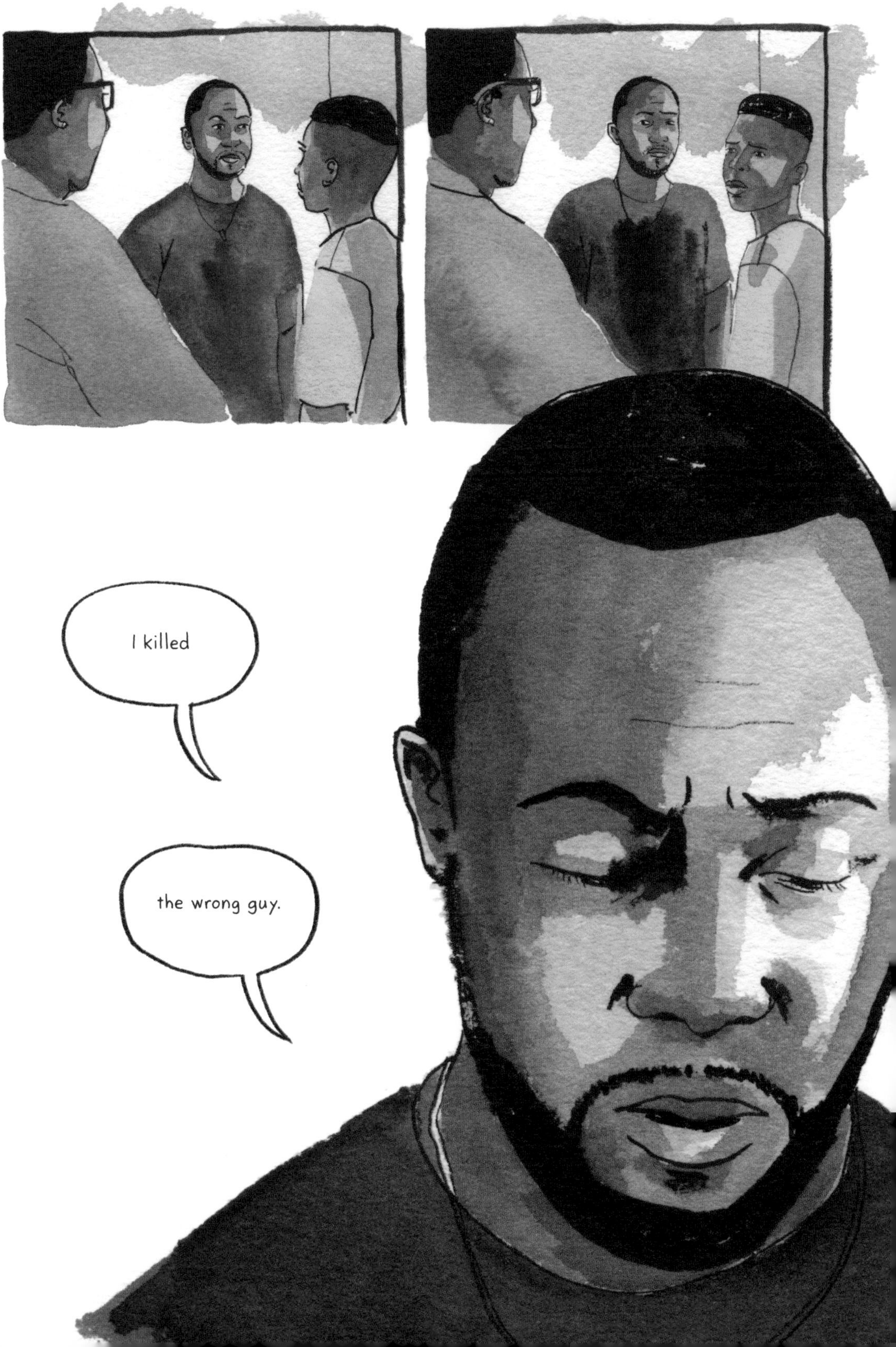
I killed
the wrong guy.

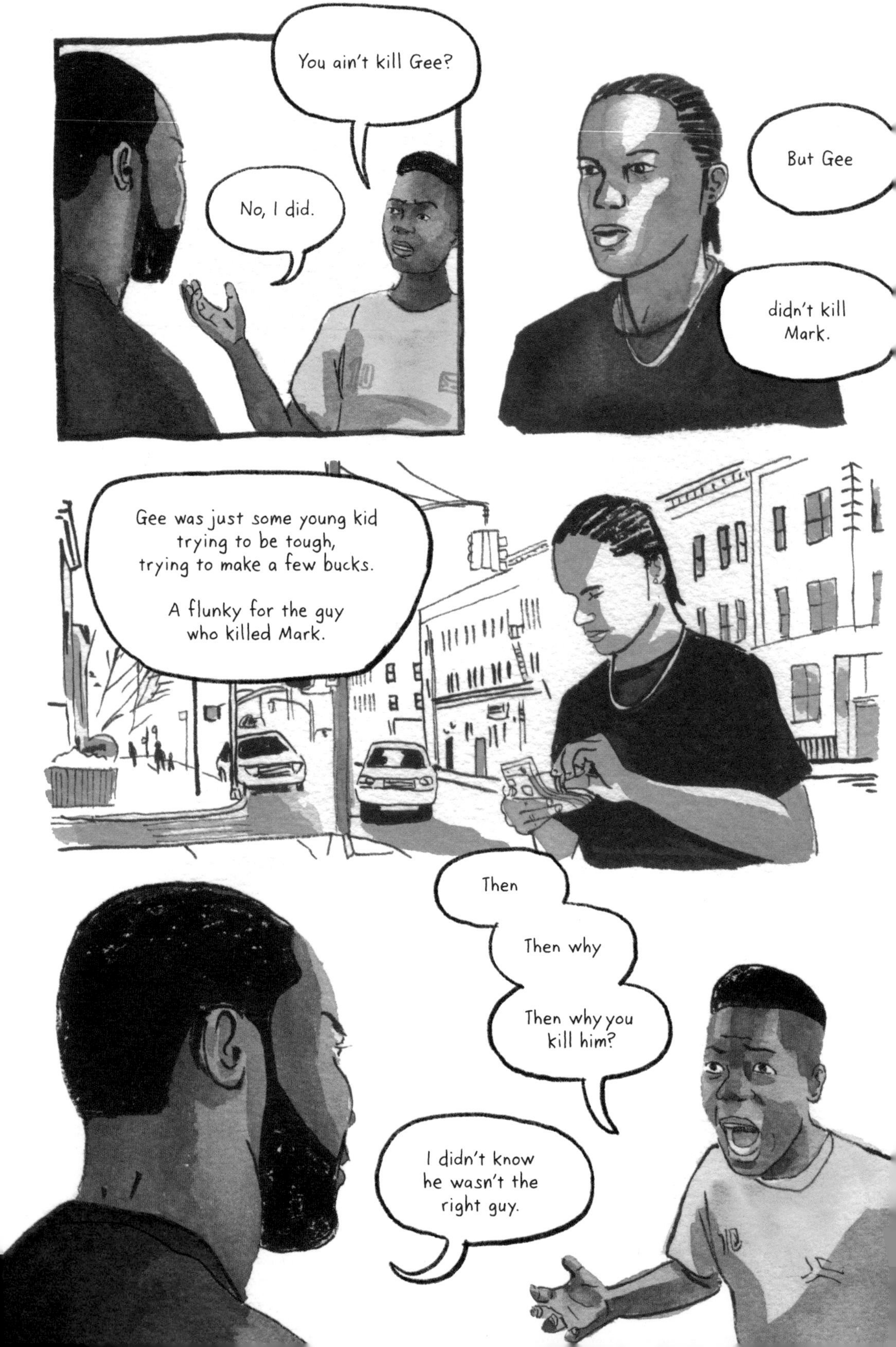
You ain't kill Gee?
No, I did.
But Gee
didn't kill Mark.
Gee was just some young kid trying to be tough, trying to make a few bucks.
A flunky for the guy who killed Mark.
Then
Then why
Then why you kill him?
I didn't know he wasn't the right guy.

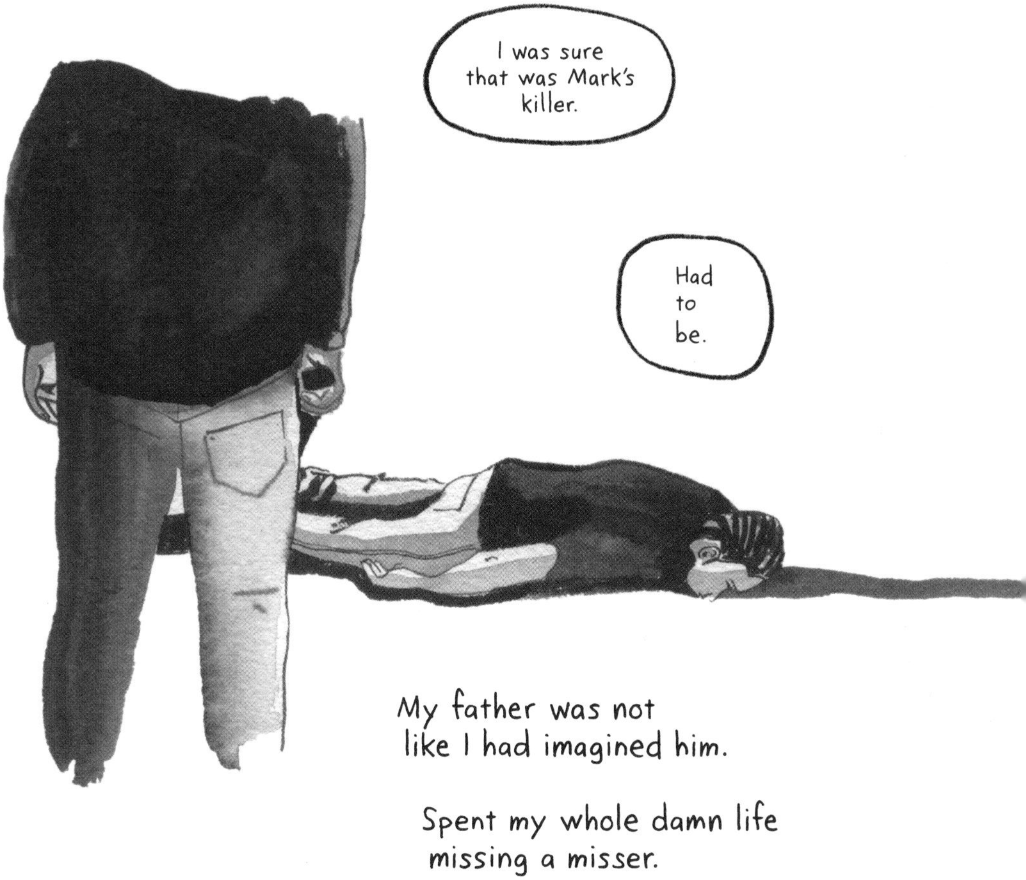
I was sure that was Mark's killer.
Had to be.
My father was not like I had imagined him.
Spent my whole damn life missing a misser.

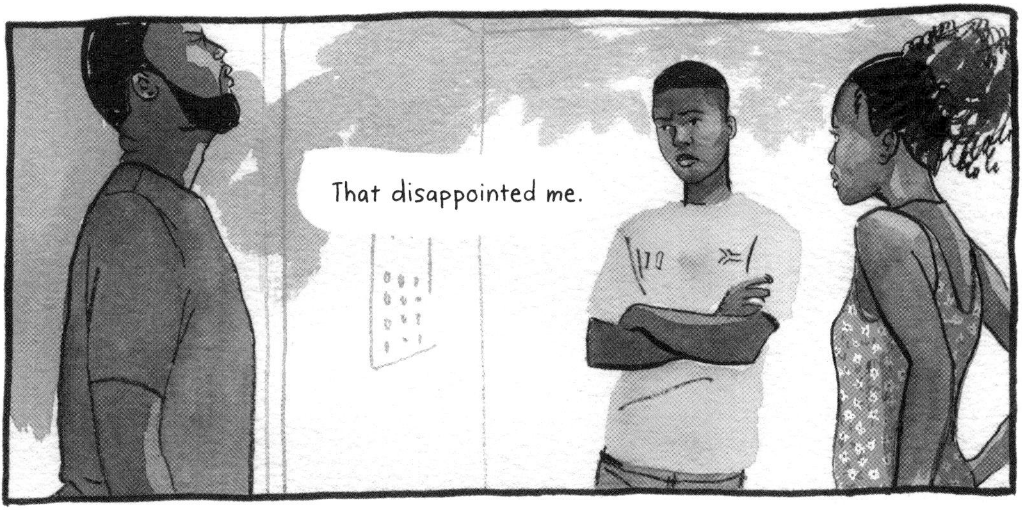
That disappointed me.

Wasn't sure what
he was thinking.

Maybe that I was
exactly how *he* had
imagined.

Maybe that
disappointed him.

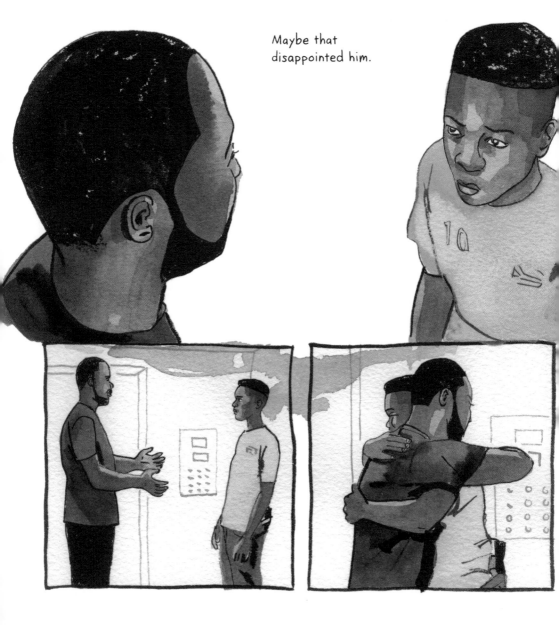

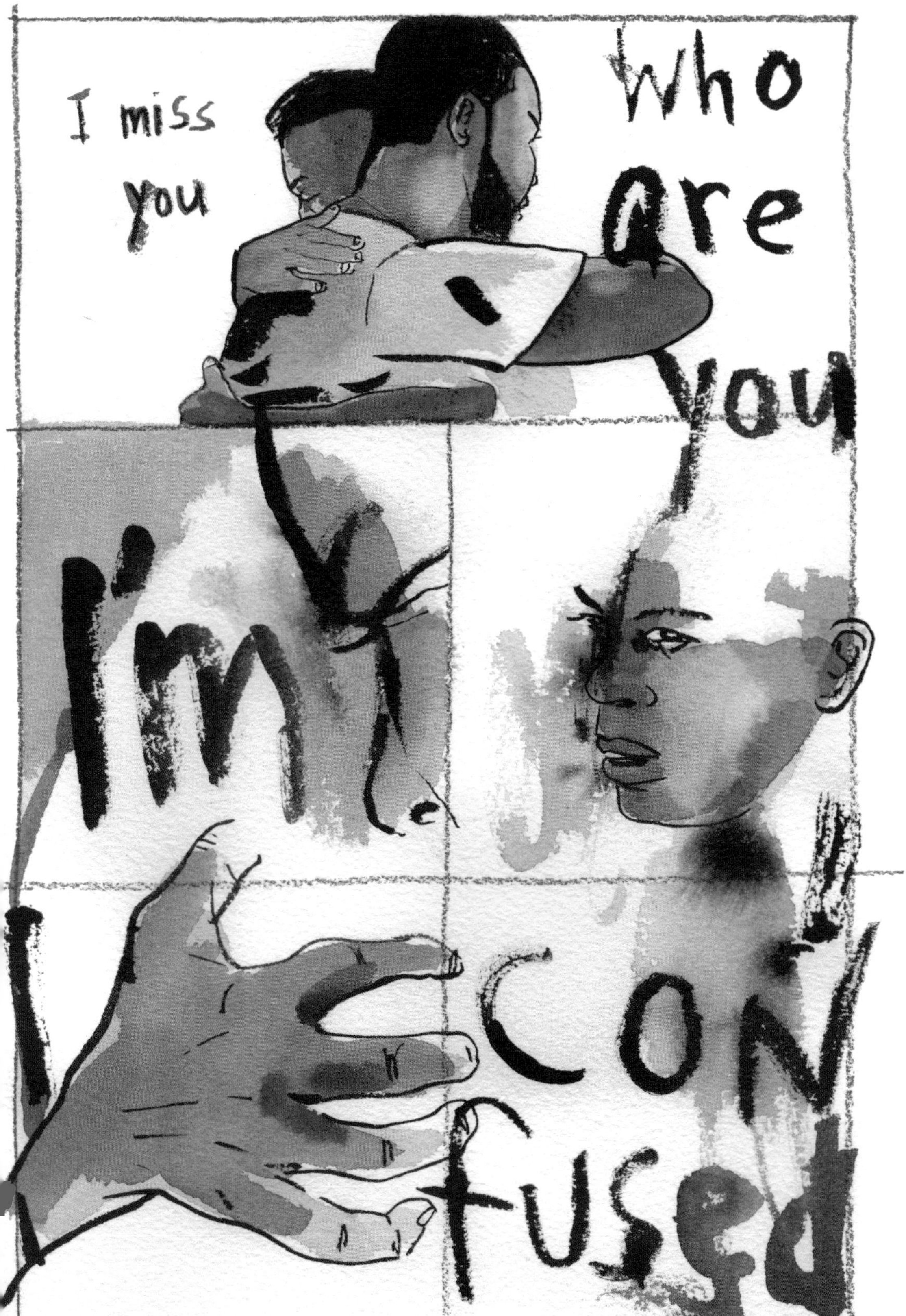
I miss you
Who are you
I'm
I'm con fused

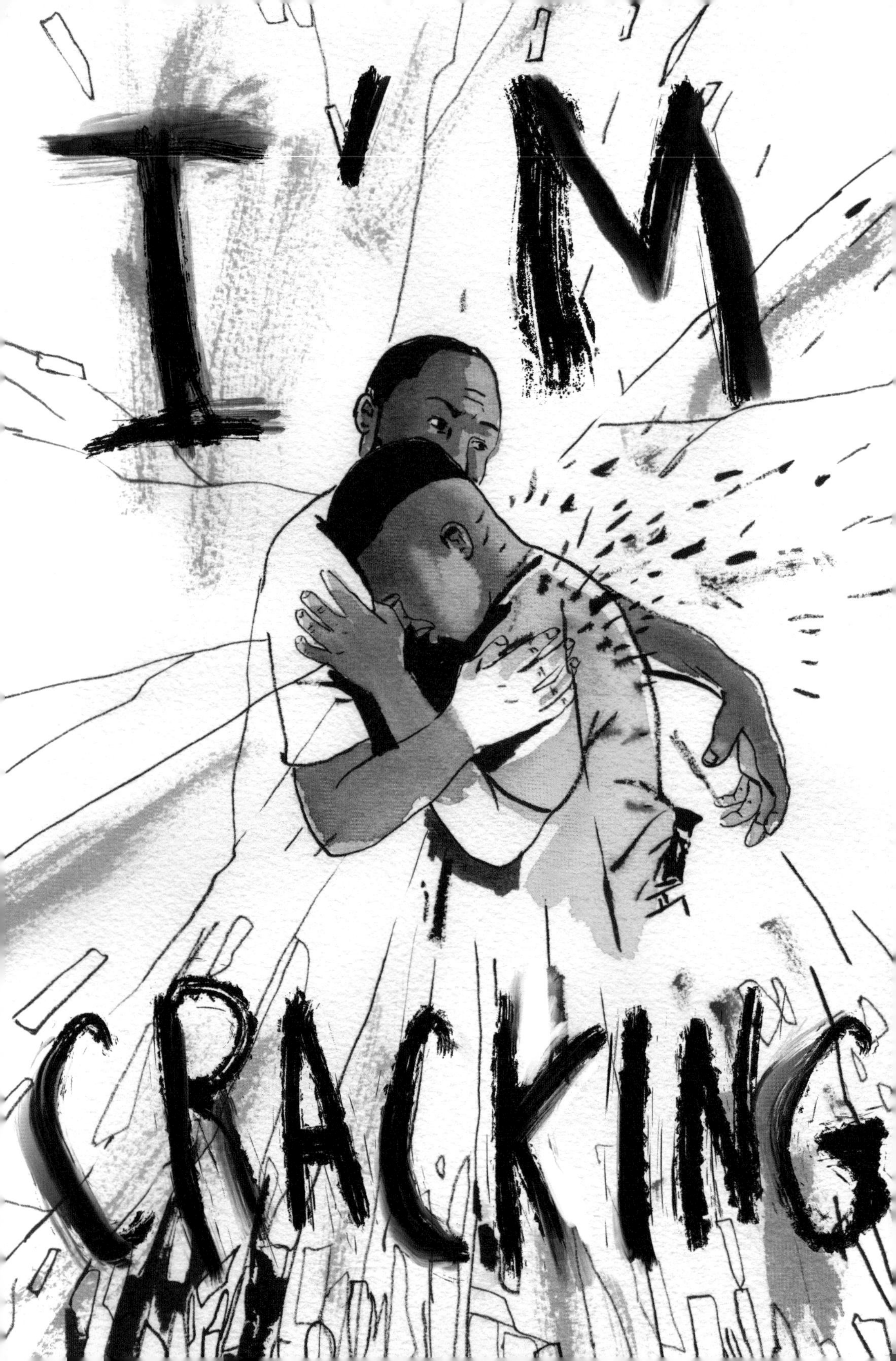
I'M
CRACKING

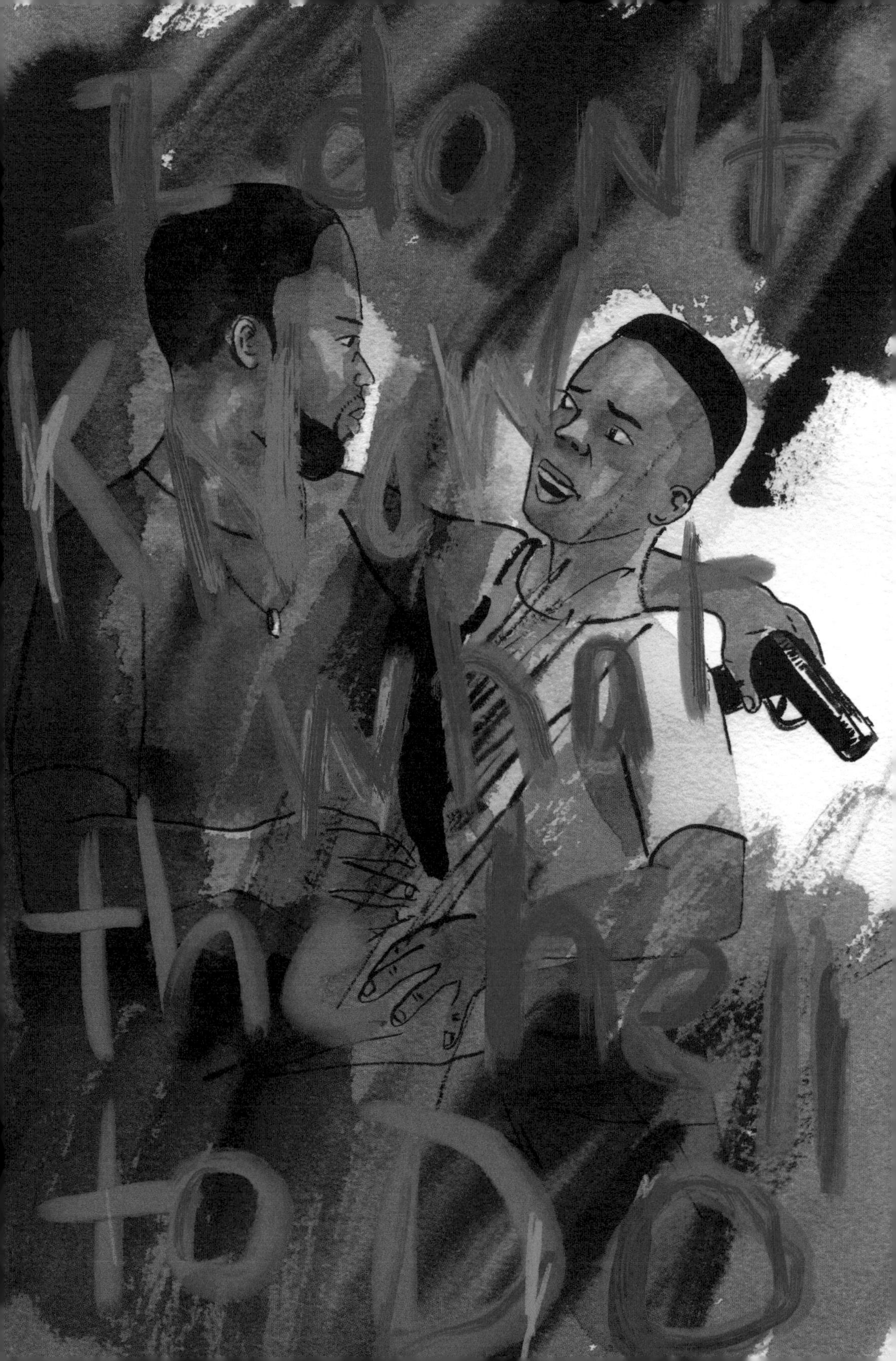
I don't know what the hell to Do

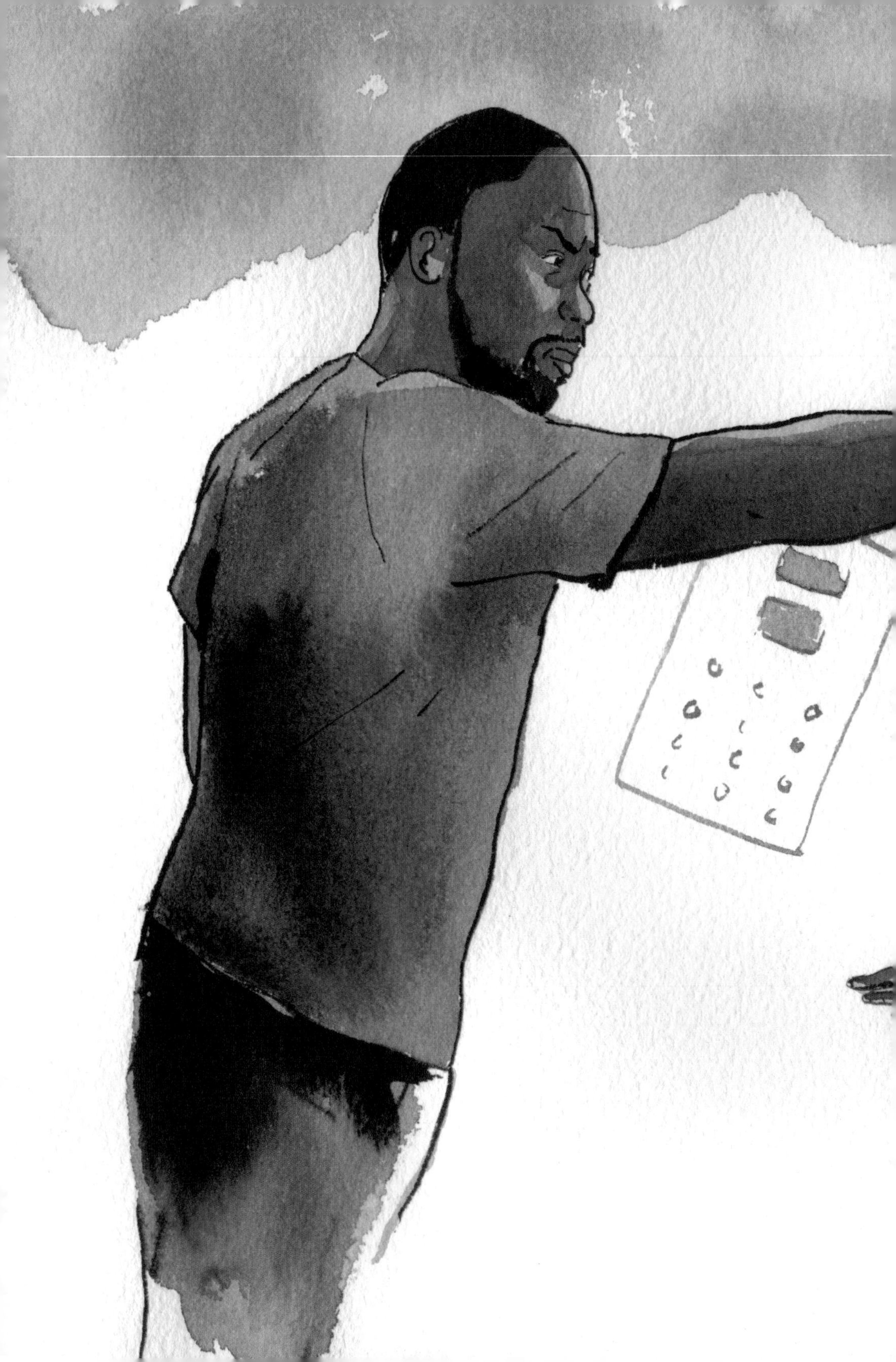

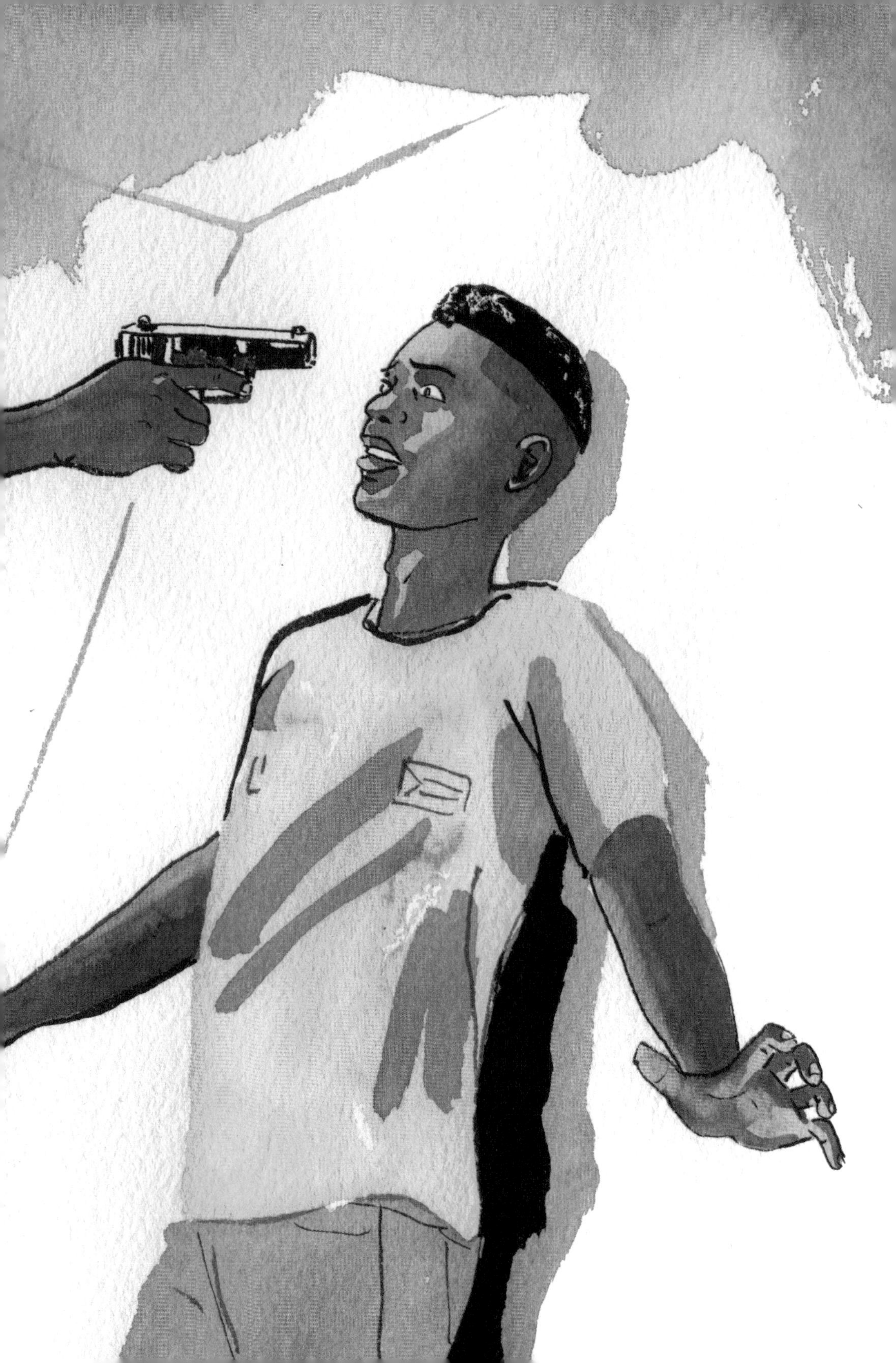

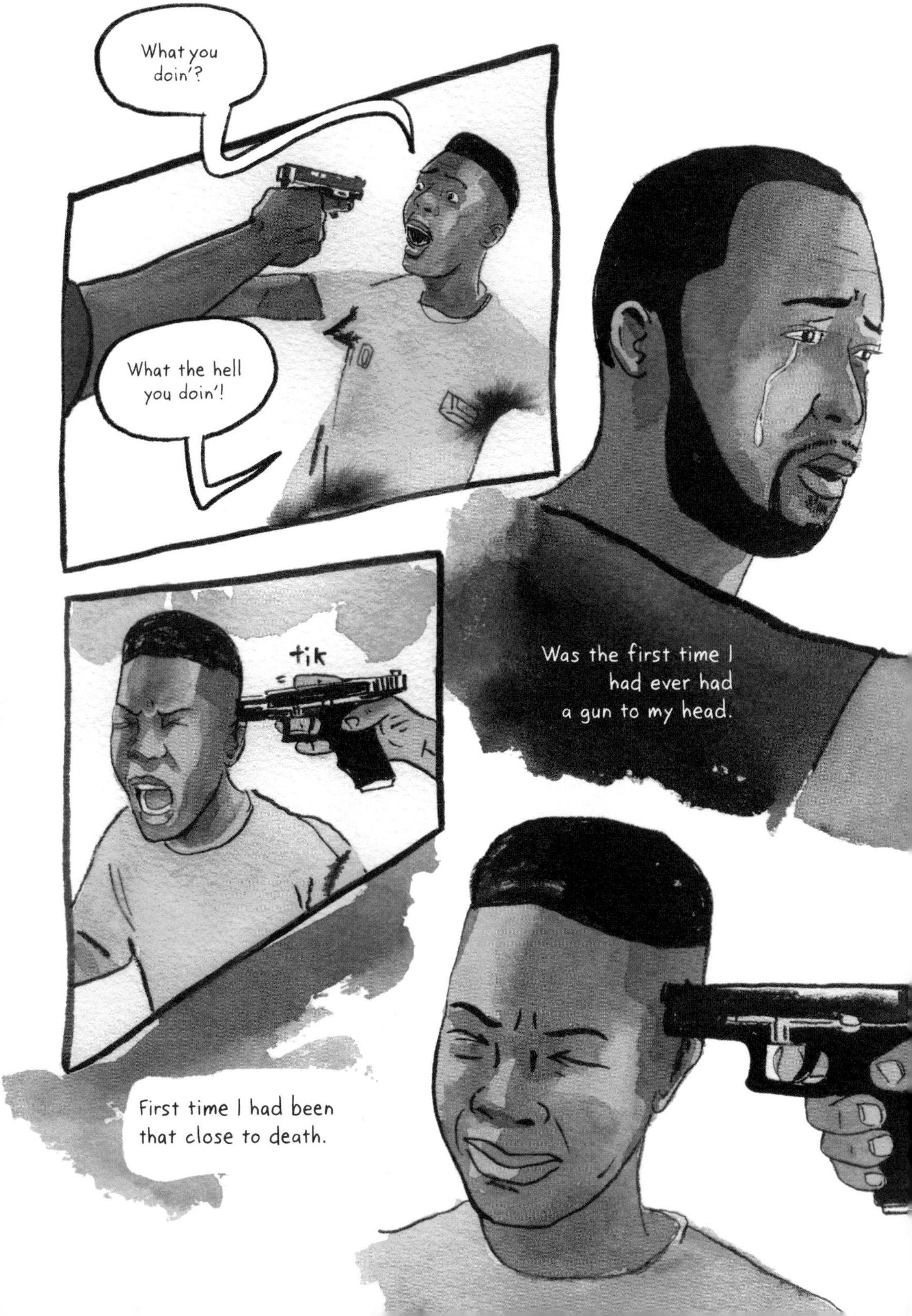
What you doin'?
What the hell you doin'!
tik
Was the first time I had ever had a gun to my head.
First time I had been that close to death.

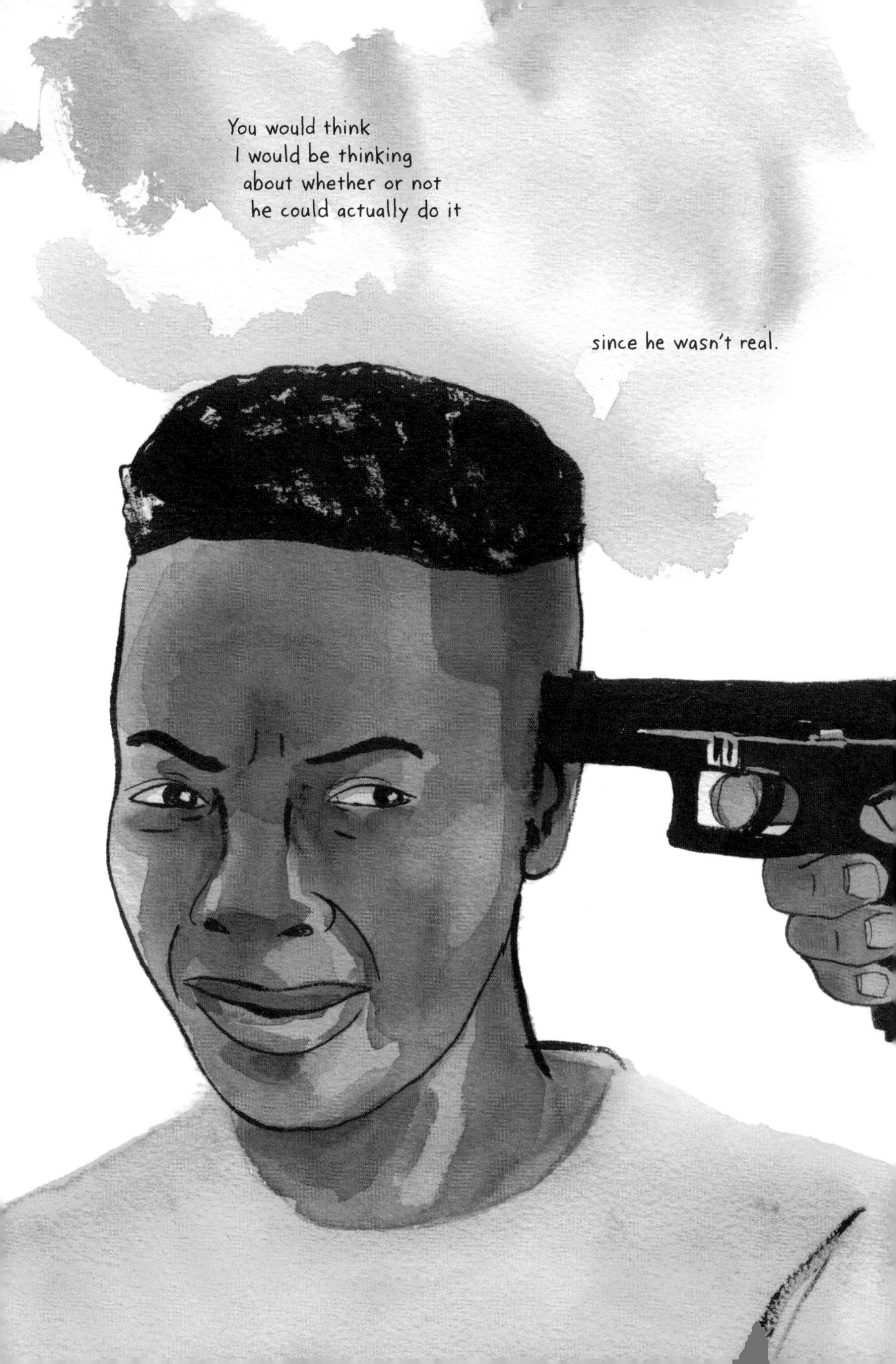
You would think
I would be thinking
about whether or not
he could actually do it
since he wasn't real.

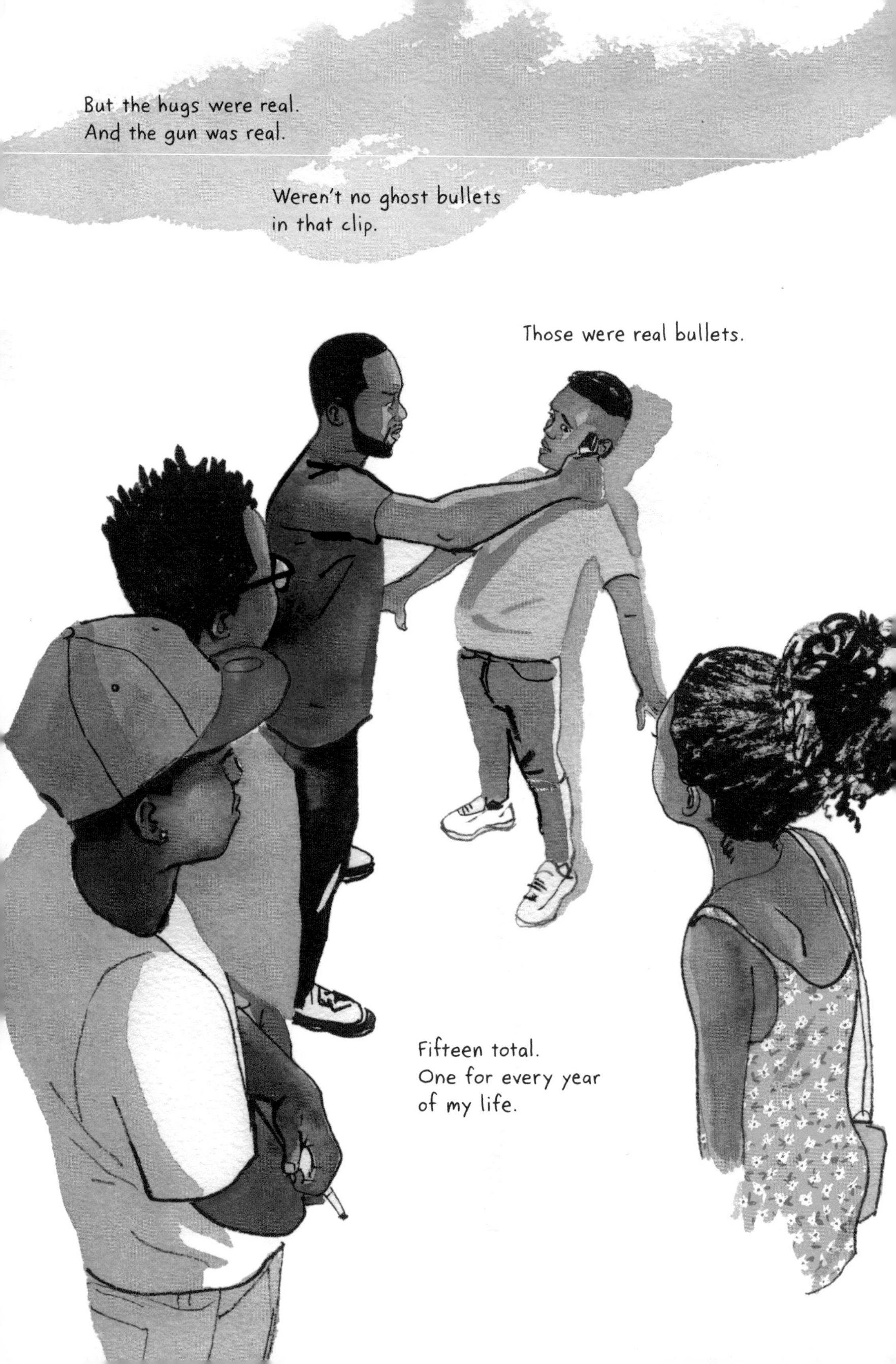
But the hugs were real.
And the gun was real.
Weren't no ghost bullets
in that clip.
Those were real bullets.
Fifteen total.
One for every year
of my life.

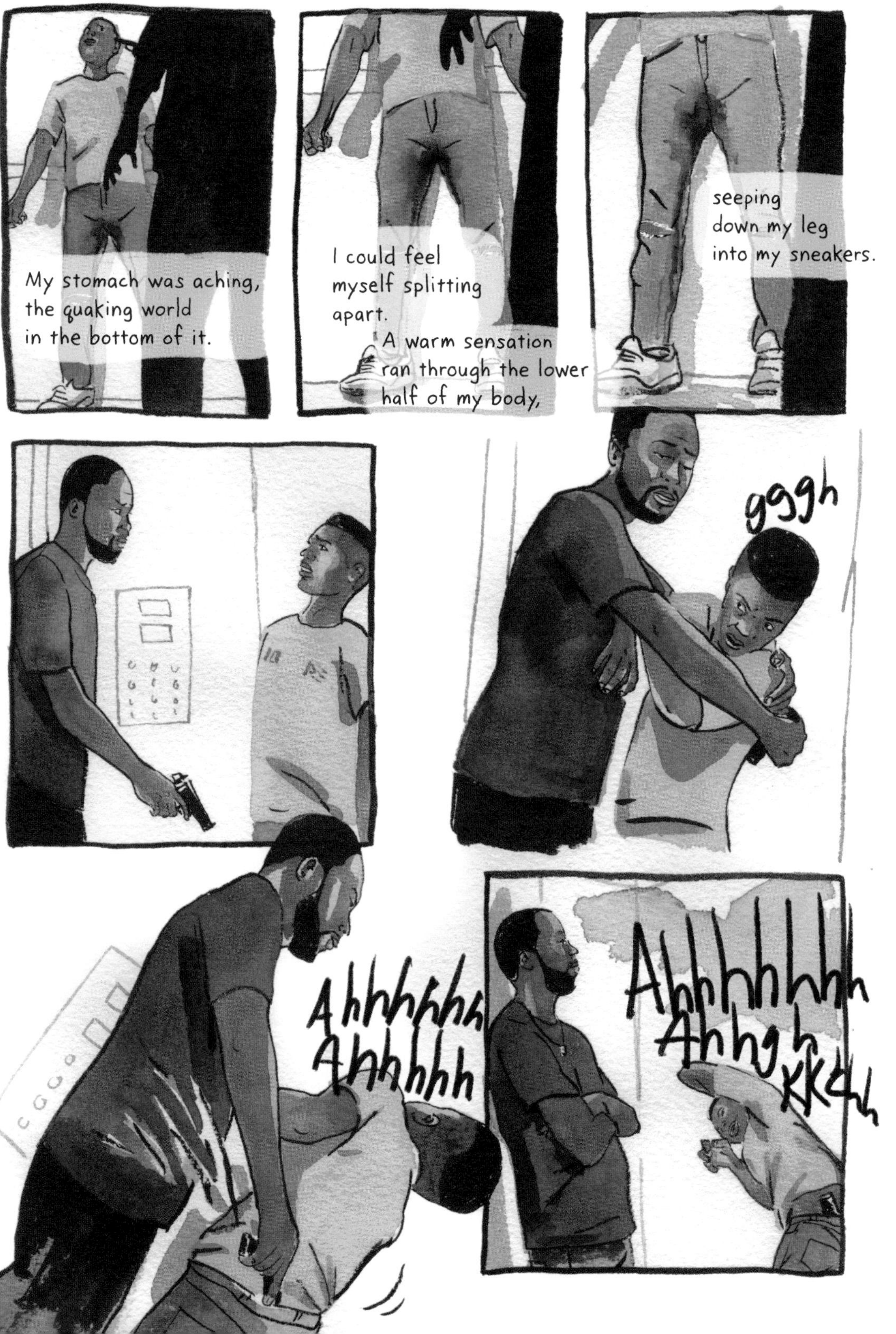
My stomach was aching, the quaking world in the bottom of it.
I could feel myself splitting apart.
A warm sensation ran through the lower half of my body,
seeping down my leg into my sneakers.
gggh
Ahhhhhh
Ahhhhhh
Ahhhhhhh
Ahhgh
KKchh

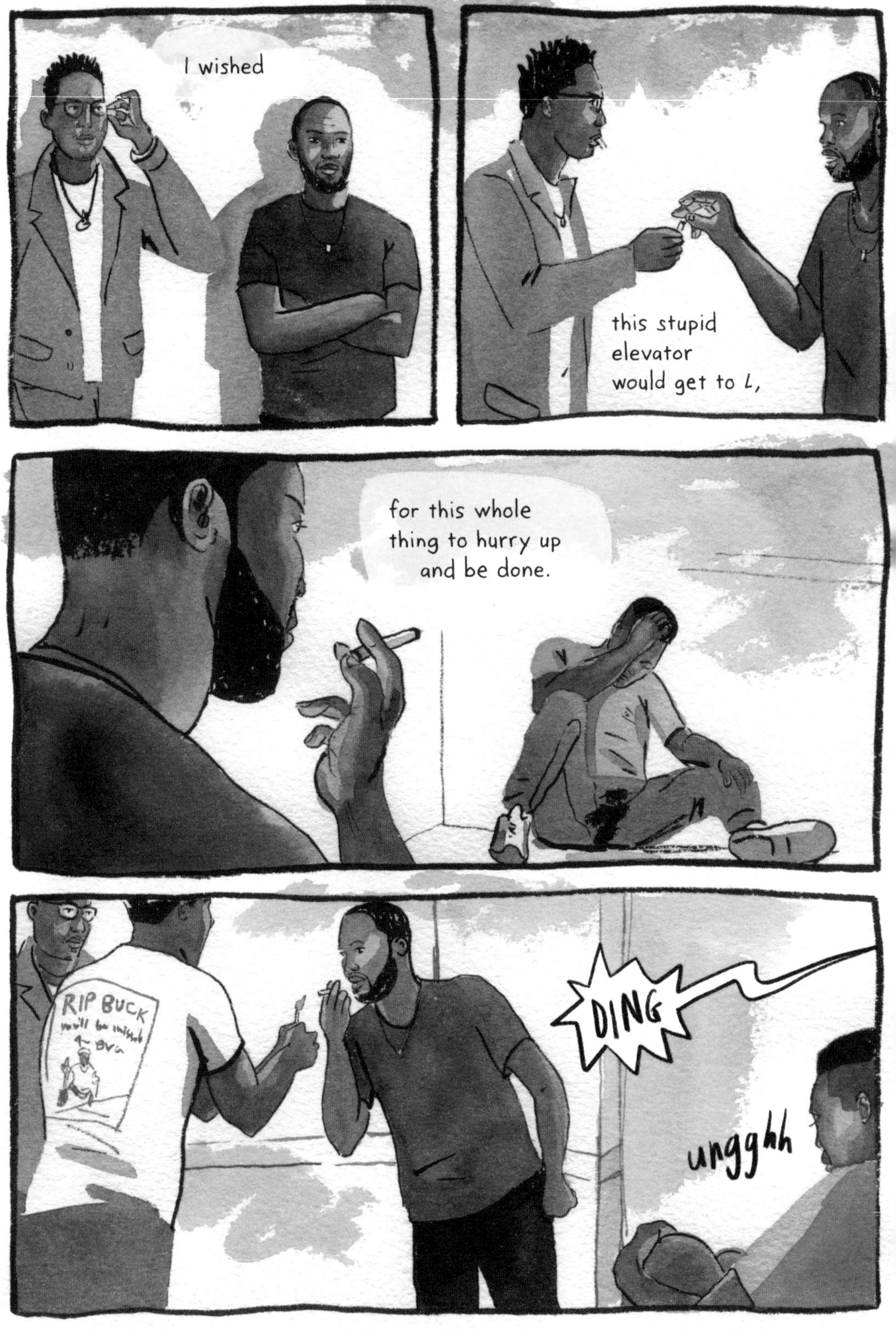
I wished
this stupid elevator would get to L,
for this whole thing to hurry up and be done.
RIP BUCK
DING
ungghh

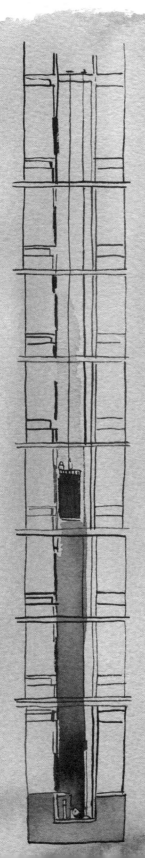

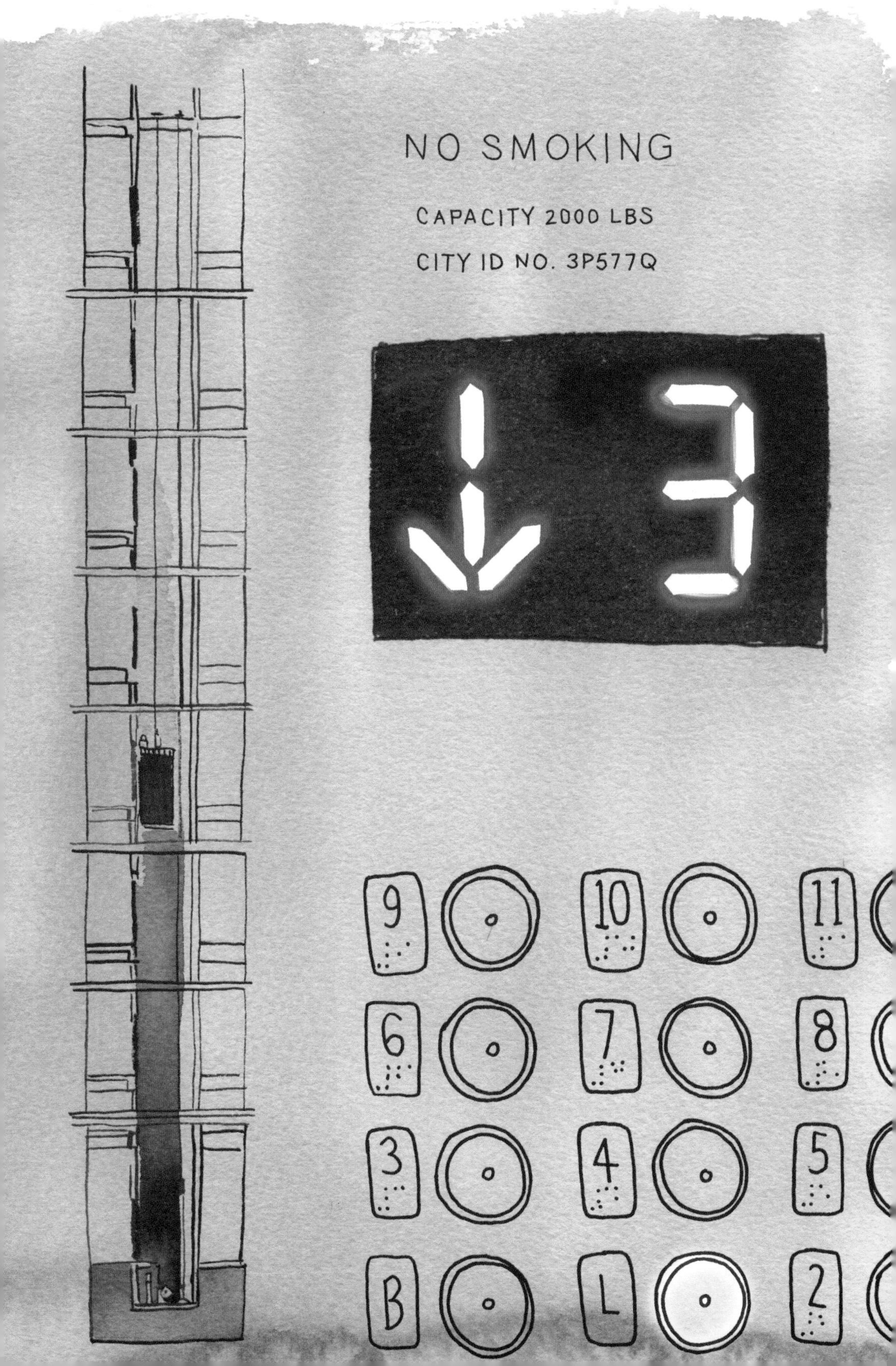

NO SMOKING

CAPACITY 2000 LBS

CITY ID NO. 3P577Q

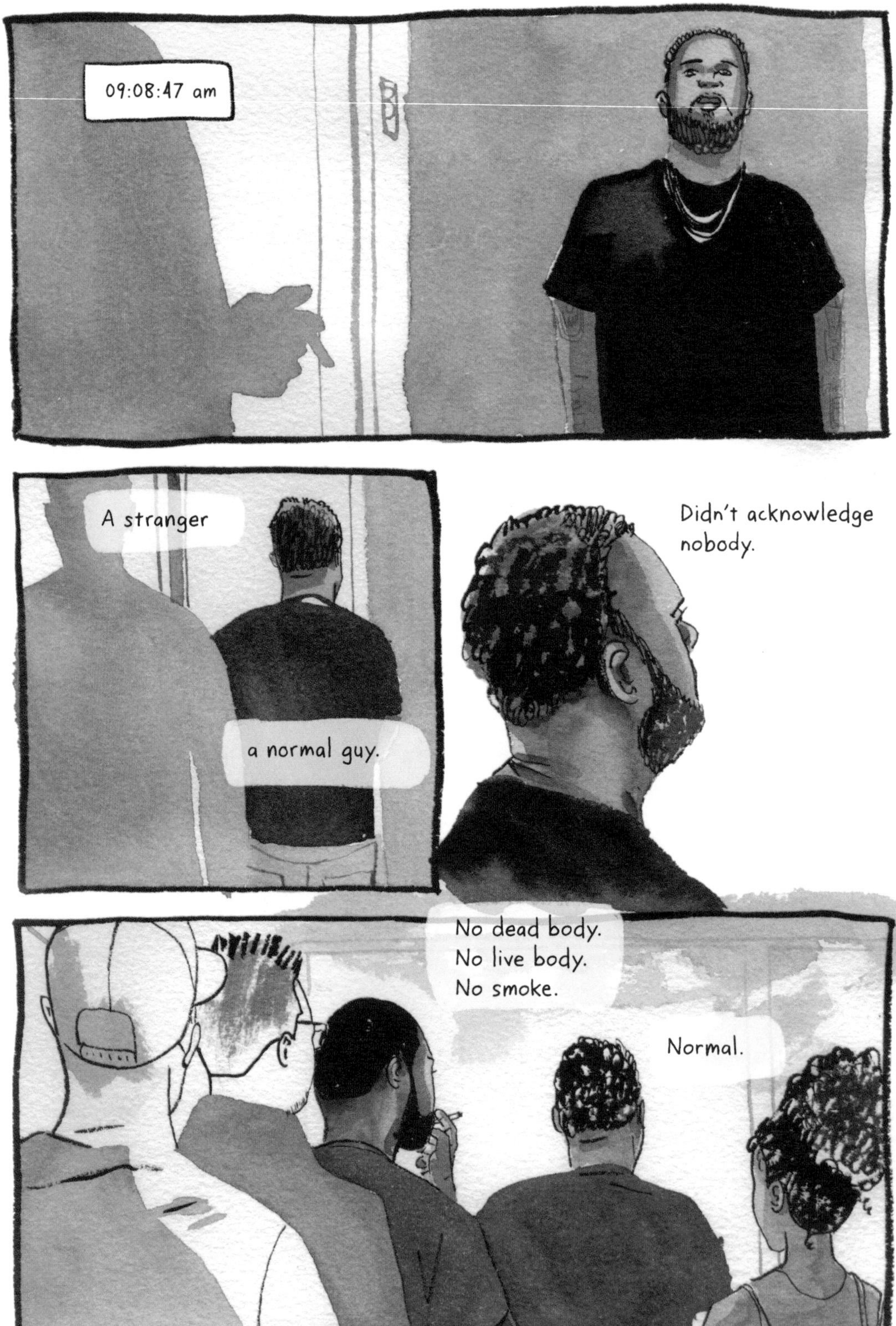
09:08:47 am
A stranger
a normal guy.
Didn't acknowledge nobody.
No dead body.
No live body.
No smoke.
Normal.

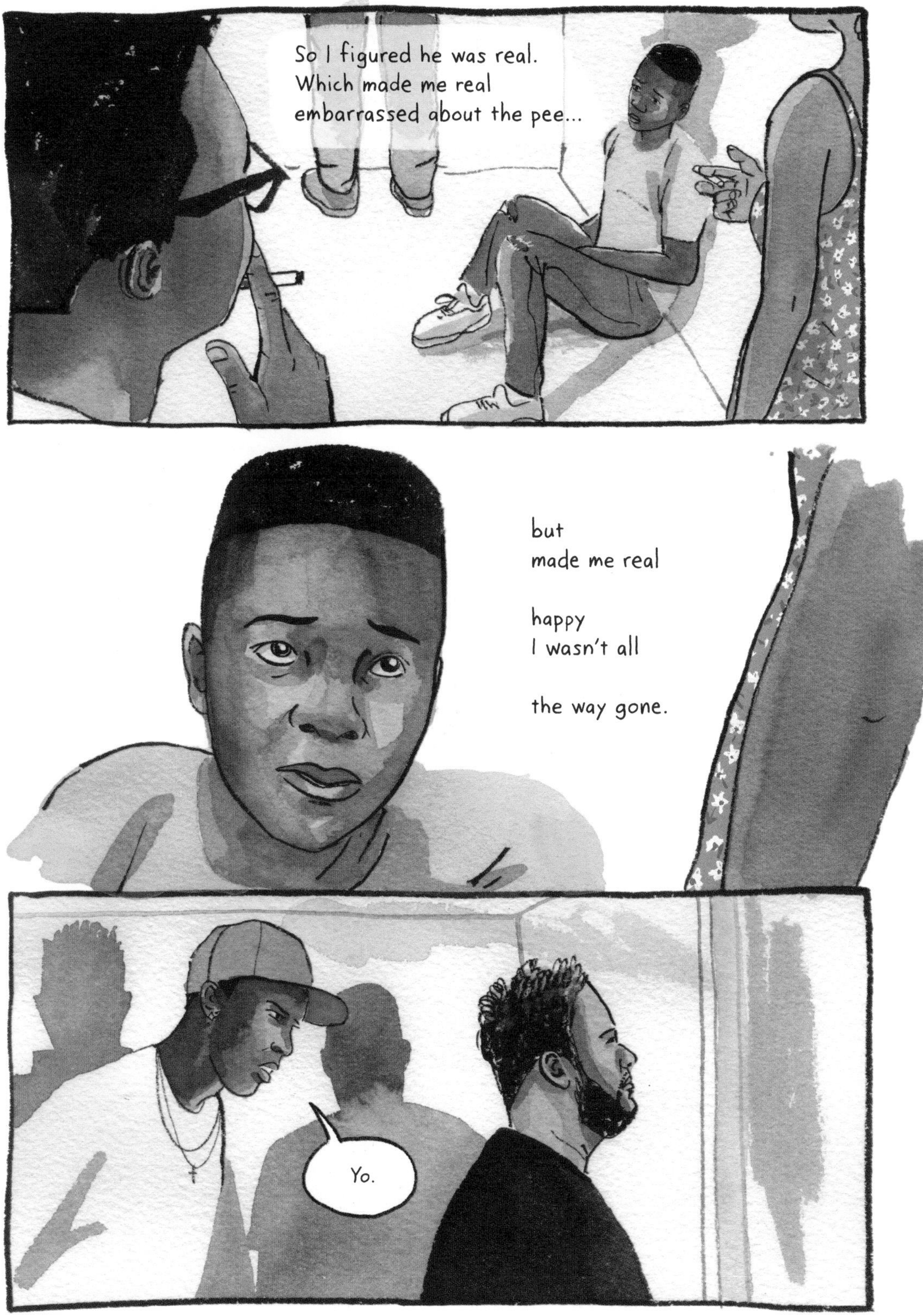
So I figured he was real. Which made me real embarrassed about the pee...
but made me real
happy I wasn't all
the way gone.
Yo.

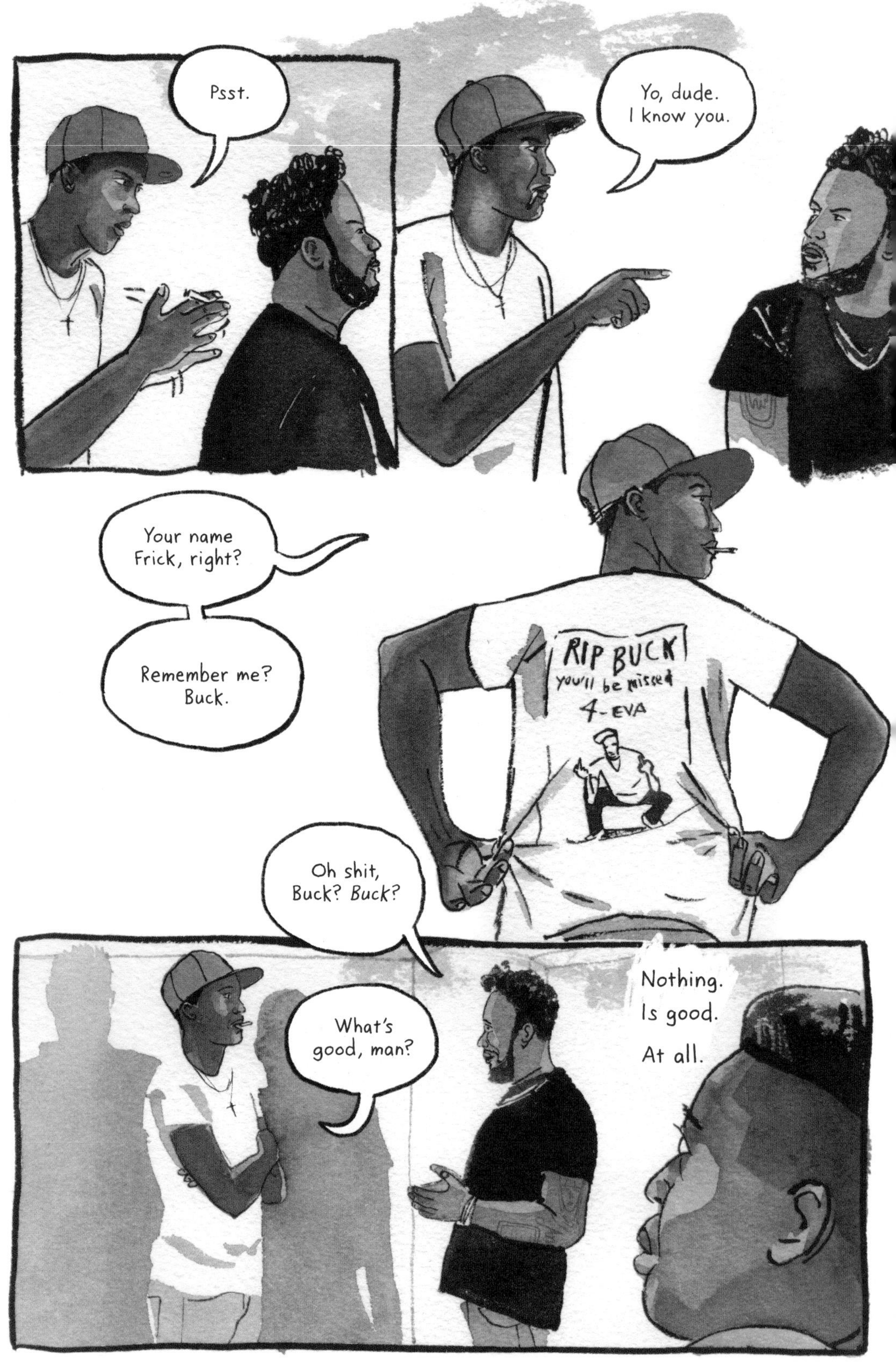
Psst.
Yo, dude. I know you.
Your name Frick, right?
Remember me? Buck.
RIP BUCK you'll be missed 4-EVA
Oh shit, Buck? *Buck*?
What's good, man?
Nothing. Is good. At all.

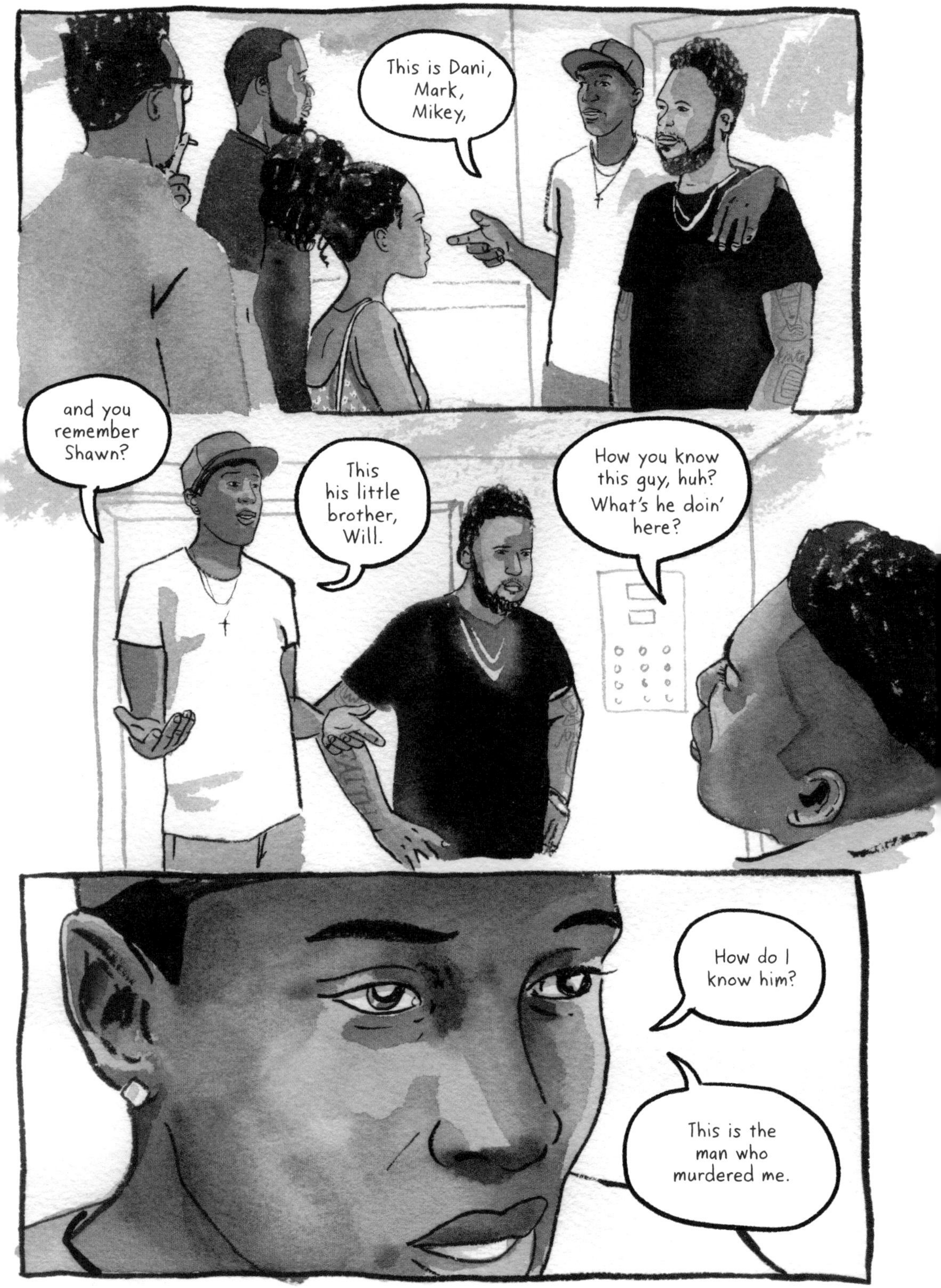
This is Dani, Mark, Mikey,
and you remember Shawn?
This his little brother, Will.
How you know this guy, huh? What's he doin' here?
How do I know him?
This is the man who murdered me.

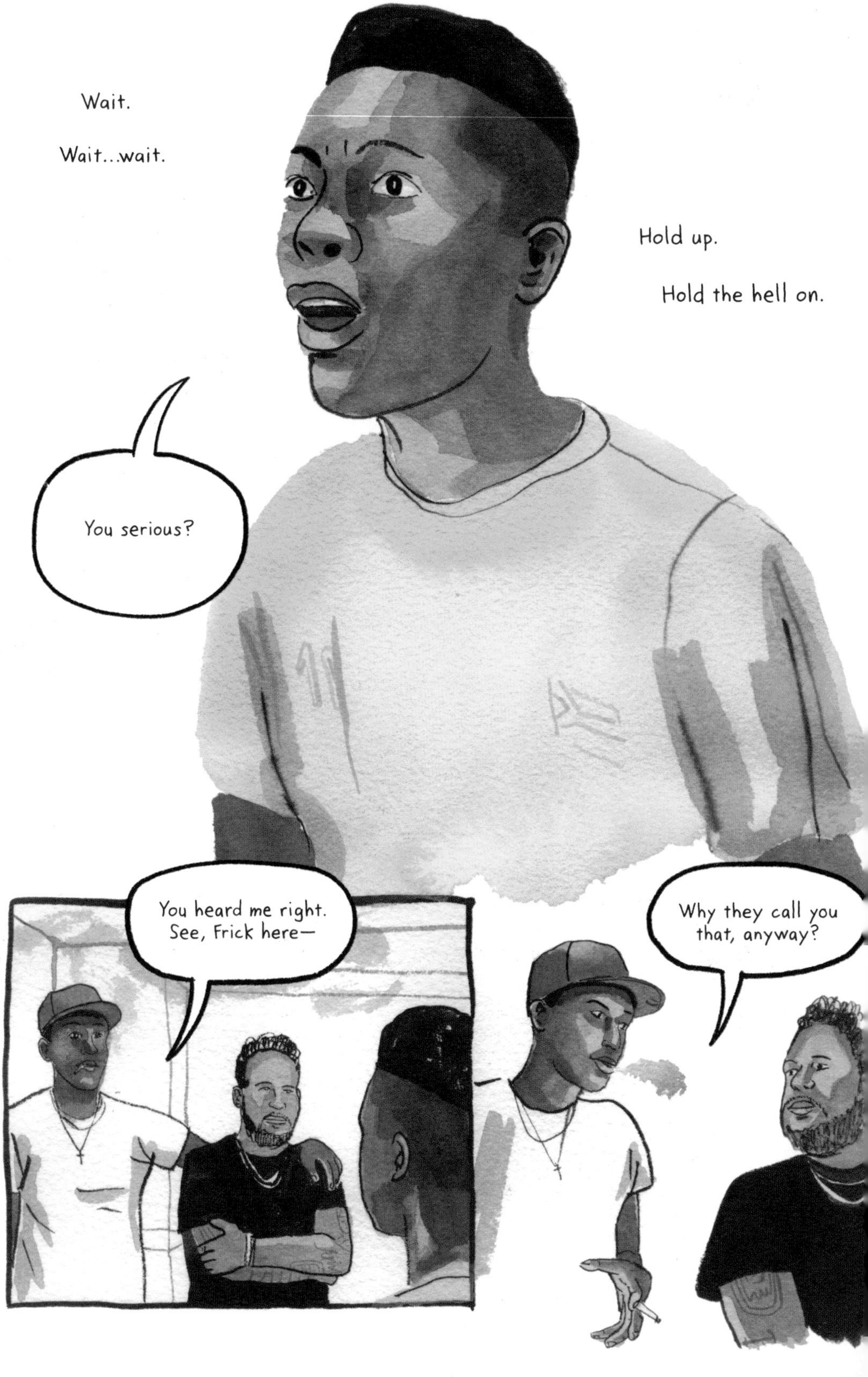
Wait.
Wait...wait.
Hold up.
Hold the hell on.
You serious?
You heard me right. See, Frick here—
Why they call you that, anyway?

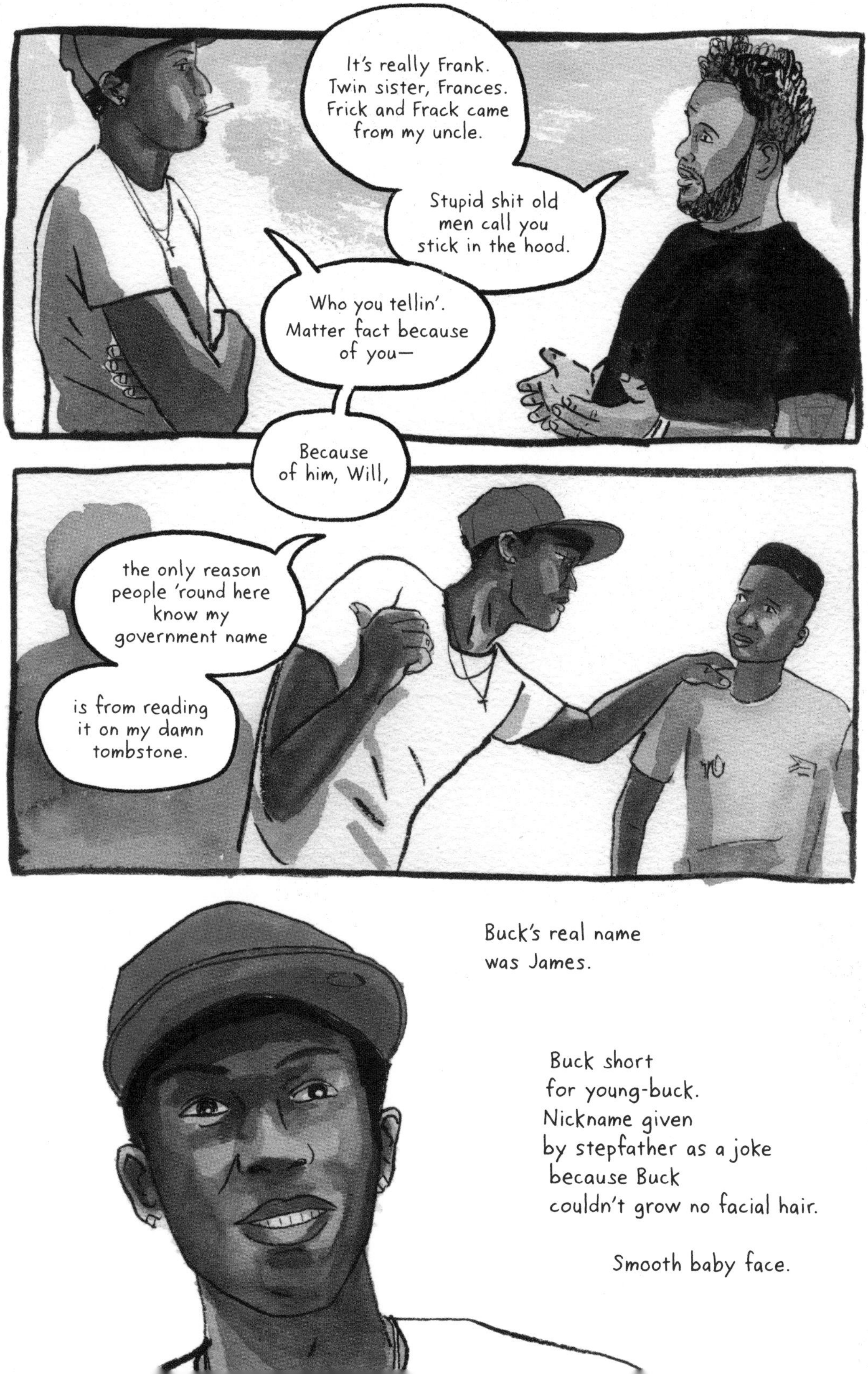
It's really Frank. Twin sister, Frances. Frick and Frack came from my uncle.
Stupid shit old men call you stick in the hood.
Who you tellin'. Matter fact because of you—
Because of him, Will,
the only reason people 'round here know my government name
is from reading it on my damn tombstone.
Buck's real name was James.
Buck short for young-buck. Nickname given by stepfather as a joke because Buck couldn't grow no facial hair.
Smooth baby face.

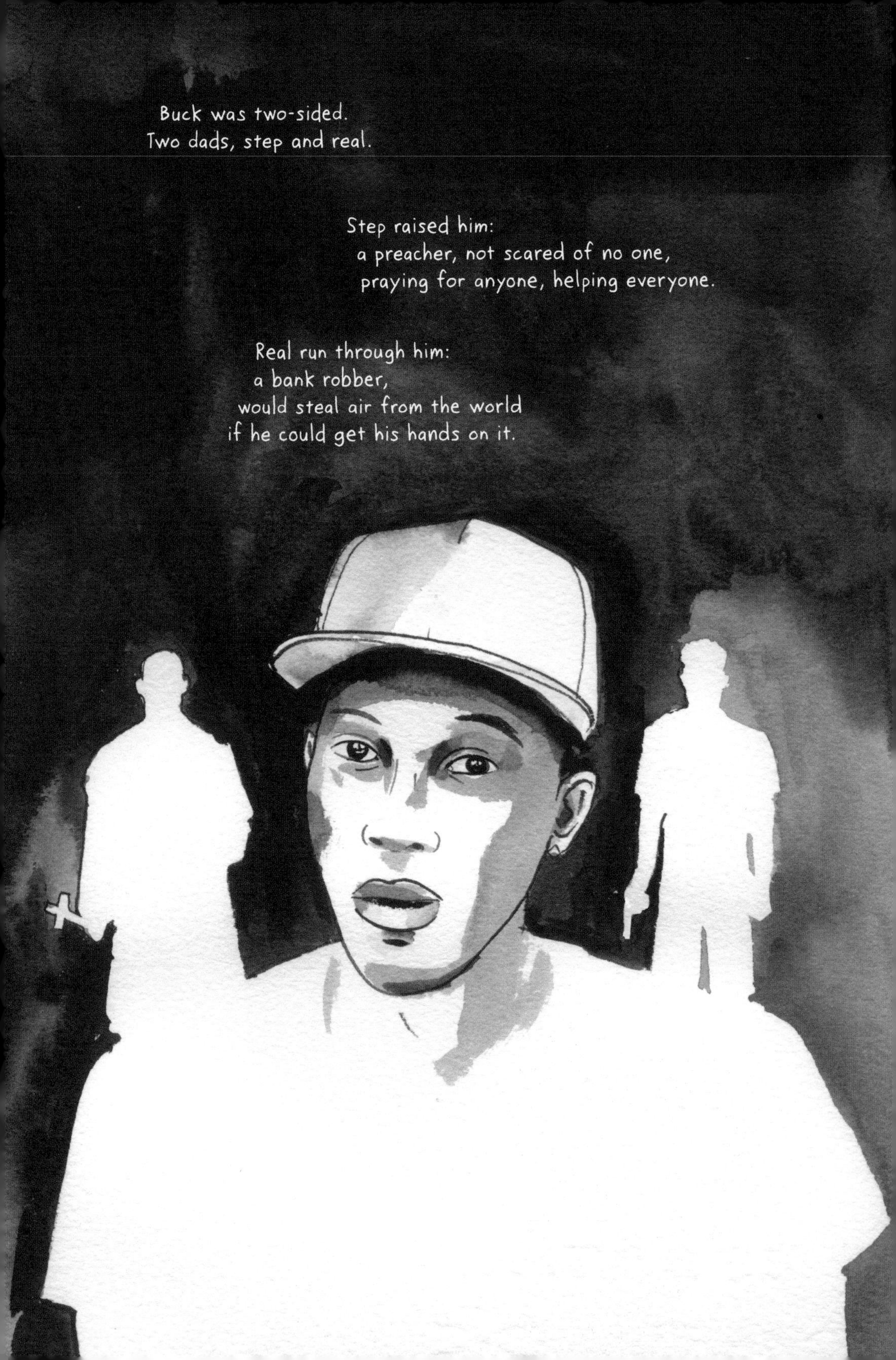
Buck was two-sided.
Two dads, step and real.
Step raised him:
a preacher, not scared of no one,
praying for anyone, helping everyone.
Real run through him:
a bank robber,
would steal air from the world
if he could get his hands on it.

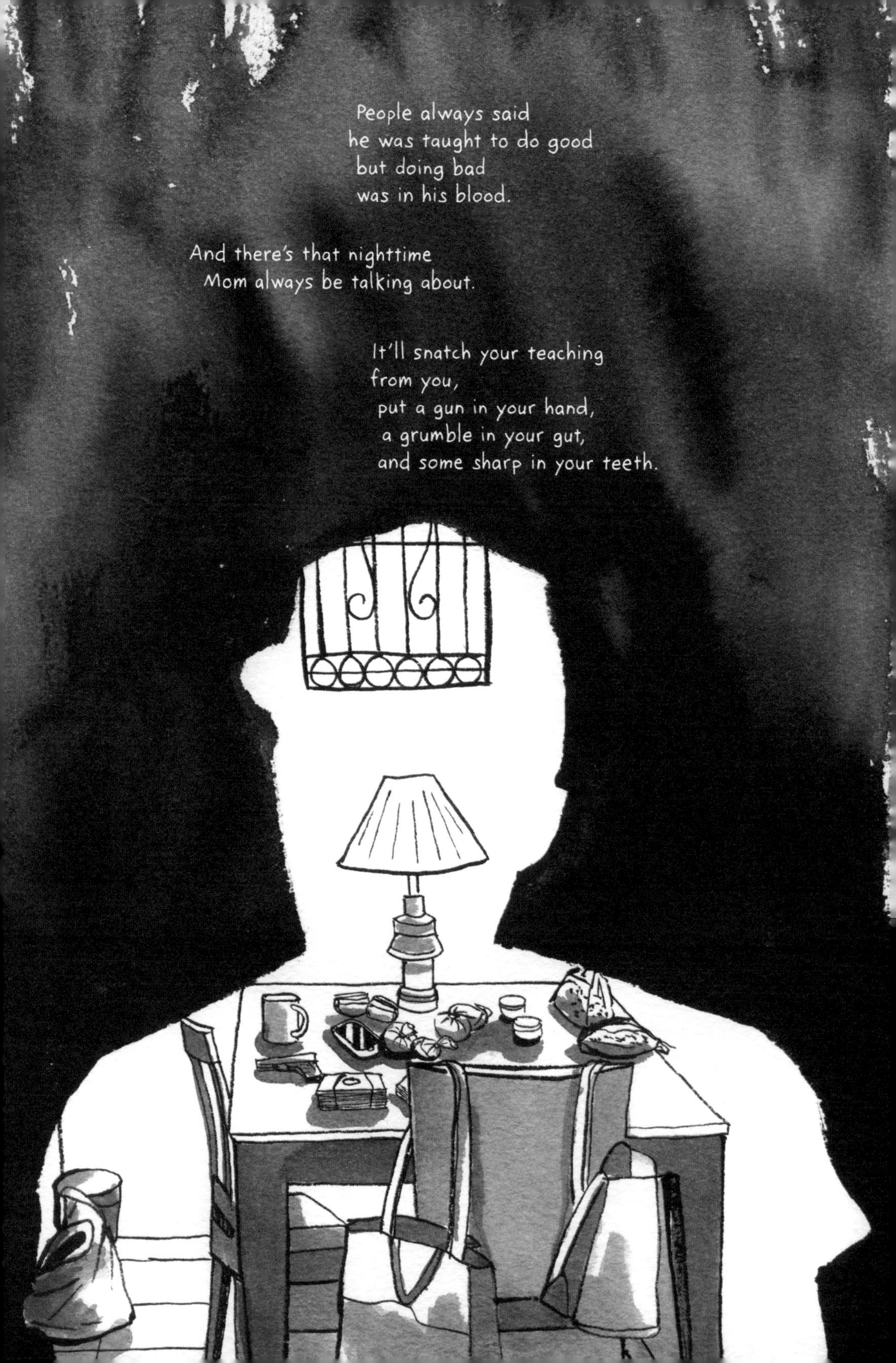
People always said
he was taught to do good
but doing bad
was in his blood.
And there's that nighttime
Mom always be talking about.
It'll snatch your teaching
from you,
put a gun in your hand,
a grumble in your gut,
and some sharp in your teeth.

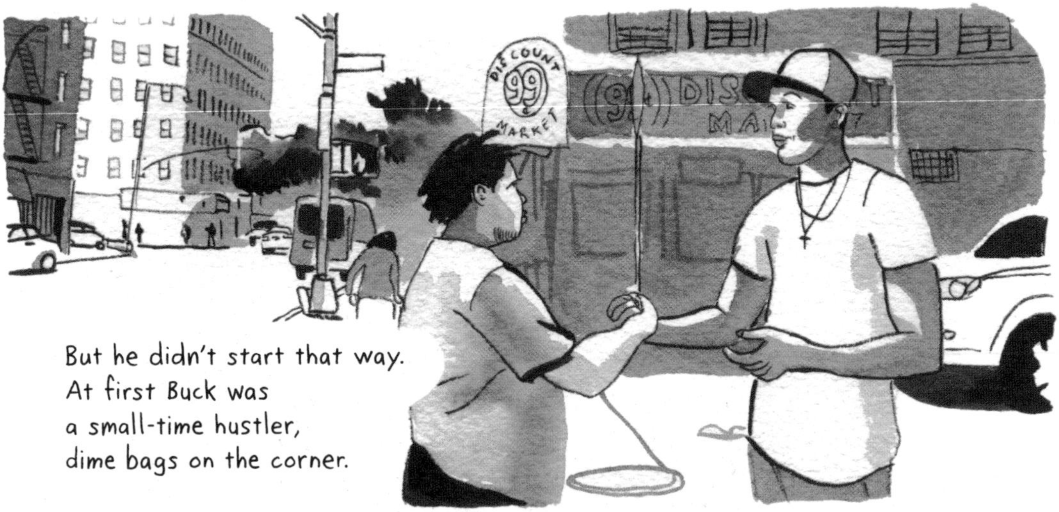
DISCOUNT
99
MARKET
But he didn't start that way.
At first Buck was
a small-time hustler,
dime bags on the corner.

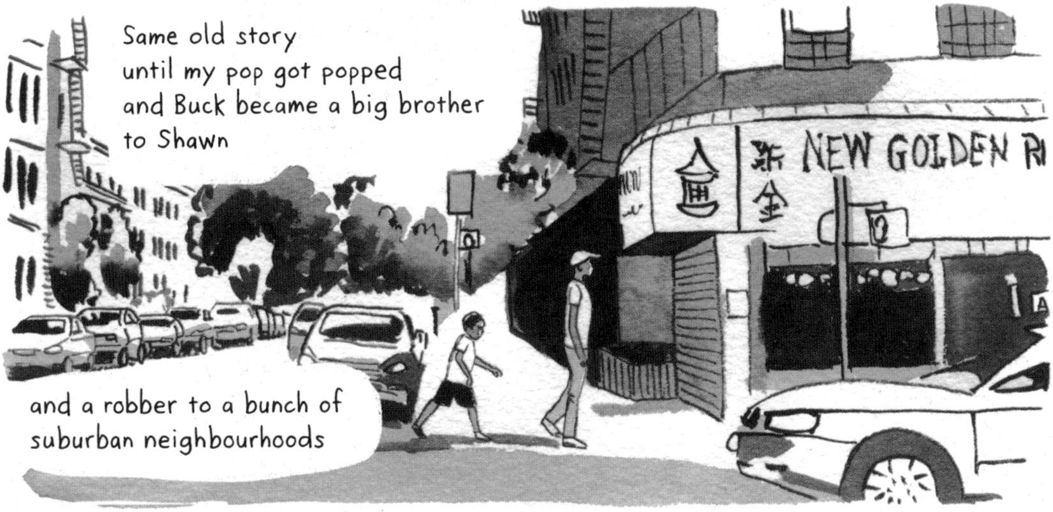
Same old story
until my pop got popped
and Buck became a big brother
to Shawn
NEW GOLDEN
and a robber to a bunch of
suburban neighbourhoods

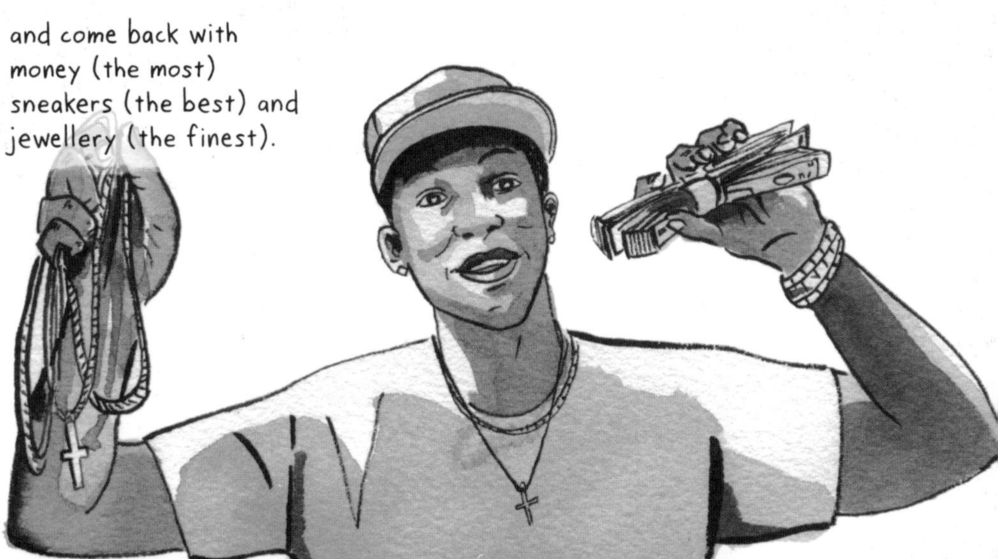
and come back with
money (the most)
sneakers (the best) and
jewellery (the finest).

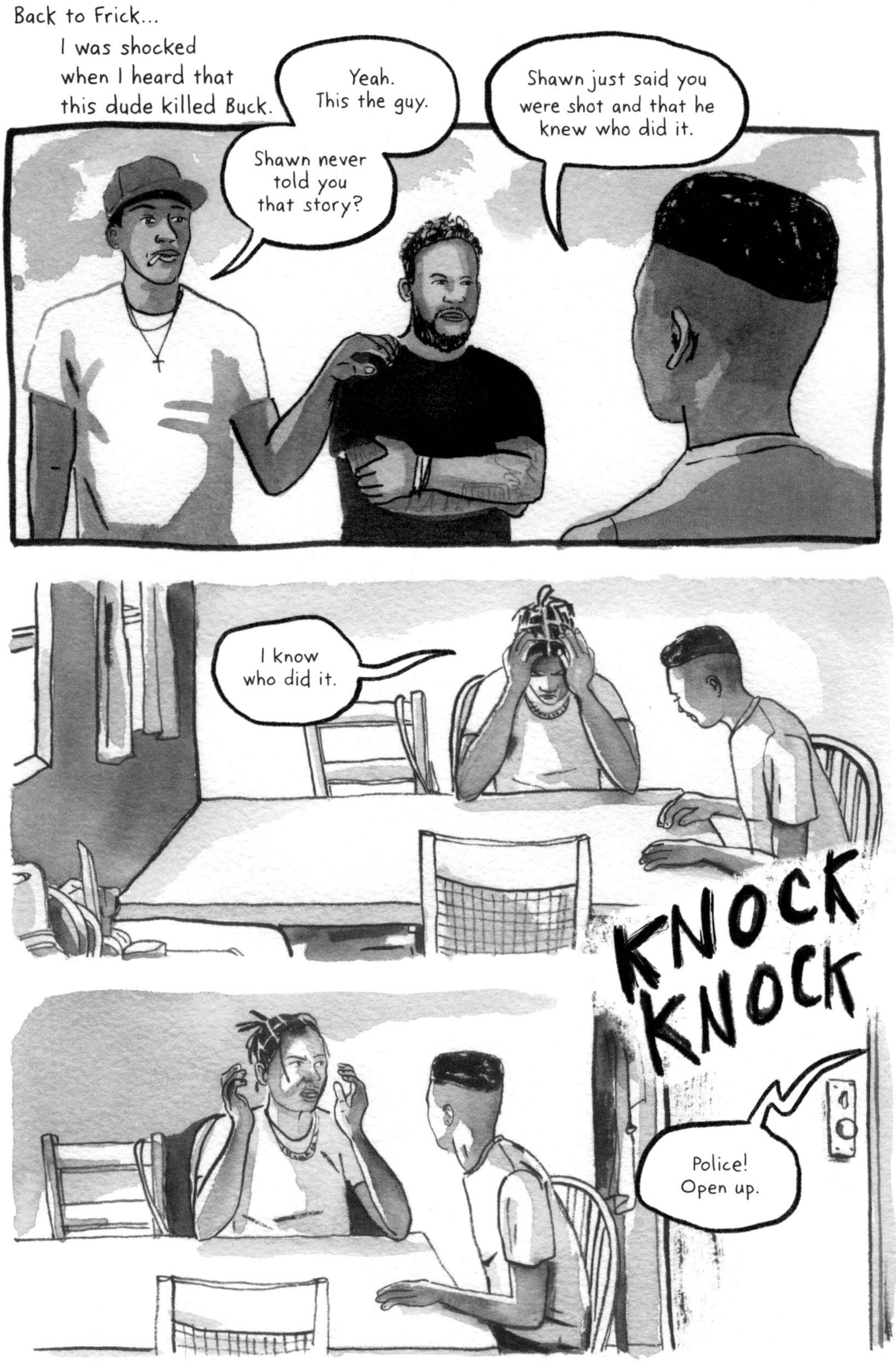
Back to Frick...
I was shocked when I heard that this dude killed Buck.
Yeah. This the guy.
Shawn never told you that story?
Shawn just said you were shot and that he knew who did it.
I know who did it.
KNOCK KNOCK
Police! Open up.

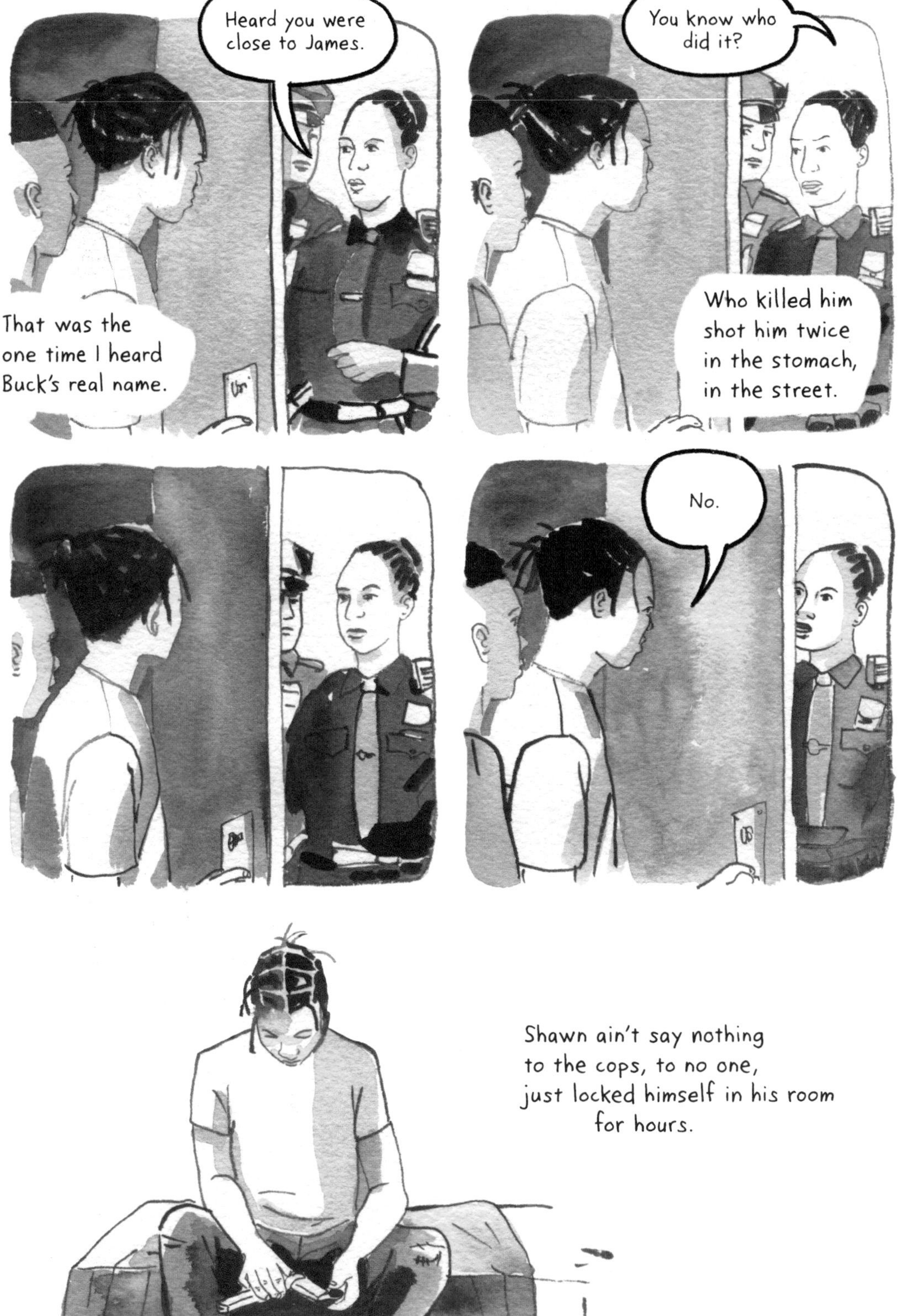
Heard you were close to James.
That was the one time I heard Buck's real name.
You know who did it?
Who killed him shot him twice in the stomach, in the street.
No.
Shawn ain't say nothing to the cops, to no one, just locked himself in his room for hours.

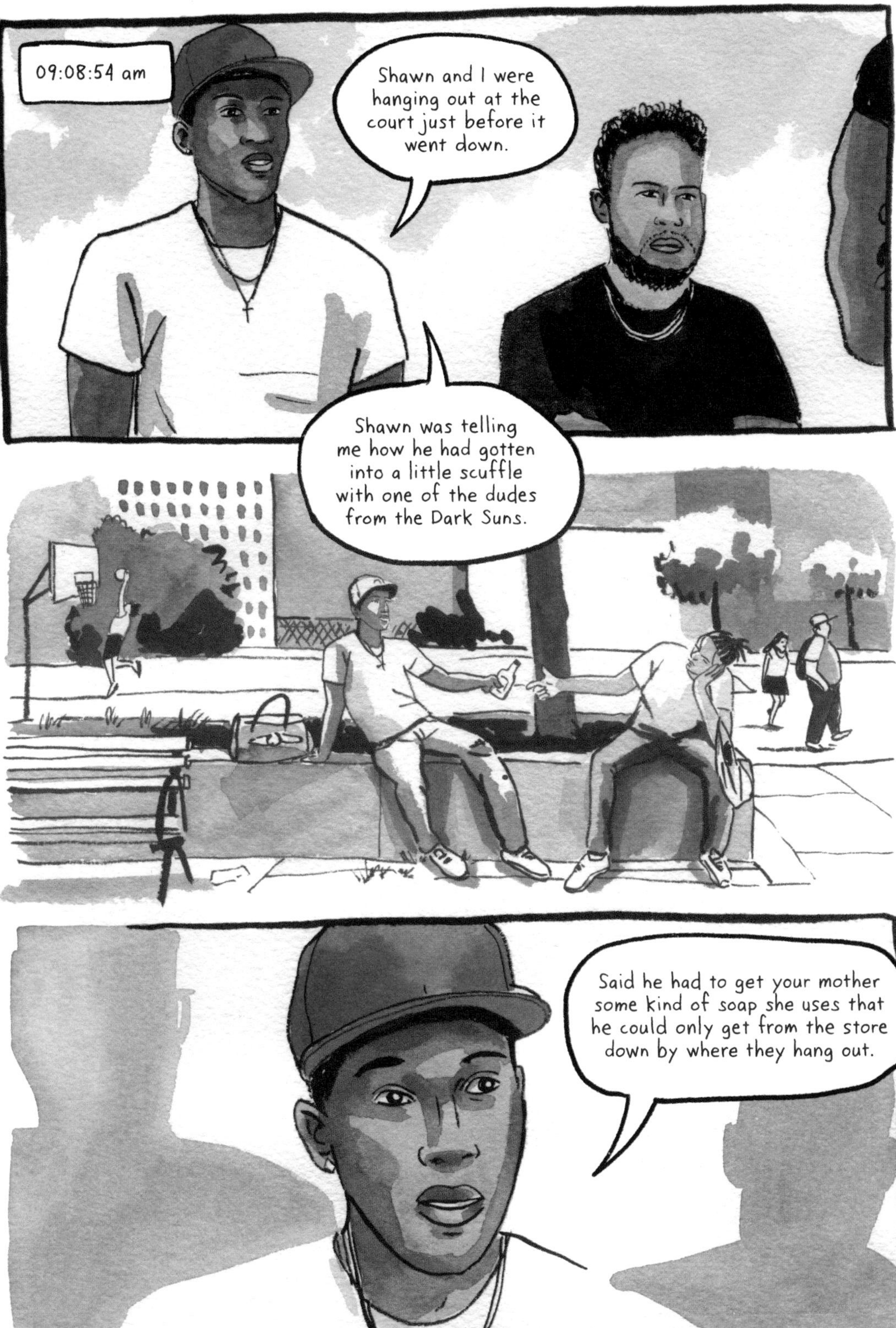
09:08:54 am
Shawn and I were hanging out at the court just before it went down.
Shawn was telling me how he had gotten into a little scuffle with one of the dudes from the Dark Suns.
Said he had to get your mother some kind of soap she uses that he could only get from the store down by where they hang out.

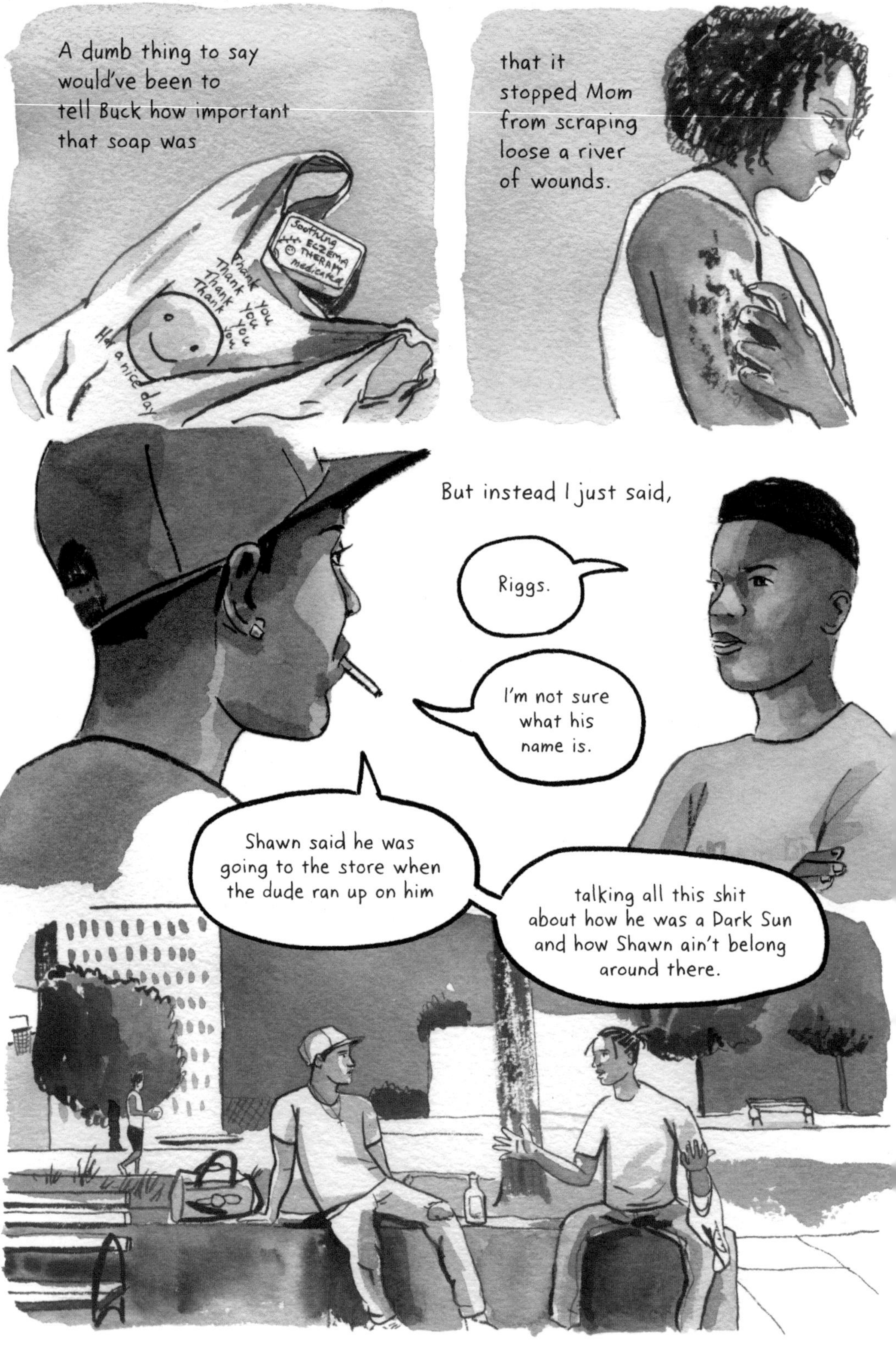
A dumb thing to say would've been to tell Buck how important that soap was
Soothing ECZEMA THERAPY medicated
Thank you
Thank you
Thank you
Thank you
a nice day
that it stopped Mom from scraping loose a river of wounds.
But instead I just said,
Riggs.
I'm not sure what his name is.
Shawn said he was going to the store when the dude ran up on him
talking all this shit about how he was a Dark Sun and how Shawn ain't belong around there.

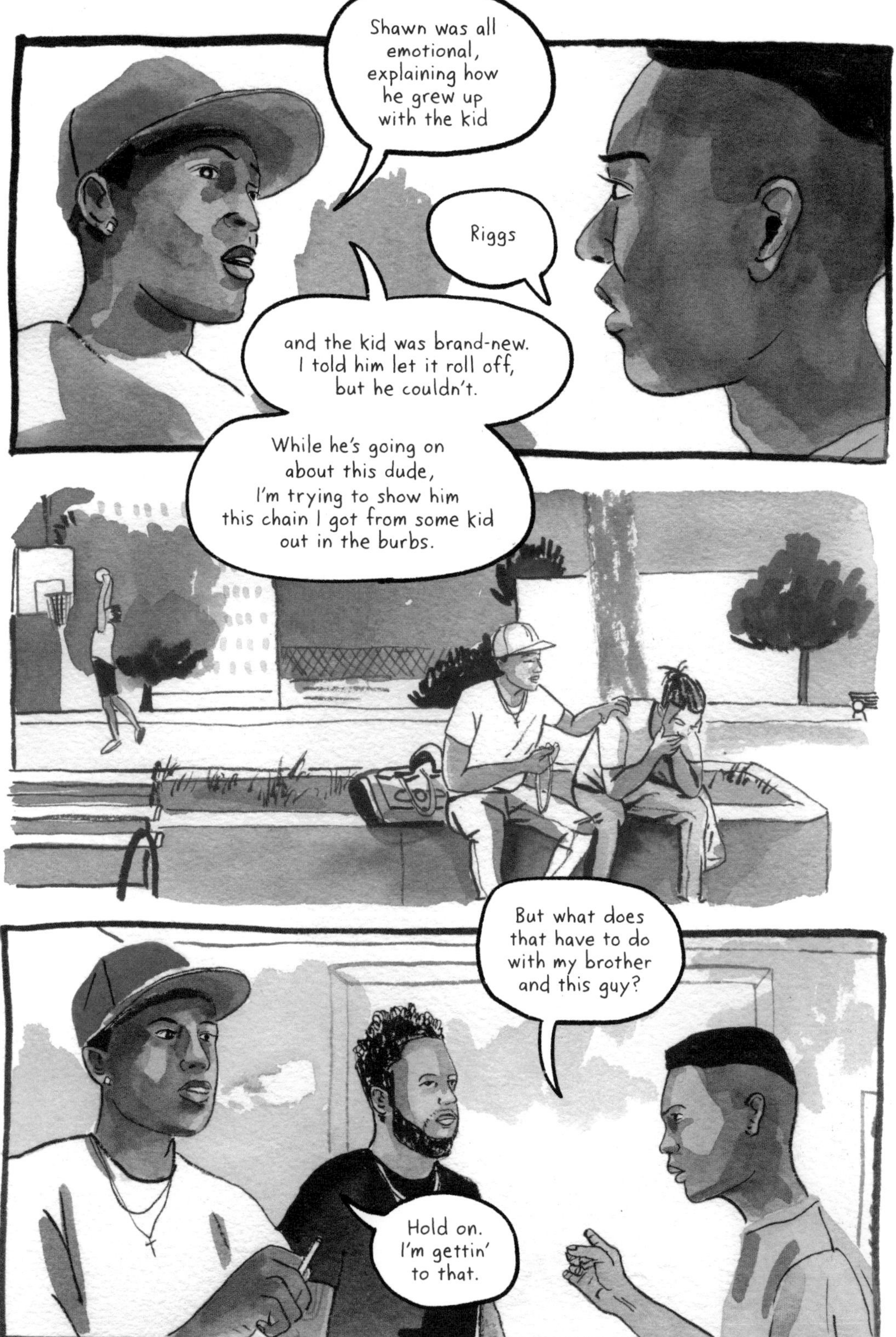
Shawn was all emotional, explaining how he grew up with the kid
Riggs
and the kid was brand-new. I told him let it roll off, but he couldn't.
While he's going on about this dude, I'm trying to show him this chain I got from some kid out in the burbs.
But what does that have to do with my brother and this guy?
Hold on. I'm gettin' to that.

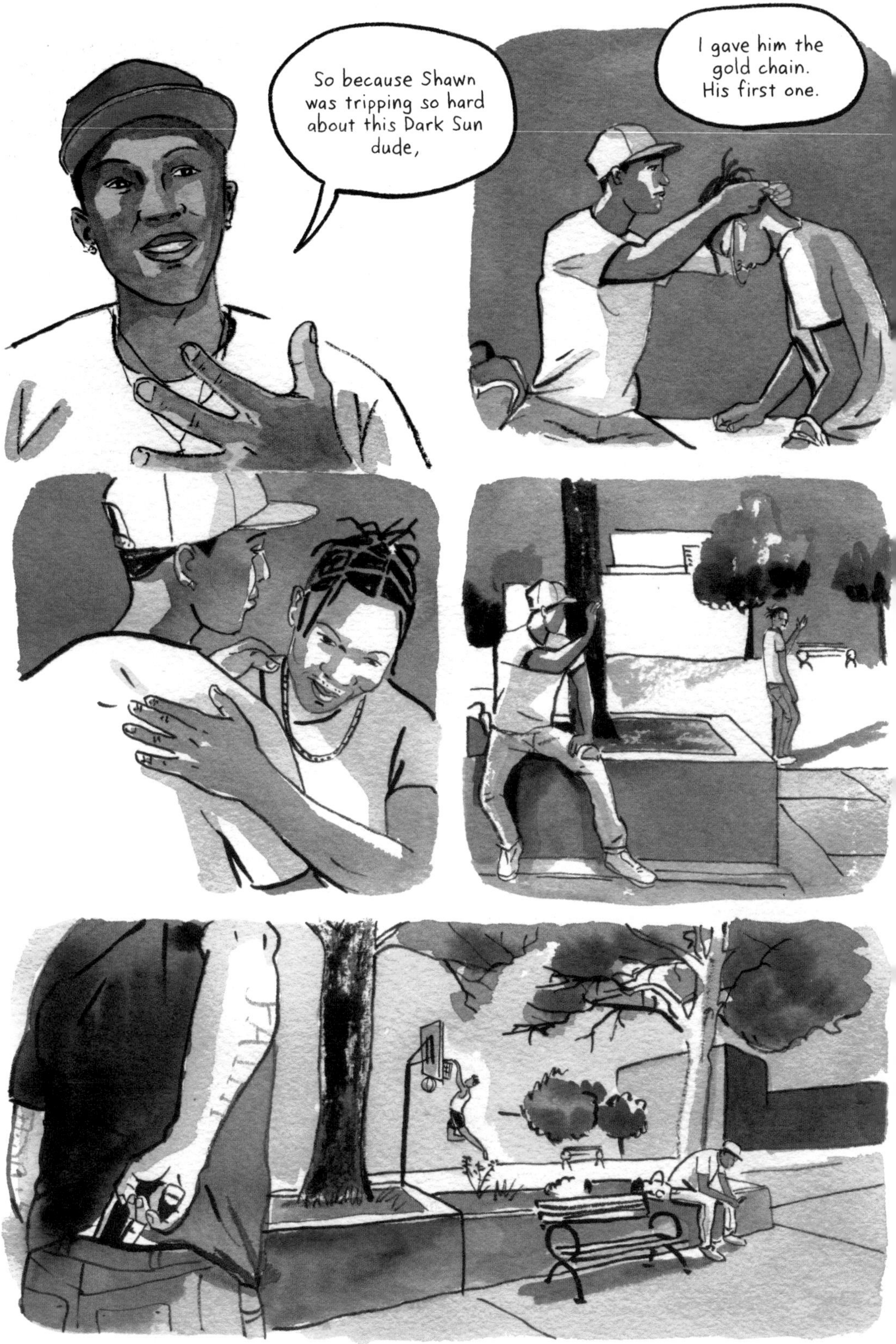
So because Shawn was tripping so hard about this Dark Sun dude,
I gave him the gold chain. His first one.

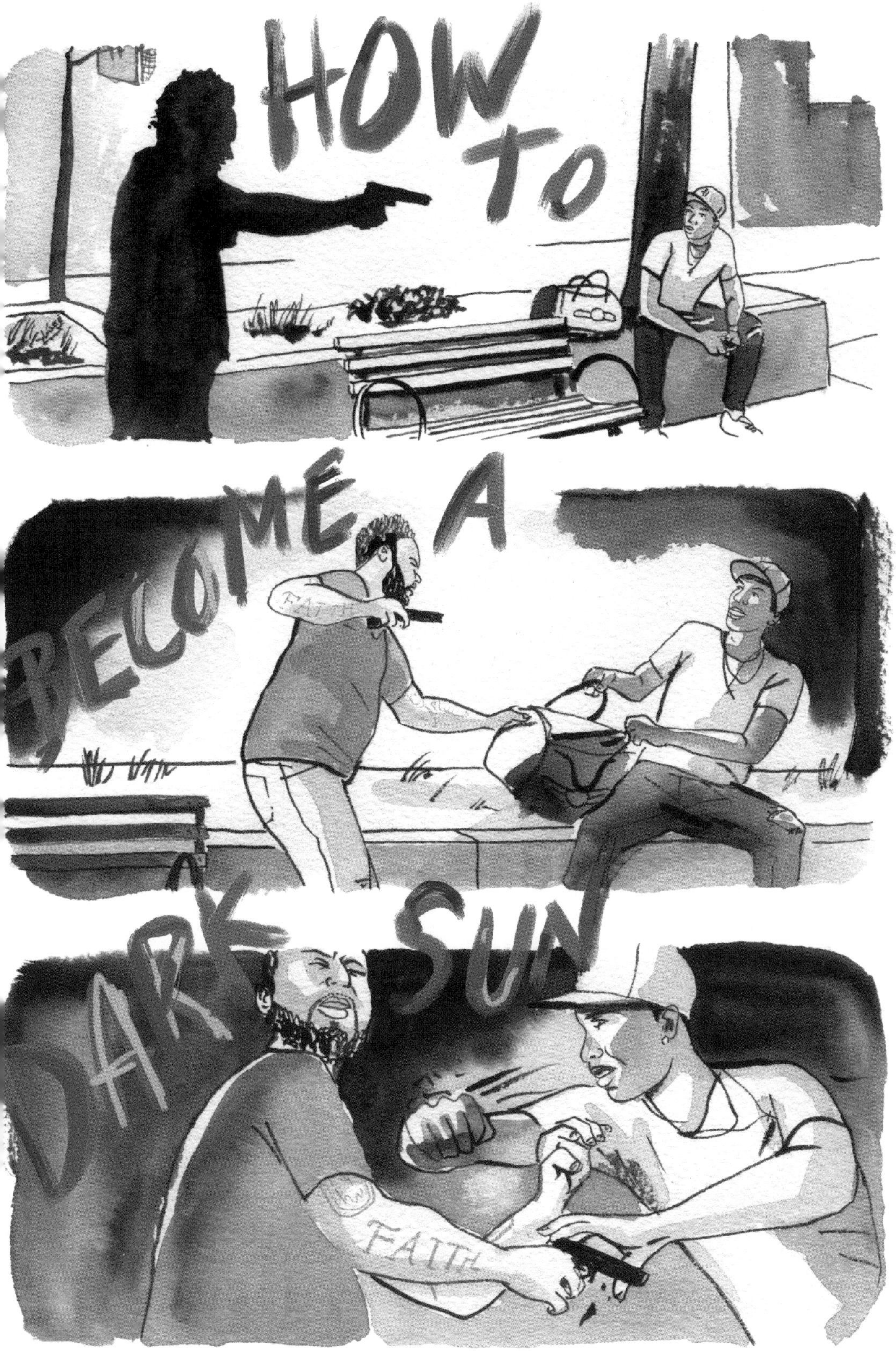
HOW TO
BECOME A
DARK SUN
FAITH
FAITH
FAITH

No.1: TurF

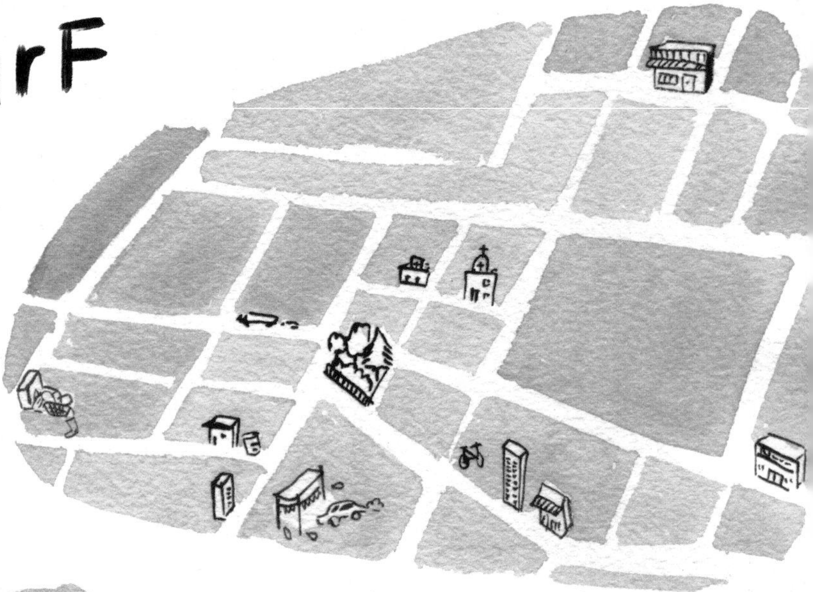

nine blocks from
where I live.

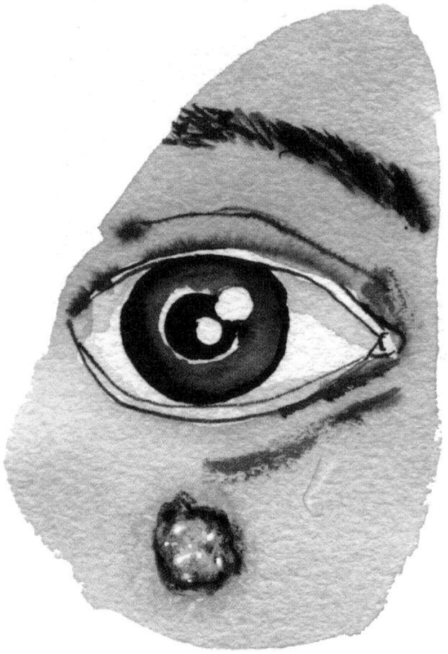

No.2: The ShiNing

a cigarette burn
under the right eye.

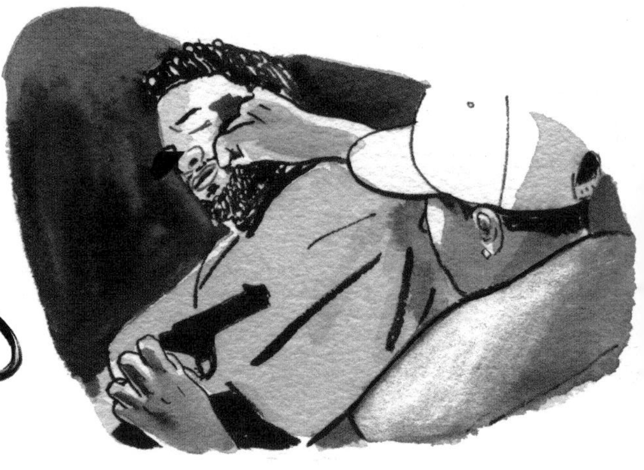

No.3: DARK DeeD

robbing someone,
beating someone,
or the worst,

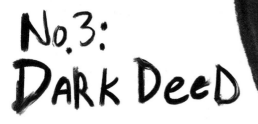

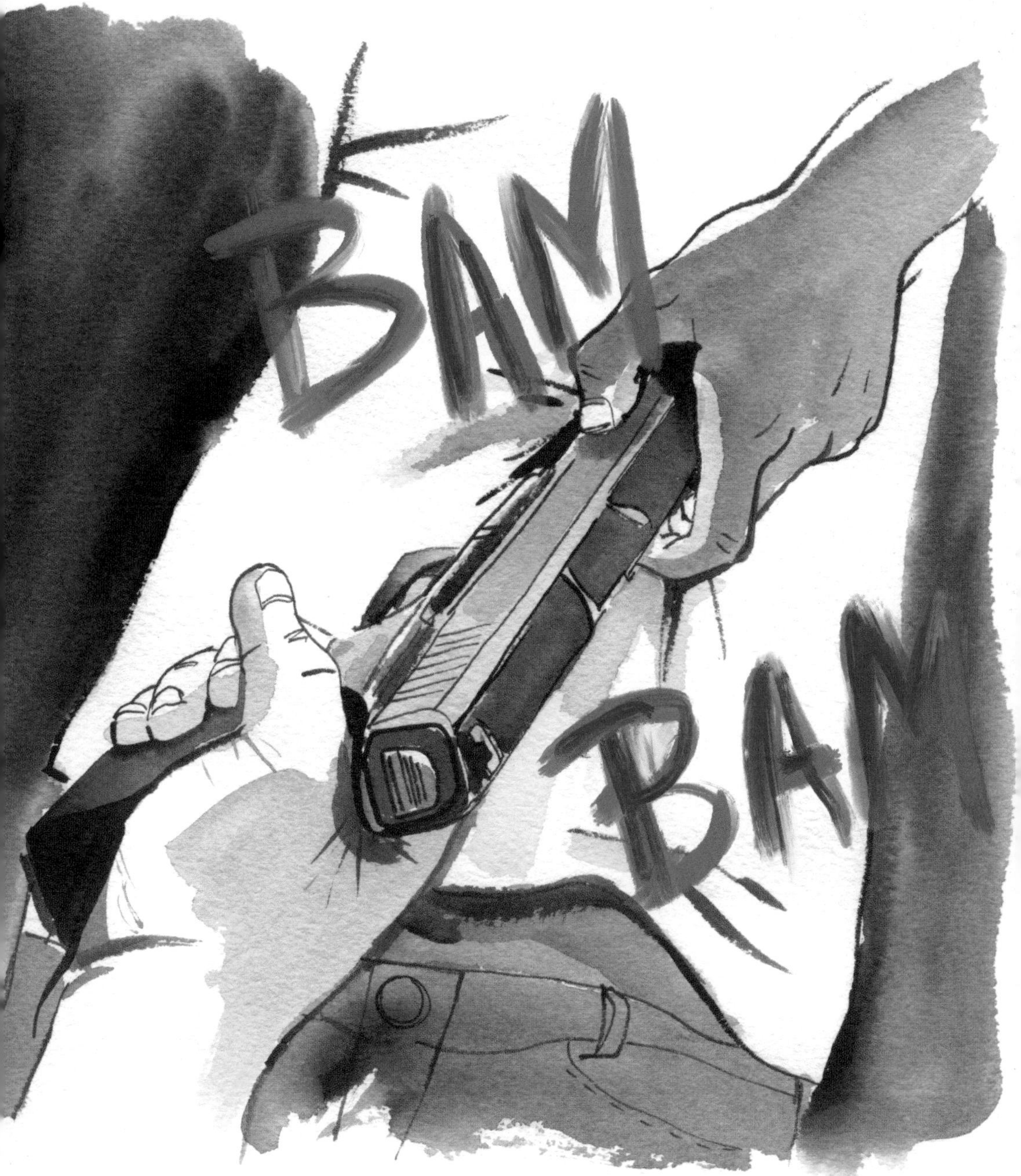
BAM
BAM

Killing Someone

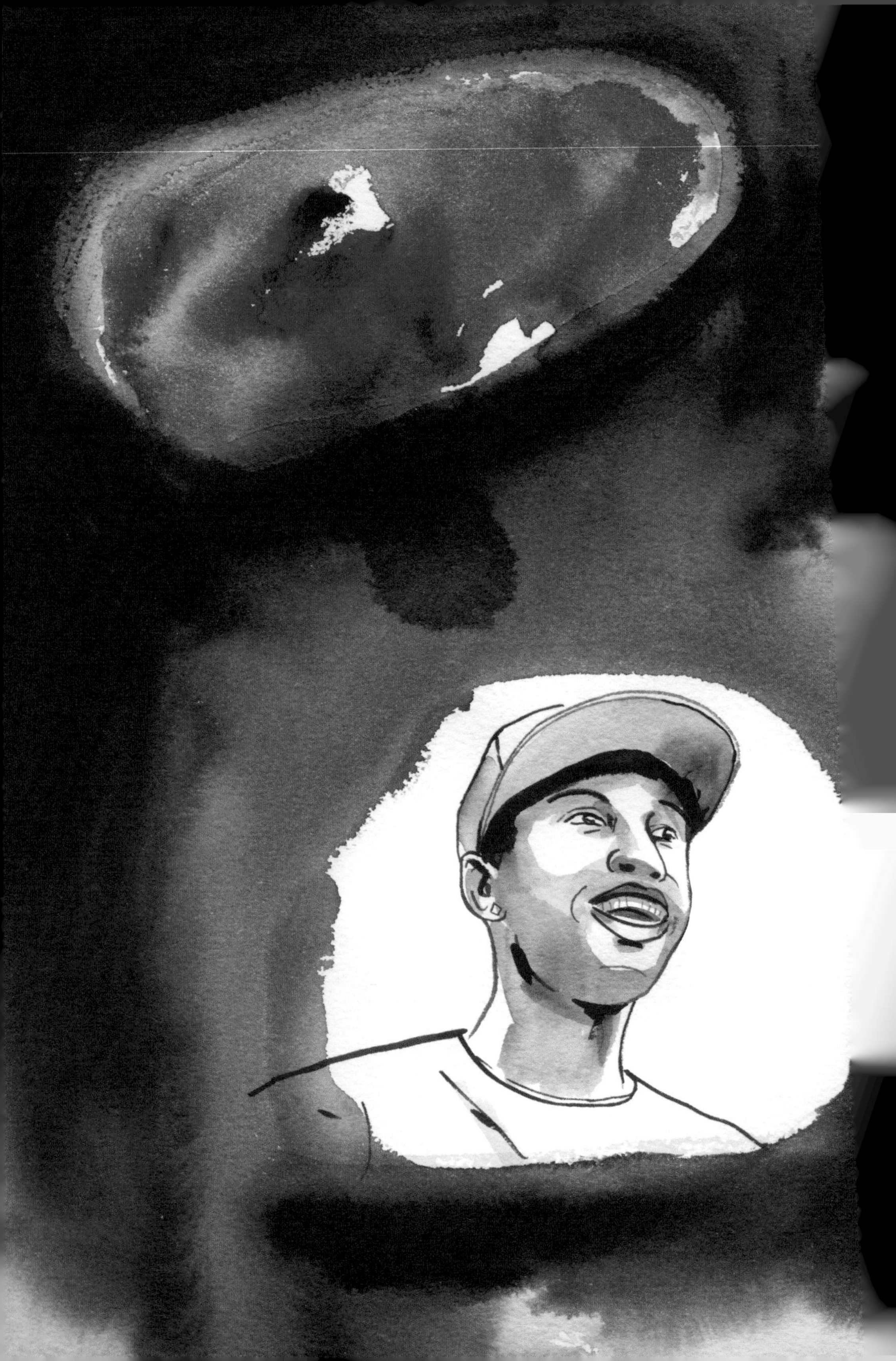

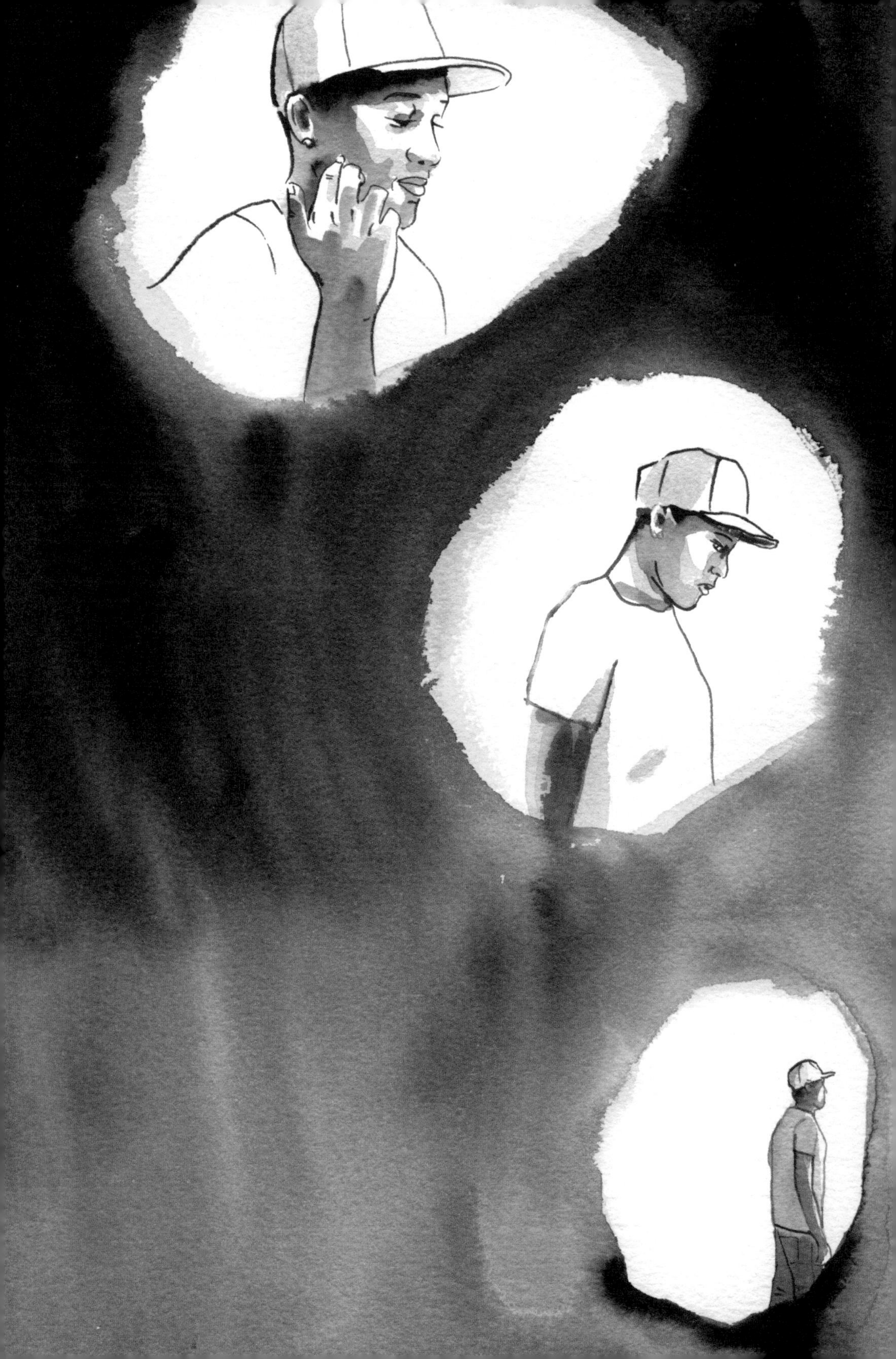

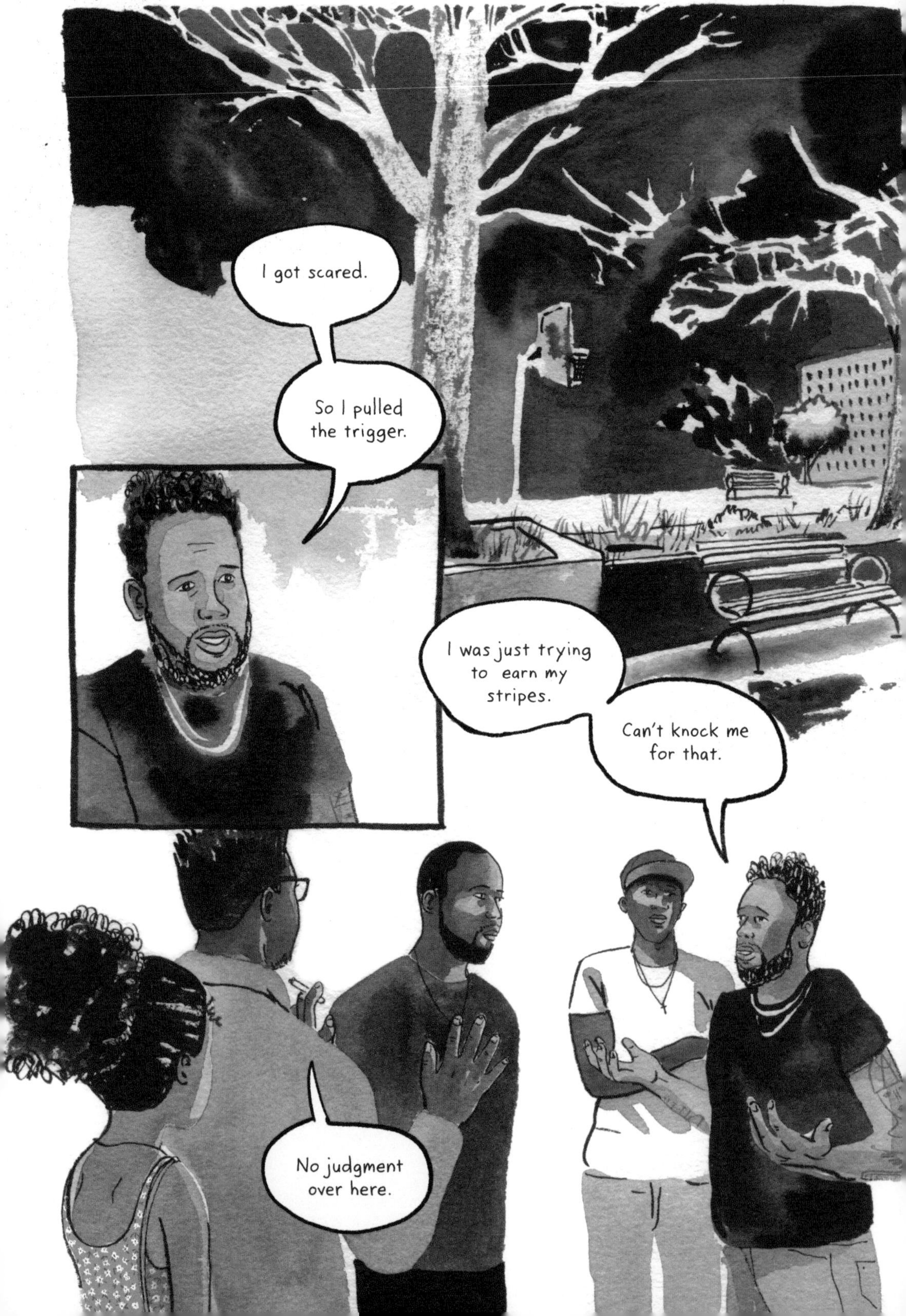
I got scared.
So I pulled the trigger.
I was just trying to earn my stripes.
Can't knock me for that.
No judgment over here.

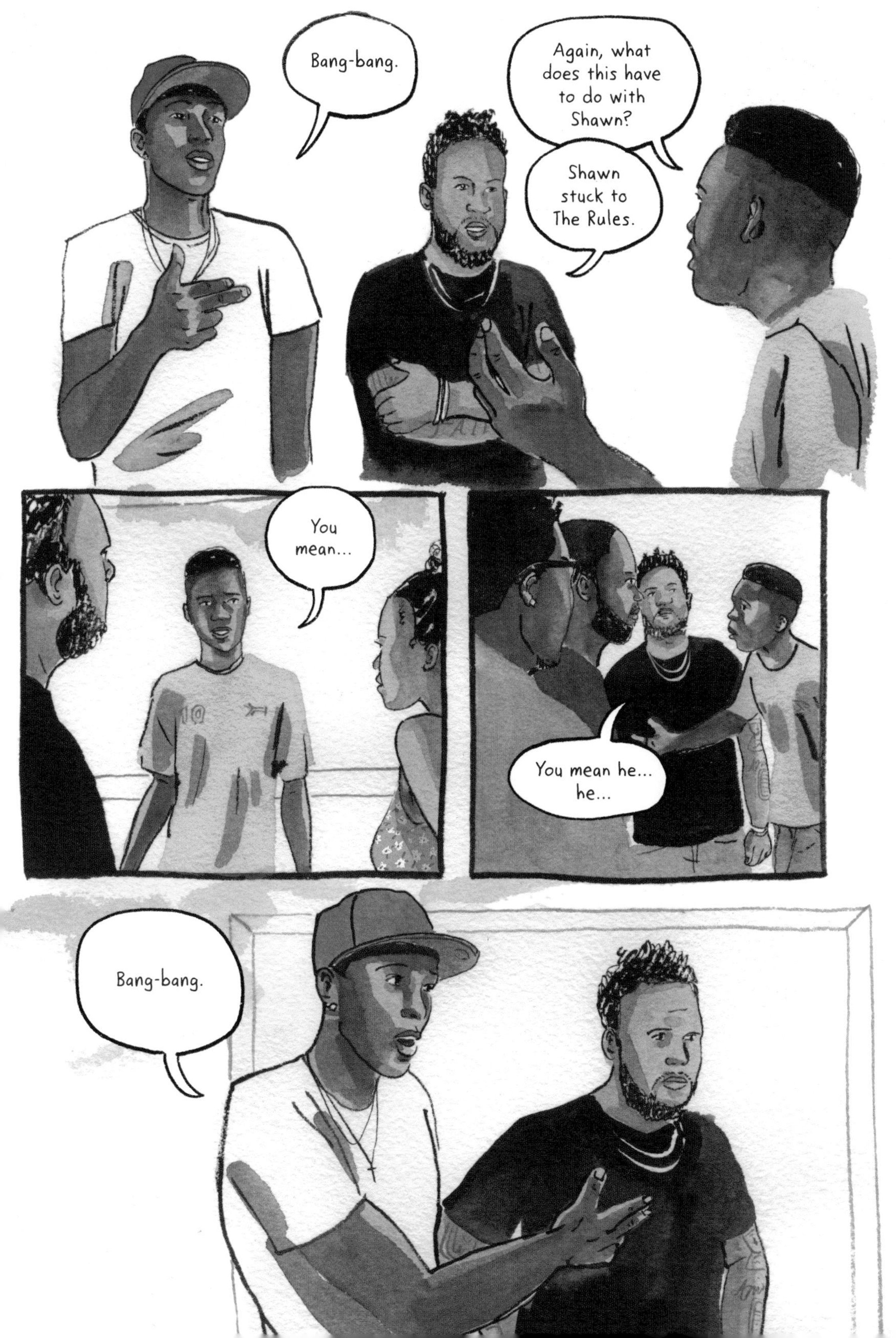
Bang-bang.
Again, what does this have to do with Shawn?
Shawn stuck to The Rules.
You mean...
You mean he... he...
Bang-bang.

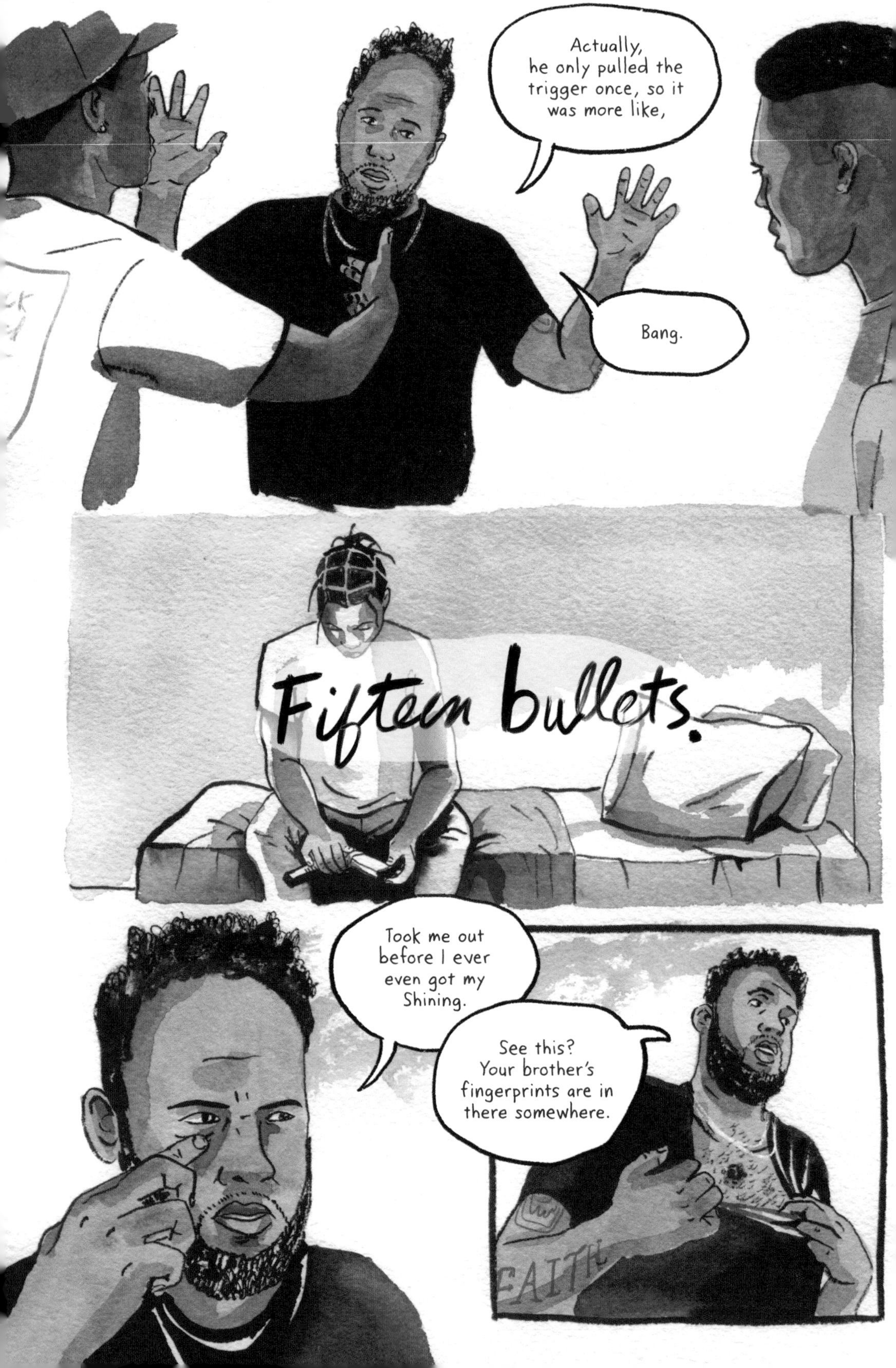
Actually, he only pulled the trigger once, so it was more like,
Bang.
Fifteen bullets.
Took me out before I ever even got my Shining.
See this? Your brother's fingerprints are in there somewhere.
FAITH

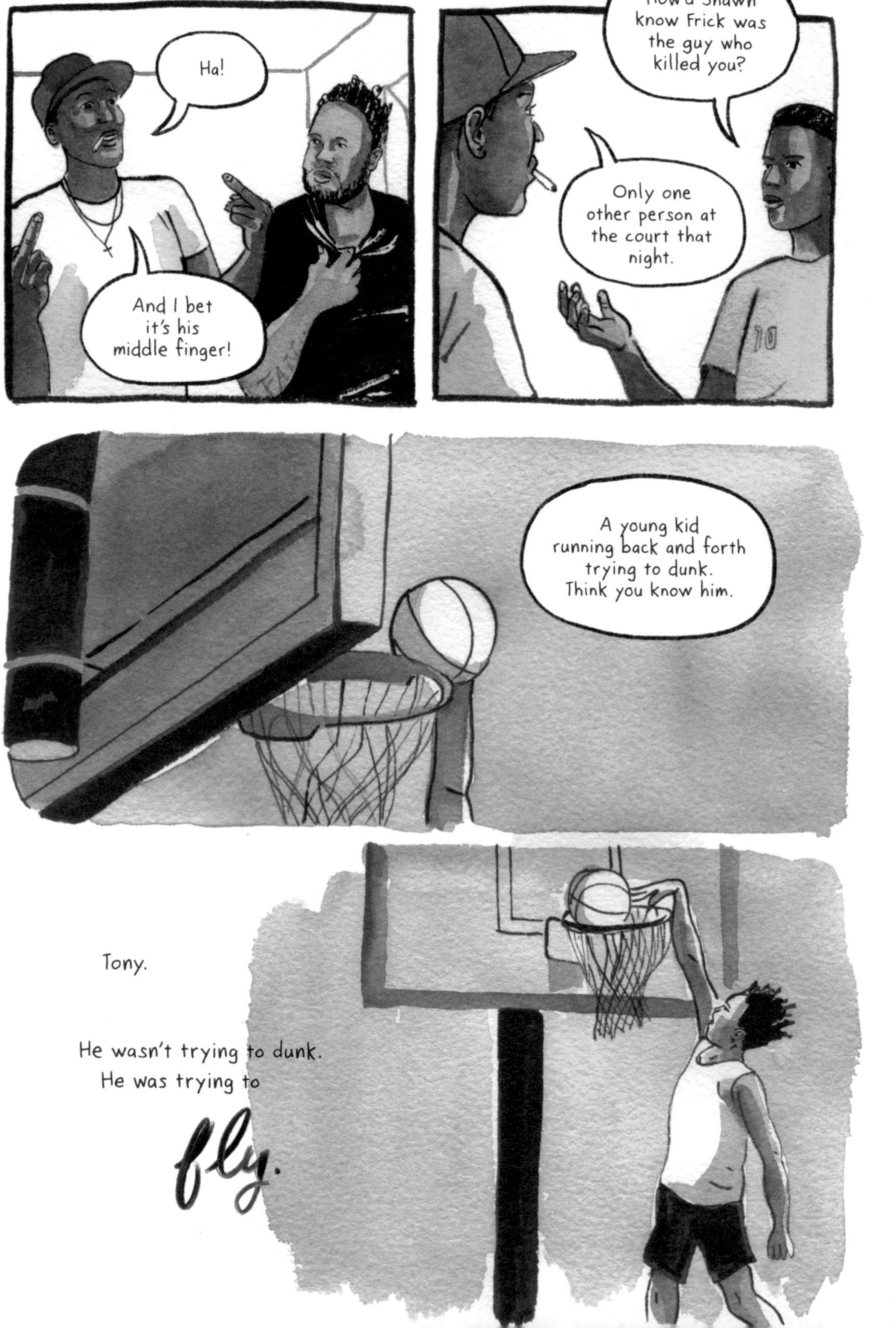
Ha!
And I bet it's his middle finger!
How'd Shawn know Frick was the guy who killed you?
Only one other person at the court that night.
A young kid running back and forth trying to dunk. Think you know him.
Tony.
He wasn't trying to dunk.
He was trying to
fly.

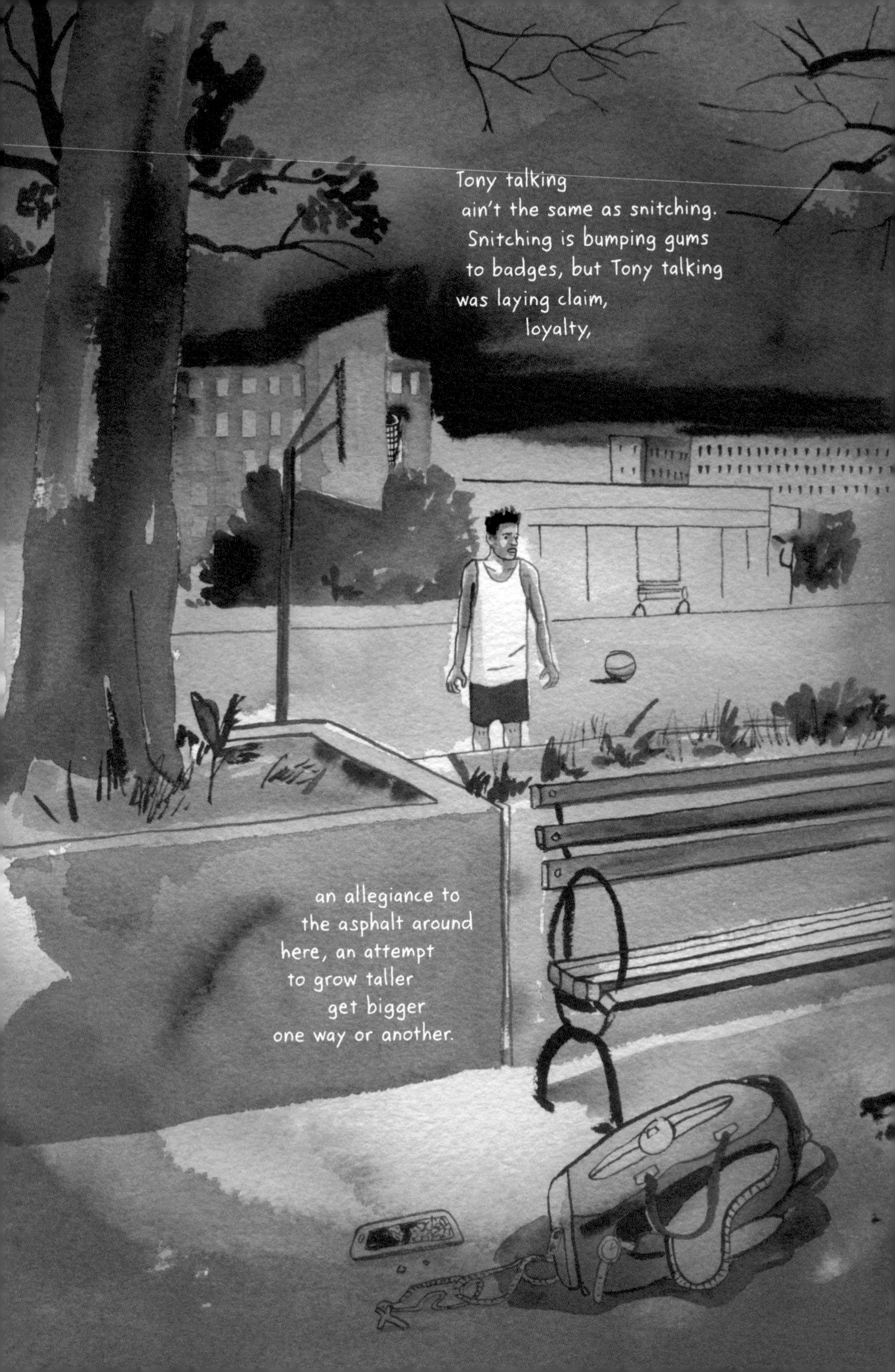
Tony talking
ain't the same as snitching.
Snitching is bumping gums
to badges, but Tony talking
was laying claim,
loyalty,
an allegiance to
the asphalt around
here, an attempt
to grow taller
get bigger
one way or another.

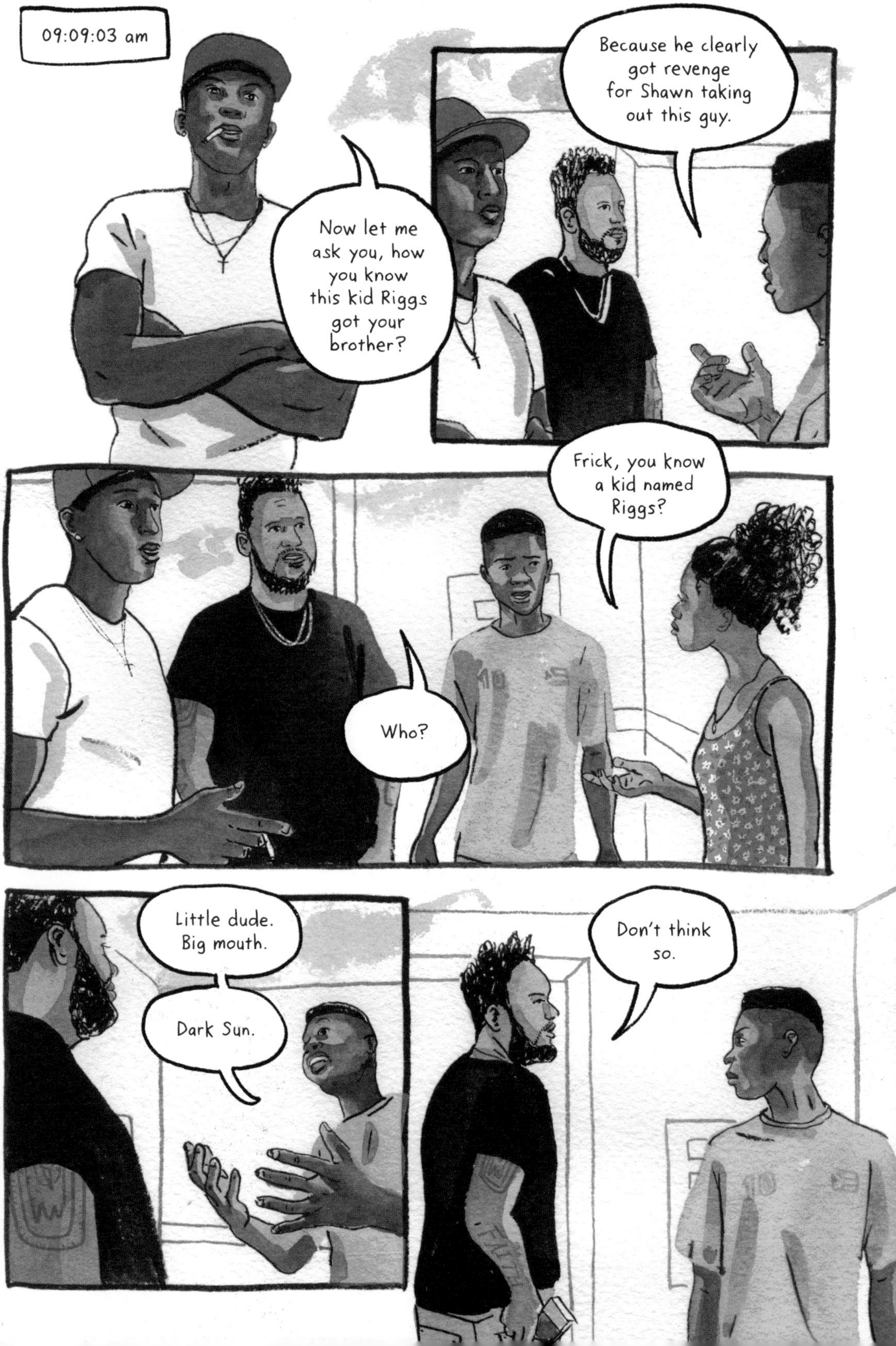
09:09:03 am
Now let me ask you, how you know this kid Riggs got your brother?
Because he clearly got revenge for Shawn taking out this guy.
Frick, you know a kid named Riggs?
Who?
Little dude. Big mouth.
Dark Sun.
Don't think so.

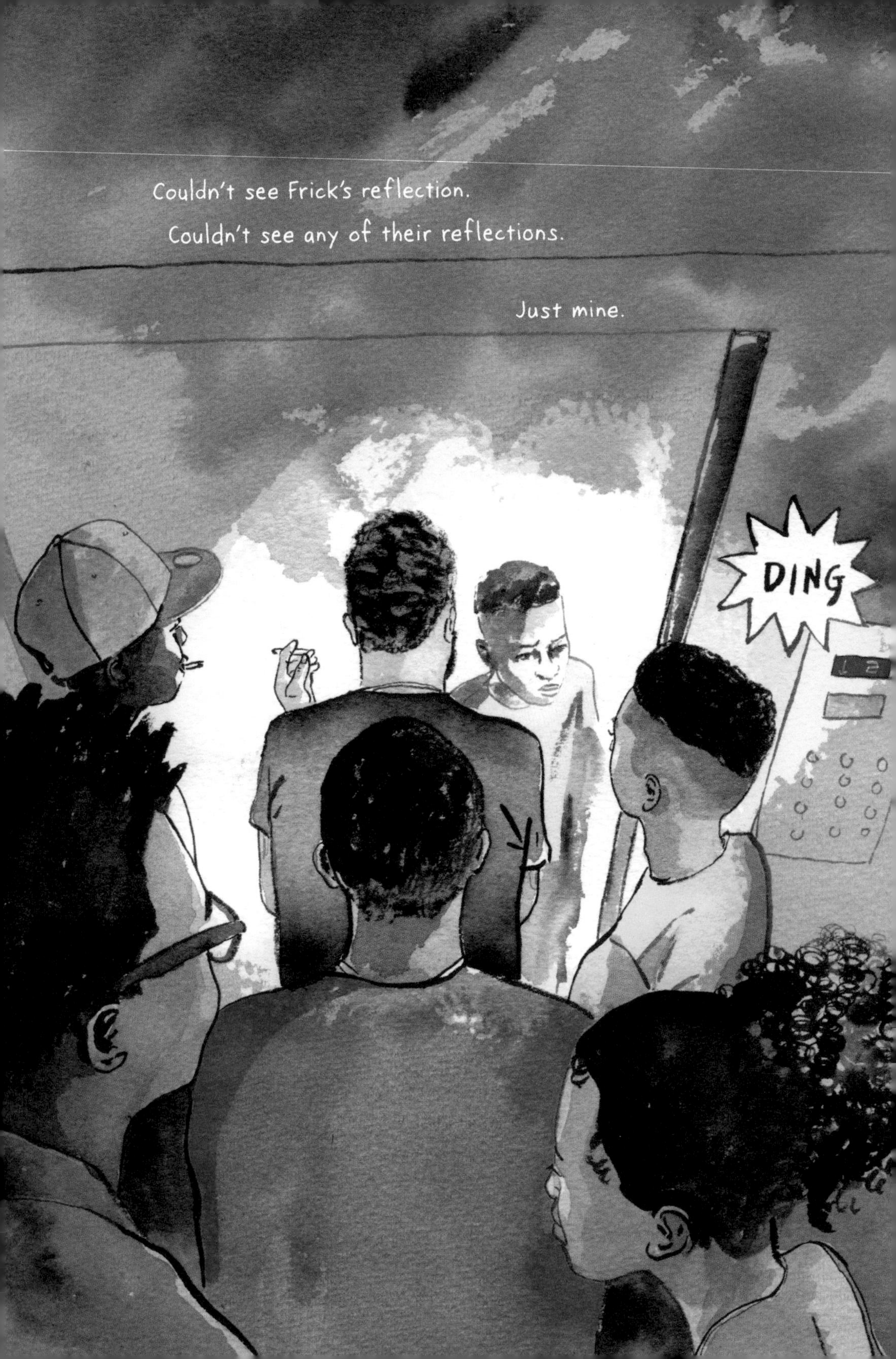
Couldn't see Frick's reflection.
Couldn't see any of their reflections.
Just mine.
DING

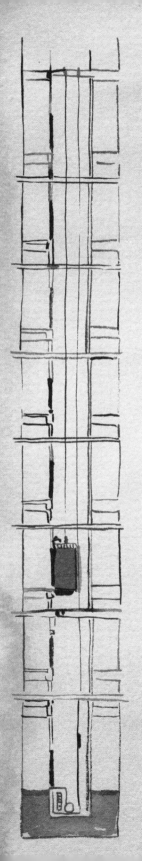

NO SMOKING

CAPACITY 2000 LBS

CITY ID NO. 3P577Q

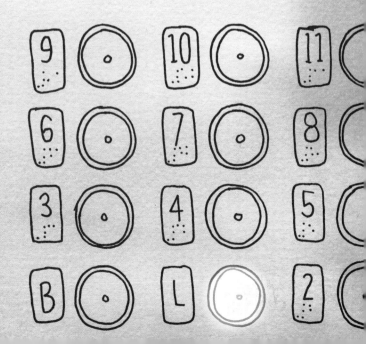

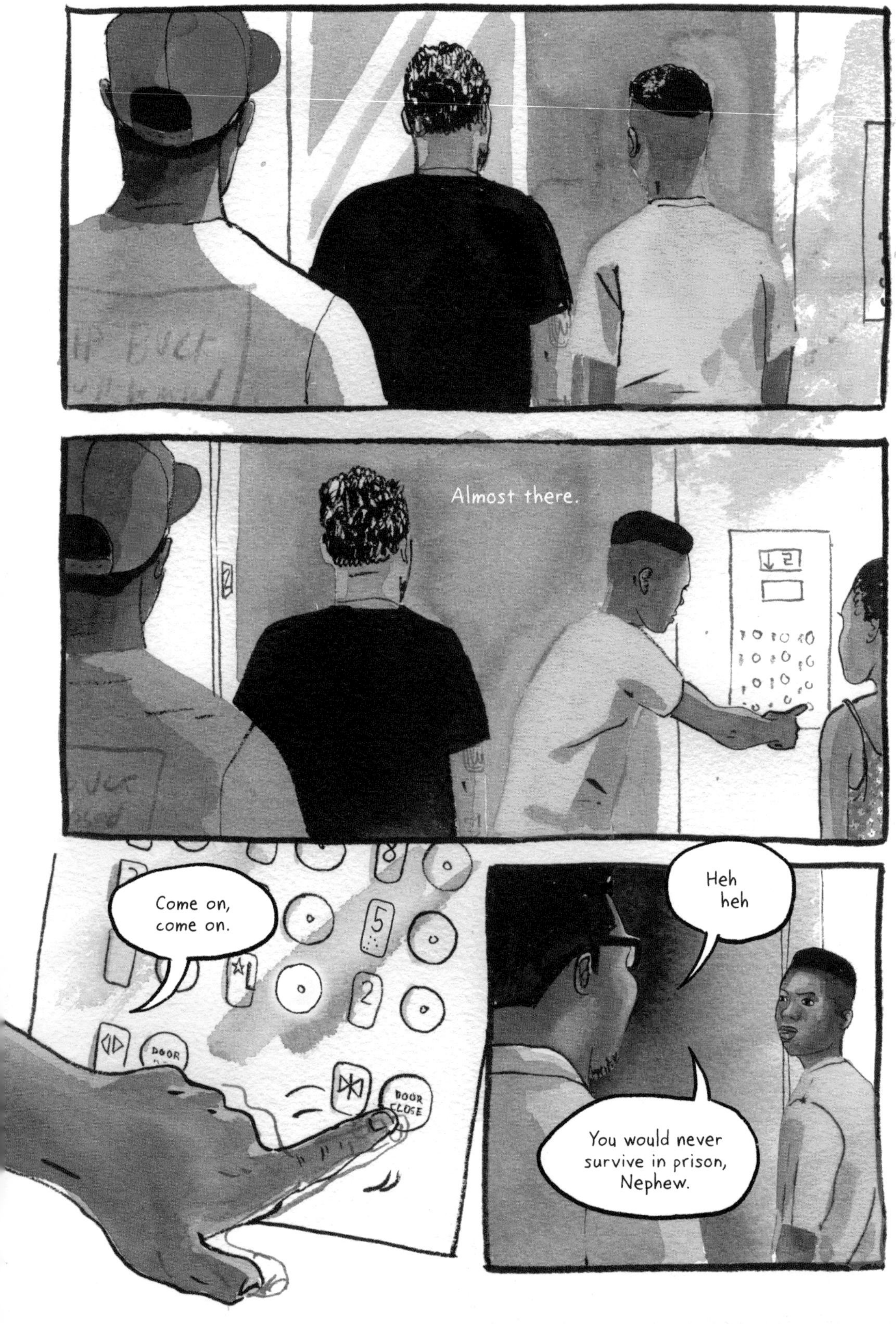
Almost there.
Come on, come on.
DOOR CLOSE
Heh heh
You would never survive in prison, Nephew.

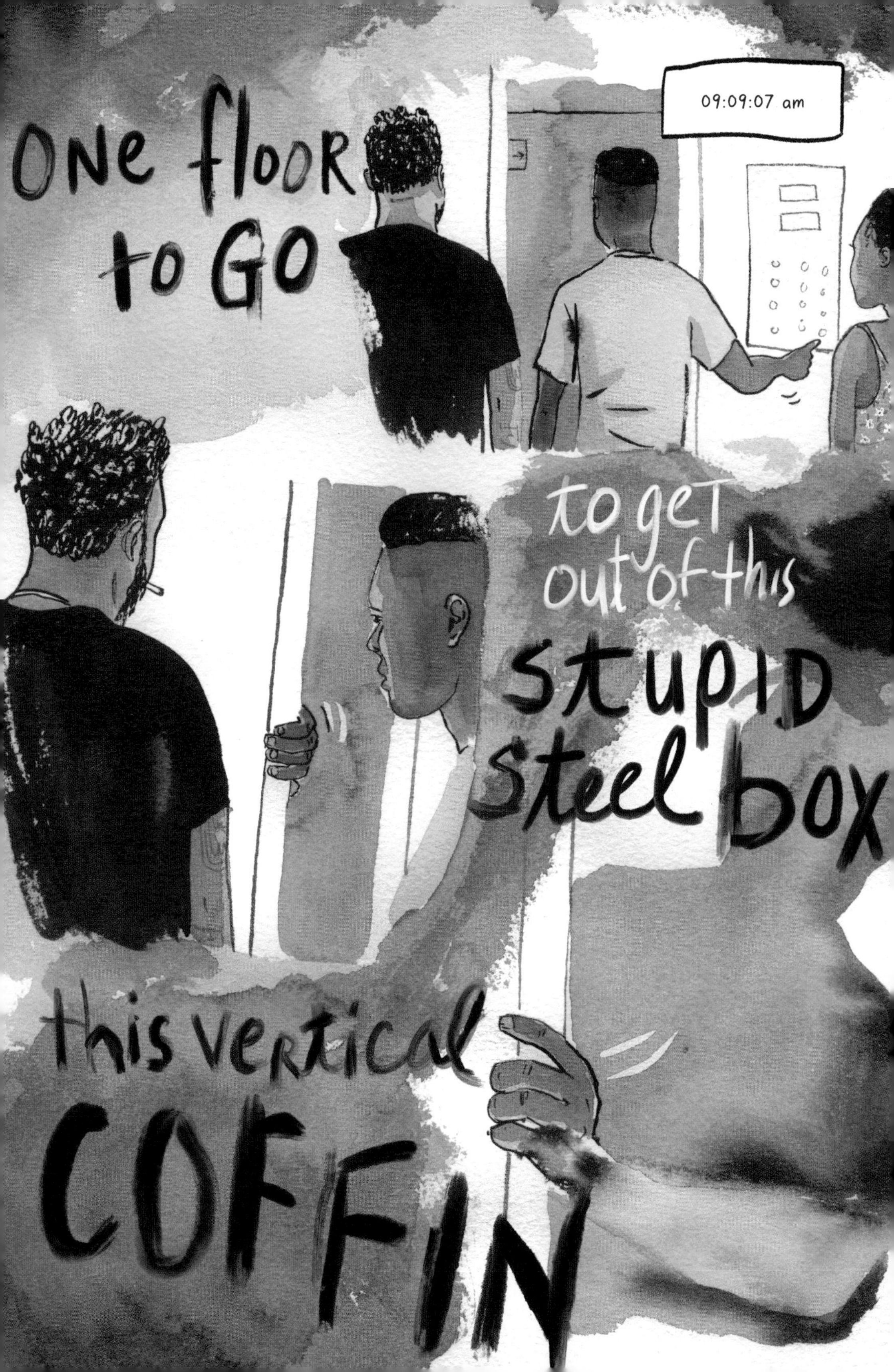
09:09:07 am
One floor
to GO
to get
out of this
stupid
steel box
this vertical
COFFIN

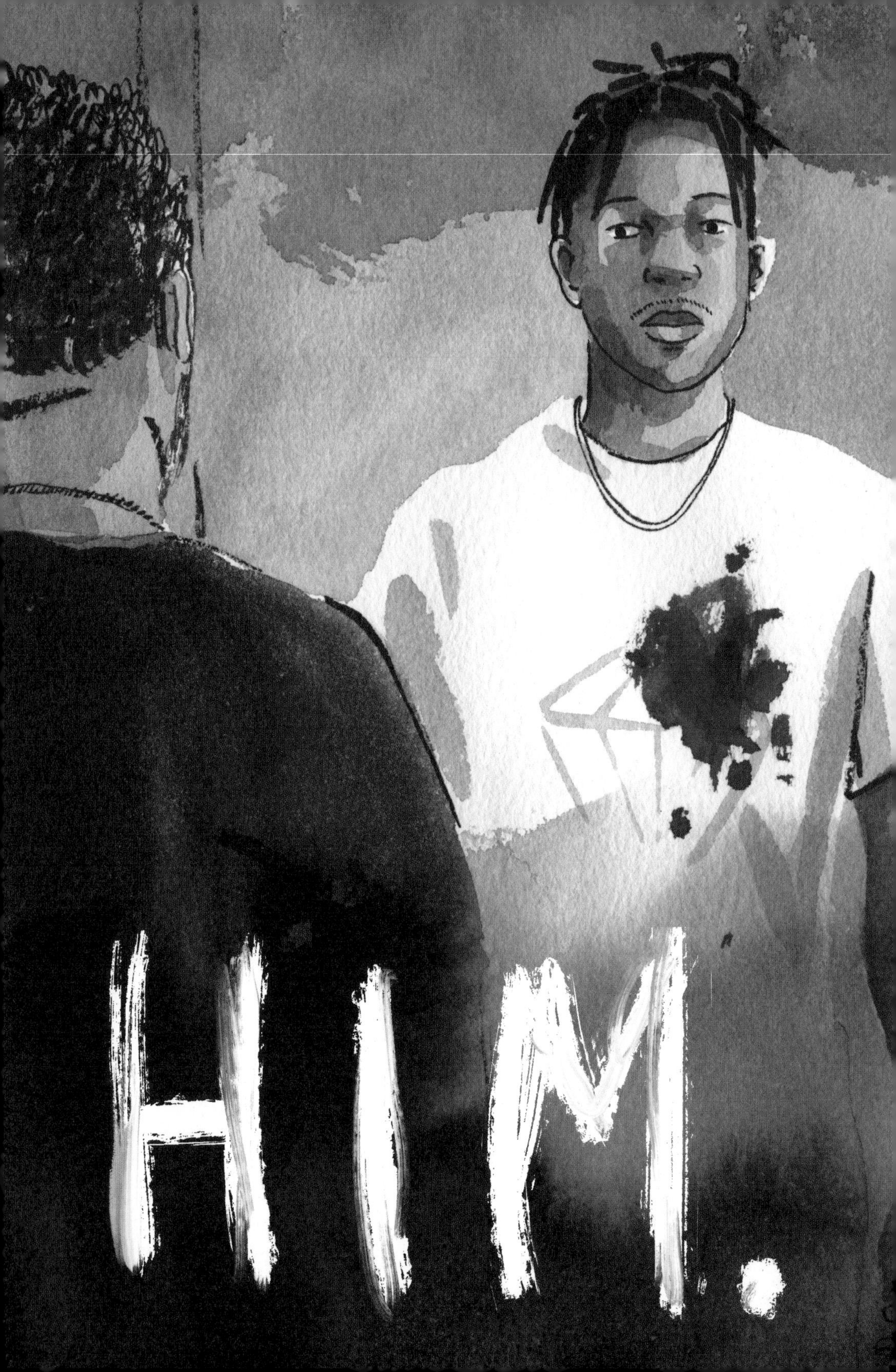
H.I.M.

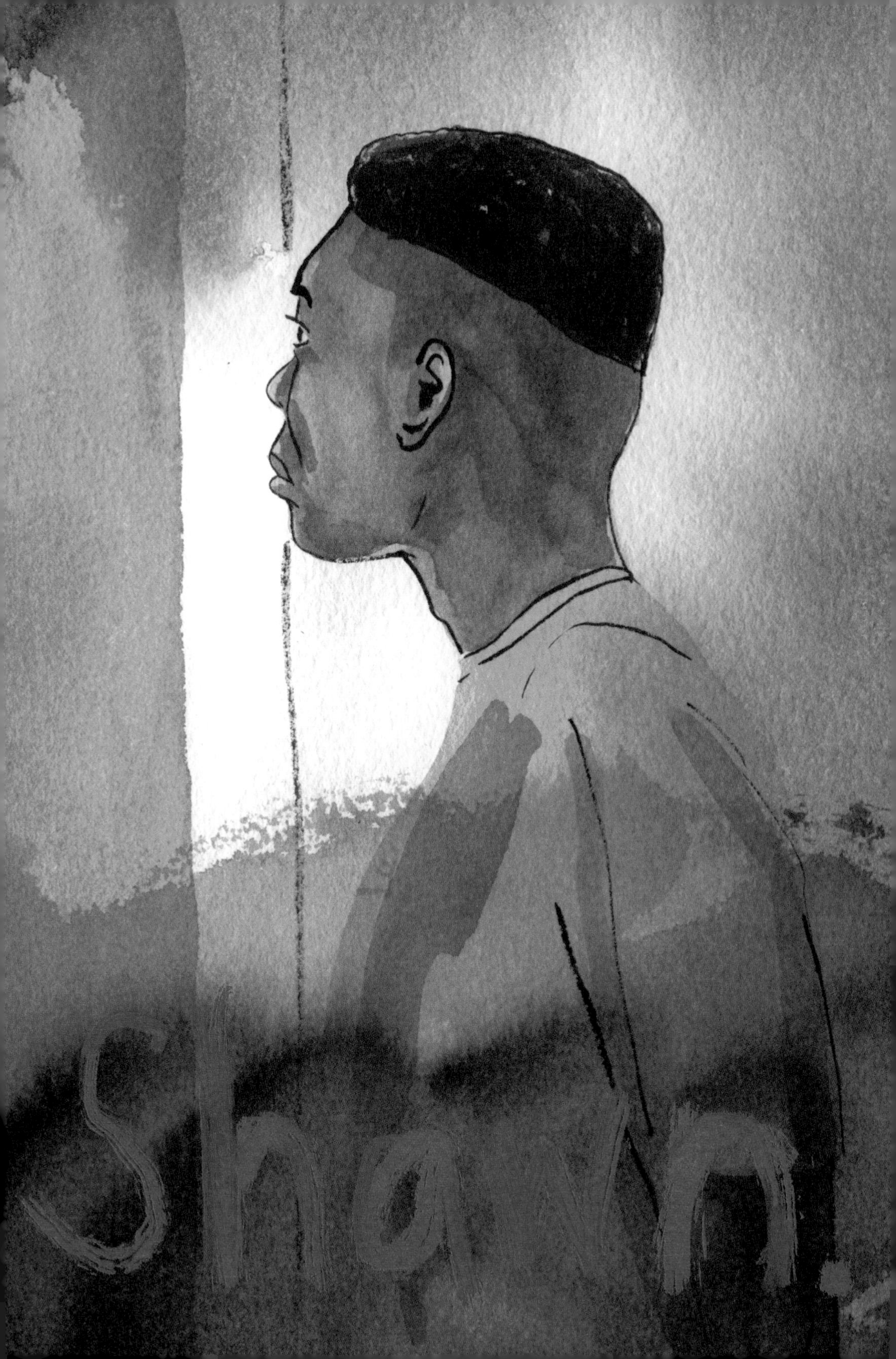
Shawn.

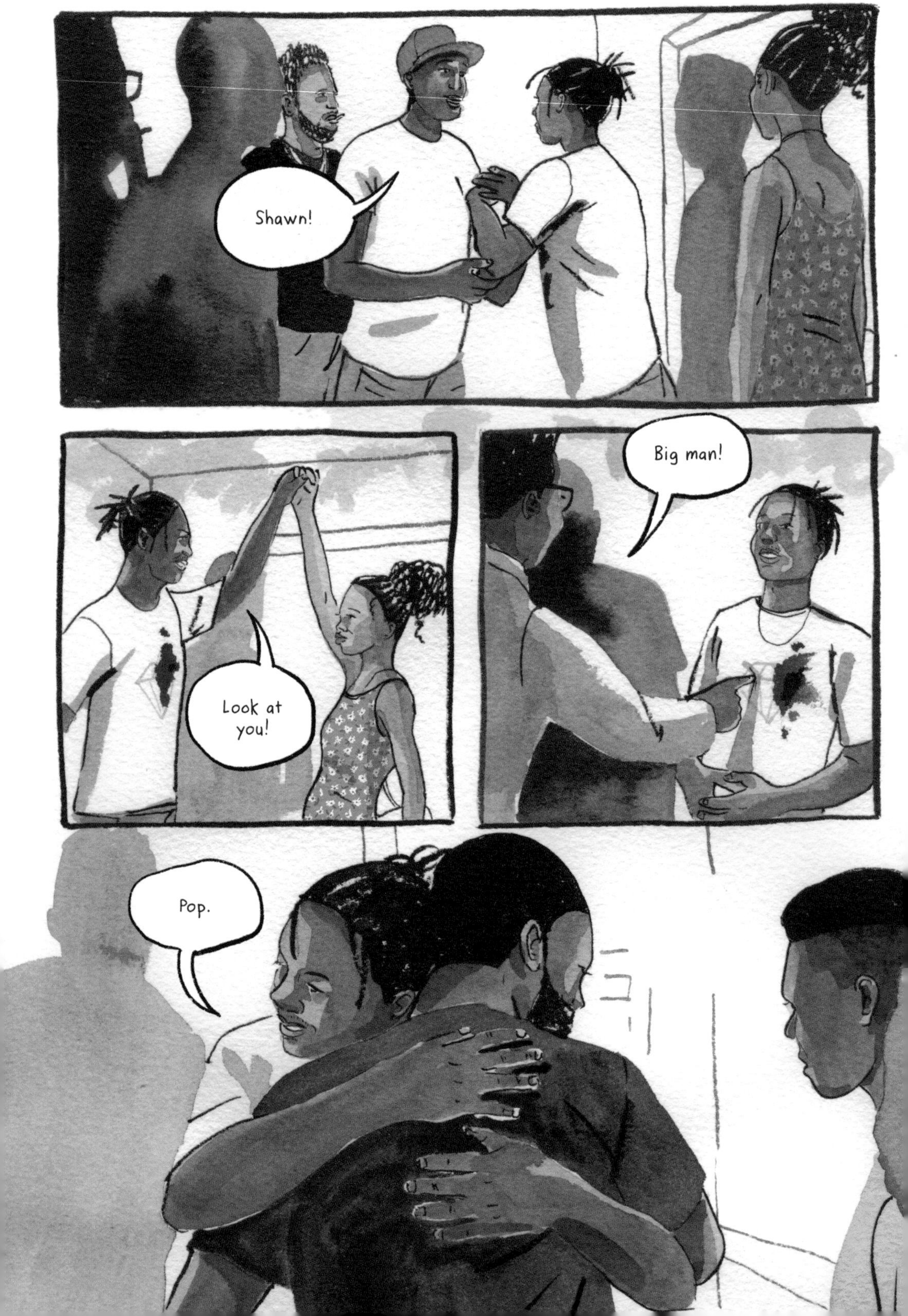
Shawn!
Look at you!
Big man!
Pop.

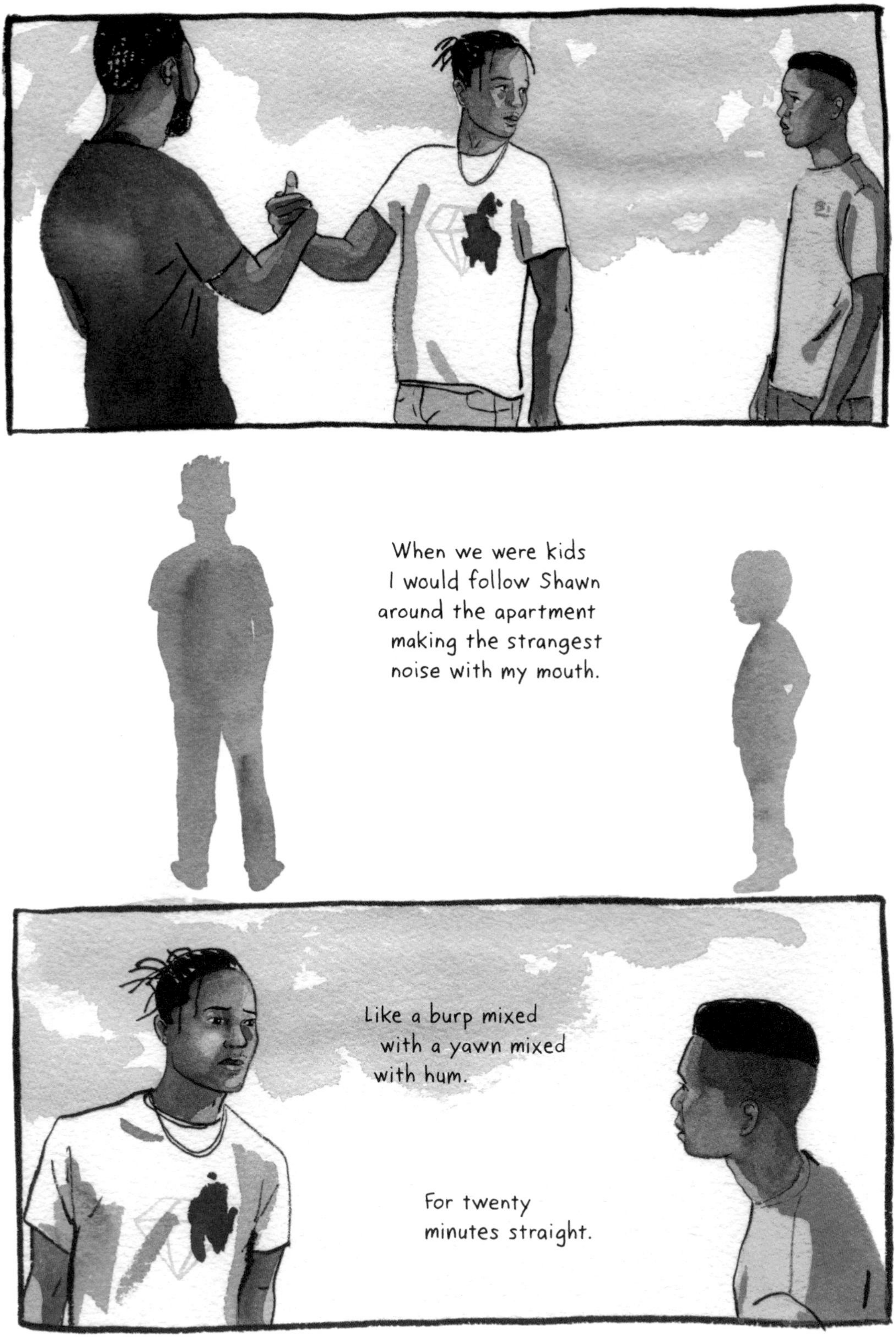
When we were kids
I would follow Shawn
around the apartment
making the strangest
noise with my mouth.
Like a burp mixed
with a yawn mixed
with hum.
For twenty
minutes straight.

To punish me,
he would wait for me
to run out of steam

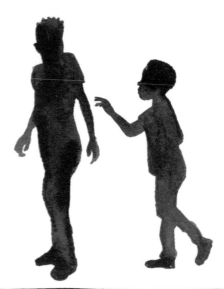

and then, to my surprise,
he wouldn't say a word to me
for the rest
of the day.

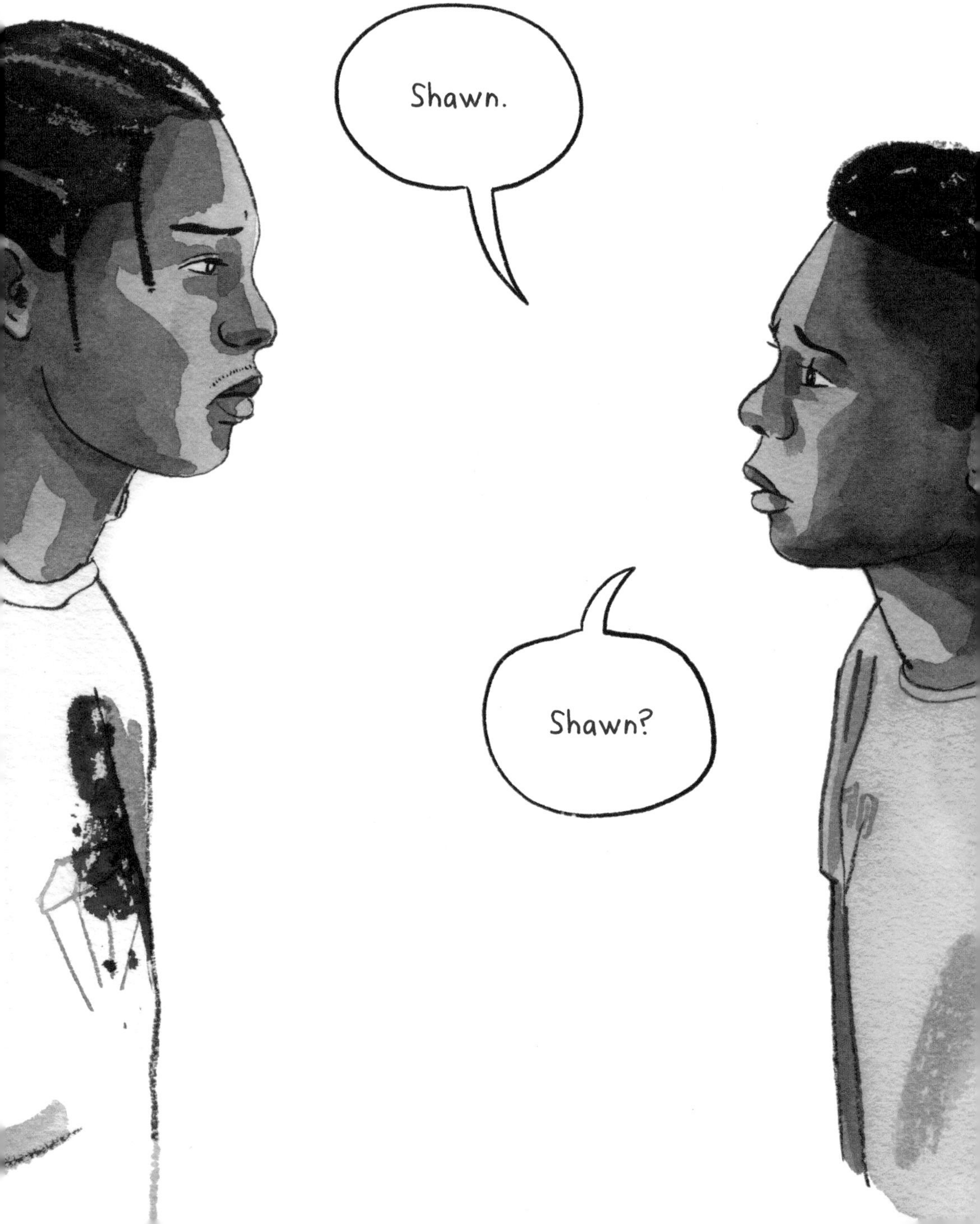
Shawn.
Shawn?

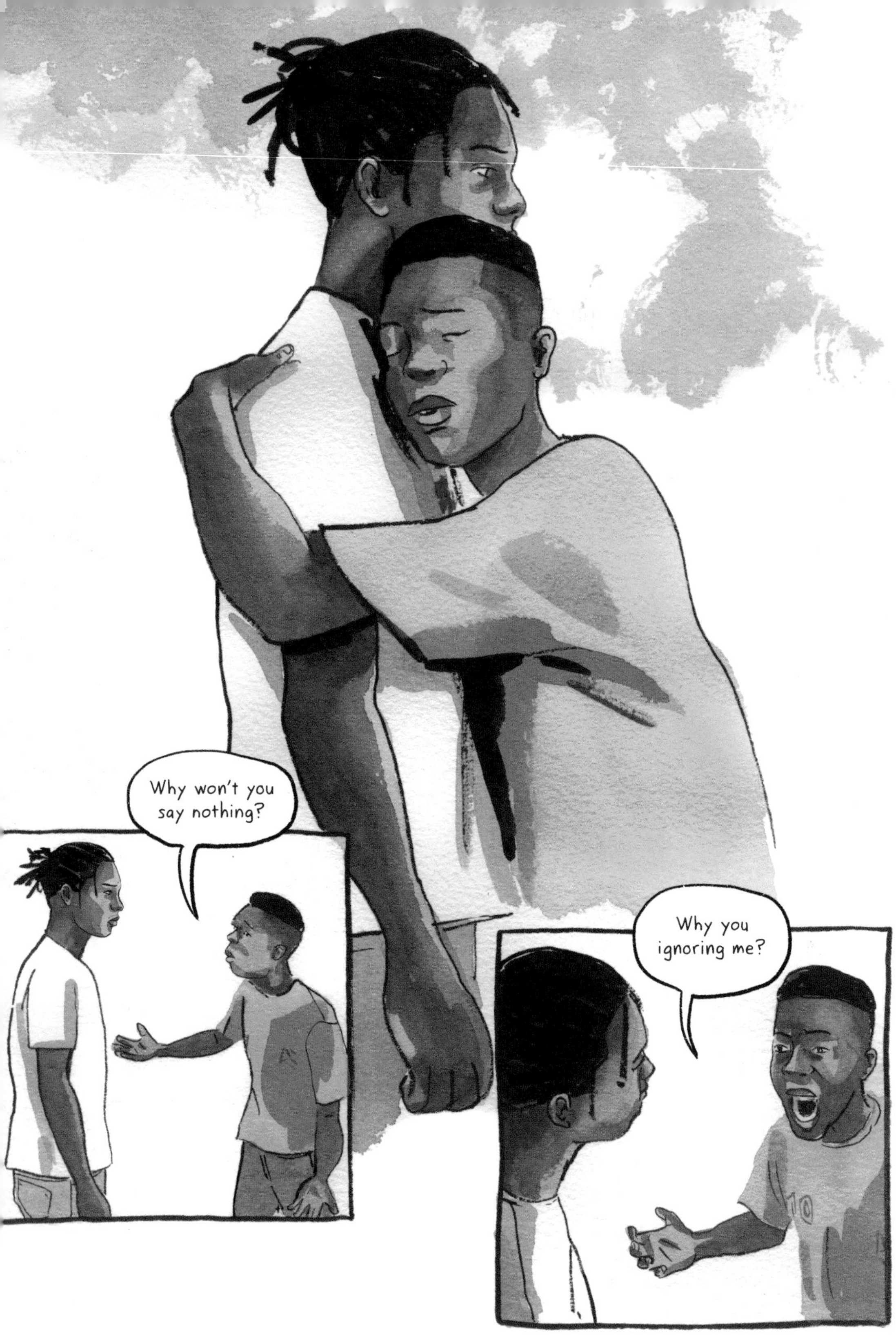
Why won't you say nothing?
Why you ignoring me?

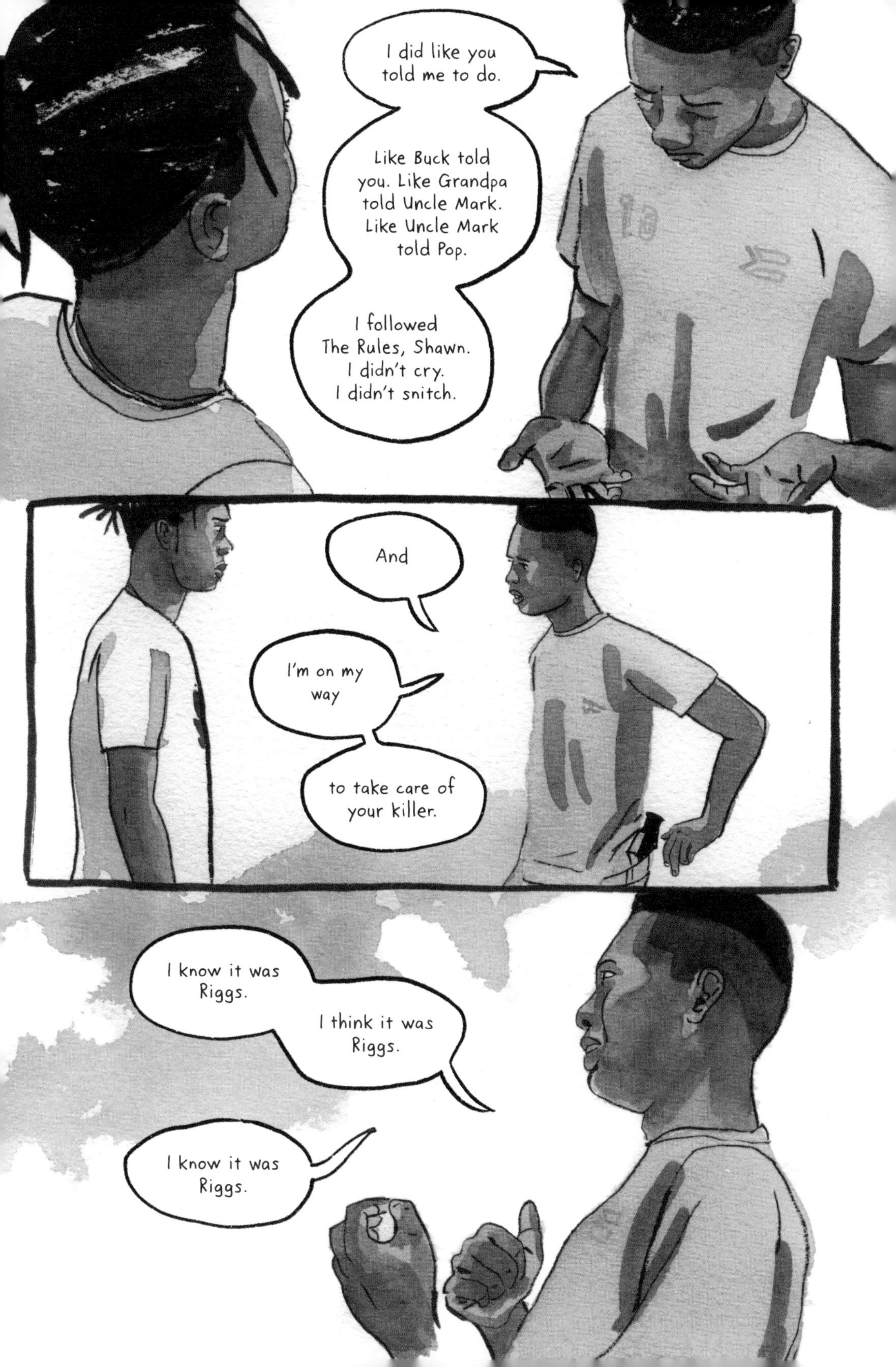
I did like you told me to do.
Like Buck told you. Like Grandpa told Uncle Mark. Like Uncle Mark told Pop.
I followed The Rules, Shawn. I didn't cry. I didn't snitch.
And
I'm on my way
to take care of your killer.
I know it was Riggs.
I think it was Riggs.
I know it was Riggs.

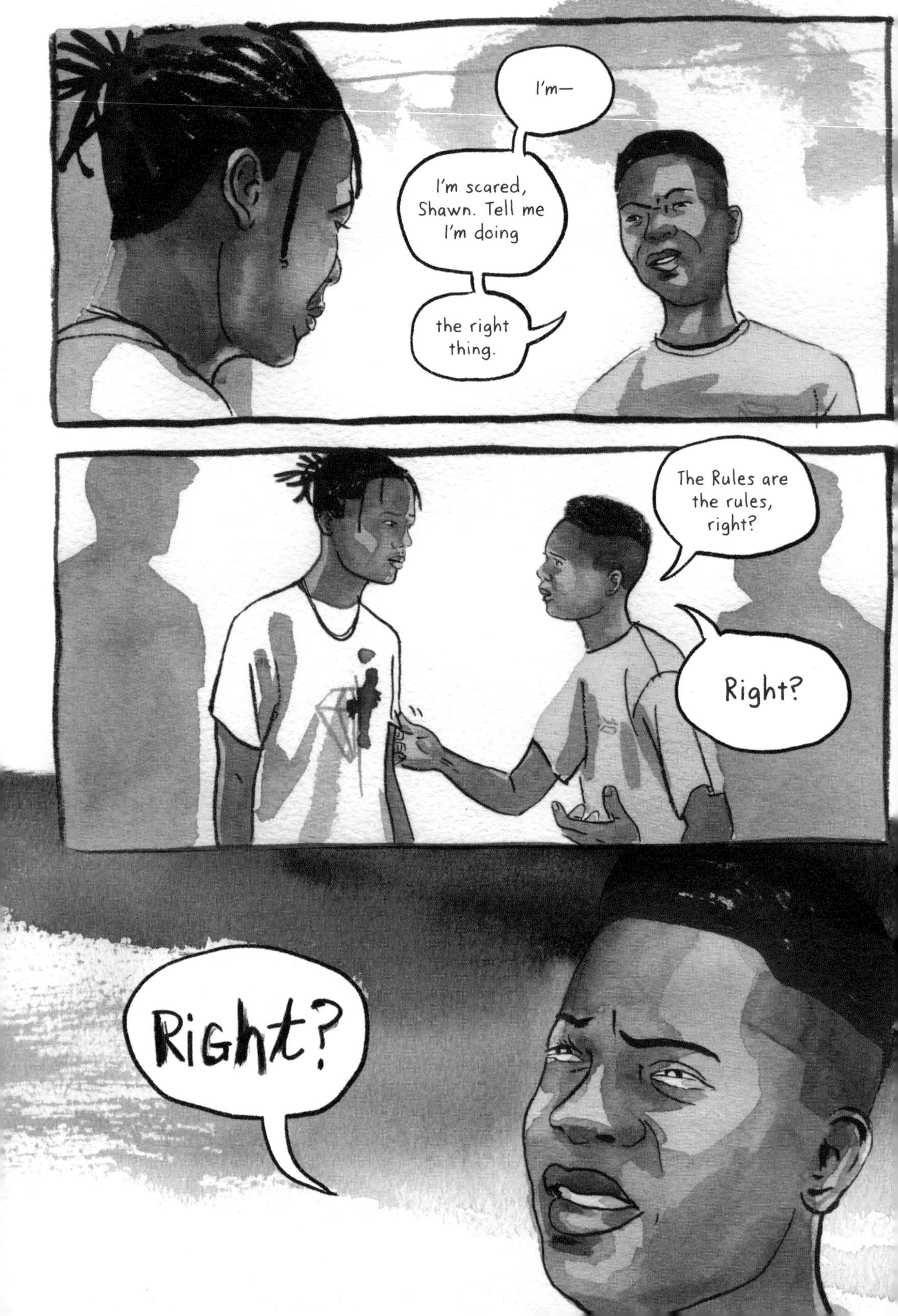
I'm—
I'm scared, Shawn. Tell me I'm doing
the right thing.
The Rules are the rules, right?
Right?
Right?

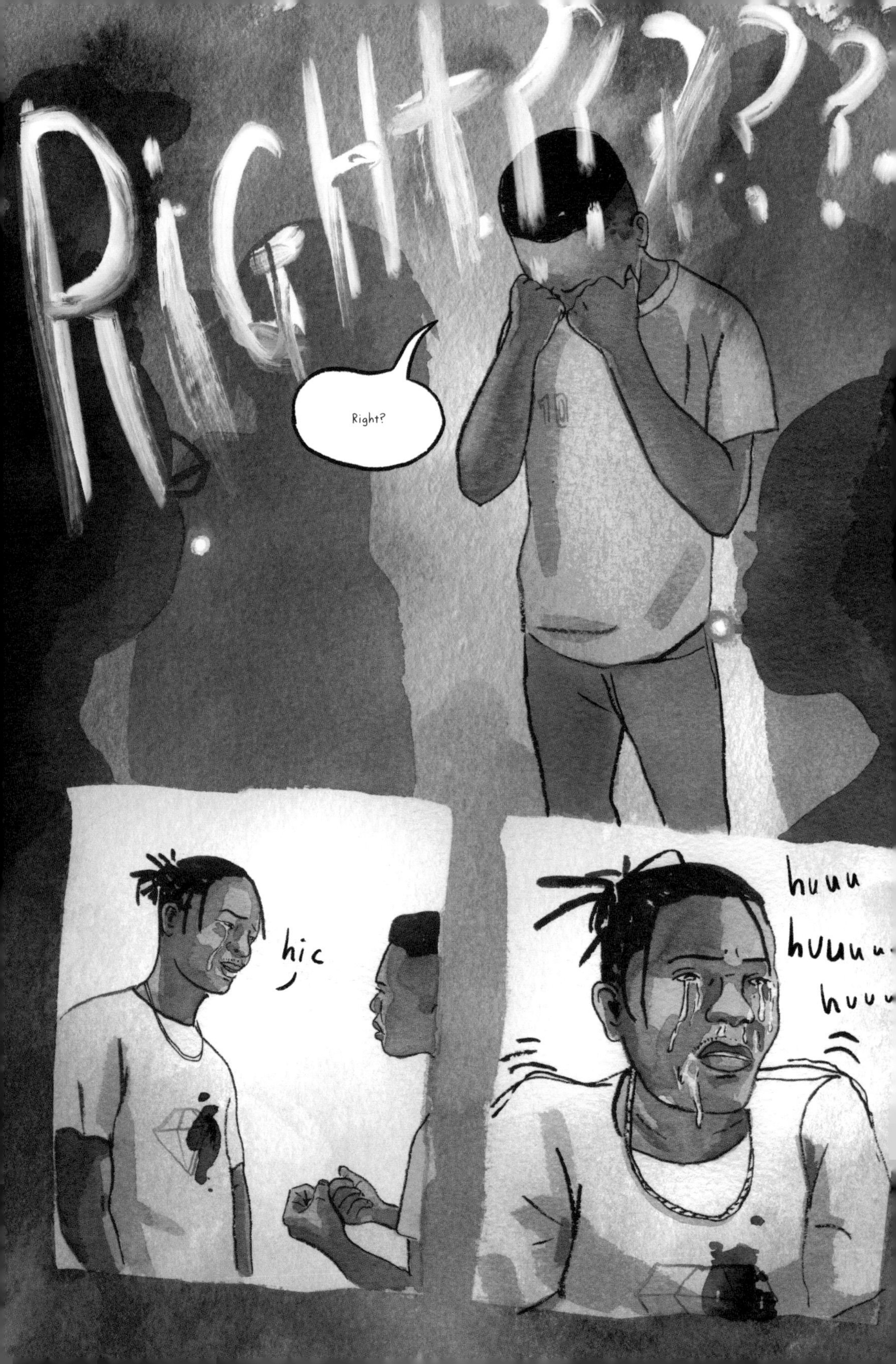

RIGHT???
Right?
hic
huuu
huuuu
huuu

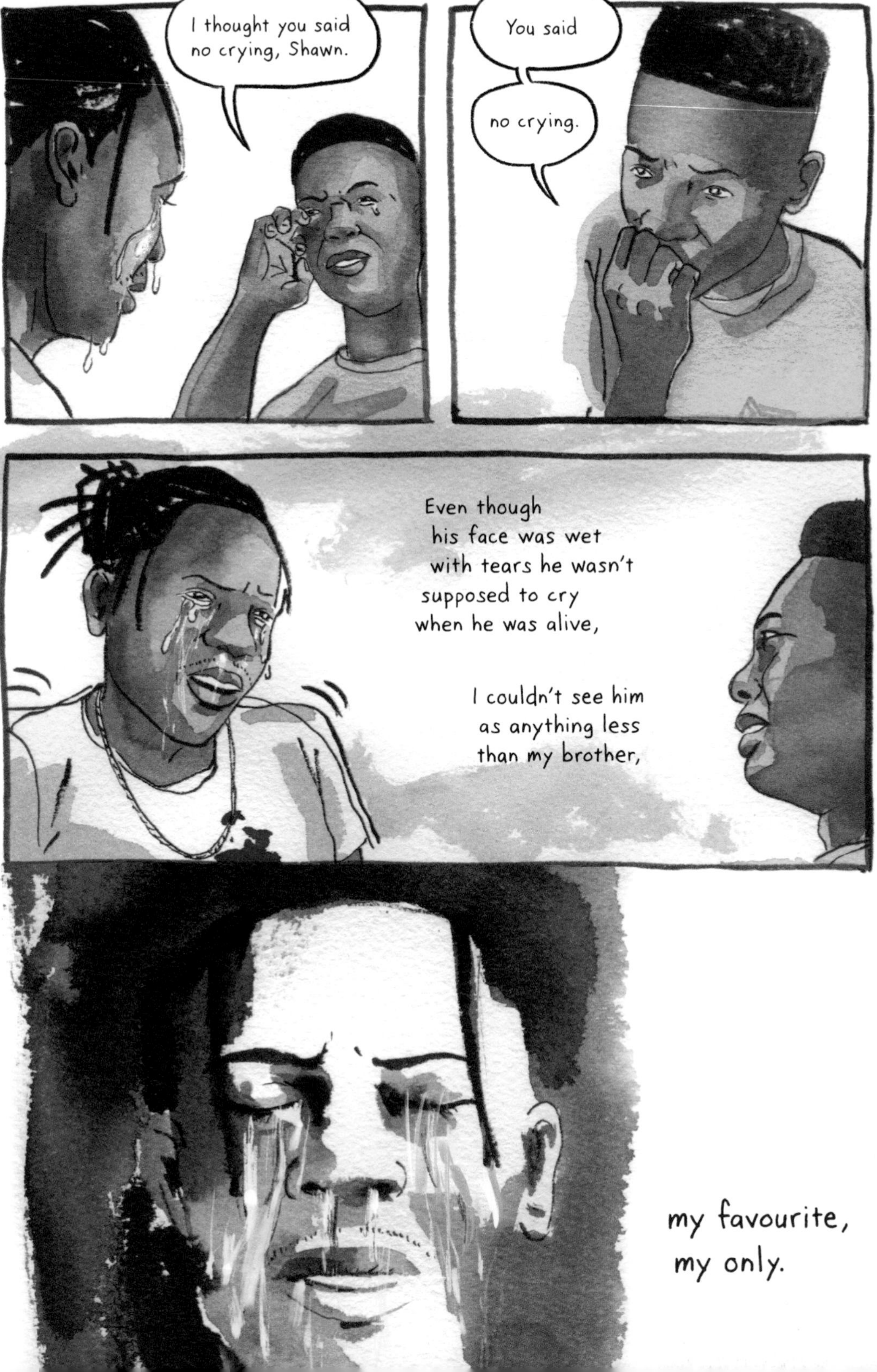
I thought you said no crying, Shawn.
You said
no crying.
Even though his face was wet with tears he wasn't supposed to cry when he was alive,
I couldn't see him as anything less than my brother,
my favourite, my only.

And there was a sound like whatever makes elevators work,
cables and cogs, or whatever,
grinding, rubbing metal on metal
like a machine moaning but coming
from the mouth from the belly
of Shawn. He never said nothing to me.
Just made that painful piercing sound,
as suddenly the elevator came to a stop.
DING

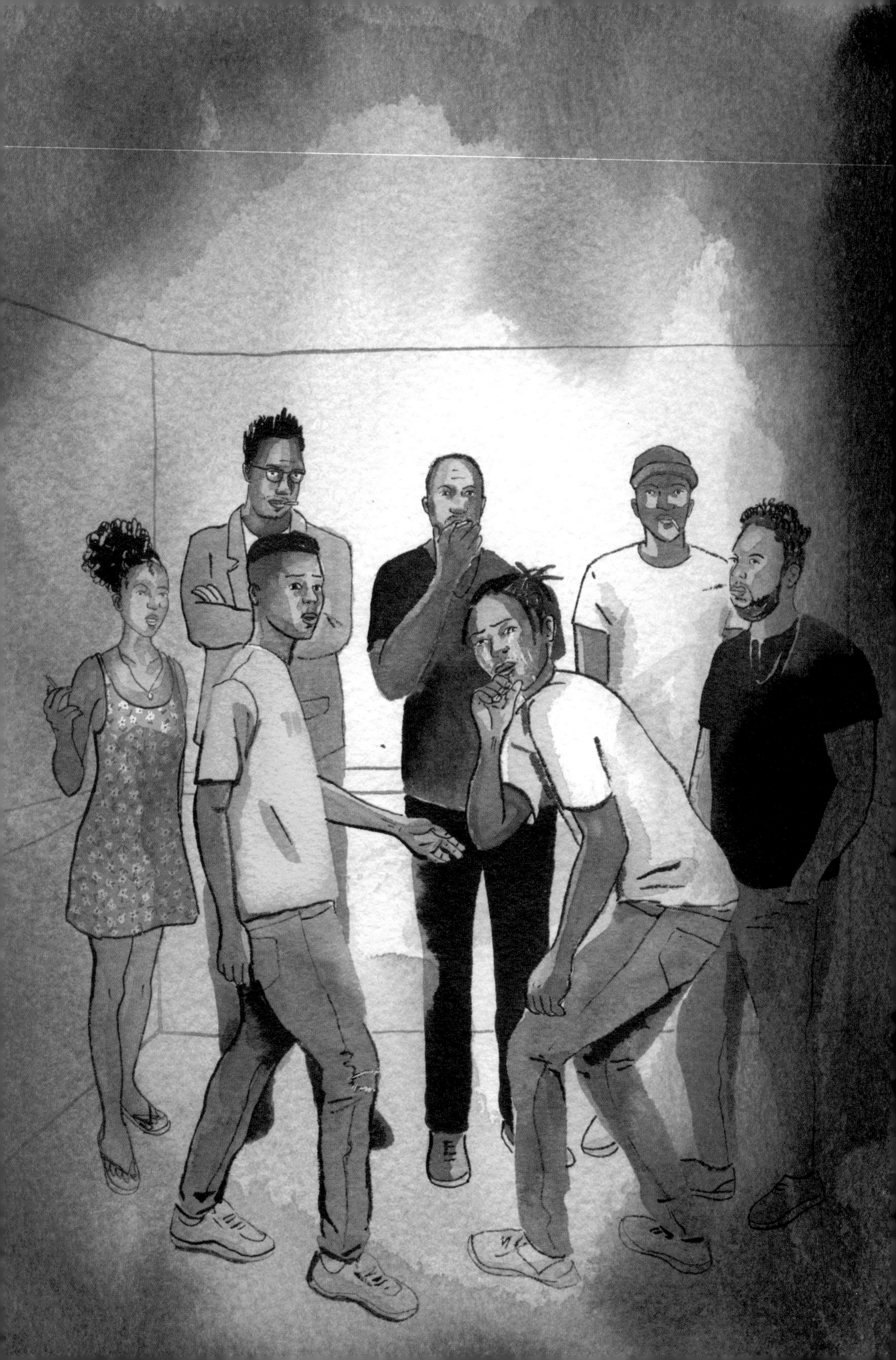

NO SMOKING

CAPACITY 2000 LBS

CITY ID NO. 3P577Q

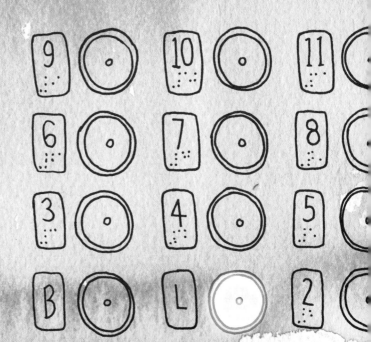

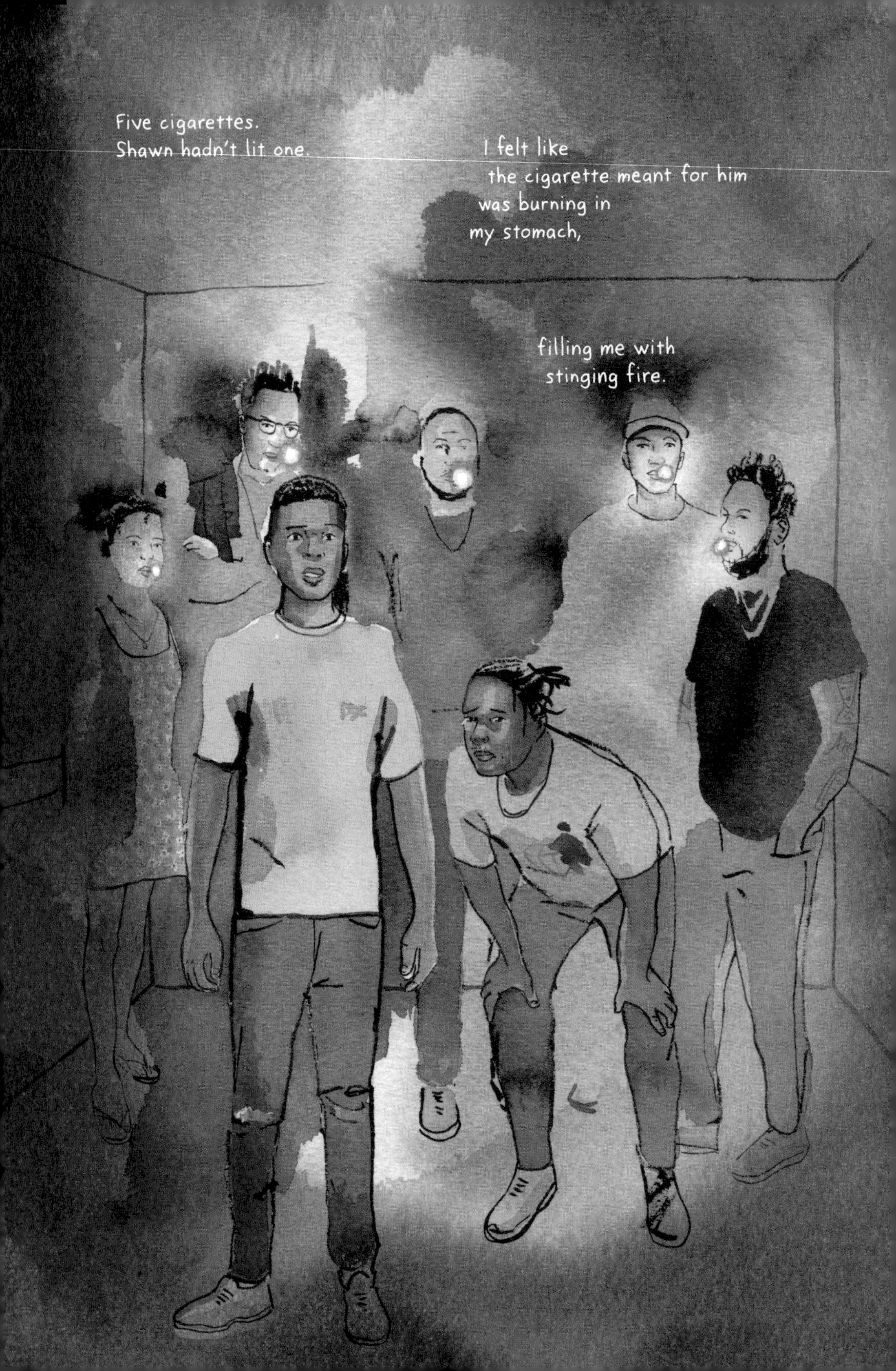
Five cigarettes.
Shawn hadn't lit one.
I felt like
the cigarette meant for him
was burning in
my stomach,
filling me with
stinging fire.

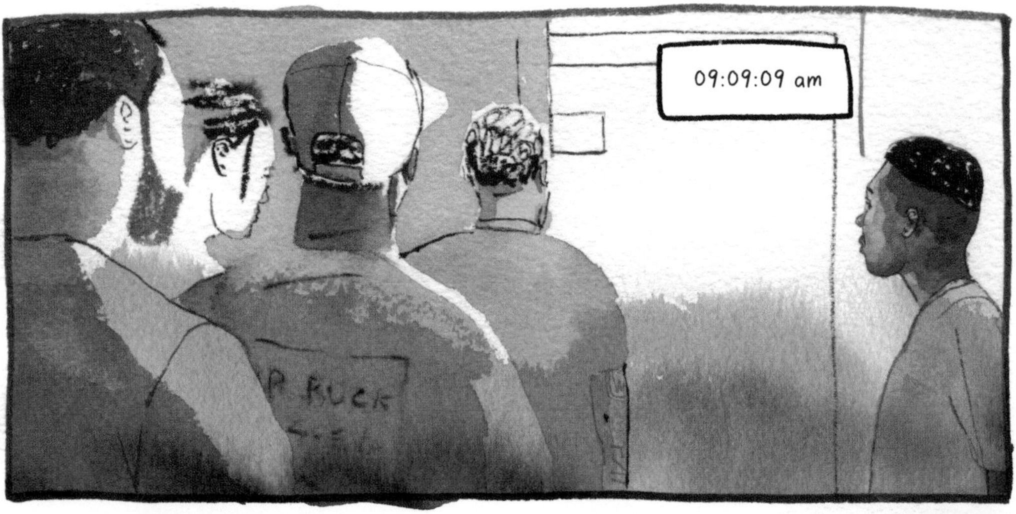
09:09:09 am

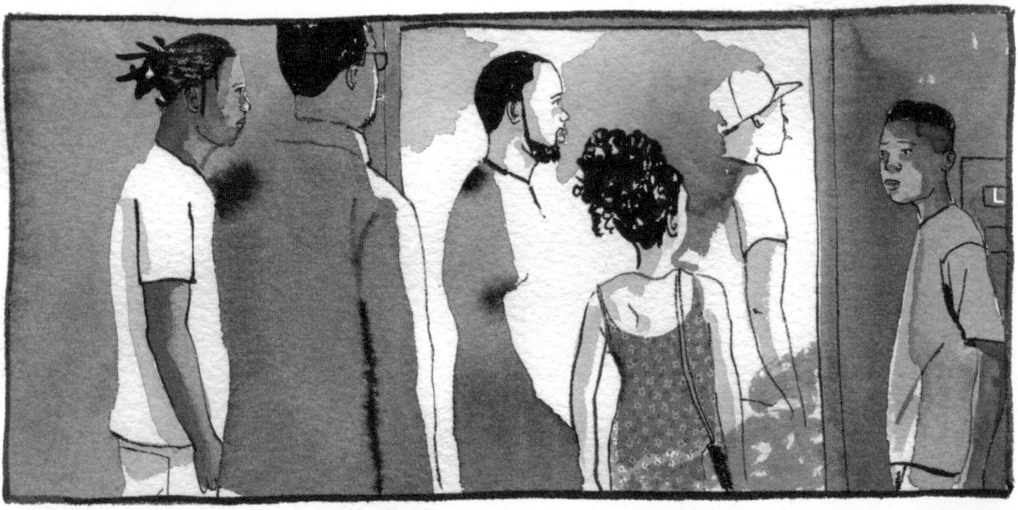

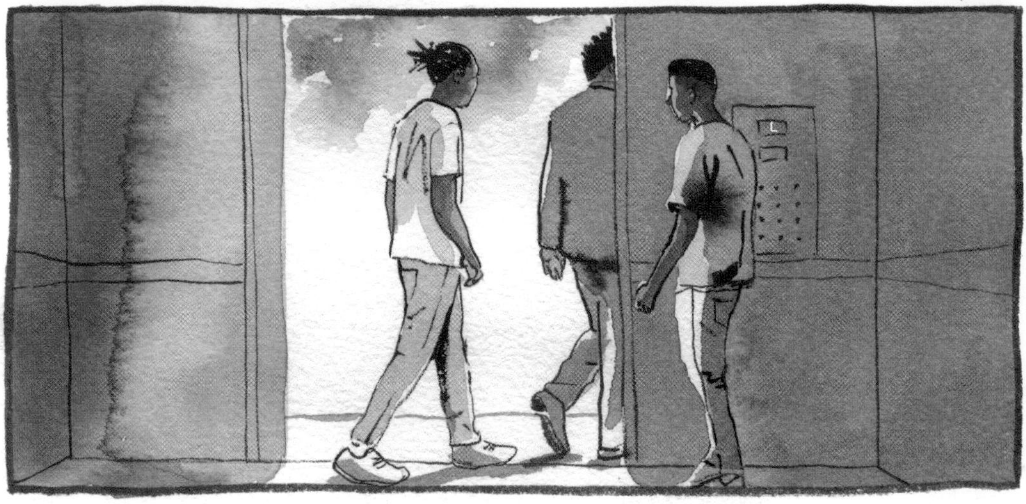

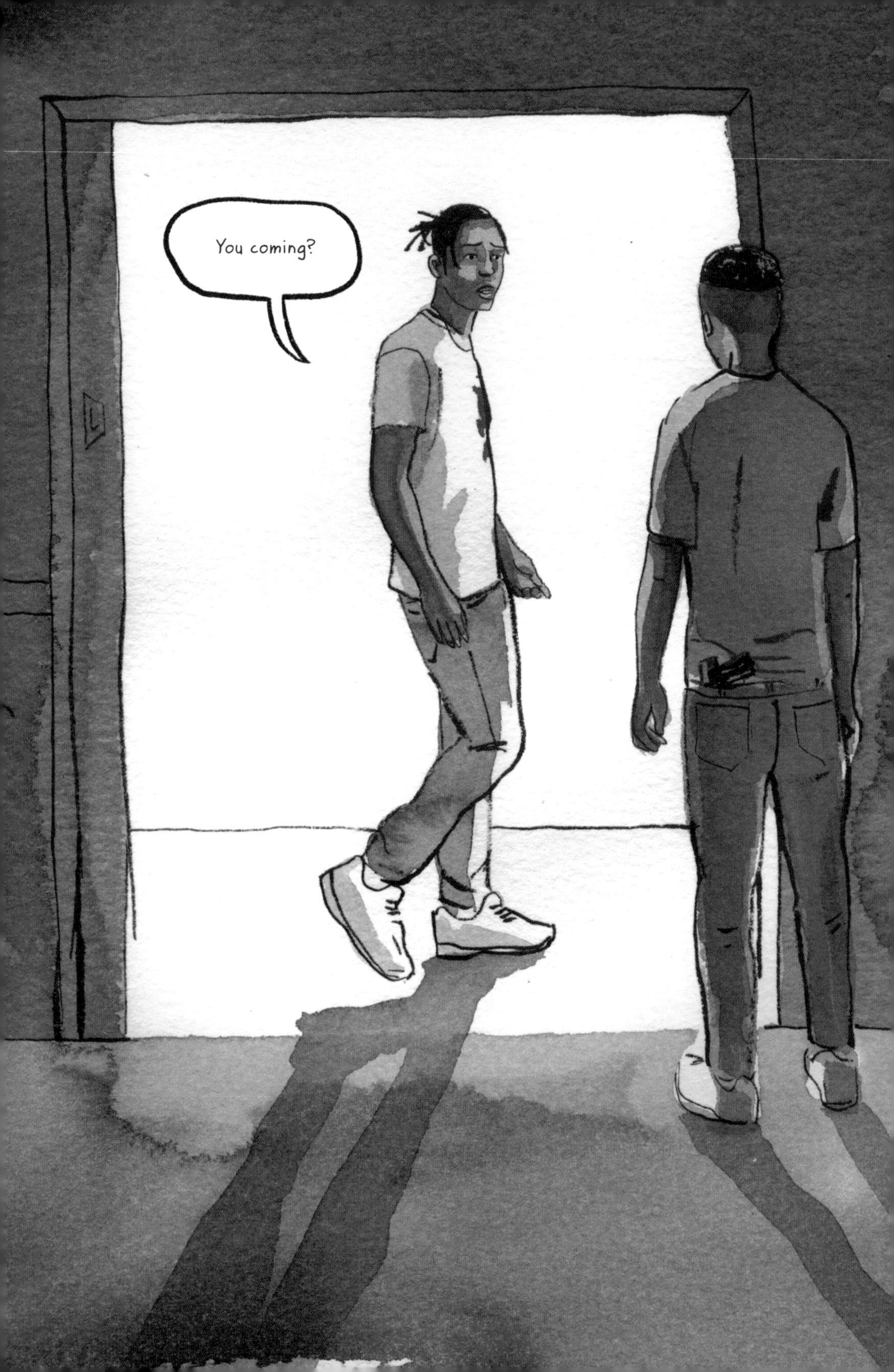
You coming?

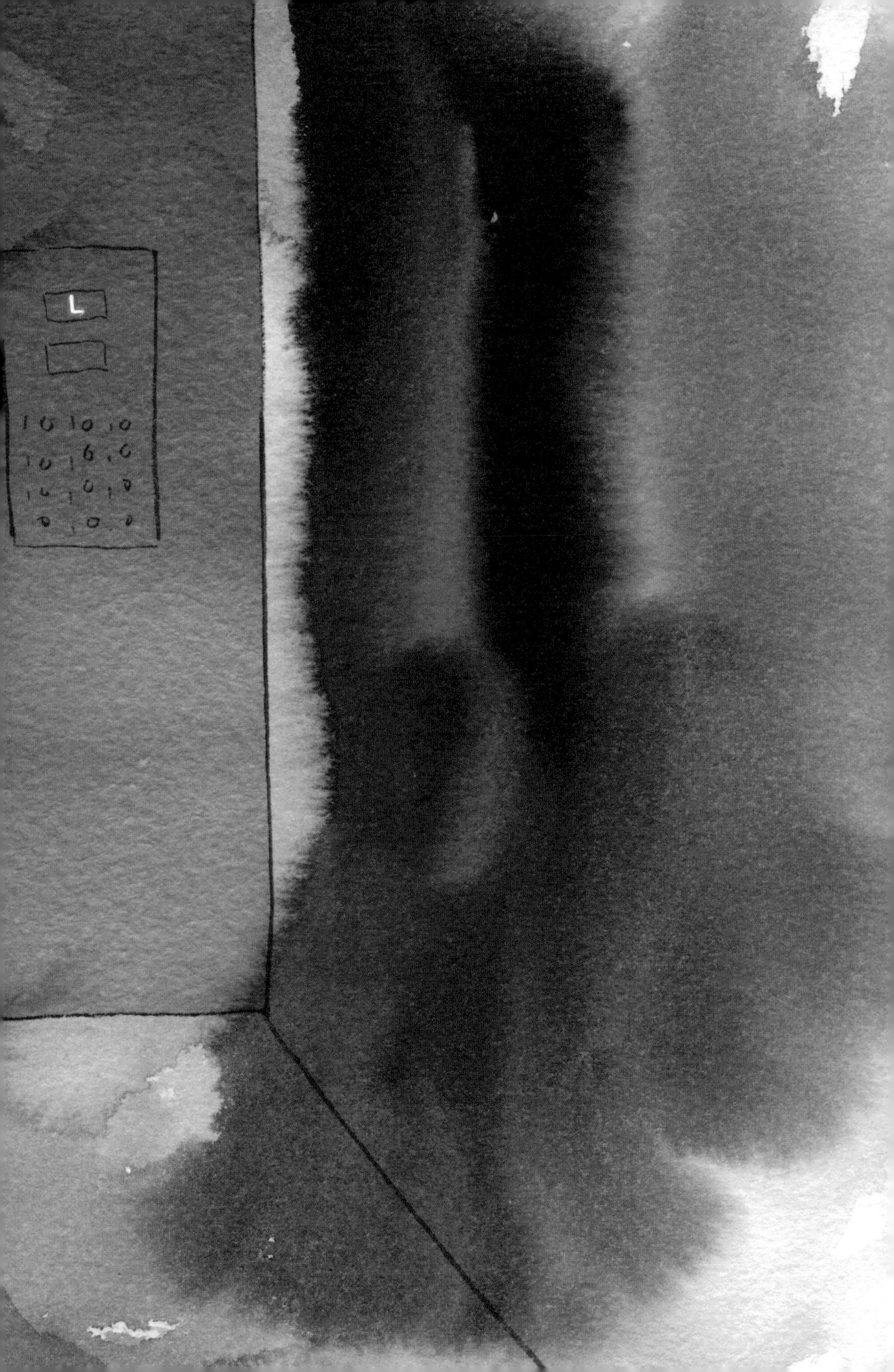
L

Also by Jason Reynolds

The Boy in the Black Suit

All American Boys

Long Way Down

For Every One

Look Both Ways

The Track Series:

Ghost

Patina

Sunny

Lu

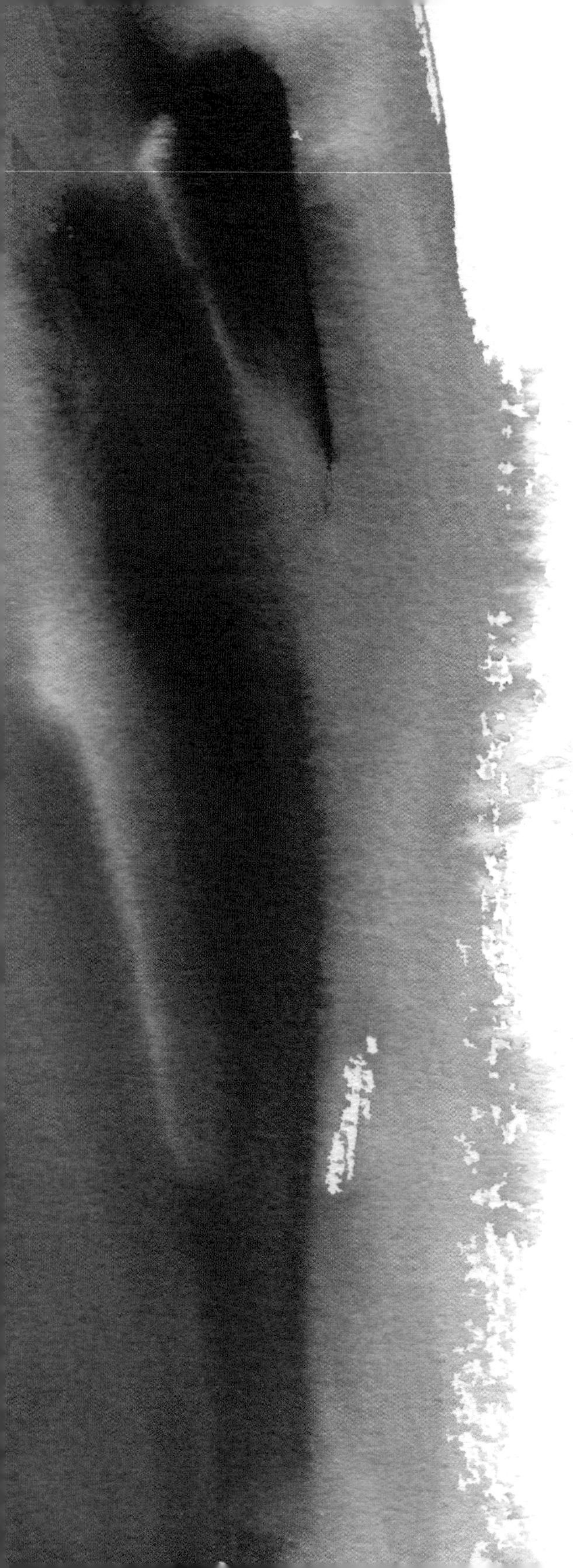

FABER has published children's books since 1929. T. S. Eliot's *Old Possum's Book of Practical Cats* and Ted Hughes' *The Iron Man* were amongst the first. Our catalogue at the time said that 'it is by reading such books that children learn the difference between the shoddy and the genuine'. We still believe in the power of reading to transform children's lives. All our books are chosen with the express intention of growing a love of reading, a thirst for knowledge and to cultivate empathy. We pride ourselves on responsible editing. Last but not least, we believe in kind and inclusive books in which all children feel represented and important.